STORMVALOR

STARR Z. DAVIES

First published in the United States in 2025 by Character Assassin Books an imprint of Starr Z Davies, 1328 Lynn Avenue Altoona, WI 54720 USA. Email: starr@starrzdavies.com

Cover illustration by Kateryna Vitkovskaya Art
Chapter headers and breaks by Therena Carlin
Cover typography by MIBLArt.com
Divica logo design by GreenPik Studio
Book layout and design by Starr Z Davies & Atticus software
Maps, glyphs, and illustrations relating to maps by Starr Z Davies & Inkarnate software

ISBN (Hardback) 960-7-026000-11-6
ISBN (Paperback) 978-1-965603-00-0
ISBN (eBook) 978-1-965603-01-7

www.starrzdavies.com

BOOKS BY STARR Z. DAVIES

<u>Divica Stormborn Chronicles</u>

Stormvalor

Stormveil

Stormcrown

Stormvoid

<u>Divica War of Two Crowns</u>

Volume 1: Darkness Falls

<u>Powers Series</u>

Ordinary

Unique

(extra)ordinary

Superior

<u>Powers Origins</u>

Miller: Origin

Enid: Origin

Celeste: Origin

<u>Powers Legacy</u>

Powers Legacy: The Prequel

Desolation

Infiltration

Insurrection

Invasion

<u>Fractured Empire Saga</u>

Daughter of the Yellow Dragon

Lords of the Black Banner

Mother of the Blue Wolf

Empress of the Jade Realm

Prosperous Eternity

<u>Stand-Alone Stories</u>

Stones: A Steampunk Short Story

LUTHIA
RUINS OF KRUOS
GALAN BLUFFS
PAL KA'IKO
SARAK DUNES
GOKA'ATUN
ULA'AN UUL
N
W
E
S

VARYOVA ICE CAP
RIDGEBACK ICE MOUNTAINS
MURANDY HILLS
ELYSIA
BLEAKBURN
ELPISIO
VOROVESTI
MORDELIC
CLIFFS OF HOPE
GREAT RIVER
CROWTOWN
LEMHELLER GAP
STORMVALOR
UMBR
DEADWOOD
PORT VERIX
MT. FJAROE
BARDEN
NOVAVITO
SEORAS PLAINS
OSHON
ARYTH MOUNTAINS
ARITHIA
LAGO
ISLES OF STORM
CAVERN OF LOST SOULS
DIVICA

Contents

Trigger Warning

Stormvalor is an exciting epic noblebright fantasy with dark themes throughout. The book is set in a brutal, bloodthirsty world and includes elements such as intense violence, brutal injuries, blood, dismemberment, murder, death, graphic language, loss of family, grief, psychological and physical torture, psychological abuse, perilous situations, and sexual activities that are shown on the page. Readers who may be sensitive to these elements, please proceed with caution.

And prepare for an epic adventure.

The whispers of the gods faded into echoes, and the balance of power teetered on the brink of collapse.

It was a time foretold by the sages, a time when the balance of the world would be shattered.

The people forgot the warmth of the sun, the comfort of knowledge, and the beauty of the earth.

The world plunged into darkness, not of shadow, but of the heart.

In the heart of this darkness, it was foretold that a single light would rise to restore brightness and hope to the world.

His name shall echo where valor is shown, his heart burning with fury.

And at that moment, the skies answer.

Chapter 1

A Trail of Shadows

Beneath the cloak of darkness, Bast Blackblade found liberation, his footsteps silent against the city's quiet streets as he navigated the labyrinthine alleys and hidden passages that crisscrossed Arithia's heart.

Killing was not a choice for Bast. It was a necessity. And Bast excelled at it more than anyone else in the realm. Everyone except Emperor Oxon's Black Guard, who could hunt and kill without question or emotion at their emperor's command.

For the last two weeks, Bast Blackblade observed his mark, making note of the man's habits and the guard shifts he kept around him, as well as where those guards were posted at any given time. Bast studied the sprawling mansion for weaknesses and potential traps. Rarely did he ever get caught in a trap laid around a mark for protection, and he was not about to make that mistake with this one. Not with the payment he would receive upon completing the task.

A fine mist blanketed Arithia tonight, making the lights across the city glow like wide orbs ringed by thin halos of mirrored light. The city was always beautiful in the dead of night when people were bedded down, taverns were closed, and a tranquil peace settled over the streets. It was a far cry from what Bast encountered in the light of day.

Bast embraced his magic, pulling cautiously from the well within. Shadows shifted around him, eagerly forming his own guard of darkness. No one understood shadows like he did, the life that hummed its seductive song in the dark. It climbed along his limbs and brought that inner calm he would need for the task ahead.

Once satisfied with the protection the night offered, Bast shifted his black sword, Darkheart, along his back and found his grip on the outer wall of the mansion. Then he climbed soundlessly, sticking to the path he carefully selected. A neighboring mansion with tall towers cast long, high shadows along this section of wall. His magic had little work to do to keep him invisible to the eye.

Still, those shadows sang to him, sustaining the mesmerizing calm that accompanied them. He left a trail of his own shadows in his wake for a quick emergency exit.

Bast reached the mansion rooftop in less than a minute. He crouched in the darkness, surveying the ground and walls, seeking any potential threats.

He had climbed this wall a few days ago when scouting the best route to Lord Corinth's balcony. None of the guards noticed him moving in the shadows that night, but he had spotted a pair of guards patrolling the perimeter wall, as well as the mansion courtyard. When he had reached Lord Corinth's balcony, he had observed the movements in the courtyard, the best route down to the stone railing, and how to slip in without a sound.

What he hadn't expected to find a few nights ago on that scouting mission had been Lady Corinth changing for bed... alone. Bast had enjoyed watching her change, had allowed his gaze to slide along the supple curves of her body.

The couple was young for their position, and from what Bast learned, they had only married two years ago. She and Lord Corinth had no children yet, though not for lack of trying, Bast knew. He heard and occasionally caught glimpses of those attempts as he scouted for this job. Once he finished the job tonight, the line would die with Lord Corinth. No doubt that was why he was hired. Someone was making a power play for Lord Corinth's control over Arithian textiles—and possibly his stunning wife. Not that Bast could blame any man for desiring Lady Corinth and that dark, smooth skin.

Bast was actually glad she wouldn't be present tonight. Killing her would be a tragedy.

Once the pair of guards rounded the wall and disappeared from his path, Bast continued along the rooftop, keeping a low profile and using the shadows to his advantage.

As he neared his drop point over the balcony, Bast spotted the single rooftop guard he had expected. He waited until the guard turned his back to peer out at the courtyard and the lord's balcony below. Then, Bast slipped into the shadow of the chimney near the guard. How many nights did this guard have to listen to the Corinths ravishing one another while he stood watch on the roof? He wouldn't see anything from here, but those sounds definitely drifted up here when the couple had grown heated.

As Bast pressed his back into the chimney shadows, he reached out with those same shadows, his magic trilling in delight. The guard's mouth opened in a cry as the darkness wrapped around his throat and cut off his ability to make a sound. The guard reached up with both hands, scratching at the strangling arm as if he could pull it away. But his fingers met his own skin as his face turned red.

Bast crept forward as the shadows hummed for him alone. The guard slipped from consciousness. Bast caught the guard before he could pitch forward into the courtyard and he dragged the guard back toward the chimney, laying him face-down as he tied the guard's arms behind his back and connected the rope to his ankles. The guard would wake with a headache, unable to call for help or come after Bast.

Bast's patron would probably prefer if everyone in Bast's path died, but the payout—as generous as it was—didn't warrant unnecessary killing. Bast might be a killer, but he had a code. As long as this guard didn't see him or pose a threat to him, Bast saw no reason to kill him for doing his job. And a sucky job, at that, to be stuck on this rooftop on a misty night.

With the guard dispatched for at least an hour, Bast trailed his shadows again, then crept toward the edge of the roof and peered into the courtyard. The guards below continued their usual path. Bast would need to wait for them to venture around the corner if he wanted to slip in and out without notice.

As he waited, Bast crouched on the rooftop and gazed out over the city. Tonight offered the optimal window of opportunity. With his wife visiting their country estate with her sister, Lord Ned Corinth would be alone. That also meant her absence would lead to depleted guard shifts.

Lord Ned Corinth's mansion nestled beside the Great River, barely a stone's throw from the Assembly House—a sign of the young lord's power and influence in the kingdom, if nothing else was.

In the moon's silvery glow, the city transformed. Its spires cast long shadows across cobblestone streets. Arithia stood as the radiant jewel within the crown of Novavito. Its breathtaking spires and opulent mansions kissed the heavens. Each edifice whispered tales of a bygone era.

Waterfalls born from the bosom of the lush green Aryth Mountains that enveloped Arithia cascaded in a symphony. The Great River, a shimmering ribbon of life, pulsed through the very soul of Arithia, a liquid lifeline connecting the peaks of the palace to the grandeur of the Assembly House before spilling out into the southern ocean. Where ocean met land, waves caressed sandy beaches.

To the casual observer, Arithia shimmered, its beauty unfurling like a lover's embrace. Crisp white buildings adorned with verdant foliage spilling from windowsills and climbing towers stood as monuments to the harmonious coexistence of nature and civilization.

For Bast Blackblade, the night held a promise of freedom, a respite from the suffocating embrace of daylight's expectations. He found solace in the embrace of darkness. For beneath the veil of night, Arithia revealed a different beauty—a beauty born of whispered secrets and clandestine rendezvous which served him well in his work. This city, like all others, prospered on the backs of the less fortunate, and the royal family had done little in the past century to initiate change.

The guards below disappeared and Bast moved into action. In seconds, he descended the stone drain that sloped down from Lord Ned Corinth's balcony roof. Bast's black boots touched the pristine white stone without a sound. He listened for three beats to the sounds from beyond the open balcony doors as he left a trace of his shadows in place once more.

Only the occasional, soft snore of Lord Corinth broached the silence. The lamps had been extinguished some time ago. Bast hopped off the rail, casting a glance over his shoulder to the courtyard.

Nothing.

With a shake of his shoulders, his magic stirred off the water clinging to his black oiled cloak and boots. He had no intention of leaving incriminating footprints behind.

The instructions were explicit. Lady Corinth was to be spared—the very reason he had waited until she left for the country. No one was to see him go in or out. No traces could be left behind. He would have to wait three days after completing the job before he could collect his final payment—so serious was his patron that no hints be left behind. If he screwed up, he wouldn't be able to collect his money.

This kind of killing would raise suspicions. Whoever hired Blackblade wanted people to know this was personal. Such specific instructions for how to kill only indicated something personal. Quick and sure. A dagger straight to the heart.

Bast hugged his shadows around him like a second skin before stepping inside on silent feet. Lord Corinth didn't stir, didn't stop his soft snoring.

Lord Corinth laid in bed with his limbs sprawled out and most of the blankets kicked off, likely because of the humidity in the air. Only a thin sheet covered his bare body, twisted around his lower half. Ned Corinth was in good shape for a lord—probably because he was still so young. The more these lords aged, the less fit they became, used to their life of lazy entitlement.

Bast crept toward the bed, avoiding the path of any lights from beyond the open balcony doors. The last thing he needed was Lord Corinth startled awake and calling for his guards because Bast's form passed through the light.

He paused beside the bed, and a blade slipped silently into his hand from the sheath along his armguard. Bast drew in a steadying breath, reveling in the song of his shadows in his own soul. Then he slammed the knife true to the mark.

Lord Corinth's eyes shot wide. His mouth opened. In that final moment, Lord Ned Corinth's gaze met Bast's and his eyes widened. Then they glazed over in death.

Bast carefully withdrew his knife, wiping it on the blanket before slipping it into his sheath.

He had no need to steal a token of evidence that the job had been completed. By morning, news of Ned Corinth's death would be on everyone's lips.

With a gentle tug on his shadows, Bast Blackblade disappeared from the lord's bedchamber, sliding along the trail of shadows he had carefully left when he entered the grounds.

In less than a minute, he strolled away from the walls of the mansion precisely where he had entered.

No alarms sounded.

No calls rang out.

No one had any clue Lord Ned Corinth was dead.

CHAPTER 2

Princess of the Sword

The early spring morning air remained cool as Aslyn Kiernan joined her family on the garden veranda for breakfast. Only her father was absent, no doubt called away on business early this morning. Aslyn kissed her mother on the cheek as she passed and assumed a patio seat at the table across from her younger brother, Dorin.

While her mother sat resplendent in a breezy early morning breakfast dress of green, Dorin Kiernan appeared as if he hadn't slept all night. His brown gaze flitted to their father's empty seat, and Dorin shifted in his chair as a servant poured him a glass of cool summer tea. His ebony hair hardly maintained a sense of order, as if he woke late and ran his fingers through it on the way to breakfast instead of taking time to get himself properly ready for the day.

The late-night mists had cleared the humidity from the air, and so high up in the palace, a beautiful spring frost tipped the courtyard grass. Soon, the sprawling gardens would unfurl in a riot of color, their fragrant blooms perfuming the air with the sweet scent of jasmine and rose.

The garden veranda secluded itself from the palace, like a private corner of their world where no other eyes but the gods could see them—assuming any gods remained to watch over them at all.

Aslyn smiled pleasantly at her mother, Queen Giata, as she plucked a delicate pastry off the tray and added it to the plate of eggs Benedict a servant placed in front of her. She waved off the summer tea in favor of fresh-squeezed orange juice.

"Where is father this morning?" Aslyn asked, keeping her tone light.

"Called off to business early," her mother replied.

"Why would he not summon me to shadow him?" Aslyn asked. As part of her training as heir to the kingdom, Aslyn spent more time shadowing her father's business these days than doing anything else. Except, maybe, avoiding Ambassador Umbogo—Emperor Oxon's man. Umbogo shadowed her in ways that made Aslyn uncomfortable.

Dorin made a nearly imperceptible noise of derision on the back of his throat, smearing a far too generous portion of jam on his toast as he responded sharply. "Maybe this is one of those tasks his precious princess is too soft to handle."

Someone woke up on the wrong side of the bed. Aslyn arched a brow as she studied her brother again. Those amber eyes lined with exhaustion. The downward slope of his strong shoulders. The paleness of his chiseled face. Come to think of it, was he wearing that shirt yesterday?

"At least he would have found me in *my* rooms, where I belong," Aslyn replied. The words were barbed, but she delivered them with a casual honey-sweetness that made her mother sigh.

"At least I have other rooms to be found *in*," Dorin muttered.

Aslyn bristled. Dorin knew nothing of her chosen bedmate. No one did, which was for the best. He was her guard, not a true future prospect. Aslyn understood how to be discreet, unlike her brother. She opened her mouth to snap at Dorin and tell him exactly what she thought of his evening escapades, but Queen Giata cut her off.

"That's quite enough." The queen fixed them both with a look Aslyn knew all too well. Their mother had patience in a lot of their banter, but some days she was just too worn out to deal with it. "Aslyn, if your father wanted you to shadow him, he would have summoned you."

Dorin stuck out his tongue so childishly Aslyn wanted to stab it with her fork.

"Dorin, you are a prince and your sister's chief guard," Queen Giata said sharply. Dorin winced, knowing what came next. "What would happen if she were in danger and you were bucking about in the stable with that *boy* like a stallion in heat?"

Dorin flushed. "He's not a boy."

"Or if word got out that you preferred the warmth of men in your bed?" their mother continued. Dorin dipped his head toward his plate, shoving a sausage link in his sour mouth. "Your father is tired of covering your tracks so no one finds out."

"I never asked him to," Dorin muttered under his breath.

"You will be expected to sire children at some point. Who would ever agree to marry you if they knew you preferred men?"

"I prefer what I like, regardless of parts." Dorin's jaw twitched. "I'm in love."

The words were so heartbreakingly sincere as he muttered them that a flash of sympathy for her brother's plight rushed through Aslyn. She tried to offer him a comforting smile, but he refused to glance her way.

"Such things fade," Queen Giata said so matter-of-fact that Aslyn winced. Was marriage so doomed? "Passion doesn't last forever, and that love you think you feel now will become little more than passing companionship. If you think you will be allowed to marry for love—and marry *him*—you are in for a very rude awakening. Your father and I are trying to protect you from making a mistake."

Dorin's jaw twitched. Aslyn nudged her shoe against his under the table. He finally lifted his gaze to meet hers, and the sorrow there broke her heart again. She wanted her brother to be happy, and she knew that *boy* was the only thing that brought any light to his face. If she were queen, she would allow him to marry whomever he wanted.

But she wasn't queen. Not yet.

"He's not a mistake," Dorin muttered so quietly Aslyn hardly heard him, and she was certain their mother hadn't. "And I don't need protection."

A few years ago, Dorin had a close relationship with Lady Dalma Vinto. Aslyn knew Dorin preferred the company of men even then, but Dalma hadn't minded. Aslyn was fairly certain Dorin and Dalma had worked out some kind of agreement that might lead to marriage one day. Then, her family sold her off in marriage to the young, quickly-rising Ned Corinth. And their father, the king, hadn't lifted a finger for Dorin.

Ned was only a few years older than Aslyn, and he had been close friends with Dorin. When Ned married Dalma, something in Dorin broke. It had been another two months before Dorin finally fell apart, as if the reality finally crushed down on him. Losing Dalma had been harder on Dorin than Aslyn had anticipated. Some part of him must have truly loved Dalma to react the way he had.

Aslyn had tried to talk to her brother about it, but Dorin shrugged it off. It wasn't long before he started spending more time with that stable boy he so loved now. At social gatherings, Dorin avoided the new Lord and Lady Corinth, but Aslyn occasionally caught her brother staring at the couple with longing and jealousy in his brown eyes.

"I believe this season you should procure a husband, Aslyn," her mother said casually. But the way her mother eyed her made Aslyn nervous.

Dorin choked on his summer tea.

"A husband?" It was all she could say. *Procure*. It made the entire thing sound like she was buying her mate instead of entering a partnership. Not that anyone she married would ever be a true partner. He wouldn't rule as she would. While her husband would have responsibilities to Novavito and its people, only she would truly rule the kingdom. Still, Aslyn had yet to meet a nobleman with the qualities of a suitable King Consort.

"Yes, so that we can see our future queen settled into marriage before the next winter." These weren't the words of her mother. It was Queen Giata commanding the heir to prepare to produce more heirs. Her mother sliced through her egg whites a touch roughly. "And maybe I will have grandchildren before I die." She threw a pointed glance at Dorin, too, as if to say, *I know* you *won't give me any grandchildren*.

Silence settled over the table as the three of them continued their breakfast.

Aslyn had no desire to marry. Not yet. She was barely twenty, with plenty of good child-rearing years ahead of her. While she understood that this day might come, Aslyn had hoped for a few more years of freedom. She certainly had her own plans for the future.

After that disastrous breakfast, Aslyn needed to work off some of her anger, so she marched to the lower courtyard near the guard quarters to train. The early-spring frost had melted away by the time her boots crunched on the gravel path leading to the sparring ring where a guard training session was already well underway.

While Aslyn looked every inch the princess she was in front of the public, she was anything but soft—as her father sometimes implied. A princess needed to know how to defend herself just as much as a prince, so she had spent years training with Shino, Captain of the Guard. Though she was nowhere near a weapons master, Aslyn could hold her own in a fight... and often did here in the training ground.

Her appearance on the training ground didn't startle any of the guards. They knew when she had that kind of burning fury on her face to steer clear of jovial comments.

To her disappointment, Captain Shino left the palace grounds early on business for the king, taking his second and several of the guards with him. It left Aslyn with far fewer suitable options for sparring, but she made do.

After a brief prayer to Justis, the god of war, Aslyn tucked her necklace safely in a pocket. Then, she began her warmups with her practice sword, working through the forms Captain Shino taught her slowly at first to be certain she had each motion right. Then, she increased speed until she had worked up a sweat in her training leathers.

Princess of the Sword, the guards called her with increasing pride. She bore the title with honor, thrilled that they would see her as so skilled to deserve it.

It was in this sparring ring that she had met Elisio and taken a liking to him. He was just as young and spirited as her, but honorable. It had taken her months to work up the courage to make a move. He had been shocked and horrified at first. Not because he wasn't interested in her, but because she was the crown princess and he was a lowly guard.

On the one-year anniversary of when they first met, Aslyn invited him into her room, into her bed. Elisio had been hesitant to accept, but she had found ways to make that hesitation vanish.

Where is Elisio today?

He was almost always near the sparring grounds, ready to challenge her. But not this morning.

The practice sword had been crafted to match the size and weight of Nova, Sword of the First King, though the practice sword edges were dull to avoid true injury. One day, she would take up Nova in defense of her kingdom. Though right now, it belonged to her father, King Novin. The sword she would use until that day—Vito, Sword of the Crown Heir—also followed the tradition of being passed from one heir to the next, and it matched the balance of Nova as well.

After finishing warmups, a handful of eager guards jumped at a chance to train with Aslyn when she demanded a good workout. Not because they wanted to be closer to their beautiful princess, but because entering the sparring ring with her had become a badge of honor and could elevate them if they did well and the captain found out.

The first guard Aslyn trained with had massive shoulders and thighs the size of a tree trunk. He pressed his attacks with brutal efficiency, but he lacked the skills the princess had become accustomed to competing against.

In just two minutes, she had him in the dirt with her sword poised over his heart. The others cheered her victory, and he offered her a forced smile as he submitted. But Aslyn saw that anger burning in his dark eyes. He didn't like losing to her.

Aslyn offered him a hand up. The burly guard appeared ready to brush her hand aside but seemed to think better of it. He pulled at her as he rose, and she had to adjust her own balance to keep him from yanking her off her feet. A purposeful move on his part, she was certain.

For the next half hour, various guards—both men and women—challenged their future queen. Aslyn's limbs trembled from exertion, but she continued working the muscles. She didn't slow as the sweat rolled down her spine beneath the leathers, as her knees trembled from exhaustion, and as the sword became increasingly more of a burden to bear.

All of these guards displayed their own skills, but none of them were a true match for Aslyn. Where were the more skilled guards?

After an hour, the gates near the guard courtyard opened, and Captain Shino rode in with his soldiers—Elisio among them.

And they weren't alone. King Novin rode astride his own mount at the captain's side, their heads together in hushed conversation, faces grim.

Aslyn grinned at the guards surrounding her and said, "Thank you all for humoring me today."

They all offered their own kindness, some sporting fresh bruises from her strikes.

It took considerable effort to march to the rack and put the practice sword where it belonged without showing anyone her exhaustion.

Aslyn hustled over to her father as quickly as her unsteady legs would allow. As she moved, she pulled the leather strap from her ebony hair and re-adjusted her ponytail to something at least a little more respectable.

Captain Shino noticed her approach first and fell silent after a quick word to King Novin. Just behind the two of them, Elisio rode with a grim look in his eyes.

By the time Aslyn crossed the courtyard to reach their sides, all the men had dismounted and stable hands retrieved the horses.

King Novin failed to mask his inner anger. The set of his stare softened at the sight of her, but his soulful eyes always gave him away. Captain Shino was no better, his muscles tense, his salt and pepper beard twitching at his jawline. Elisio met Aslyn's gaze and his lips tightened.

"What is it?" Aslyn asked softly, understanding in less than a second that something horrible had happened.

Her father simply tilted his head toward the palace. Whatever they uncovered, he didn't want anyone else to hear of it yet. Aslyn's stomach sank.

A cool breeze chilled the sweat on her skin as she matched her father's stride into the palace. He moved with purpose, a man on a mission. Captain Shino gave the men who had escorted him and the king a few quick commands, and Aslyn swore she heard the words "discretion" and "silence" in the mix. Elisio caught her eye once more before he turned to follow his orders. They would talk in private later. She knew it for certain.

Aslyn had been around such dealings her entire life. She knew that other lords had spies in the palace walls, seeking any information that might help their position at court. If her father kept matters this quiet, it meant the court would somehow benefit from the news.

As she marched silently beside her father, the captain catching up and trailing them like a shadow, Aslyn combed her memory for anything that might have happened, any hints she might have previously gleaned.

Had Emperor Oxon's Black Guard taken another trove of hidden magic users? Magic was rare anywhere in the realm of Divica, and King Novin had always been careful to serve Emperor Oxon, but Aslyn knew there were certain practices—such as detaining and killing anyone with magic—that her father despised. But no one dared speak out against the Imperial Seat in Umbr. Any who did either died or vanished without a trace. King Novin had warned Aslyn that if she didn't follow his example, the emperor would find ways to ensure she never took the throne. Especially if Dorin proved more amenable.

Aslyn had her own future plans for the kingdom of Novavito. She prepared herself for the day she would be crowned, the day she would have to bow to the emperor, and what she would say and do when that day came. By that time, his son, Prince Valen, would reach the transition age, forcing Emperor Oxon to retire and crown the new emperor. Aslyn intended to make Prince Valen her ally... even if it required using her feminine wiles to sway him. Surely a young prince newly risen to his rule over the five kingdoms would see the benefits of what she could offer.

Aslyn once more glanced at her father from the corner of her eyes as they climbed the wide marble steps leading to the council chamber.

A guard opened the chamber door for them, bowing deeply to the king and his heir. Aslyn followed her father inside. Captain Shino paused at the door, whispering commands to the men on guard, then he closed the door behind himself.

The moment the door closed, King Novin turned, pressing the tips of his fingers against the tabletop. Those brown eyes met her gaze urgently.

"As if rumors of rebels to our crown weren't bad enough..." King Novin's jaw tensed, then he said, "Blackblade is in Arithia."

Aslyn's blood ran cold at the mention of the infamous assassin. No one knew who he was. He only went by the name Blackblade—a moniker granted to him because, if stories were to be believed, his blades all absorbed light.

She licked her lips to steady her breathing. Yes, the rumors of rebels against the Novavito crown were troublesome, but with their resources they could root out the problem. But Blackblade... Her heart hammered. If he was within the city walls, they were all in danger.

"Who would send him here?" she asked, hating the slight tremor in her voice. "Is he linked to the rebels?"

The king shook his head. "Doubtful. The better question is, why was Lord Corinth selected as his target?"

The room tilted. Blackblade in the city with Ned as a target could only mean... "When?"

"In the middle of the night," King Novin said.

Dalma Corinth had gone to their country estate with her sister just yesterday. It couldn't be a coincidence that Blackblade would strike the same night she was gone... not if whoever sent him wanted the lady alive. But... why would she be spared?

Captain Shino positioned himself between the door and his king and princess, as if doing so could prevent Blackblade from getting to them. But he wouldn't take the door, would he? Not if stories were to be believed. He could walk through the shadows along the walls, invisible and untraceable.

Aslyn didn't bother asking how Blackblade slipped in when Ned Corinth's mansion was so heavily guarded. It was a stupid question. Blackblade could walk through shadows, appearing and disappearing at will. It made night his best ally. According to stories, he could walk through walls themselves.

Captain Shino broke down the details of what they had learned. The maid discovered Ned dead in bed just before dawn, when she came to his chamber to draw his bath and prepare him for breakfast. Only one wound had been inflicted. A slice straight down into his heart. His eyes were wide open in alarm, as if he saw his death coming, but hadn't time to move before it was done.

Aslyn sank into a seat at the council table as she listened.

A knife to the heart. Not a slice across the throat.

"Dalma…" Aslyn said.

"I will dispatch a messenger to her this morning," her father replied, understanding in his brown eyes.

Aslyn cleared her throat as if it could remove the dread clawing at her veins. "Let me send the message. Please." He nodded once in agreement.

"This was not an outside job," the captain said.

"How do you figure?" Aslyn asked, straightening in the chair and trying not to ruminate on Blackblade loose in her city.

"Outsiders would gain little by killing him," Captain Shino explained. He spoke so calmly and rationally. Though he sounded at ease, his eyes continued watching the windows and shadows for signs of danger.

He's worried Blackblade will strike us next, Aslyn realized in alarm. Not that it was outside the realm of possibility, but striking them now, in daylight, didn't seem like Blackblade's style.

"Whoever paid to have Lord Corinth killed wanted to be sure it was done, and was willing to pay a hefty sum to make sure the assassination went smoothly," Captain Shino continued. "Whoever killed him stood to gain something from his death."

Aslyn snorted and rolled her eyes. "That's any of the nobles." Ned recently gained control over the textile factories, making him one of the wealthiest men in the city… the kingdom. With him out of the picture, any of the other noble houses could swoop in to take his place.

"The captain is worried the nobles will whisper Dorin's name," her father cut in. His fingers pressed so hard into the tabletop his knuckles turned white, the only sign of his worry. "It's no secret Dorin had a connection to both Ned and Dalma before the marriage. And he didn't exactly hide his jealousy for a while after, either."

Aslyn laughed at that. She couldn't help herself. Dorin was a lot of things, but not a murderous, jealous lover. The humor died quickly as she studied the seriousness of their expressions.

"Oh come now, father, you can't honestly think—"

"No," he said quickly. "But Lady Corinth just happened to be gone. If she were there, Blackblade would have killed her, too. Which means her survival was not an accident." He leaned toward her, urgency bleeding off of him. "Do you think Dalma would have done this to gain her husband's wealth, so she could then marry your brother?"

Aslyn opened her mouth, but floundered. No. No, Dalma wouldn't dare. She loved her husband. Aslyn was certain of that from the many conversations they had these past two years. She shook her head. "No. She adores Ned."

Her father and Captain Shino exchanged a knowing look Aslyn couldn't read. Some silent conversation passed between the two of them.

"Then we need a strategy to protect your brother from suspicion," King Novin said at last.

The way his expression hardened made Aslyn's skin crawl, but it was nothing compared to the terror his next words invoked within. "And for the time being, we all sleep with our lights on."

Blackblade would have a harder time striking them when shadows were few.

Aslyn would do more than sleep with the lights on. She would insist on Elisio as her night guard and he would spend those nights so close to her Blackblade wouldn't be able to touch her without a fight.

As soon as the coast was clear, Aslyn summoned Elisio into her room. She wanted to know everything he had learned about Ned's murder. Surely there had to be some clue who was responsible.

The grim truth Elisio shared with her brought a fresh bout of tears to her eyes. Ned's wide-eyed shock. The knife wound straight to his heart. The mess of blood staining the mattress.

"It's some small mercy, I think, that he would have died quickly," Elisio said solemnly.

Aslyn swallowed her sorrow and cleared her throat. "The weapon?"

He shook his head. "No forced entry, and no witnesses, either. A guard was found unconscious on the roof, soaked to the bone. He was a mess. He said something choked him, but when he reached for his assailant, there was no one there."

Aslyn's stomach churned. "Magic?"

"Your father thinks so. It would explain how Blackblade moves without notice." Elisio closed the narrow gap between them, cupping her face tenderly and tilting her chin up toward him. "He won't touch you, Aslyn. He will have to go through me first."

Aslyn offered him a soft smile, stroking his hand against her cheek. "I know." Except if the stories about Blackblade were true, Elisio would die before he even knew the shadow assassin was in the room.

Their lips met, and she didn't know if she kissed him or he kissed her first. It didn't matter. She needed his closeness and comfort.

After a moment, Aslyn broke the kiss long enough to whisper, "Stay with me."

"As you wish, Your Majesty," Elisio murmured affectionately.

Then they kissed once more.

CHAPTER 3

Patience of a Saint

Bast seated himself at a corner table of the common room in The Supernova Inn, positioned so he could see most of the open space and hear what he couldn't see. The shadowy corner at his back offered a means of emergency escape, should anyone come looking for him.

As the dinner hour approached, the aroma of hearty stew wafted from the inn's kitchen, enticing hungry travelers to feast. Servers bustled back and forth, delivering steaming bowls of stew with crusty bread to eagerly awaiting tables. The stew was hardly a feast. In fact, it was a staple dish at any inn no matter where Bast traveled. Stew was cheap to make and often watered down or over laden with spices to mask the lack of real meat or fresh produce. Often places that boasted meats lied about the true source of that meat. Bast knew a lot of the time it came from rats, rabbits, or squirrels. Only the rich could afford real meat, such was the low production and high demand in the slowly dying world.

As Bast choked down his dinner, he covertly listened to the conversations all around the tavern. Most of it was meaningless banter about the daily grind. Climbing market prices. Diminishing goods. Speculation on how the realm might change when Prince Valen became the emperor. Bast restrained himself from an exaggerated eye roll at that. The Imperial Heir wouldn't care about the slow decay of the fields or meats any more than his father had.

All emperors were the same, born and bred for rule and cruelty. No doubt that was why no one saw the princes until they were about to become emperor, to ensure they would carry on the brutal legacy appropriately. Why did anyone think that would change?

No one knew much about Prince Valen, nor had they seen him. Only rumors of his young Oshon princess-wife dying of the withering disease that plagued some people of Divica. The emperor's heirs were always kept within the palace walls in Umbr until he rose to power over all five kingdoms of Divica. Prince Valen would look just like his father—just like all the heirs over the centuries all bore the same look. Snowy blond hair. Hard, soulless black eyes. The resemblance from one generation to the next was uncanny. Younger, to be sure, but a spitting image of his father... always.

And always male.

Other kingdoms had seen both kings and queens over the centuries. But the whole of Divica was always ruled by a male. An emperor.

People assumed all of this meant the bloodline was strong. In Bast's opinion, these emperors were all weak.

All Bast wanted was to remain outside the reach of the emperor—present and future.

Magic was forbidden ever since the war against the Kruos elves more than a millennium ago. Anyone who showed magical gifts faced capture by the emperor's Black Guard and were taken to Umbr for sentencing, never seen or heard from again.

Killed, most likely, though a few desperate soulless men might have been converted into Black Guards.

Bast sometimes wondered if those poor souls ever reached the palace high in the Umbr Mountains, or if the Black Guards killed the prisoners and dumped their bodies elsewhere.

If Emperor Oxon or his precious prince ever learned the kind of magic Bast could wield, he doubted the Black Guards would bother taking him to the palace. They would likely try to kill him on sight.

Thankfully, no one knew who he was. In public, he went by many names. What he did, the moniker he acquired, meant people only knew the name—Blackblade. Even the contacts between himself and his patrons were a few steps removed.

A young man in a nice jacket strolled in, joining a table of guards with a jovial grin on his face. He settled on the bench with the men, an air of self-importance surrounding him.

"Did you hear about Lord Corinth?" the young man asked his friends. They all fell silent, shaking their heads. "Surprised it hasn't reached The Supernova patrons yet. He's dead. They're holding a funeral for him along the Great River to the Hall of Honors as soon as his widow returns from their country estate."

Another man snorted. "So? Another snooty lord died. Good riddance."

"Sure, but he was our age," the young man said. "Younger, maybe. What are the odds he just kicked the bucket in the night?" He leaned closer. "I think the Kiernan family is covering something else up."

The Kiernans. Royals. Did they cover up Lord Corinth's murder so people didn't know Blackblade was near?

Bast focused on his ale, acting casual so no one knew he was listening.

"Did you notice the palace lights stayed on all night long?" the young man continued. "What do you suppose was going on up there that they would leave the palace in light all night?"

"Maybe Blackblade is after the royal family," a companion said, mockery bleeding into his voice. "They left the lights on to keep him away." He shrugged.

As if lights would keep Bast away.

The young man thanked the barmaid, Evette, for the drink as she delivered it, giving her a coin. Her face as she pocketed it and turned away made it apparent his next drink would have spit in it. The young man had the audacity to slap her on the ass like he had given her a generous tip.

Bast's jaw twitched. He took a slow drink to cool his rising temper.

"Good riddance to them all," the young man said, raising the cup to his lips as he settled back comfortably in the chair. "Except that princess. Blackblade can leave her for me." A devious grin split his ugly face.

Bast wanted to throw a knife into the asshole's eye. Or maybe down his throat.

"Oh please," a companion said. "Like the princess would ever look at an ugly fucker like you."

The rest of the men roared with laughter.

Bast remained in his seat, fingers tightening around his mug of ale. Someone needed to give him a medal for having the patience of a saint with men like these.

Sure, Bast bedded his share of women—probably considerably more than all those men combined—and yes, he rarely returned to the same girl. Better that they not grow attached. But at least he had respect for the women he did bed. And he didn't harass or force his presence on anyone not interested in him.

But men like these... Bast grew more certain by the moment that consent was not a necessity for them.

He called Evette over for another drink and drank slowly as the conversations continued. A musician entered the tavern just after the dinner hour. After a brief conversation with the innkeeper, the older gentleman took his place near the warmth of the hearth and opened with a warmup song that drew more attention to his performance.

As the music carried on into the night, the sound drew people in from the streets seeking warmth, drinks, entertainment, and company. All who entered The Supernova Inn found themselves welcomed with open arms and a warm smile, ready to savor the simple pleasures of food, drink, and fellowship amidst the enchanting backdrop of good music and stories.

This was Bast's fourth inn over the past few weeks. Experience taught him to keep moving, to not stay in one inn for more than a week at a time, or people started asking questions about his business and if he needed a room to rent in a house or apartment block instead.

Distracted by the way the young man wrapped an arm around the barmaid and slid his hand down her hip and outer thigh, Bast's vision narrowed on the two.

Evette was a pretty girl with thick red lips, a narrow waist, and wide hips. Dust auburn hair was tied back from her face in a braid, but on a busy night like tonight, a few hairs came free and clung to her face.

The common room joined the musician, singing the chorus to the song with such vibrance he flinched. It wasn't until the girl pulled away with a forced smile that he even realized the song the patrons bellowed into the rafters.

He suppressed a groan.

Blackblade stalks the shadows deep. A phantom's touch, a secret keep. Cloaked in darkness. Silent night. Fear his name. The endless fright.

It was one thing to allow the legend to grow. That reputation served his business well. It was another thing entirely to sit in a common room while people sang stupid songs about him.

Bast glanced to the side again to see the young man missing from the table. He grimaced, knowing what he had to do next.

Patience of a lost god, more like, Bast thought as he downed his drink in a gulp and rose from the table. Screw the gods. They never did him any favors.

Evette was missing as well.

He doubted Evette would have followed the young man anywhere. More likely, he had followed her. Which meant she would have gone somewhere meant for staff.

Bast reached into that well of magic within and the shadows sang with life around him. With a glance over his shoulder, he slipped into one in search of the missing barmaid.

The shadows sang, spoke, guiding his silent steps as he entered a narrow hallway near the back of the tavern. Several doors off the hallway likely had rooms belonging to the owner, as well as storage spaces. He approached the second door on his left, not needing his shadows to hear Evette's muffled protests on the other side.

Bast couldn't barge in with a weapon in hand and shadows around him. No one could know he was here or his payday would vanish. Tomorrow, he would have his coins. But today... tonight... if he killed this entitled prick, he risked everything.

Instead, Bast pushed the shadows back and adopted an inebriated façade. He stumbled into the door, throwing it open with drunken confidence.

Evette trembled against a cask of ale where the jerk had her pinned, his hand over her mouth. Her eyes widened seeing Bast stumble into the room, blinking dumbly at them. The man jerked around, glaring at Bast with his teeth bared.

"This isn't my room," Bast mumbled.

"Get out," the man growled.

"Yeah. Right. M'kay." Bast blinked slowly, listing to the side. "Which way might that be?"

Confident in his dominance at the moment, the young man did exactly as Bast predicted. He stomped toward him, grabbing an arm to thrust him back out the door.

A dangerous mistake.

Bast moved with lightning quick reflexes, rotating the grip so that he had a firm hold on the man's arm, then he wrenched it behind the man's back. In a heartbeat, the man was pressed face-first against the doorframe. Bast drove against the back of his head, forcing the edge of the doorjamb into his face.

"—the hell?" the man yelped, his words as distorted as his lips were pressed up against the frame.

"Seems to me Miss Evette has no interest in where your hands were," Bast hissed into the man's ear. He shifted slightly so the tip of his dagger subtly pressed against the man's side.

All twisting resistance in the man winked out the second he felt that blade pinch his side.

"And even with too many drinks in me, you don't stand a chance," Bast said, letting a dark chuckle roll out. "Touch her again, and I'll enjoy pulling your guts out through your mouth."

Bast pulled back and shoved the man into the hallway with enough force the body slammed against the opposite wall and rebounded. The man's arms flailed as he fell on his back. In a second, he was scrambling to his feet, glaring at Bast.

"My friends will be back with me," the man threatened even as he stumbled down the hallway away from the open door.

"Good. It might be a fair fight then."

The man disappeared into the common room.

Evette sniffled behind him.

Bast half turned, looking her over for signs of injury. He couldn't see anything obvious.

"Are you alright?" he asked gently.

Evette swept tears from her cheek and sniffled again, but her eyes cleared as she studied him uncertainly. "What... what do you want?"

"A room would be a good start."

Evette's spine stiffened as she adjusted her clothes, big eyes locked on him. "I will not—"

"For me. Not you."

She edged toward the door, keeping what she assumed was a safe distance from him, and glanced toward the common room.

"He will bring his friends," she murmured.

"I can handle them," Bast replied. "But if I hire out a room for the night, I would prefer he not know where."

She studied him once more. Whatever she saw seemed to satisfy her because she gave him a tight nod. "This way."

The two made their way along the hall and up a set of stairs at the back of the inn and up three flights of stairs, music fading as walls and floors separated them.

"How do you know my name?" she asked.

"The innkeeper called you by name several times tonight." He couldn't help watching the way her apple-bottom moved with each stair she climbed.

"Do I get to know your name?"

"Bast."

"No last name?"

"Arrd."

She stopped at the top of the stairs, eyes narrowing in suspicion. "Your name is Bast Arrd?"

"I blame my parents." A lie. He didn't know his real parents, and the ones who did raise him were hardly worthy of the title.

At the far end of the hallway, she opened a door for him.

Bast stepped into the doorway, examining the room. One window was closed and curtained with a lock engaged inside. A full-size bed with more than enough space for him. A nightstand with a lamp beside the bed. A chest with spare blankets at the foot. He nodded. This would be good enough.

"This will do fine. Thank you, Evette." Bast lifted her hand and slid coins into it. "For the week."

Evette pocketed the coins with a nod. "Thank you."

"I would suggest not returning to the tavern until he and his friends are gone." Bast strolled across the room. He leaned Darkheart carefully against the bedside table, thankful for the sheath that covered the black blade. Seeing that might be too much of a giveaway on a night like tonight, when people were already whispering his name.

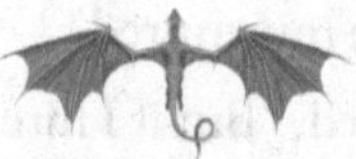

After using the washbasin to clean himself off, Bast dressed and strapped his weapons on. Nothing would be left behind in the room. He traveled with what he could carry and nothing more. It made it easier for him to move quickly should he need to flee.

Bast fastened his belt, then hooked Darkheart in place at his hip before strolling out the door.

If gossip in the common room last night was to be believed, the heat from Lord Corinth's death would cause considerable trouble. It was best to leave right away and escape the heat.

I'll collect my payment and leave the city, he thought.

Bast slithered out the back door of The Supernova Inn and slipped along the alley into the street, his hood down to avoid raising curious glances. A man in black leather with a sword on his hip was not so odd—hunters and swords for hire did it all the time. But having a hood up in broad daylight would attract unwanted attention.

In the early morning hours, Arithia exuded a vibrant energy that pulsed through its sun-kissed streets. Golden sunlight filtered through the verdant canopy of foliage, casting dappled shadows upon the cobblestone pathways below. Shops and market stalls opened their doors, their colorful wares spilling out onto the bustling thoroughfares.

Merchants called out their wares, their voices blending into a melodic symphony that filled the air with anticipation and excitement. Aromas of freshly baked bread, exotic spices, and fragrant flowers mingled together, tantalizing the senses and beckoning passersby to indulge in the delights of the day.

Bast made his way along the streets with the flow of the crowd, buying breakfast pastries from a bakery street vendor. All the while, he listened to the gossip among the people, moving closer to the heart of the upper-class section of the brilliant city.

Amidst the hustle and bustle, street performers entertained the swelling crowds with their colorful antics while artists captured the beauty of the city with strokes of their brushes and pens along the banks of the Great River. Children darted through the throng, their laughter echoing like joyful peals of bells as they chased one another through the sunny streets.

All of it was a mask, a carefully crafted illusion to cover the true dangers of the city... of the dying world. Nowhere was safe. Arithia might appear to flourish, but Bast had seen the darker side of every city. People still starved, and the royals did little to help. The few soup kitchens run by greedy, self-serving patrons in the crown's name served little more than broth.

As the city came alive with the promise of a new day, the vibrant pulse of Novavito's wealthy capital filled the air with a sense of vitality and possibility.

Noblewomen and gentlemen clad in fine silks and shimmering jewels traversed the streets, their careless laughter ringing out in the crisp morning air. Carriages drawn by sleek horses clip-clopped along the thoroughfares, their occupants exchanging pleasantries and gossip as they journeyed through the city.

Bast leaned against an arching pillar that served as entrance to a bridge spanning over the mighty river. To passersby, he looked like a man enjoying his pastry in the shade beside the river. But it was the opposite side of the water that caught his attention. City guards cleared the path along the road between the palace high above and the Hall of Honors beside the river. And milling among those guards were pale men clad in black uniforms with wicked swords, overseeing the work.

Black Guards.

The emperor's Arithian might flexed its muscles to once more remind the people who truly ruled over them all. Bast's jaw twitched as he watched. How he would love to take all of their heads and dump them at the base of the Umbr palace.

Yet he had a job to finish... or better yet, to collect.

After another two hours wandering the streets for whispers of Blackblade or rumors about Lord Corinth, Bast knew that the truth of what Blackblade had done was covered up. Yes, people knew Lord Corinth was dead. But many believed he died in his sleep of a mysterious ailment. Some blamed it on the wasting illness, but most knew better. Lord Corinth was young and healthy. Wasting took at least a year and quickly became evident.

Bast made his way toward the market where he would find the contact who brokered this deal.

If Emperor Oxon's Black Guards were putting on such a display of superiority, it was better he collect and disappear before they caught his trail all over Arithia.

Bast reached the tailor's shop, but the moment he opened the door and stepped into the dim shop, his senses came to dark life.

None of the lamps used to illuminate the cloth were lit. No one exited the back room to see who had walked in. The bell over the door that warned the tailor someone had entered was gone.

Bast dipped his fingers in the well of his magic and wrapped a hand around Darkheart. With silent, cautious steps, he eased deeper into the shop, not daring to call out in case an attacker awaited. The toe of his boot kicked the bell across the floor, making it chime softly and pitifully as it rolled away.

Fabric fluttered as he unsettled the air around it. Bast glanced at the front entrance once more, but people streamed past the shop without so much as a glance into the massive glass windows.

That warning in his veins screamed at him to leave, but he had to know. He had to confirm that instinct clawing its way through his gut.

With his free hand, Bast eased the back door of the shop wider so he could slide through.

The smell hit him before he spotted the source. A metallic tang crusted the air in the back room, slamming against him.

Bast checked the room for attackers before giving himself a moment to take in the scene.

On the back wall of the tailor's workshop was the tailor himself, stretched out like a piece of morbid art. A thin man in his forties with years still ahead of him. But his eyes were open, milky with death. Metal spikes through his wrists and ankles pinned him to the wall like a bolt of his own fabric. A final spike had been driven through his open mouth.

Bast pulled his shadows closer, creating a protective shield.

Someone knew. They had to.

Why else would this tailor be targeted?

Avoiding the pool of blood on the floor, Bast edged closer.

A parchment note was attached to the spike through the tailor's mouth. Bast winced as he pulled it off and read the warning.

We have found you.

Bast cursed viciously.

Bright light flashed in the back room and he dropped the parchment to cover his eyes as the shadows wrapped around him screamed in pain.

Before he could move, the entire shop trembled.

CHAPTER 4

Eyes of Sun-Kissed Amber

Aslyn Kiernan, Crown Princess of Novavito, hated Emperor Oxon's Arithian ambassador. Her dealings with him had been minimal at her parents' request for years. But she could only avoid Ambassador Umbogo for so long if she was ever to take the throne. And with the death of a High Lord—an assassination courtesy of Blackblade—Aslyn could avoid Umbogo no longer.

The emperor's ambassador moved around the throne room as if *he* were the king, ordering servants about and putting lesser nobles in their place. Only when one of the royal family approached did he become more subservient.

The throne room of the Arithian palace stood as a breathtaking testament to the kingdom's grandeur and majesty. Its pristine white walls, adorned with intricate gold filigree, gleamed under the soft glow of crystal chandeliers that hung from the vaulted ceiling like celestial stars.

At the heart of the chamber, upon a raised dais of polished marble, sat the throne of the king, a magnificent seat of ivory and gold that commanded reverence and respect.

The tall windows on one side of the chamber provided a view of a cascading waterfall, with its crystalline waters tumbling gracefully down the mountainside before spilling into a series of cascading fountains that adorned the lower levels of the palace. From there, the waters flowed further still, coursing through channels that wound their way down into the heart of the city below.

The air was heavy with the scent of exotic flowers and the gentle murmur of cascading water, lending an aura of tranquility to the proceedings.

But that tranquility fell flat on Aslyn.

Tomorrow would be the funeral. Dalma had only been a day from Arithia when she received the message about her husband. Aslyn had offered her most heartfelt apologies in the letter and asked her to come straight to the palace upon arrival, where she would be taken care of during her period of mourning. It was the least Aslyn could offer.

Besides, she was sure Dalma would not want to return to her bedroom in her own home, where her husband's blood still stained the mattress.

Dalma hardly said a word when she arrived at the palace late the previous night under heavy royal guard. She had ignored Dorin when he attempted to greet her, his face streaked with tears. Aslyn didn't understand why he was so upset over Ned's death. He had been fiercely jealous of the marriage. Her only conclusion was that Dorin felt the grief for Dalma, his dear friend.

But Dalma had given him the cold shoulder, devastating what little remained in Dorin. Aslyn's heart broke for her brother as she watched his face shatter at the dismissal, the way he appeared near collapse.

Queen Giata insisted Dalma be given a day to herself to mourn before being put on display in front of the kingdom, and Aslyn couldn't help but agree.

Tomorrow, Dalma would commit her husband's soul to the goddess Astra in the Stellar Passage funeral. "So he might find his way and guide us all safely home," Dalma had said through her grief. And that was all she had said before closing the door to her guest suite. Already, city guards worked with Black Guards to prepare the funeral route.

Aslyn oversaw the organization of the event alongside the king and queen... and Umbogo. Several other lords and ladies ventured into the palace to assist, but Aslyn was fairly certain as she mingled that they were simply seeking favor from the Kiernan royals. After all, a major position had just become available.

Aslyn wanted to punch all the sniveling sycophants in the face. She understood why they held court—so that these nobles could have answers to some of their questions and to assuage fears. Doing so would keep those questions out of the funeral proceedings tomorrow.

Aslyn snatched a drink off a passing serving tray and meandered toward the window overlooking the waterfall and the city below.

The palace was not so far up that everything looked small, but it certainly made her feel small to peer over everything from such a distance. She watched the river roads that passed by the palace and out toward the ocean, noting the black figures "helping" the city guards.

Emperor Oxon's men. His presence in this city was endless, with his own soldiers always watching, always waiting somewhere in the shadows. She almost feared them more than Blackblade... almost.

As the crown princess, it was Aslyn's duty to move through the room and engage in conversation, establishing alliances with these nobles. But she just couldn't make herself care. Her mind continued to drift to Ned. To Blackblade.

Where was Blackblade now? Was he still in the city?

She heaved a sigh that seemed to come from her toes.

"Such a heavy sigh for such a light thing." Umbogo's voice slid across her skin like slime.

Aslyn schooled her features calm, pleasant even, and turned to face Umbogo as he joined her beside the window.

"That's quite a view," he remarked.

"I suppose," Aslyn replied, wishing she could throw her drink in his face and walk away. But her father would flay her alive. "I find little joy in it today, though."

"You weren't particularly close to Lord Corinth, I thought?" Umbogo shifted closer, watching her and not the view.

Aslyn threw her gaze at the city once more. "I am friends with his wife. I should think that's cause enough to feel mournful today."

He nodded, then glanced at the rest of the nobles mingling in the room as if searching for eavesdroppers. Umbogo leaned closer and lowered his voice. "I've heard a rumor that Blackblade might be captured today."

Aslyn had been in the middle of taking a drink and nearly choked on the sparkling juice. Worse, Umbogo ran his hand along her back as if trying to help her.

The ambassador was fairly new to his post, and perhaps only five years older than Aslyn. His sharp, dark eyes stood out starkly against that pasty skin. There was a deadly beauty to the hard lines of his face. Nothing Aslyn ever wanted to become further acquainted with, though. Nothing more than she had to, anyway.

But she had to form a relationship with Umbogo. At his age, he would likely serve during most of her reign. Which meant they would work closely for a very long time to come.

He seemed to read her train of thought, because he said, "I've been trying to gain an audience with our future sovereign for some time." He cocked his head slightly, studying her eyes intently. "You have such... unique eyes, princess. Like eyes of sun-kissed amber." She didn't like the intensity of that stare. "Such beautiful, unique eyes. I believe it would behoove us both to... get to know one another better."

She had no interest in finding out just what he meant by that. Aslyn changed the subject. "Why do you think Blackblade will be captured?"

A knowing smile curved his sharp cheekbones into something truly menacing. "Call it a hunch. But I intend to ensure you have a long and fruitful reign, princess. What better way to offer my humblest allegiance than with such a precious gift?"

He stepped closer, placing a hand against her lower back as he pointed out at the city. Not just anywhere. His long, thin finger pointed with purpose. "Watch right there. If you see it, then you know I have a rare gift for you indeed."

She attempted to pinpoint what he indicated, craning her neck slightly for a better view of the city.

Umbogo whispered in her ear, "And then we can talk about just how we might solidify this alliance... together."

Aslyn turned to push him off and tell him just what she thought of his presumptuous behavior, but Umbogo had already strolled across the throne room to engage in a new conversation.

How could he possibly think of capturing a ghost, a shadow? And just what did he think she would see?

But Aslyn was rooted. Her curiosity peaked by his cryptic words. She stared at the street he had indicated, unable to look away.

"What are we looking at?" Dorin asked as he joined her. He sounded utterly exhausted and broken. "You've been standing here for half an hour now. Our mother is worried."

"I don't know. Umbogo said..." But how could she explain? Especially if Umbogo was doing little more than blowing smoke up her skirt.

Dorin waited, downing his mimosa and handing it off to a servant passing by. When Aslyn glanced at him again, he had a fresh glass.

"Slow down, Dorin. Please."

He responded by taking a sip as if to prove he could. "By the way, I thought I would warn you. Mother was talking about your marriage again."

Aslyn groaned. "Who is it this time, Umbogo?" She was only partially joking, truly worried that her parents saw true merit in marrying her off to Emperor Oxon's ambassador.

He snorted. "No. Father said he wants to stick a pencil through the guy's eye."

Aslyn choked on a laugh. "Amazing, I was just thinking the same thing." She glanced over her shoulder at the throne room, spotting Umbogo watching her from across the chamber. She fought the urge to shudder. "Keep those comments to yourself, though. I swear he hears everything."

Dorin nodded in agreement. "I think our ever-reaching mother is trying to arrange something with Vorovesti."

Vorovesti! Who would even be suitable for her from that kingdom? Certainly not Crown Prince Gannon. He would have his own kingdom to rule. But whoever it was, he had to be connected to the royal family somehow. A cousin, perhaps?

"They're getting ready for the Stormvalor tournament in Vorovesti," Dorin said, keeping his voice down. "I think she means for you to find someone suitable there."

"A brutish idiot with muscles and no brain? No thanks."

The Stormvalor tournament took place every ten years in the spring, and warriors from all five kingdoms would venture to the city of Stormvalor in Vorovesti to compete against one another to be crowned champion. Aslyn had no interest in brutes. Of course, she always knew she couldn't marry Elisio—not that she wanted to—but could she dare to keep him to warm her bed in ways she was sure a brutish husband would be incapable of?

Dorin released his own exasperated sigh. "If only we could both be so lucky."

Aslyn nearly laughed at that, but from the corner of her eye, she spotted a commotion in the city below. Her heart stopped.

If you see it, then you know I have a rare gift for you indeed.

City guards and Black Guards surrounded a building. Aslyn and Dorin edged closer to the window and squinted. The building the men surrounded was little more than rubble.

But it wasn't where Umbogo had pointed. It was across the city, in a high-end tailor district Aslyn knew well. She couldn't tell which shop suffered the collapse from here, but she was certain of one thing...

Something in that building had gone terribly wrong. Was this Umbogo's doing?

Dorin simply cocked his head and smiled to himself, then strolled away toward the exit, drink in hand.

She glanced over her shoulder in shock, her eyes meeting Umbogo's. He simply smiled that sharp, angular smile.

There was no way.

He couldn't have truly done it.

He couldn't have captured the famous shadow. But if he did...

Aslyn very much wanted to meet this Blackblade and *thank* him for all he had done.

CHAPTER 5

The Odds in Good Favor

The palace of Vorovesti stood at the heart of Mordelic. Lord Aethan Starkling loved everything about the palace. The imposing onyx walls, veined in silver and gold, were only breached once in thousands of years, during the War of Two Crowns. Legend claimed the breath of a great dragon forged the walls. The sloping rooflines and jutting spires added an air of grace to the onyx walls.

Silverbark trees adorned the palace grounds. The trees grew only on the palace grounds, and master smiths, jewelers, and carpenters all vied for wood from the trees. Aethan coveted a rare silverbark handle sword, just like everyone else, but they were so rare he was certain he would never get one. When a cool spring breeze made the budding leaves dance, the silver veins of the young leaves caught in the light, creating a kaleidoscope of bewitching light on the path in front of his horse.

Aethan breathed deeply, reveling in the sweet yet earthy scent of the trees. No small amount of his Vorovesti pride had to do with the grandeur and awe of this place. The palace was a testament to the power, majesty, and history of Vorovesti, its beauty rivaled only by the grand noble houses that surrounded it. He would gladly pledge his life to the defense of Mordelic and this historic palace.

His horse plodded along the path leading from the guard gate to the stables, hardly needing direction any longer. Aethan had ridden this path more times than he could count. Every day for the past twelve years—since his tenth birthday—he reported to the royal Master-at-Arms for weapons training just like any other young Vorovesti lord.

A few of the ladies trained as well, but only if their parents permitted. Where a son was prized for his continuation of a family line, a daughter was prized because of the alliances she could bring to the family. A few families saw merit in their daughters learning to fight, but far more believed their daughters should be raised to keep the home running and raise strong children.

Lady Iskra Pridell was one of the latter. Aethan winced when he reached the stable by the training grounds, remembering the fight he had with Iskra as he prepared to leave this morning. What a fool he had been.

A host of young ladies had already gathered near the training ground. Aethan eyed them as he dismounted and handed over the reins. He didn't need to see his cousin to know what had all the girls whispering and giggling and staring with those dreamy doe eyes.

Gannon, Crown Prince of Vorovesti and Aethan's cousin, stretched his muscled limbs to prepare for the practice to come. A sheen of sweat already made Gannon's shirt cling to his skin. Aethan shook his head as he pulled off his riding gloves and shrugged out of his fine sapphire jacket.

He strode toward his cousin.

"You look like you want to skewer something, Aethan," Gannon remarked as he noticed his cousin's approach.

"How far did you run today?" Aethan asked, not eager to rehash the argument with Iskra. Especially knowing how poorly he handled himself.

"Only eight kilometers." Gannon rolled his neck. "I assume your absence for the run means you were otherwise occupied?" The smirk on Gannon's face made Aethan's face heat.

"I was, but I have a feeling I won't have that problem in the future." Aethan tossed his jacket over a bench, hoping his cousin couldn't read his irritation too clearly.

Gannon scrunched his nose. "It couldn't be that bad. Iskra adores you."

Aethan snorted. He highly doubted she thought so much of him anymore. "She wanted me to withdraw my name from the Stormvalor Tournament," he said a touch more sharply than he should have.

"Why would...?" And judging by the way Gannon's sea-green eyes shifted, it dawned on him. "Ah. So she heard the rumors then."

"It would seem so." Aethan threw his gloves on the bench hard enough that the leather smacked against the stone. "The very notion is ridiculous. She should know better. And she should know me better! I've been waiting for the year I could enter the tournament. I won't give that up."

Iskra knew how important this tournament was to him. Since he was a little boy, he had trained for it, dreamed of competing, of winning.

His father's advisors watched the competitors closely—usually because fortunes could be won betting on the right person—and this time, all signs pointed to Aethan as the victor. There were a few other potentials, but Aethan grew more confident with every passing day that he could beat them. He could win. He *would* win. Iskra couldn't ask him not to. She couldn't stand in his way, ask him to give up on a lifelong dream, and expect him not to be angry.

Iskra had insisted Aethan withdraw and wait for the next tournament. But in ten years, he would be too old to compete, and she knew it.

At first, she had made excuses. He wasn't ready to compete—a lie if he ever heard one. She wanted to marry before he competed. That, he was sure she meant, but only because Stormvalor competitors were often sought for marriage by anyone able to make a good offer. It was a badge of honor to marry a competitor. Especially one who finished high in the tournament. It was no wonder Iskra wanted to marry him first, so no other woman could come along to steal his interest. As if any could.

The list of Iskra's protests had seemed endless... And then the truth of her worry came to light.

"I'm competing." Aethan produced his practice sword hard enough to make the entire rack rattle.

"And losing," a familiar male voice called.

Aethan turned toward the sound of boots crunching gravel as his best friend, Trystain, joined the two of them, sandy hair tied back and ready to begin.

A broad grin split Trystain's face. "My father told me about the rumor as well. Seems word is getting out that Queen Giata is looking to select a competitor for her daughter, the crown princess. And I've heard she's a beauty."

"You forget my sister so easily?" Aethan snapped, in no mood to listen to Trystain talk about another woman.

"I adore Sybil, but a future queen..." Trystain shook his head. "You know my father won't let that chance pass. No matter what I say."

As if sensing the tension building in Aethan, Gannon cleared his throat. "Maybe we should start training."

"Yes, let's." Aethan gladly stomped toward the practice ring. The tone of his agreement had Trystain hesitating. That momentary worry on his face made it clear he knew he couldn't beat Aethan in a fair fight.

If Trystain truly considered ditching his sister for a princess, Aethan would make him pay for it. Today would be a taste of what Aethan had in store for Trystain.

The trio fell into an easy rhythm of combat, a dance they had executed for years now.

Aethan poured his frustration into each strike, not bothering to pull any of his blows to Trystain as punishment for even hinting that he might break his word to Sybil in favor of a crown. *Prick.*

But Trystain was not the only one worried about that crown.

When the truth came out, Aethan had grown more furious with Iskra. She didn't worry that Aethan wasn't ready for the tournament. She worried that he was *too* ready and didn't want him to know that she wanted him to withdraw from the tournament because she thought he would turn his attention away from her in favor of a princess, a crown, an alliance through marriage between Vorovesti and Novavito.

Certainly, his own father would suggest it. His uncle, King Orrin, likely would as well. But neither of them would force him. Apply pressure, yes. Force, no. Iskra must know he loved her. He wouldn't leave her for some mysterious foreign princess he'd only met twice in his youth, on the heels of his cousin.

This was his year. The odds were in good favor of his victory.

Aethan had said all the wrong things and none of the right ones in the argument. Instead of reassuring Iskra that he loved her, that he could never imagine being with another woman, no matter the crown on her head, he had told Iskra that he had no intention of pulling out of the contest. Not for her.

That didn't mean Aethan didn't love Iskra. But it didn't mean some princess destined to become queen would sway him. He had no interest in the princess.

Which, in hindsight, is probably what he *should* have told her instead of calling her selfish.

Aethan Starkling thrived in combat, like a part of his soul came alive anytime he had a weapon in his hand and an opponent in front of him. He raised his shield to block one blow and deftly dipped his sword around on his other side to block an attack from behind. The attack forced him to push his body forward with the shield to avoid a follow-up strike against his spine.

Aethan's muscles protested, exhausted from the extensive training, but they didn't fail as he pushed hard against Trystain's entire body. His friend stumbled back with a grunt, his footing slipping on the gravel beneath their feet. Aethan didn't have time to see how well Trystain would recover as he heard the boots rush toward him from behind. He twisted his body as he clipped the shield to his back, then raised his practice sword as Gannon's sword came within a breath of his practice leathers.

Trystain grumbled under his breath as he climbed to his feet again, now at Aethan's back. A shadow of Trystain's blade fell over the ground as Aethan pushed Gannon back to open more space to maneuver.

In a smooth, practiced motion, Aethan crouched low as he spun around, swinging one leg out against the gravel to kick dirt in the air and keep Gannon out of range. At the same moment, Aethan thrust his practice sword up into Trystain's exposed side beneath the arm—much harder than necessary. Trystain cursed as he stumbled back, knowing he was eliminated from the match with that death blow.

Aethan didn't have time to gloat. Gannon's sword came down toward his neck. Aethan merely winked at Trystain before rolling over the shield on his back to avoid the death blow.

Gannon was quick on his feet, pulling his swing the moment he knew he would miss and turning with as much grace as Aethan would expect from the Crown Prince of Vorovesti.

In a heartbeat, the two were locked in a sword fight that made Aethan's aching muscles protest every blocked blow and smooth strike. It transformed into a dance between two matched foes. Step left, twist right. Strike, block, armguard. Their practice swords sang through the air, and Aethan was well aware that they had an audience.

Not just other men training. Courtly girls whispered, giggled, and fanned themselves as they watched their Crown Prince and his cousin spar.

"You're making me look bad," Gannon teased, then grit his teeth as Aethan's strike made his muscles tremble as he blocked.

"I think nothing would make you look bad in their eyes," Aethan remarked, grinning as an idea struck him. "One girl looks ready to devour you whole. No doubt you could win her into your bed with your princely charms."

Gannon stepped back as their feet shifted in the continued dance of swords. "Who?" He glanced toward the gathered ladies.

Aethan waited for the moment Gannon's gaze shifted to the girls lining the courtyard. The practice sword shifted from one hand to the other, where he plunged the tip into the leathers at Gannon's back.

Gannon grunted against the blow, then turned to Aethan, lowering his weapon. "That was low."

Aethan chuckled as he straightened. "I know the Master-at-Arms taught you that any distraction is deadly. Maybe you should have listened a little more closely."

Gannon threw a very unprincely vulgar gesture at Aethan with a tight laugh. Even that had some girls sighing.

The three men strolled toward a servant holding a tray of ice cold water for the prince and his companions. The eyes of all the ladies followed them.

"If your father saw that he would have a heart attack," Aethan laughed. The exercise had done his foul mood some good. His head cleared and his anger abated. He would apologize to Iskra, crawl to her and beg forgiveness for calling her selfish... as long as she could understand he competed for himself and her and nothing more.

To his credit, Gannon had the good sense to scan the courtyard for signs of King Orrin's presence.

Aethan waited for Gannon to take his water before accepting one for himself—as was proper. Each of the three of them grabbed a towel to mop the sweat off their faces and necks.

From the corner of his eye, Aethan caught Emperor Oxon's ambassador lingering near a pillar, hidden beneath a palace walkway. His gaze fixed on the three of them, and something about that calculation in those black eyes gave Aethan chills. Aethan was loyal to the Divican Empire as much as the kingdom of Vorovesti, but that ambassador always gave Aethan a sense of dread. Like something lurked just around the corner.

Aethan pulled his gaze away, trying to ignore the ambassador, and he ran a hand through his pale blond hair. No one in any of the kingdoms had hair like the Starklings except Emperor Oxon, and, according to rumor, his heir Prince Valen—who both had hair as white as snow. Others had varying shades of blond, sure, but none as pale as theirs. Not his mother, Olivya—King Orrin's younger sister. Not even his father, Lord Lux Starkling. Though his father's hair darkened only a few shades from his children, it still held some hallmarks of the pale color. Aethan and Sybil shared their father's sky-blue eyes and long face. Aethan had the same sharp jawline as his father, too.

A few of the ladies eyed him as he ran the cloth along his sweaty neck. If the Crown Prince wasn't a prize for these ladies, Aethan knew he was. But these ladies also knew he gave his heart to Iskra years ago. They weren't married yet, but that was just a matter of time.

Lord Starkling had been in negotiations with Lord Pridell for months, haggling over petty crap that kept Aethan's engagement from being official. But it hadn't been enough to keep Iskra from sharing his bed.

Though Aethan was fairly certain their fight this morning would fix that problem.

"I don't think any Stormvalor competitors stand a chance against Lord Aethan Starkling," one of the ladies crooned.

"Do you so easily ignore my skills with a sword?" Trystain asked, and the way he met her gaze hinted at something more.

Aethan's jaw tensed slightly.

"I think you might overestimate your skills a touch, Trystain," Gannon teased.

Trystain raised an innocent hand in defense. "I *did* bring the distinguished Starkling heir to his knees just last week. Have you forgotten already?"

Aethan's lips thinned in a cross between amusement and suspicion.

But it was hard to stay mad at either of these two for long. They weren't just his cousin and best friend. They were his brothers. The closest he could have hoped for.

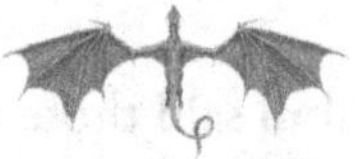

After cleaning up from training and changing into fresh clothes—a suit cut from fine sapphire cloth embroidered with gold along the lapels, and boots of pure black—Aethan followed a servant to the king's council chambers.

Upon entering, he noted the king's advisors already gathered, as well as Prince Gannon, Lord Starkling, and Ambassador Zambul—the emperor's ambassador for Vorovesti. Those black eyes rose to meet Aethan's and a chill settled on Aethan's skin that had nothing to do with the cool spring breeze blowing in the window.

The topic revolved around the Stormvalor Tournament. While competitors from each of the five kingdoms would compete, Vorovesti played host in the city of Stormvalor, the seat of Starkling house power.

Many believe the city to be the home of Justis, God of War and Storms. The people of Vorovesti devoutly followed the teachings of Justis—the value of honor, courage, and physical prowess.

Every ten years in early spring, competitors from each kingdom engaged in mock battles to prove their abilities. The first tournament reportedly took place a year after Justis' grand victory over the dark forces that threatened to consume the land to commemorate Justis' valor and role as protector of the realms. Competitors would partake in jousting, archery, sword fighting, and tactical challenges. The winner would be crowned as Stormvalor Champion.

That was the *only* title Aethan coveted.

Throughout the conversation, Ambassador Zambul's gaze remained fixed on Aethan. The continued attention unnerved him. What did Zambul suddenly find so interesting about the Starkling heir?

For the past ten years, Zambul had shown some interest in Aethan and even sometimes engaged him in conversation. Aethan always assumed it was because of his link to the royal family. This intense interest, though, felt very different. Like Zambul saw something in Aethan's visage that he considered immensely intriguing.

"Bring your kingdom and your family honor in the tournament, Lord Aethan," Zambul said as the meeting concluded and everyone prepared to leave. "Make your emperor proud."

Something about the way Zambul said those words made Aethan's skin crawl. But Aethan gave the ambassador a respectful nod, hand over his heart, as he said, "For the good of the empire and the realm."

The words were automatic—spoken a hundred times in his life—but Aethan sensed that something had just happened and he didn't even know it. His father certainly didn't look pleased by it.

Aethan stepped out with his father. He couldn't leave fast enough. The two of them made their way to the stable to retrieve their horses, then left the palace grounds with few words exchanged. The hard silence from his father made Aethan uncomfortable. Had he done something wrong?

The streets of Mordelic wove like intricate tapestries, a labyrinth of cobblestone paths that wound and twisted through the heart of the city. Towering buildings adorned with ornate carvings and intricate mosaics lined the streets, each telling stories of a bygone era when magic and mystery intertwined with daily life.

Life thrived within the city walls, with merchant shops packed with eager shoppers in the middle of the day. Some corners of the city played host to performers seeking to entertain the crowds and earn extra coins. Aethan had watched several of the performances over the years, whether they be musicians, illusionists using sleight-of-hand tricks and not forbidden magic, or acting troupes weaving grand stories of bygone eras.

Aethan breathed it all in as they rode toward home, reveling in the comfort of this city he loved so much. Aethan could never imagine leaving.

Beyond the lively streets lay the city's defensive ring, massive walls of onyx nearly as thick as they were tall. That ring formed a protective barrier to encircle the city, keeping it safe from invading forces.

The outer walls of Mordelic formed a formidable barrier that stood as a testament to the strength and resilience of Vorovesti. Towers and battlements rose high, manned by vigilant guards who kept a watchful eye on the horizon, ever ready to defend against any threat that may dare to approach the city.

Aethan had walked those walls with his father, uncle, and cousin hundreds of times. He knew the ins and outs of the city walls as well as his own hand.

And soon, he would leave.

In a week, Aethan would depart for the tournament. Nothing in his life would be the same when he returned, which was why he felt the need to press his father once more. "Father, is there any chance we can get the marriage contract signed before the tournament?" Aethan asked, breaking their tense, silent ride home.

Lord Starkling eyed Aethan, his lips thin. "We've been through this, Aethan."

"I owe Iskra."

"And why is that?" The cutting look his father shot at him made Aethan stiffen in the saddle.

"She's been so patient," Aethan said, quickly covering his tracks. Because if his father knew how often he and Iskra had lain together, he would be livid. While it might bring about a marriage, it would be for all the wrong reasons. And his father would never let him forget it. "I made her promises. I gave her my heart years ago. She's waited so patiently for us to create an agreeable marriage contract with her family."

Lord Starkling's jaw tightened, making the angles of his face almost deadly. "You aren't just anyone, Aethan."

"I know that."

"You are nephew to the King of Vorovesti."

"I am aware."

"Which means you are in line for the throne should anything happen to the royal family. Your marriage has to be a carefully agreed upon arrangement."

"And why would anything happen to the royal family?" Aethan snapped.

Lord Starkling gave Aethan a hard look, one Aethan knew far too well. Pushing this subject would not end well for him. In fact, if he pushed hard enough, his father might be inclined to refuse the marriage altogether.

Aethan fell silent, eyes fixed forward with determination. Because if he looked at his father right now, this would turn into an argument in the city streets.

Lady Iskra was beautiful and smart and so much more than Aethan felt he deserved. She had a good heart and put the needs of others ahead of herself time and again.

Strength. Honor. Valor.

The Starkling family motto. Iskra embodied those words. She fit perfectly into the family in every way. Aethan couldn't understand why his father deliberated for so long about this. It couldn't just be about his place in the line of succession, because the odds of him ever taking the Vorovesti throne were slim to nil.

He contemplated this as they entered their manor walls, and he dismounted alongside his father.

Lord Starkling paused, facing Aethan. "We can revisit this conversation after the tournament."

Before Aethan could argue, his father stalked away, greeted in the entryway by his assistant.

After the tournament...

Aethan's heart sank to his feet as the truth settled over him.

Iskra was right. Aethan wasn't after a crown. He didn't want a crown. But a royal marriage would solidify a slipping accord between Novavito and Vorovesti.

Aethan was little more than a prize stallion. The choice was an illusion.

He never truly had an option.

CHAPTER 6

Before the Fallen Gods

Seeking solace and a few minutes alone, Aethan Starkling entered the family temple. Sunlight streamed through the stained-glass windows set into the stone walls every ten feet. It illuminated dust motes floating in the air, as well as sections of the floor to ceiling mural. That mural had adorned the walls of the small family temple for as long as the Starkling family maintained the estate—perhaps even longer.

The stained-glass patterns had been designed over a millennium ago by expert craftsmen so that light moved along the celestial mural painted on the walls, floor, and ceiling at certain times of day.

Lord Starkling had once told his young son that the family believed the mural a gift from the goddess Astra herself. Artists entered the temple every generation to touch up worn surfaces, but never changed the mural itself.

Other noble houses had temples on their grounds as well, each with altars of worship to each of the seven gods. Once upon a time, people worshipped all seven of the gods. Now, most were content to ignore the gods just as the gods had ignored them.

Most of those temples had been casually neglected in the past century as the gods slowly faded from the world and left the people to fend for themselves. Sure, they maintained the buildings enough to keep them from collapsing and clear decay—what a scandal it would be if the gods returned to find their temples in ruins!

Only the royal family and the Starklings kept their temples pristine. And only the Starklings had such a magnificent mural.

Aethan settled on the only bench in the small temple, raising his gaze to the mural around him as the scent of stone and candles tickled his nose.

Most days and nights, the stained-glass windows lent the interior of this small temple enough light to see by. Only on the darkest of nights were candles truly necessary.

Aethan studied the only large stained-glass window depicting an image of Solisina, goddess of light and knowledge, holding her stone of light aloft to chase off creatures of shadows.

The image could be found on tapestries in all five kingdoms, a famous moment in the battle between darkness and light.

The gods worked together to protect the realm. Solisina came to Justis' aid as the god of shadow and death spread his dark minions across the realm. Morumbris, that dark god, suffered defeat when Solisina used her stone of light to force him and his minions back into the darkness deep beneath the earth. Then Fiara, goddess of fire, melted the stone over the tomb. Coravita, goddess of life and the sea, quenched the molten stone with her life-giving waters. Terralibra, goddess of earth and balance, covered that tomb with miles of earth, never to be uncovered again.

When the battle was won, Solisina cast her light into the heavens. But every night, Morumbris searched for an exit from his eternal tomb, so Astra, goddess of the stars, created the moon to reflect Solisina's light and keep Morumbris away. But death still came for all mortals, pulling souls into the underworld.

Aethan knew the story well. Everyone did. But as a boy, Aethan had been fascinated with the tale. He studied everything he could find about the gods. Their creation. Their balance. Their war. Their continued vigilance...

Their downfall at the hands of the first emperor of the five kingdoms of Divica.

A shudder rolled down his back. Aethan gripped the edges of the stone bench in his fists so hard the grains of the underside of the stone dug into his fingertips.

Narcisse the Godslayer.

Aethan knew that history just as well. The dark prince who rose to power. Conqueror of the lands. Destroyer of magic. Exterminator of the elves. Slayer of the gods.

That last title was little more than whispered stories. No one could find any evidence that it was true.

But it was not until after he became Emperor Narcisse that the power of the gods, their touch on the world, began to fade. Whether he truly was a godslayer didn't matter. The gods were gone. The evidence of that was hard to ignore.

And without the gods to maintain a balance between shadow and light against the forces of ruin, the world would fall into darkness. It had already begun. Aethan knew the people suffered because of slowly depleting harvests each year. Most of the huntable wildlife was thin, too. And Aethan couldn't remember the last time he saw a clear blue sky without traces of gray. Perhaps he never had. Perhaps blue skies were myths shared in stories to give people false hope.

The stark truth was, if the gods remained, they had forsaken their world completely. How long before the world died for good?

Aethan didn't come to the temple weekly to feel the grace of the gods. No one could claim that any longer—though the Matriarch and Patriarch in Elysia certainly insisted the gods still spoke to them.

The temple offered Aethan little more than clarity of spirit. It remained the one place on the family estate he could sit and think without his father intervening.

He closed his eyes as the warmth of the sun through the windows heated his face.

Somehow, he had to fix things with Iskra. But how could he when his own father had all but hinted that he wanted to wait and see what other marriage offers would come from the Stormvalor Tournament?

After the tournament... Those three words spoke volumes.

If he ran off and married Iskra without consent, his father would disown him and name Sybil heir. Aethan wasn't sure he minded that so much. His sister was capable of the role. But the Novavito royal family didn't just have a daughter. They had a son. One close to Sybil's age. One not waiting to inherit a throne.

Selfishly marrying Iskra to have what he wanted would only place his sister in his position.

Solisina, Astra, whomever might still listen, he thought, opening his eyes to take in the stained-glass goddess, *if you remain, I could use your guidance.*

Silence.

Nothing but dust motes and slowly shifting rays of sunlight across the celestial mural.

Aethan remained on the bench, unmoving for some time as he observed the slow progression of light across the paint.

Foolish to pray to gods who've abandoned us, he chided himself.

"Aethan?" Sybil's gentle voice called to him as she glided quietly across the stone floor toward him.

He glanced over his shoulder at his sister.

Sybil could've been his twin. They shared the same pale blond hair and the same sky-blue eyes. Even their faces were remarkably similar, though Sybil possessed a feminine grace.

"You've been in here for hours," Sybil said, settling beside him.

Aethan's hands hurt as he uncurled them from the bench and brushed them off. How long had he been clenching the bench in that vice-like grip?

"I don't think our father intends to agree to my marriage with Iskra," Aethan admitted. Speaking the words aloud cracked something inside of him apart. He swallowed thickly.

"I know." Her gentle admission made him glance at her from the corner of his eyes. Sybil slid an arm around his shoulders.

"I love her, Sybil. I can't... Living without her would be like living without the sun." He sagged against Sybil, comforted by her presence, as he often was. "I'm tempted to perform poorly in the tournament just to spite him."

Sybil nudged him with her shoulder. They pulled apart, but her blue eyes peered into Aethan with so much clarity. "That wouldn't be you, Aethan. You've too much self-respect and honor to throw your chance at becoming the Stormvalor Champion out of spitefulness."

He took his sister's hand, giving it a small squeeze. "I hate when you're right." His gaze shifted once more to the goddess watching over them. "Do you think the stories are true? That the gods are dead?"

Sybil didn't respond for several minutes. When Aethan examined her, she didn't peer at Solisina, as he had. Her gaze drew downward to the illuminated section of the floor mural. What did she see when she studied the art? To him, it was merely a mural of the celestial body that surrounded their world. But when Sybil examined it, he knew she observed something more.

She harbored a deadly secret. One the Starklings and their royal cousins guarded closely. Sybil possessed the gift of foresight. If Emperor Oxon ever found out, he would kill her. Possessing any form of magic had been outlawed by the first emperor, Narcisse the Godslayer, a millennium ago. It was a certain death sentence. Above all else, Aethan had to keep Sybil safe.

The two fell into agreeable silence, neither having a suitable answer to his question. No one did.

After some time leaning against one another, Sybil shuddered.

"Are you alright?" he asked as he sat upright and swept his gaze over her, seeking any signs of weakness.

Something about Sybil had changed in those moments of silence. While her body trembled slightly, her back straightened. The color in her eyes deepened. Aethan frowned.

"Sybil?" *Oh no. No, it's happening now...*

Aethan slid off the bench and kneeled in front of her, taking her hands.

Her gaze snapped to his, eyes wide. Something like wonder—or maybe fear—shined in her clear blue eyes. She rested a cold palm against his cheek.

"We all have a path to walk, Aethan," Sybil said, breaking her strange silence. "Stay the course. No matter what. For me."

Aethan frowned. What did that mean?

"Promise me, brother," Sybil whispered urgently. "Promise me you will stay the course, that you will carry on with strength, honor, and valor."

Those final words made him flinch. The ominous nature of her words awakened something inside of him. And the way she used the family motto to bind him did little for the sudden fear clawing at his gut.

But he couldn't deny her. Not just because she beseeched his true nature, his integrity, with her plea... but because more than anyone else, more than Iskra, he adored his sister.

Aethan could deny her nothing.

"I promise."

A sad smile perched on Sybil's lips as she leaned forward and pressed a gentle kiss to his forehead.

And he could swear that kiss bound him to his promise more certainly than the words spoken.

CHAPTER 7

Like a Shadow in the Night

King Novin Kiernan paced the dais in the glittering throne room, his face red with rage. Sunlight caught on the gemstones encrusted in his golden crown, making the curved wings at the front of the crown appear as if they stretched to take flight. The tails of his ivory suit jacket flapped each time he spun on his heel, also mimicking flight. Aslyn wondered what sort of bird her father would be. Something large and fierce, but also loyal. A fabled phoenix, perhaps. Fire certainly seemed to trail in his furious wake.

Aslyn observed each movement her father made from the corner of her eyes, trying to be the calm, composed crown princess she was meant to be. Yet she could barely contain her satisfaction knowing Umbogo became the focus of her father's wrath.

Were Umbogo any other man, he would be imprisoned or dead already. But being Emperor Oxon's ambassador warranted Umbogo more leeway from punishment than anyone else, if only because King Novin hoped to keep the emperor's eye off Novavito's throne.

The Arithian Black Guard captain had received a tip that Blackblade maintained several contacts throughout the city—a dozen, perhaps more. Men of seemingly innocent trade who acted as brokers for the assassin. Such as the tailor whose shop had been destroyed by the Black Guard.

"You put the lives of my people in danger with your stunt!" King Novin roared at Umbogo.

After hours of searching the rubble, the only body recovered from that tailor shop had been that of the already dead tailor.

Blackblade killed his broker—probably after receiving his payment—and somehow escaped the trap. He must have known the tailor had informed the emperor's captain or the city guard. No doubt the tailor's murder had been in retribution, as well as self-preservation.

While Aslyn would have enjoyed asking the assassin questions regarding Ned's murder, she also experienced waves of relief knowing that Umbogo's ploy for power and position had failed so spectacularly. It served him right.

Umbogo stood at the foot of the dais, spine straight, completely unruffled by the king's fury. His hands remained folded behind his back and a mask of calm smoothed the hard lines of his angular face.

"They are Emperor Oxon's people," Umbogo corrected. If Aslyn didn't loath the snake so much, she would have envied the way he faced her father without breaking. "And the captain and I were perfectly within our rights to execute this mission without your approval."

Aslyn tensed as her father's steps halted and he turned slowly toward Umbogo like a predator stalking its prey. It sent ice through her veins.

The king paused on the dais stairs. Close enough to kill the ambassador swiftly if only he drew Novo from his hip. Instead of lashing out, King Novin asked through his teeth, "How many?"

Umbogo cocked his head to the side. "I'm sorry?"

"You said the Black Guard captain uncovered several of Blackblade's brokers," the king's voice held a lethal calm. He sought someone to punish for what happened in the tailor district. If he couldn't punish Umbogo, he would find someone else. Like the brokers. "How many did he learn of?"

"Ten."

"I want them brought to me alive for questioning," King Novin growled.

Yes, Aslyn was certain now that her father wanted someone to punish.

"The captain has already brought them to the Black Guard headquarters and begun interrogations," Umbogo said, somehow remaining steady and calm with the king only a breath from him. Judging by the gleam in Umbogo's black eyes, Aslyn knew those brokers were being tortured for information. "Only four remain in custody. The rest, unfortunately, died during the attempted arrests."

Died... or were killed? Aslyn knew better than to speak up at this moment, but she suspected the Black Guard tortured some of those brokers on site for information. Perhaps that was even how they uncovered so many. One led to the next, and the next...

No, that would be sloppy on Blackblade's part to allow his brokers to know one another, Aslyn realized.

"When the captain is through with them, I will have him send the survivors your way," Umbogo finished.

Survivors... Aslyn almost snorted at that.

King Novin bared his teeth at the ambassador. He knew as well as Aslyn that there would be no survivors left to question. The Black Guard were experts at torture. They could dissect a man for days—weeks—without killing their captive.

"I want them alive," the king hissed. "They are my people, and Blackblade killed one of my lords. I will get my answers."

Umbogo simply raised a brow, as if he knew something they didn't. As if he thought himself above the Crown of Novavito.

Emperor Oxon was cruel and had a zero-tolerance policy for failure among his own men. Surely Umbogo knew what withholding this information could do to him—the failure it could make of him.

Yet still, he stared down the king of Novavito as if he had no fear of him.

"I am still the king," her father said with lethal calm. "And as long as I sit atop this throne, those are still my people, and *you* are little more than an ambassador. You live under my roof, eat my food, and breathe my air solely so that you may act as a mouthpiece for the emperor."

Nova, the sword of the first king, hung from King Novin's belt, and for a moment, Aslyn was certain her father grabbed the hilt to execute the ambassador. Instead, his grip only tightened until the leather wrapping creaked.

"You extend your hand farther than your reach, King Novin," Umbogo said boldly, not flinching in the slightest. "It would behoove you to remember who allows you to sit atop that throne."

King Novin descended a step, every movement of his muscles lethal and graceful. "Will you now threaten me, ambassador? I am not nearly as replaceable as you."

Umbogo's gaze flicked to Aslyn. "No?"

That ice in her veins melted under the heat of Umbogo's black-eyed stare. He assessed every inch of her boldly in front of her father.

No, hate was not the right word for how she felt about Umbogo. Aslyn wanted to grind him to dust and bury his remains in the earth. How dare he look at her like a prized mare?

"Continue looking at my daughter like that and I will send your head back to the emperor in a golden box," her father growled.

Umbogo offered a slight bow to Aslyn, but he didn't act the least bit ruffled by the king's threat. "Apologies, Princess, if my gaze has offended you." He straightened, ignoring her father completely. "And I am also most aggrieved I could not fulfill my promise. Rest assured, I will."

"What promise?" King Novin whirled on Aslyn, narrowing his eyes. "What have you done, Aslyn?"

"Nothing." Aslyn waved the question off. Because she had done nothing nor promised Umbogo a single thing. Not even a continued position as ambassador. "Not only did you fail to catch Blackblade, ambassador, but you didn't even direct my attention to the right part of the city. He slipped right past the Black Guard, past you, like a shadow in the night. How thoroughly the assassin has shamed you and the Black Guard. It seems you have little to offer your future sovereign. Unless broken promises are a skill with which you excel."

For the first time since entering the throne room, Umbogo's pale face flushed with anger.

Aslyn offered him a smug yet sweet smile. Oh, it warmed her so much to know *she* could get to him when even her father could not. "Should my father and I warn the city guards that other buildings might be in danger of collapse as well? Perhaps in the fisherman's district?"

Where he had actually directed her attention.

Where nothing had happened.

Umbogo's jaw clenched so tight the sharp lines of his face became more pronounced. But he raised his head as if trying to scrape his pride back together again.

"I hope, Princess, that you will realize I am human, just as you are," Umbogo said.

You are nothing like me, worm, Aslyn thought. But she bit back the words before speaking them aloud.

"I meant every word I spoke earlier." Umbogo took a bold step closer, despite the king's growl of warning or hold on Nova. "I believe we will have a long and fruitful working relationship."

"I hardly see how," Aslyn retorted.

Umbogo flinched, then his dark eyes flared with anger and... hunger.

King Novin placed himself between the two of them, and Aslyn nearly sagged with relief. She wasn't sure she would sleep knowing Umbogo prowled the palace halls.

"The emperor's Black Guard," King Novin interjected, "will clean up your mess. Not my men."

The ambassador opened his mouth to reply, but the king didn't give him a chance to speak before he growled his final warning. "And you, Umbogo, will not so much as *look* at my daughter before she returns from the Stormvalor Tournament."

Aslyn nearly groaned at the reminder of the upcoming trip. Her mother would, indeed, force her to choose a husband soon. It seemed her father agreed.

"Now get out of my throne room before I have my men throw you out," King Novin commanded.

Umbogo bowed, but as he turned toward the door, he smirked ever so slightly. "The throne you sit upon was a gift to your forefathers from Emperor Narcisse, and his heirs have a long memory."

The doors to the grand chamber groaned closed behind him, but the words lingered.

What did that mean?

Aslyn studied her father's hulking back as he steadied his anger. Did he understand that final declaration? Was that a threat against the crown? Could it be possible Umbogo had a hand in the rumors of rebellion against the Novavito crown?

"What, exactly, did he say to you earlier today, Aslyn?" The worry in King Novin's voice made Aslyn's heartbeat increase. Why was her father scared? "And how did you respond?"

Concerned she had, in fact, unknowingly agreed to something—though she could not imagine what it could have been—Aslyn carefully recited the conversation between herself and Umbogo earlier in the day, word for word.

King Novin settled on his throne and observed her as she spoke, taking in every detail. That careful consideration terrified Aslyn.

When she finished, the king's gaze drifted somewhere distant. His silence stretched and unnerved her.

"Father?" Aslyn reached for his hand.

King Novin wrapped his fingers around hers. "I'm so relieved you're smarter than your brother. Dorin would have unknowingly given the kingdom away. But I cannot see any fault in what you said to him. No promises you unwittingly made."

She shook her head. "I would never make promises to Umbogo."

"Be wary of your words around him, Aslyn." The way he tightened his grip on her fingers made Aslyn's already racing heart thunder. "Emperor Oxon's ambassadors are not like other men. The wrong words in the right place can bind you in an oath to them."

Aslyn refrained from rolling her eyes. That had been drilled into her for years. Ambassadors were clever with words and wits and could use those words to draw out promises that bound the promiser to their words forever. There would be no escaping an Ambassador's Promise. None but death.

"I know, Father," Aslyn sighed.

The king chewed his lip, then ran a hand through his ebony hair, making the gray roots more prominent.

"We are running out of time, Asy," he admitted, and his shoulders sagged. The grip on her hand slipped as he sank into his throne.

Asy. That nickname was reserved for when he teased her... or when his words were grievously serious. Her dinner churned in her stomach.

"After the funeral, you leave for Stormvalor with your mother," he said, and as he spoke his words picked up confidence.

But Aslyn knew what he would say next, and she felt anything but confident.

"You need to choose a husband. We've waited as long as we can. But Umbogo made it clear he is hoping to catch you off guard." He turned brown eyes on her, and more than worry shone in them.

"You're afraid he will trick me into marriage, into an Ambassador's Promise, and I will have no choice but to marry him," Aslyn breathed. She was going to be sick. The idea of marrying Umbogo, let alone sharing a bed with him and making heirs... "But he can't... he can't become a king beneath me as long as he's ambassador." She bit her lip, suddenly uncertain. "Can he?"

King Novin unstrapped the sword from his waist so he could lean back properly on his throne. "It has never been done to my knowledge, but I have been advised that there is no law against it. In fact, I dare say that's the very reason Emperor Oxon sent him. Do you truly believe it's a coincidence he was appointed to this position in Arithia at the same time you came of age and entered your first season of eligibility?"

Aslyn struggled for breath. Her parents didn't keep Umbogo away from her just because they didn't like him. They worried she hadn't matured enough to know what she said around him. That he would trick her into the Ambassador's Promise and bind herself to him much sooner.

The only way to keep Umbogo from trapping her unwittingly was to choose a husband before he bound her to an oath. Once she was promised to another, Aslyn could not be tricked into Umbogo's bargain.

Which meant, whether she liked it or not, Aslyn had to attain a husband.

"You are twenty, Asy." He drew in a breath, then let it out slowly. "It's time. We cannot delay any longer. I wish you had time to find love like I did, but it seems Umbogo has other plans."

All of it made horrible, perfect sense. Umbogo would get Aslyn to agree to marriage, then dispose of her father. *It would behoove you to remember who allows you to sit atop that throne.* If Emperor Oxon wanted Umbogo as king of Novavito, he would send him here, to Arithia, to the palace, to enact that exact plan.

"Should I keep my eyes on anyone in particular?" Aslyn asked, her throat suddenly parched.

"There are a few your mother will verse you about on the way to Stormvalor," her father replied. "But word is King Orrin's nephew is entering the contest this year, and he has good odds to win."

Great. What was worse than a brainless brute? An arrogant, royal one, she told herself bitterly.

But it would be a match that even the emperor couldn't argue against.

Unless he thought the kingdoms of Novavito and Vorovesti uniting in marriage was a threat to him.

Good thing Prince Valen will take his place soon, she told herself.

"I hear he's a good man," her father said sadly, as if trying to convince himself as much as her. "It may be a good match. Just... follow your mother's advice."

Aslyn nodded. "I will do what I must. Meanwhile, I will keep my distance from Umbogo and speak no words to him before I depart."

She rose from her throne, smoothing out the skirt of her dress and running her hands over her roiling stomach. After a kiss on her father's cheek, Aslyn turned away from him to leave the throne room. The sorrow bleeding off of him broke her heart.

King Novin was no more ready for his daughter to marry than she was.

Elisio hounded Aslyn's steps all the way back to her suite. If she was to leave for Stormvalor, Aslyn had a lot of packing to do. She would need Kaiti's help. Miraculously, Elisio said nothing in the halls.

Aslyn stopped in her doorway, holding it and barring his entrance. Whatever had been between them had always been doomed to end. She knew it. He knew it. They had discussed it and accepted it before he ever climbed into her bed. But as he attempted to push his way in, Aslyn knew the years had changed him.

"I need you to remain out here and see that Kaiti comes to help me pack," Aslyn said, forcing him a step back instead of allowing him into the room.

Elisio's jaw tightened and twitched, then he said, "You can't be serious about this. Do you know the kind of men who participate in these competitions?"

"It is for me to judge who would be best suited for my future, not you," she replied.

He edged closer, peering down at her with heat in his eyes. "Did this mean nothing to you?"

Aslyn swallowed and shook her head. "That's not fair and you know it. We discussed this long ago, Elisio. This was always inevitable."

Seven Gods help her. If he didn't stop staring at her like that, her will would crumble. Not because she loved him—she cared deeply for him, but she refused to allow herself to love him. No, her will would crumble because she knew what he could do to her, and she did love that.

"Please see that Kaiti arrives quickly."

"I know we talked about this possibility," Elisio admitted, staring at her lips. Her pulse quickened. He brushed his thumb over her lower lip, and it was all she could do not to tremble. "I guess I just hoped that, after all this time, something might have changed. That you might have changed your mind." He leaned closer.

Aslyn swallowed again, caught in his spell. Then his words pushed through the haze of growing desire in her mind. Aslyn stepped back from his touch, his lips, his body, and blinked to clear her thoughts swiftly.

"I have not," she said firmly. "And I think it's best if you don't come to Stormvalor as my guard. It isn't fair to make you watch other men court me. You will remain here when I go."

Elisio's broad shoulders sagged as his arms fell limp at his sides. "I will see to your safety."

"You will not. There are plenty of guards to watch over me. I'm trying to do you this kindness, Elisio."

"Kindness..." His face twisted as if she had stabbed him in the gut. "So not only are you banishing me from your bedroom, but from your service as well?"

Aslyn recoiled. Did he truly not understand? "Banishing? Elisio, I'm trying to spare you as much pain as possible!" Aslyn took a deep breath, then stepped toward him, brushing a hand along his cheek.

The agony in his twisted features smoothed at her touch.

"I care for you, Elisio, but I have no choice in this. Far worse will happen if I postpone any longer. I need a husband."

"What about me?" Elisio's question cracked Aslyn's heart.

"You know I can't. There are laws about this sort of thing." Aslyn leaned in and kissed his other cheek, then whispered, "Please stay in Arithia when I go. For both of our sakes."

Before he could argue further, Aslyn withdrew and closed the door, then leaned back against it and closed her eyes.

I should have known better, she thought. She had never wanted to hurt him, but it had been childish to believe this would end in anything but pain.

CHAPTER 8

The Bill is Due

Escaping the Black Guards surrounding the tailor's shop had been tricky, even with Bast's shadow magic. They could trace the use of magic, so Bast had to invert everything he did carefully. He had used a shadow to draw them away from him and only wrapped silence around his boots to avoid making noise as he walked. Thankfully, they had made enough noise stomping over the rubble that they hadn't heard him clawing his way out from beneath the ruins. Then Bast had sent a gust of wind through several fluttering and frayed blots of cloth to block him from sight just long enough to slip around a corner.

After that, he was forced to venture into the sewers. Black Guards were watching rooftops, so that path of escape was out of the question.

Getting cleaned and patched up proved difficult when all the city guards were searching for him. Bast had used his thieving skills to lift the supplies he needed, then broke into an empty house on the edge of Arithia.

After inverting his magic to avoid detection, then setting shadow alarms in case anyone entered the house, Bast drew himself a bath. Water from the aqueduct system throughout Arithia ran cold, but he didn't dare heat it. Every ounce of magic he used could alert the city guards—or worse, the Black Guards. Heating it the traditional way would take too long.

His blood colored the water of the tub, but it would be easier to clean the mess and leave no evidence behind if he did everything in the water.

Once the dust from the tailor's shop had been washed away, making the pink-tinted water murky, Bast retrieved the wound adhesion he left beside the tub and examined the gash in his side. The bleeding had been minimal, but the cut was deep enough that he knew he couldn't ignore it, or it would rip open wider.

The salve was hard to acquire. Healers with the skill and materials to create the wound adhesion salve were rare and generally only sold to the highest bidder—the nobles and royals. Bast had worked his only charms on one of those healers to get his hands on a tin. He hated using it, resorting to more traditional stitches whenever possible.

But he would need to move quickly to find out what had gone wrong, then get out of Arithia before the guards tracked him down. Stitches wouldn't work. Not this time.

After making certain the wound had been properly cleaned, Bast applied a little of the wound adhesion salve. The mixture had herbs to combat infection, as well as a rare gum that held the wound firmly closed so the body could do its job.

After drying off and cleaning any traces of himself from the tub, Bast donned the Arithian commoner clothing he nicked off a cart. The man had been selling his wares for far too much, anyway. He could afford to lose a little. It would serve him right for gouging the hard-working people. Bast rolled up his leathers and tucked them into the pack he pilfered.

In ten minutes, he was clean, patched up, and ready to head out on the hunt.

Someone turned him in.

Bast would hunt down the snitch and finish him.

And hopefully find another way to retrieve the rest of his payment for Lord Corinth. If there was one thing Bast Blackblade hated, it was being stiffed on a bill.

Bast had spent the last eight years building his network across the whole of Divica. He had carefully vetted each broker in his network. In exchange for their service and discretion, they received a generous finder's fee. Men and women with connections to all the right people, and just enough fear for their own skins that they would never dare tell anyone.

He didn't really trust anyone. Trust created more problems than it helped.

The system worked. None of the brokers knew one another. None of the people who hired him knew what he looked like, where he came from, or even if he would take their job until that down payment disappeared from their accounts.

All the brokers thought Bast was another agent working for Blackblade, because that's what he told them. Another step removed from the Shadow himself. He even donned disguises sometimes to keep guards off his trail.

Bast routinely poked at his own network, seeking holes to shore up. Only once had he ever been forced to kill one of the brokers trying to sell him out... and everyone the broker might have told.

Word of that butchering spread throughout his network, and he never had a problem again. Putting themselves at risk was one thing. Putting everyone they knew at risk was another. No one wanted his vengeance to fall over their heads.

Somewhere in his Arithian network, someone had sold Bast's information to the Black Guard. There could be no other way for them to track down the tailor and have time to set a trap.

Every broker Bast dared to visit turned up the same. Their locations were crawling with Black Guards, like monstrous crows picking over the remains of dead men and women.

One after another, all around Arithia, Bast found repeated images. Black Guards. Dead or broken brokers. How had his network been so thoroughly uncovered?

Bast watched as some brokers were beaten bloody in the street as Black Guards questioned them about Blackblade in front of passersby. Then they were forced into the waiting prison carriage.

Instincts warned him to forget the bill still due and leave the city immediately. But Bast couldn't flee like a coward. He couldn't allow anyone to get away with this. He needed to send a message so this didn't happen again.

He had to find the rat and give it the treatment it deserved.

Moving at night would be better than in broad daylight. He could vanish into the shadows at night.

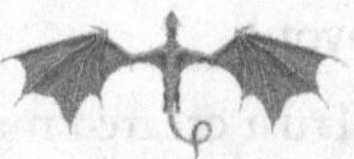

Aslyn couldn't sleep, haunted by the pain she had caused Elisio and the danger looming in her own palace. She tossed and turned until she couldn't stand it any longer. Umbogo wanted to trap her, which meant he either worked against Emperor Oxon's commands—unlikely as it was—or the emperor wanted her under Umbogo's thumb. Neither prospect made her stomach any less uneasy.

The sooner she could leave for Stormvalor, the better.

Anxious and restless, Aslyn tossed off the blankets and slid her feet into the velvet-lined slippers beside the bed. Then she slipped out, ignoring the startled night guard who followed a respectable distance behind her, and headed for Dorin's room.

Elisio's absence worried her. Had he gone off to lick his wounds? Would he now avoid her utterly before she left for Stormvalor?

As she raised her fist to knock, Aslyn prayed he didn't have company. Dorin didn't dare to bring his lover into his room often. But some nights, when their parents were sound asleep, he would sneak the young man in late at night and have him out before dawn.

Aslyn knocked gently, yet firm enough for Dorin to hear. Without waiting for an answer, she slipped into the suite.

The main room of Dorin's suite reflected his position as a prince of Novavito clearly. Gold gilded lamps and décor covered every surface. A fine rug of pure white covered the floor in the center of the room, surrounded by emerald green furniture with gilded arms and legs. Dorin always had expensive taste.

To the left, Dorin's door stood slightly ajar. Aslyn sighed as she edged closer. "Dorin?"

Murmurs from the other side of the door had her pausing on the plush white rug. She chewed her lip as she listened to the whisper of bare feet over marble.

A moment later, Dorin emerged in a silk robe embroidered with golden swirls. His dark hair was a mess, his amber eyes blurry from exhaustion.

"Asy?" He covered his yawn. "What time is it?"

"I can't sleep."

Dorin made a sound in the back of his throat, then eased his bedroom door closed and shuffled to the sofa, pulling Aslyn down beside him. "Stormvalor?"

Aslyn nodded, leaning against his side as Dorin wrapped his arm around her. Then she told him everything she worried about. The marriage. Umbogo's intentions. The emperor's possible plans for their throne. The threat of rebellion.

For all his faults, Dorin remained one of Aslyn's few trusted friends. Most of the ladies in her court simpered and cooed at her, more interested in their positions and in pleasing their future queen than being genuine. Aslyn had few others in her life besides her family and her ladies... and the guards, but even they showed her deference outside of the sparring ring. Elisio only treated her differently in private. In public, he respected her and his position guarding her.

Dorin, though, always spoke frankly with Aslyn, always listened to her fears. She adored her brother.

Dorin hummed as she finished spilling her fears. After a moment of consideration, he kissed the top of her head, hugging her tighter against his side.

"You know, I've heard about Aethan Starkling," Dorin said, practically sighing like a girl. "Fierce and intelligent and beautiful. They say his eyes are like a clear sky and his hair like a cloud among that sky—lush and fluffy and soft."

"Maybe you should marry him," Aslyn muttered.

"If the rumors are true and I could..." Dorin shifted, nudging Aslyn to sit up a little straighter. His amber eyes shone with sincerity. "Look, our parents haven't agreed to anything. They're just asking you to consider your options, to consider him. Keep an open mind."

Aslyn knew Dorin was probably right, but to hear even him suggesting she consider marrying this lord from Vorovesti... She had hoped he might be the voice of reason, or at least have an idea for how she could escape all of this.

Perhaps it was idealistic, but Aslyn had hoped to marry for love. She should have known better. As the future queen, love had never been in her future.

Arithia had been asleep for more than an hour. Even some of the more rowdy taverns quieted this late at night.

Bast had passed the time in a whorehouse. The women there would sell him out if they knew who he was. But with a little bit of coin, the women were quick to make him comfortable and ignore the scars on his body, as well as the fresh wound in his abdomen.

He left two women in a deep slumber when he slipped out to continue his hunt.

With Black Guards on alert, as well as city guards, Bast didn't dare leave a trail of shadows to use in case he needed a quick escape. If they caught the trail, it would lead them straight to him.

This time, Bast knew where he was headed.

Another benefit of whorehouses was the idiots who spoke too freely within the walls. Bast struck up a casual conversation with the girls he hired about the rumors that Blackblade was in the city. The women had shared what they knew.

One of their friends had told them that yesterday her patron had flashed coins and bragged to her that he was paid handsomely to help aid in the capture of Blackblade. Their friend had laughed it off and done her job, but when news of Lord Corinth's murder reached their ears, their friend packed her bag and fled the city.

No doubt she feared Blackblade would come for her just for knowing who the contact was. And he might have. But she had left enough clues with her friends about who she had shared that bed with for him to know where to go tonight.

Bast perched on the sloped roof of the building across from the broker's apartment. The man might be dumb enough to boast, but he wasn't so dumb to spend all of his money like some of the others. Until today, that was.

This broker, Benji, hadn't been the most lucrative of his contacts in Arithia. Most of the offers Benji brokered were petty and offered little coin. Wives seeking vengeance on a cheating husband. Family members looking to cash in on a family inheritance.

If Bast learned anything from his trade, it was the deeply petty nature of humans. No other species was so driven by greed or wrath to kill. Not like humans.

He hated people, in general, for exactly that reason.

Bast's stepfather had been an abusive bastard prone to drinking and fits of rage. One of those fits had cost his mother her life when Bast was only eight. His stepfather accused his mother of whoring around, and often pointed a finger at Bast the Bastard, roaring about how she came about the child. Bast wasn't sure if any of his accusations were true. His mother certainly denied ever cheating. But she also never spoke of where Bast had come from.

He truly was a bastard.

Bast had run away at twelve when his dark magic manifested for the first time. He had been terrified that his stepfather would discover what he could do and turn him over to the Black Guard—to the emperor.

So Bast fled in the night.

It hadn't taken him long to figure out how to survive on his own. Especially not with the new magic swelling within him. The trick was to remain unnoticed. After a few near misses with the Black Guard tracking his magic, Bast learned to use it cautiously and wisely.

Bast's first kill had been an accident, a fight over a near-molding loaf of bread with another street kid in Elysia. His shadows had lashed out during that brawl, strangling the other boy, snapping his neck.

The bread had been salty with his own tears.

The memory hit him hard as he watched the street below for signs of the Black Guard. Bast had killed more people than he could count in the last ten years. So many that he was beyond numbed to the sight of death. But that first kill still rattled him.

He took a deep breath to keep his nerves calm and centered himself.

Enough waiting.

Bast checked the street once more to make sure no one would spot him. Then he leaped from the rooftop onto the small balcony across the street. Darkheart bounced against his back. But he wouldn't use the sword. Not tonight.

With a flick of his knife through the crack in the doorframe, he unlocked the balcony door and slipped into Benji's apartment.

Only the curtain stirred.

Benji's apartment was small. A joint kitchenette and sitting room. A latrine and a single bedroom off the main sitting room. Little furniture to speak of.

The apartment was so quiet Bast could hear Benji's soft, slumbering breaths from the bedroom. He strode silently across the hardwood floor and into the room.

Benji laid atop his blankets in his night clothes, head back and arms splayed out at his sides. Bast smirked, risking a touch of his magic to coil bindings around Benji's wrists and ankles.

By the time Benji's eyes shot open, Bast hovered over the man, his hood up to cover his face and a black knife at Benji's throat. The mattress sagged under Bast's knee.

Benji tried to slither away, then yelped as he realized he was bound in place.

"Justis help me," Benji whimpered.

Bast almost laughed at the prayer to the god of justice and war, as if he thought he deserved to be saved. As if he thought the gods still existed.

"The gods can't save you," Bast hissed. He allowed the edge of the knife to kiss Benji's throat.

"P-Please. Don't kill me!" Benji squeezed his eyes closed.

"A job has been completed, and the bill is due," Bast said, keeping that low hiss in his voice to mask it. "But the broker is dead."

"I didn't... I didn't..." Benji trembled violently. Fat tears streamed down his cheeks into the pillow beneath his head.

Pathetic.

"No..." Bast cooed with dangerous intent. "Of course you didn't, Benji. Nor did you sell information about Blackblade to the Black Guard, did you?" The edge of the knife bit into Benji's neck, drawing blood. "What did you tell them?"

Benji attempted moving, but the paralytic on the blade that bit into his neck worked quickly. A confession spilled from Benji's lips like he thought the words might actually save him. But he was already a dead man. Bast couldn't allow him to live after this.

Benji had told the Black Guard everything he knew. That Blackblade had brokers all over the city. That those men and women arranged the payments for him. Then Blackblade's agent would come to collect the final payment when the deed was done.

"Th-they said they just wanted to question the agent," Benji stuttered.

"How did the Black Guard find so many of the brokers in less than a day?" Bast asked.

Benji squeezed his eyes closed, forcing more of those fat tears down his cheeks. "Please. I didn't... I don't know anything else."

Liar.

"What do you know about the last job?" Bast asked, sliding the knife down Benji's torso.

Benji whimpered, then sobbed, "Nothing. Nothing!"

Another lie. Bast knew it with certainty. Benji must have realized his error, because he opened one eye slowly, warily, peering into the shadowed hood as if he could see Bast's face. But Benji would see nothing but darkness.

Bast shifted the tip of the knife, poised right over the parts Benji favored, then pressed gently enough for Benji to know he meant business. Benji choked on his own sobs. A sharp tang clouded the air. The idiot pissed himself. Bast curled his nose in disgust.

"I expect the truth," Bast said darkly.

Benji just sobbed.

Bast didn't have time for this. He struck. With a flick of his wrist, he sliced a warning cut along Benji's precious parts. Benji screamed, but Bast shoved shadows down his throat to gag the sound.

He waited a moment, then leaned closer. "Tell me what you know and I'll make it quick. Otherwise, we are in for a very long night. Do you know who contacted the other broker for the job?"

Benji blinked rapidly.

Bast loosened the shadow gag.

"There were... r-r-rumors. The... the..." Sweat beaded on Benji's brow. "Another b-broker." It took far too much effort for Benji to describe where the broker had come from, that he had contacted several of Bast's own brokers for a third party.

"Javon..."

Bast's blood curdled. He only heard of one man named Javon in Arithia with the means or connections to carry out the deal.

"The bill is due, Benji," Bast said darkly.

And before the other man could respond, Bast sliced his throat.

Javon Nadier. Finance Advisor to King Novin Kiernan.

CHAPTER 9

Leavetakings

The palace courtyard burst with activity as Arithian guards saw to the horses. Servants fastened trunks of clothes and jewels to the carriages. Aslyn Kiernan stood on the stairs of the palace, watching as enough wealth to feed a kingdom loaded up for the queen and crown princess.

Ned's funeral had passed without incident or the appearance of Blackblade. Not that Aslyn expected the assassin to show up and proclaim his victory. Dalma had said little and the moment it was over, she vanished back into her suite to grieve alone. Aslyn hated leaving the city while her friend needed her, but there was nothing she could do about it.

Aslyn had selected her most comfortable riding dress and insisted her favorite horse accompanied them on the trip. If she was to travel more than halfway across the realm, her horse would come as well.

After a fierce argument with her chief maid, Kaiti, Aslyn had wrapped a couple of ladies' daggers in silk and hid them in a trunk. Her mother would chide her if she had dared to wear them beneath the folds of her dress. Surely a future queen had every right to protect herself. It was a long road ahead. Anything could happen.

Javon Nadier, her father's financial advisor, conversed with the king off to the side. No doubt reminding her father of just how much wealth accompanied the crown princess on this northward journey.

Aslyn admired Javon's no-nonsense approach to the kingdom's finances. Not only did he know at all times how much remained in their coffers, but he somehow also knew how much something would cost them before they even asked. And not all costs were financial. The man was a wizard with figures.

Aslyn descended the steps and strode to the fountain fed by the waterfalls from the mountains. She slid her fingers along the water. Next time she saw this fountain, her entire life would look different.

Movement across the bustling courtyard caught Aslyn's attention. While every part of the palace hustled on urgent business to prepare for the leavetaking of the queen and princess, something about this movement made Aslyn's bones chill.

But when she stepped around the fountain to get a better look, all she saw were shadows beneath archways.

Shadows watching them.

Watching her.

Aslyn strained her focus on those shadows, knowing something watched her. She could feel it in her prickling skin. Her heart beat harder against her chest. The Jewel of Arithia warmed against her skin where it hung around her neck. That had never happened before.

Yes. Those shadows had shifted. Just slightly.

One alcove darkened more than the others. It was a subtle difference, but now that she watched it, that difference appeared so obvious to her.

Nervous—terrified for reasons she couldn't wholly explain—Aslyn licked her lips and dared a few steps closer, drawn toward that darkness.

"Princess."

Aslyn jumped, whirling to find Umbogo approaching. Her already racing heart slammed wildly against her breast and she was sure her face heated.

Instead of acknowledging the ambassador further, Aslyn once more peered toward that darkened alcove.

"What's wrong, princess?" Umbogo asked, stepping up beside her. His black eyes peered toward the alcoves curiously.

"Nothing."

Nothing remained. Aslyn's amber eyes darted from one alcove to another, but that sense that she was being watched vanished.

Umbogo emitted a small, curious hum, but he didn't question her further. "I had hoped we could speak for a few minutes before you leave for Stormvalor."

Aslyn pulled her gaze from the alcoves, giving up her hunt, and glared at the ambassador. "No."

"But—"

"Your Majesty?" Elisio materialized from the mess of royal guards. She should have been furious that he was there, but now she was thankful for his interruption. Elisio beckoned her toward the carriage, eyeing Umbogo suspiciously. "It's time."

"I'm afraid I don't have a moment, ambassador." Aslyn left it at that, turning on her heels. She marched toward the carriages, leaving a glowering Umbogo behind.

The moment they were out of earshot, Aslyn hissed at Elisio. "I told you to stay."

"Sadly, Your Majesty, your father and my captain supersede your command," Elisio replied, a harshness in his tone. "They insist I'm the best equipped to protect you, and I don't disagree."

Aslyn's jaw twitched in irritation. He volunteered for this job, no doubt, and made his own case. All Elisio needed was her father's stamp of approval to skirt her command. It infuriated her that Elisio would go to such lengths to disobey her wishes. She only wanted to protect him from pain. Now, he would be forced to watch from the shadows as she courted men in Stormvalor. Did he not see how hard this would be for himself?

King Novin eyed the ambassador over Aslyn's shoulder as she approached. Aslyn simply kissed her father's cheek, then gave him a subtle shake to indicate she had said nothing of consequence. She had promised her father she would not speak to Umbogo, and she hadn't. Not really.

"Listen to your mother," he said instead, "and make the best choice for the future of Novavito."

"Of course, father." She briefly hugged her father, a rare public show of affection.

Dorin stood to the side. Aslyn approached her brother. A smile graced his tan face. Aslyn cupped his cheek and pulled him close, kissing his forehead.

"I'll miss you," Dorin murmured. "I love you, Asy."

"I'll only be a few months," she teased, attempting to lighten his mood. "Don't give Father a heart attack while I'm away. And steer clear of Umbogo."

Dorin grimaced as she stepped back and dropped her hand. "I'd sooner talk to a donkey than to him."

Despite her best efforts to remain dignified, Aslyn couldn't help the laugh that broke out of her.

"He is an ass," she agreed.

Dorin's lips curled up at her joke.

Queen Giata waited in the carriage by the time Aslyn joined her mother. The crown and jewels weighing the queen down seemed absurd to Aslyn. Surely wearing such things on this kind of trip would be unnecessary.

The footman closed the carriage door as Aslyn settled on the bench across from her mother and arranged her skirts.

"We have a lot of work to do," her mother said the moment the carriage lurched into motion.

Aslyn simply nodded and listened to her mother discuss the merits of the most eligible matches as they rode toward the palace gates, then along the city streets leading to the only road in or out of Arithia.

The city glimmered in the sunlight. Rays of sunshine created waves off the golden accented roofs and rails as if bidding farewell to the princess and future queen.

Such a beautiful city.

Her city.

Her kingdom.

Aslyn would do whatever necessary to protect it.

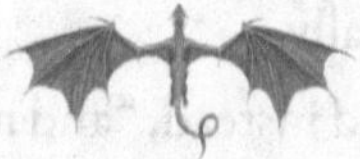

B ast had spent the morning probing the pristine, tall palace for ways inside during the funeral. It proved more of a challenge during the day. Even at dawn, sunlight shone on the white walls of the palace from the east. Since the palace faced south, it saw sunlight all day. The paths into the palace would not be the same as those he would have to find on the way out.

By the time he finally breached the outer walls, it was past midday. Bast swiftly cloaked himself in shadows among the alcoves.

The courtyard burst with activity, as if the entire palace and its staff had business in that outer yard this morning. All he wanted was a way to get closer to Javon, to find out who was responsible for his overdue payment. If the accountant cooperated, he might be allowed to live.

The accountant lingered near the king on the palace steps, their heads bent together. Had the two of them worked together to entrap him? It would make the Novavito king much more fearsome an enemy if he could boast of taking down Blackblade himself. But why would he target one of his highest ranked, most loyal lords to trap Blackblade?

Bast moved to another shadowy alcove to get a better look at the king and his advisor, perhaps even close enough to hear some of their conversation.

But when he moved, the crown princess looked over.

Right at him.

Bast froze, carefully masking himself in the shadows of the alcove. There were enough guards in the courtyard that, were he spotted, his chances of escape were slim at best.

But no matter how long he remained frozen, staring back at the princess, she didn't turn away.

She couldn't see him. There was no way.

Yet there was no doubt she looked directly at him.

Why hadn't she called for the guards?

Because she doesn't see me, he realized. The princess only sensed something, no matter how precise her gaze was.

Something in the courtyard beckoned him like invisible tendrils of temptation attempting to draw him in. What sort of dark, forbidden magic was it? Perhaps he had underestimated the palace defenses. That call tugged at his heart and mind, and it was all he could do to resist.

One of the emperor's ambassadors approached the princess, but she was in such a trance, staring at *him*, that she hadn't noticed the pale young man's approach.

The moment her gaze moved off of him, Bast dipped around the corner. It was better to wait until the commotion ended. Then he could try this again.

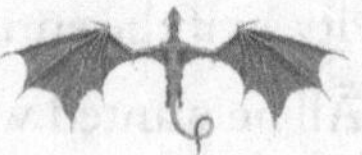

King Orrin of Vorovesti held a farewell banquet for the young men leaving for Stormvalor. Aethan Starkling had attempted to speak with Iskra before the banquet, but the Pridell house guards had turned him away at the gate, saying that the lady was unavailable.

Iskra had not returned the message he sent to her, either.

But all the nobles were required to attend the banquet.

The palace ballroom burst with eager young lords and ladies. Some of the young men boasted about the tournament or groused that their parents didn't deem them prepared. Aethan engaged in conversation, food, and drink when necessary. He even exchanged a few pleasant words with Borin and Calvin, the two other competitors who would join him and Trystain in the tournament.

Older lords eager to remind Aethan that a fair fortune rode on his performance in the tournament foiled every attempt to get close to Iskra all night. Younger lords wanted a moment with the king's nephew to make friends before leaving for the tournament. Young, eligible ladies asked for a dance or insisted on sharing a drink.

Aware that his father's eyes were always upon him, Aethan did his duty. He engaged in pointless conversation, joked with eager lords, young and old, and humored the young woman with the courage to approach him. Each time, he found polite ways to duck out as soon as etiquette allowed.

By the time he found a free moment to himself, Aethan could no longer see Iskra's strawberry blond head or ruby red dress.

Sybil hustled over, politely curtseying to a lord who eyed her in ways Aethan loathed.

"Did you speak with her?" Sybil asked, watching the rest of the nobles milling around them.

"I've been trying all night, but I can't get close to her," Aethan admitted. "Do you know where she is?"

"She's leaving right now, Aethan."

His heart sank. No. He wouldn't leave Mordelic without speaking to Iskra. He had to make up for his idiocy.

"Lord Aethan," a deep voice said from behind Aethan.

He turned to find Lord Cyrus, Trystain's father, looming with a dark drink in his hand.

"Lord Cyrus," Aethan said politely, inclining his head as much as propriety demanded. He hated Trystain's father. The man was needlessly cruel to his son and applied unreasonable expectations on Trystain's shoulders.

"I imagine you've heard this from a few others already," Lord Cyrus said. "But I have a good deal riding on your success in the tournament."

Aethan's mouth went dry. Lord Cyrus bet against his own son? Did Trystain know that? "I hope I won't disappoint my king," Aethan said carefully. "To me, that's what matters most."

"Yes." Lord Cyrus's lips thinned. He looked so much like his son, but with a razor-sharp edge that Trystain wholly lacked. "Just don't embarrass my son."

Aethan attempted to make light of the moment despite his anger, glancing at his sister. "I wouldn't dream of embarrassing my sister's future husband."

Sybil slid herself into the conversation smoothly, taking Lord Cyrus by the arm and turning him away from Aethan. As she beamed and pushed all her charms on Lord Cyrus, Sybil gave Aethan a subtle nod to go after Iskra.

He didn't waste the opportunity, moving to the edge of the room and following the black onyx walls to the massive double doors open to the night.

Iskra stood with her parents, waiting for their carriage.

Aethan jogged over, calling her name.

Iskra turned toward him slowly, the hem of her red dress sweeping the stones beneath her with a soft swish. Her strawberry blond hair piled on her head, shimmering in the torchlight like flames of their own. The green rim on her hazel eyes flared with life as she peered at him.

Iskra was, as always, breathtaking. Aethan couldn't help but stare.

"Don't leave yet," Aethan pleaded, aware of the way her parents studied him. "Please."

"I'm not sure what else there is to say, Aethan," Iskra said. The sorrow in her voice cracked his heart open.

The carriage arrived. Her parents climbed in first. Iskra took a step toward it to join them, but Aethan grabbed her arm.

Iskra glared at his hand on her skin, then lifted those fierce, beautiful eyes on him.

Aethan didn't back down. He didn't let go. No, Aethan stepped closer.

"I told you what I want," he said, desperate to get her to understand before he left for Stormvalor. "It's you, Iskra. It's always been you." His hand slid along the smooth skin of her arm into her hand. "I swear it." He leaned in closer, eager to capture her lips. "You and me."

Some of the fury dimmed in her eyes, but she shook her head and pulled away to avoid the kiss. "We both know your father won't allow it. It's better if we admit the truth now."

"Don't do this." Aethan's voice cracked over the words. "Iskra, I lo—"

She pressed her fingers against his lips, cutting off the confession. Pain made the lines around her eyes more pronounced. Lines that he had created. Pain because of him. Aethan couldn't bear it.

"Listen to me, Aethan." Her words were soft.

He shook his head, closing the gap between them, needing her body close to his.

"We've lived a beautiful, glorious dream for three years now," Iskra said softly. He could hear her pain in each word. "But I think I always knew, deep down, how this would end."

"It doesn't need to end," Aethan said. He ran his hands along her arms, afraid he would never get to touch her again, knowing where this was headed and refusing to accept it. He shook his head.

"It does."

Again, he shook his head, this time more fiercely. Tears brimmed his eyes. He loved her. Iskra had stolen his heart and he refused to take it back.

"We both know you will likely win the tournament," Iskra continued, and her own pain thickened her voice. "And your father will use that to leverage a... better wife."

"Then I will refuse."

Iskra smiled sadly, caressing his cheek, wiping away his tears.

"Please." He hardly recognized his own voice, the desperation anchoring to him.

"You won't refuse him." Iskra leaned closer and kissed him softly, a whisper of what they had shared and nothing like the kiss he had wanted to give her. It was a sad goodbye. "We both know you won't."

"I will," Aethan said, fiercely determined to hold on to her for as long as possible. "I will, for you. You are not selfish. You are kind and fierce and beautiful inside and out. I didn't mean what I said. Not a word of it."

"I know."

Aethan slid his fingers into the hair at her nape, pressing his forehead to hers.

"If it's meant to be, it will be," she breathed.

And she believed those words. He heard it in every sound from her luscious lips.

But she didn't believe it would happen.

"What will be, will be," he said, fighting back his sorrow.

Iskra nodded.

Then she pulled away.

His hands fell from her body, hanging limp and lifeless at his sides.

Aethan watched helplessly as Iskra climbed into the carriage. She paused before dipping inside, turning back to him.

"I think it's only right to tell you..." Iskra's voice cut out. She swallowed, and the pain in her eyes tensed something inside of him. "...I will be there, at Stormvalor. I will cheer you on, Aethan, but if this is the end of us, I need to secure my future somewhere."

Secure her... Aethan shook his head.

But before he could respond, Iskra said, "I'm sorry." And she meant it.

Iskra dipped into the carriage and the footman closed the door.

Aethan remained in that spot, unable to move, to think, to breathe as the truth of her words fell over him.

If she couldn't marry *him*, Iskra intended to find someone else. One of his competitors at Stormvalor.

Aethan's fists clenched at his sides.

He would destroy all the competition before he lost her to one of them.

CHAPTER 10

To Honor Vanished Gods

The journey from Mordelic to Stormvalor only lasted two days, but for Aethan Starkling, those two days felt like an eternity. He rode with the other Vorovesti competitors, each with a wagon or carriage bearing their armor sets, weapons, and clothing. Everything else would be provided. Food, shelter, a personal squire.

Each of the five kingdoms were allowed only five competitors to keep the numbers balanced and manageable for the Gamemaster. Four of the Vorovesti competitors were from Mordelic. One would travel from Murandy Hills further north.

For two days, Aethan examined the three men traveling with him—all from Mordelic noble houses. Trystain, he knew well. His best friend stuck close to him and covertly shared what he learned of the other two during their journey.

Aethan wondered if part of the reason Trystain stuck so close to him was as much to show the other two he held a higher position at court than them. It wouldn't be the first time someone flaunted their friendship with someone close to the royal family.

The first night, when they stopped for the night at a small village inn, Trystain had proclaimed that he would miss Sybil's company. Another flex Aethan chose to ignore. Sybil was the king's niece, so a marriage to her was as close to the royal family as any of these men could hope for.

Aethan had smiled at his friend and said nothing as they were escorted to their rooms first, where a steaming bath awaited them.

Eager to wash off the smell of his horse, Aethan cleaned up and donned fresh clothing before venturing down to the common room for a hot meal.

Calvin, a competitor chosen by House Havi for his archery and battle skills, joined Aethan first.

Aethan wondered if Calvin observed every move Aethan made as closely as Aethan observed him. The way a person moved, the way they talked and shifted and ate... everything gave Aethan clues about how they might fight in the tournament. Aethan kept his tone light, his smile free, and his movements casual as he engaged Calvin in conversation.

They weren't alone for long before Borin joined them, a beast of a young man with his wide shoulders and arms as thick as Aethan's neck. Borin moved with a predatory grace, but Aethan could tell by the way Borin approached that his speed would be affected by his size. An advantage Aethan would have to expose one of these days.

Borin spoke of his house, one of the lesser noble houses just outside of Mordelic as if it held great power in Vorovesti. Aethan humored him, but didn't dare tell the man his house barely held influence in Mordelic, let alone the whole of their kingdom.

"So," Calvin leaned against the tabletop and lowered his voice, glancing around the common room.

Since their arrival, the inn had filled with people from the village—with families eager to put their daughters on display in front of the competitors on the way to the tournament and men who likely hoped for a moment alone with one or more of them to gather their odds of winning. Aethan would place his own bet that some of those men didn't have the extra coins to lose, so he avoided any more than a tight nod and swift eye contact before returning to his own table.

"So?" Aethan peered into his mug of ale. He wasn't really in the mood for the drink, but the barmaid had been so eager to offer it he hadn't said no. Apparently, it was a local brew their innkeeper was quite proud of.

Borin grinned from ear to ear.

Aethan looked from one to the other. What were they waiting for?

"Is it true you ditched Lady Pridell on a chance to win the hand of the Novavito crown princess?" Calvin asked.

Aethan froze even as his heart skipped hard against his ribs. "I'm sorry?"

"Rumor has it you don't just want to win the tournament," Borin added. "But that you want to win a crown."

Aethan took a long drink of ale, aware that the move probably gave away the truth. But dammit if he didn't need a drink, now.

The two stared at him like eager vultures.

He ignored their stares, peering instead into the half-empty mug of ale. "The only desire I have is to be crowned the champion. The rest doesn't matter to me."

Where was Trystain? He could use his friend's support.

Borin snorted as he pushed the vegetables on his plate to the side, clearly not interested in eating them. "Sounds like a yes to me."

"How is that a yes?" Aethan asked. His hand tightened on the handle of his cup.

"Because there's no way Queen Giata would allow her daughter to marry anyone but the champion," Calvin answered. He finished his dinner, waving the fork at Aethan. "Does this mean Lady Pridell is up for grabs?"

Borin snorted again, and the sound began to grate on Aethan's nerves. He wanted to take that fork and ram it through the man's hand.

"Don't get ahead of yourselves, boys," Trystain said as he breezed into the common room. A few of the young women practically swooned as they watched him stride toward the competitors' table. "Lady Iskra Pridell would never debase herself for the likes of you lot. She has too much integrity to stoop so low."

Aethan relaxed ever so slightly, relieved to see Trystain at last.

Calvin and Borin did not appear so pleased, though. The comment, though made in jest, had clearly struck a nerve. Probably because they all knew it to be true. Iskra wouldn't just be after a competitor, but a highly ranked one.

"Oh, don't let your jealousy get the better of you before we even reach Storm-valor," Trystain teased as he sank into a seat. His gaze met one of the young women who stared at him. Trystain winked.

The woman practically fainted.

Aethan fought the urge to roll his eyes.

By the time Trystain settled across the table from Aethan, the barkeep already had a drink and plate of food in front of him. He offered her a thankful smile before digging in, oblivious to the way Borin and Calvin glared at him.

Aethan heaved out a sigh. "It might come as a surprise, gentlemen, but my interests in any women are minimal if it interferes with my ability to compete."

"A luxury the king's nephew has that the rest of us don't," Calvin replied. When Aethan cast him a curious glance, Calvin sighed and relaxed back in his chair, cradling his ale. "No offense, Lord Starkling, but you live in a whole other bubble from the rest of us. While you have more freedom to take your time and pursue your own interests, guys like Borin and me have had pressure twisted into us to make a beneficial match before this tournament ends. Before we…"

Calvin trailed off, as if finishing that sentence would cause him pain. Borin paused in devouring his meal to eye Calvin, but the flicker of mutual understanding he had with the other man was not lost on Aethan.

Did they think they would die in the tournament? No, that wouldn't benefit them when it came to making a marriage match.

Which meant their families, their sponsors, likely knew they would lose and wanted them to secure something unshakable before it happened.

"Oh, come now, it can't be that bad," Aethan said, trying to lighten the mood.

Calvin downed his ale and stood. But before he left for bed, he paused, meeting Aethan's gaze without an angry fire in his eyes.

"Just so you know, my older brother was supposed to compete this year," Calvin said, anger and indignation a cloud around him. "But when my parents found out who was competing, they instead put in my name. Apparently, my dignity is expendable to them."

With that, Calvin stormed up the steps. Aethan didn't ask who caused his parents to change their minds, to sacrifice Calvin instead of their eldest. He swallowed the lump rising in his throat.

Borin and Trystain stared after Calvin, dumbstruck. Borin seemed to calculate something, then, after a minute, he finished his drink and excused himself.

"They act like you've already won," Trystain grumbled as he ate. "I fully intend to show the world just how to bring the mighty Lord Aethan Starkling to his knees."

Aethan threw his napkin on his plate and shoved back his chair. "I'm not in the mood for your teasing tonight, Tryst."

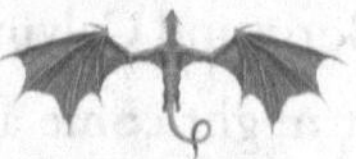

The next morning, each of the men were less conversational than they had been the day before. Aethan didn't bother apologizing as he checked his saddle, then climbed on. It wasn't his fault Calvin's family reacted the way they had. Aethan spent his life training for this, and he would be damned if he allowed anyone else to make him feel guilty for the skills he crafted through blood, sweat, and study.

They reached Stormvalor a couple of hours past midday, and their small party fell into reverent silence as they approached the northern gate into the city.

The buildings that survived the War of Two Crowns were rumored to be carved by the God Terralibra as a gift to Justis. Nothing could break the stone They hewed until that horrible war. The buildings which had been broken in that war were restored with ordinary rocks imported decades after the end of the war from the Ridgeback Ice Mountains to the far north. Any remnants of ice had long ago melted away from the stone, leaving a strange patchwork of gray and pale white stones in those repaired structures.

Despite the destruction over a century ago, Stormvalor was reborn. Green trees and vibrant spring blooms covered terraces along the streets. Thousands of people thrived in this ancient city.

Aethan's own family had long ago been given responsibility for ruling over this city. His father spent nearly as much time at Stormvalor as he did in Mordelic.

For Aethan, this arrival at Stormvalor felt like a homecoming. Not that he would return to his family estate near the arena. No, for this tournament, Aethan would be required to stay in the arena housing with the other competitors. When his family arrived, they would reside in the Starkling family suite.

The northern road to the arena in the center of the city was lined with adoring citizens. Men, women, and children cheered their arrival, tossing pale blue stardrift flowers in the path of the horses. Some called out his name, eager for a glance or nod. Some called out to Trystain, who humored the women most with smiles and winks.

Aethan simply rode with his back straight, watching the looming stone walls of the arena draw closer. He breathed in the familiar sweet scent of the stardrifts and faint hints of stone-ground bread from nearby bakeries. But his vision fastened singularly on his destination.

As he drew near the arena entrance, Aethan tipped his head back to take in the massive statue of Justis. It rose far above any of the other buildings in the city, visible even from miles away.

The weathered stone crumbled in a few places, but the imposing figure of the long-gone God of War remained vigilant.

Aethan studied the elegantly carved stone armor, the long hair streaming behind Justis as he leaned forward, sword raised and ready to defend the realm. The chiseled features and the hand around the sword suffered the worst of the decay.

But it was the eyes that made Aethan reign his horse to a halt before vanishing through the tunnel beneath Justis and into the arena.

Legend claimed those eyes once crackled with lightning. Now, they were little more than worn stone pockets. Yet something about the statue settled over Aethan like a cloak, wrapping around him, weighing him down.

A heat and fierce determination rushed through his veins, his bones, and Aethan shuddered as it passed over him. He couldn't look away, peering at the eyes of the vanished god high above. A sense of urgency to honor the vanished gods overwhelmed him.

Voices breathed from the sky like a whisper on the breeze. Aethan couldn't hear the words. He couldn't even tell if there *were* words. But he sensed... something.

Trystain, already in the tunnel, turned his mount to peer back at Aethan. "Everything alright? You look... haunted."

Aethan fought to peel his gaze away, and it felt like falling back into himself. He blinked at Trystain once. Twice.

"I'm fine."

With a nudge, Aethan sent his horse into a trot into the arena tunnel.

Aethan dismounted as they reached the mouth of the tunnel, guiding his horse at the rear of the quartet.

Borin had nudged in front of Calvin as the Gamemaster and a collection of assistants waited to greet them. Did Borin believe being first would hold any significance? Aethan knew it didn't matter. Only performance in the events would be of significance.

"Competitors of Vorovesti, welcome to the Stormvalor Tournament," the Gamemaster announced with a flourish of his long blue-gray robes. His dark gaze took each of them in with careful calculation.

The way the Gamemaster squinted slightly after studying Aethan made him uncomfortable. What did he see when he looked at them? At *him*?

"I am Gamemaster Likten," he continued, tearing his gaze away from Aethan to speak to all four of the young men before him. "Until the end of the tournament or your elimination from it, the Arena of Justis will be your new home. We are honored to host you in this sacred space."

Borin muttered something under his breath that Aethan was certain had little love for sacred spaces.

The Gamemaster ignored him—or didn't hear him at all—as he pressed on. "Each of you has been assigned a squire who will see to your needs during your stay. If you need your armor cleaned or your weapons sharpened, your squire will perform the task for you. They will manage your schedule each day in accordance with your individual requirements, per my own orders. In fact, the only person they serve above you is me."

Calvin shifted, eyeing the four waiting squires. Aethan simply nodded to the Gamemaster in acceptance and understanding.

"The tournament will require you to perform feats of strength, valor, and intelligence," the Gamemaster continued. "But in addition to these events, you will be required to attend public events as well. All of these will take place within the walls of the arena. Any competitors caught leaving the arena grounds before they are eliminated from the tournament will be removed without honors."

Again, Aethan nodded, as did Trystain. They were well aware of the rules, having had them drilled into their lessons for years now.

"Now, before we get to introducing you to your squire, I must give you one more word of advice." The Gamemaster gave each of them a hard look before continuing. "While fraternizing is not against the rules, you must remember that this tournament is about honor as much as strength. You will be expected to conduct yourself with honor in all things."

Aethan's mind wandered to Iskra and her final words to him the night before he left. Would she truly choose to fraternize with any of his competitors? The very idea of her in another man's bed fueled his jealousy.

A stable hand retrieved the reins for all four horses. Aethan unfastened his sword from the saddle before allowing the horse to be guided away. Conjuring *some* scheme to change his father's mind, Aethan fastened the sword to his hip absently.

Borin bowed to the Gamemaster, then followed his squire deeper into the arena, along the left passage. A moment later, Calvin followed another down the same passage.

When the Gamemaster called Trystain's name, Aethan's friend straightened his spine and lifted his chin proudly. After a brief introduction to the squire, Trystain was dismissed as well, walking along the passage not fifty yards behind Calvin.

"Aethan Starkling," the Gamemaster offered no deference to Aethan. Not that Aethan would receive any here. He was equal to his fellow competitors in status. Only by performing well could he rise among the ranks.

"We are honored to have our presiding Lord's son competing this year," the Grandmaster said. "Your father selected your squire himself from among my candidates."

Hand selected by Lord Lux Starkling. Great. Aethan wondered if that meant his squire would be a spy for his father, ensuring Aethan did as he was told. Particularly when it came to a certain princess.

Aethan eyed the squire. He was young, perhaps thirteen, and fit enough to handle carrying Aethan's weapons. But the way the boy cast his gaze down at his own shoes made Aethan wonder what made him special.

"Squire Roric." The Gamemaster motioned the last remaining squire forward.

The boy moved with confidence, bowing at the waist to Aethan.

"Show Master Starkling to his rooms."

The boy bowed to the Gamemaster before stepping forward and motioning smoothly for Aethan to follow him along the same passage the others had vanished into.

The wide gray stone hallway buzzed with life. Squires bustled in and out of rooms, following the outer edges of the hall to leave the pale blue rug along the center of the hallway clear for the competitors. Tapestries and stone carvings depicting glorious ancient battles of Justis adorned the walls at regular intervals along the hallway. Lamps burned brightly high up the walls, reflecting off carefully placed glass to make those lights brighter.

Aethan watched everyone move as he followed Roric along the hallway.

Roric was the only squire who dared to walk on the rug, guiding his competitor with his head held high, unapologetic even to the competitors who crossed their path.

Eyes and whispers followed them. Squires watched Aethan with open admiration. Fellow competitors eyed him like a piece of meat on a butcher block. Aethan continued confidently, gaze forward and face as unreadable as stone. He would give these men nothing to use against him, though it seemed his reputation arrived long before he did.

As Aethan looked around the hall, he noticed most of the competitors arrived for their training before the tournament would begin. Only the competitors from Umbr had yet to appear.

The tall, arching ceilings swallowed all light. The black banners of Emperor Oxon and the Divican Empire hung every hundred yards, a stark reminder of who they served.

Roric opened a door and stepped back out of the way so Aethan could enter the apartment.

Aethan had heard rumors about the comfort the competitors were afforded during the tournament, but he hadn't expected... this.

The main living space was wide, with arching double doors leading out into a private competitor courtyard. Floor to ceiling windows on the far wall allowed more than enough sunlight into the space. Even the furniture was of quality craftsmanship.

A sapphire blue banner of House Starkling hung between the windows, glowing with an almost ethereal light.

The air in the room smelled like home. Wisteria and blackberry currant. Aethan took in a deep breath as he reached the open doors, drawing the familiar smell in as deep as he could before letting out a slow breath.

"I've taken the liberty of drawing a bath for you, Master Starkling," Roric said, motioning toward the door to his right. "I thought you might like to wash the travels off before I show you to the training grounds and cafeteria."

Aethan's muscles tensed the longer he hesitated. Every part of him ached to sink into the warm water. Instead, he eyed Roric curiously.

"Tell me, Roric, what do the others say about me?" he asked as he removed his riding gloves.

Roric lifted his chin proudly, but didn't meet Aethan's eye as he spoke. "They say you are a favored champion this season."

Aethan strolled toward the squire, dropping his gloves on the smooth black walnut table as he passed. "Who says that?"

"Everyone, sire. They say you will win some men a great fortune." Roric's eyes darted around as if unsure where to look, but still, he didn't look at Aethan.

Aethan hummed in consideration. "Yes, but what do the other *competitors* say about me?"

Roric shifted anxiously, tilting his anxious eyes to the ceiling. He swallowed so hard Aethan could hear the gulp all the way down his throat. "I... have heard, only from a few, that maybe you are..."

"Go on." Aethan stopped in front of Roric, waiting.

"I don't want to, sire." Roric looked like he might vomit where he stood.

Aethan tilted his head to force the squire to meet his gaze. "First of all, I expect you to look me in the eye when you speak to me. Unless I'm truly so ugly you can't stand to do so." He offered a teasing smirk.

Roric dropped his gaze, eyes widening. "No, sire." But he did as told, meeting Aethan's eyes.

"Secondly, I will depend on you in the weeks to come for far more than cleaning my armor and sharpening my sword." Aethan rested his hand on the hilt. The black leather fit perfectly into his hand.

"As you wish, sire." Roric nodded.

"Now, tell me what the competitors say." Aethan knew it couldn't be good, judging by Roric's reaction. "And be honest. It won't do either of us any good if you keep some of the more hurtful comments from me."

Roric licked his lips anxiously, summoning his courage. "Very well, sire." The words spilled out at first with a hint of worry, but as he continued, he seemed to gain confidence that Aethan wouldn't strike out at him.

What he reported shouldn't have surprised Aethan, but it did hurt. They called him pampered. A prince without a crown. An entitled prick. Every variation of insult to Aethan's status. Most of them doubted his skills were genuine, and not some ploy for the Gamemaster to pad his own coffers on losing bets.

Good. Let them doubt his skills. He could handle that.

What he wouldn't be able to handle were the hints that he was a pampered, entitled princeling. He would skip the bath. And he wouldn't be changing his clothes either. This tournament required intelligence as well as might, and Aethan knew that included the games these men would play off the field as much as on them. He had to get a few steps ahead before they noticed him moving.

"Roric, I will need you to be my eyes and ears during the tournament as well," Aethan said. "The dangers I face are just as much outside the arena as inside it. Perhaps more so."

Roric's eyes widened. "You want me to spy, sire?"

"No. Just listen to what others already around you are saying." Roric would be around the other squires, who might let slip hints at temperaments, weaknesses, or strengths of the other competitors. He would also hear rumors Aethan would not be privy to. "If you learn anything that might help me, you tell me immediately." Aethan studied the boy's face.

Roric seemed uncertain about the arrangement, but he stood to gain a lot from Aethan's victory, too.

"Honesty, Roric. I need a vow of honesty and loyalty to me."

Roric immediately dropped to his knee, taking Aethan's hand and kissing it. "It is my honor to serve you, sire! I swear my loyalty to House Starkling."

"Good." Aethan grinned down at the boy as his first moves came into clear focus. "Because our work begins right now."

Chapter 11

The Slippery Fox

After the way the princess had peered straight at Bast in his shadows, he decided to take a more cautious approach to dealing with Javon Nadier. For the next week, Bast Blackblade observed the banker's habits. He watched when and how Javon left the palace, how many guards accompanied him, and where he went in Arithia.

Sticking around in the city had required Bast to keep a low profile. He avoided his remaining brokers both to dodge being caught and to prevent the Black Guard from discovering them. It meant walking around the city in commoner clothing and not his usual black leathers. While he might be mistaken for a hunter or sword for hire in his leathers, Bast wasn't willing to take a chance that anyone was on the lookout for a man in black leather.

Javon resided in the palace with his entire family, which made it harder for Bast to get close. But not impossible.

The Black Guard presence increased in the streets for several days after breaking down Bast's broker ring. No doubt the few who survived had been tortured for information, then killed. It was precisely why Bast made sure none of them knew who he was or what he looked like.

Bast leaned casually against the wall of a building across from Javon's favorite lunch spot, Lavender Lounge. The restaurant didn't have a reputation for being upscale. In fact, after the first luncheon Javon took there, Bast had gone in that night for dinner to learn more about the establishment. He had been firmly unimpressed with the quality of food and other patrons. Like most places, it served watered-down stew and stale bread. However, there were other "fresh produce" options on their menu. The lettuce turned out wilted and the toppings on the salad shriveled. Bast hadn't even dared contemplate the ingredients used to make the dressing atop the salad.

If Javon didn't visit the Lavender Lounge for the excellent meals, he had more nefarious reasons to be there.

Right on time, Javon's carriage arrived and he vanished into the Lavender Lounge.

Bast waited ten minutes to be sure no one would join Javon. Twice in the five visits this week, Javon had dined alone. He counted on that again today. And if Javon was not alone, Bast would try another day and another until he was.

Despite the covered trellises in front of the restaurant creating a privacy barrier, Bast's excellent sight spotted exactly where Javon sat. Alone.

Perfect. Bast smothered his smirk as he entered and turned straight for Javon's table.

Javon didn't bother lifting his gaze from his lunch as Bast approached. He dabbed a dingy white napkin to his too-thin mouth before reaching for his glass of ale.

"We are not to meet today," Javon said quietly.

Bast raised a brow. So his instincts were correct. The man came here for his own dirty deeds. "I think we are," Bast said as he sank into the chair across from the banker without invitation.

Javon's jaw tightened as he at last raised his brown eyes to meet Bast's stone-grays. He didn't bother looking alarmed. Instead, Javon's shrewd gaze assessed Bast in a sweeping motion. "Who are you?"

Bast relaxed into the chair, crossing an ankle over his knee. A knife slid into his palm discreetly enough for Javon to notice, but no one else. "A friend of a friend. And he's furious."

Before Bast even finished speaking, Javon's entire body went rigid. He scanned the dining room of the Lavender Lounge as if seeking help—or perhaps witnesses. No one took notice of either of them beyond the ordinary. Javon swallowed hard.

"What does that have to do with me?" he asked carefully. But Bast could tell Javon struggled to put on a calm façade.

The corner of Bast's mouth tipped up in a grin. "I think we both know the answer to that."

Javon set down his ale and leaned back in his chair, not daring to take his eyes off Bast. Smart. Also smart to keep a careful eye on the hand holding the knife. Not that it would save Javon if Bast decided to kill him.

"You're the agent."

"Such a formal title. I'm just the friend of a friend. One of many." Bast tapped the tip of his knife with a finger as his other hand reached for the glass of water beading condensation on the table. "He knows you owe him a debt. You have until tonight to pay or..." Bast paused, taking a slow, long drink of the water.

Javon practically fought not to shift in his chair. Sweat beaded on his forehead as he waited impatiently. But Bast wouldn't bother finishing the sentence. They both knew how it ended.

"How has he avoided the king's men and the Black Guard all week?" Javon asked, at last breaking the silence.

"Not your business or mine."

"I should think King Novin would disagree." Javon raised his chin, gathering pointless defiance. "As well as Ambassador Umbogo."

"I wonder what the king would say if he knew you brokered to have one of his highest-ranked nobles killed," Bast countered.

Javon snapped his jaw shut and glared at him. "You know nothing."

"I know enough that, one way or another, you would end up dead."

Silence settled between them. Bast relished in it, let it fester.

The longer they stared one another down, the more Javon's demeanor cracked. His confidence waned. At long last, he boldly leaned closer, eyeing the knife still in Bast's palm on the table.

Javon spoke in a low voice, watching nearby patrons for eavesdroppers. "What if I told you I could get him four times what he's owed?"

Curiosity caught Bast's attention. Normally when someone dared make such an offer, he would laugh them off. But this was the king's banker. If anyone had access to that kind of coin, it was Javon Nadier. A bold move, dipping into the royal coffers.

Bast wasn't a fool, either. This could very well be a trap for him. Still, he had to at least hear what Javon had to say.

"I'm listening."

Javon shook his head. "Not now. I will get you in contact with my patron directly if you promise to leave my family out of this."

Without a doubt, Javon baited Bast into a trap. Which meant Bast had to set the terms first.

"Tonight, two hours past dinner peak at the Slippery Fox Inn, just the two of you," Bast said, making certain Javon understood the terms were not up for negotiation. "If neither of you show up, my friend will pay your family a visit." Javon paled. "If I spot any guards at all, my friend will find out. He has no patience left for games. Someone must pay for what happened. He won't accept any less."

Javon struggled to swallow his terror and speak. Bast allowed him a moment to collect himself.

"He will want to speak directly to your friend," Javon said at last, once more watching the dining room nervously.

Bast chuckled, low and menacing. "I don't think so. I decide if this is worthwhile to him. Not you." He rose, slipping the knife back into the holder strapped under his shirt sleeve. "Tonight. Or else."

As he started to pass by toward the door, Javon's final question made the anger burn in Bast's veins.

"What's keeping me from turning you in to the guards right now?"

Bast pivoted on his heels, clamping his massive, strong hands on Javon's shoulders in what to anyone else would appear a friendly gesture. He leaned close to Javon's ear and whispered his warning.

"Because my friend knows where your children sleep and that your wife prefers to bathe when you aren't around." He let out a mirthless chuckle as he released his grip on Javon's shoulders, but not before he felt the way Javon's entire body tensed at that final warning.

He didn't need to know the truth.

Before Javon could react, Bast vanished out the door and into the street.

Choosing the Slippery Fox as a meeting place had been a very cautious choice. Bast knew the buildings, alleys, and paved roads around the inn. He knew every hiding place inside and outside of the building.

Before the dinner rush, Bast set warnings in the shadows of the alleys in case guards tried to slip in from there. He paid the young stable boy handsomely to keep an eye out for any signs of guards—royal or Black. He selected a table in the corner during dinner rush, away from prying eyes and careful of his magic protecting him from detection, then he watched everyone who came, how long they stayed, when they left, and who they left with. Bast knew which direction everyone had gone in as well.

After the dinner rush, Bast perched on the gabled rooftop in the shadows of the kitchen chimney and waited.

Precisely two hours after dinner rush ended, two men in dark and dingy cloaks entered. To anyone else, they would appear completely ordinary. But Bast spotted the salt-and-pepper hair on the banker even beneath the cowl of his hood. His companion was younger, but Bast hadn't gotten a good look before the two slipped inside.

Bast leaped from one rooftop to the next, as cautiously as possible, until he crouched on the roof across from the Slippery Fox Inn.

Once satisfied that no one else had followed the two men, Bast climbed down in a nearby alley and strolled across the street, listening for any calls. Then he hauled open the door.

While the Slippery Fox Inn was not the most respectable place in Arithia, nestled along the border between the upper-class and lower-class districts, the common room was relatively clean.

Only a few tables had patrons at this hour. Just enough customers to avoid suspicion without enough of a throng to overhear or crowd them. Bast crossed the hardwood floors, his boots sticking in places where the floors had yet to be cleaned from the dinner rush.

No one gave him a second glance as he approached the bar and ordered an ale, then made his way to the two men in the back corner near the crackling fireplace. Only the two of them cast him more than a cursory glance as he crossed the common room.

Javon, Bast had become very familiar with. The man with him, Bast didn't recognize, but his eyes shone with a curious light and not a hint of fear. His hood remained up, and the angle the man sat at the table made the lights and fire create shadows over his features. Bast didn't like it, but he didn't give any hint of discomfort as he approached.

Bast quite unapologetically settled into the vacant seat, setting his ale on the table in front of him.

"We followed your orders," Javon said, breaking the ice even if the tension remained thick around the trio.

"So it seems." Bast settled comfortably and took a sip of his ale, studying the man with Javon.

While the clothing he wore bore dirt around the lower hems and the clothes themselves were of common make, the stitching along the seams indicated a skilled hand. This man wanted to appear common but used a high-end tailor. The longer Bast stared into that shadowed hood, the more he realized Javon's patron was... young. Or at least, younger than Bast had expected. Perhaps close to Bast's age within a few years.

As if sensing Bast's conclusion, the man's jaw tightened and his dark eyes blackened a touch. A coldness rolled off of him that Bast actually admired. He would make a fine killer himself. Perhaps he had killed before. Bast had to admit he was intensely curious about this patron.

"Well? My friend is waiting for his payment," Bast said.

The man didn't flinch at the sharp threat in Bast's tone. He simply watched him, turning his own glass of knock-off Murandy Hills wine between his fingers.

Finally, he broke his silence, and he sounded just as cold as he looked. "First of all, what happened was beyond our control. Even the king had no idea the depth of the traps set for your *friend*."

Did he know Bast *was* Blackblade? *No. He couldn't.* Still, the way he said "friend" made Bast uneasy. Thankfully, he was skilled at hiding his emotions from others.

"And by the time he found out, it was too late to do anything."

"You have connection to the king yourself?" Bast asked.

The man simply stared at him as if unwilling to deign a response to that question.

"To make up for it, I'm willing to offer additional compensation," the man continued. "As a sort of restitution payment. But only if your *friend* agrees to one more job."

Bast snorted, then took a drink as he rolled his eyes.

"I was led to believe he might be amenable to this. It's why I risked everything to come here." The man glanced at Javon, daggers in his dark eyes.

"If you think he would take on a job before receiving payment for the last one, you've lost your mind," Bast retorted.

The man didn't hesitate before he pulled a hefty, large pouch from his cloak and set it gently on the table. With his index and middle finger, he pushed the pouch across the table.

Bast glowered at the man, then glanced at the other patrons. The coins certainly drew a few eyes, even if no one heard them hit the table. A pouch like this could be little else than a payoff. His jaw twitched as he snatched it and tucked it safely away. He wouldn't inspect it here with people watching.

The man simply raised his brows impatiently. The balls on this guy were impressive. Would he be so bold if he knew who actually sat across from him?

Perhaps this was the lord positioned to take Lord Corinth's power after his death. Bast didn't ask. He didn't really care about the brutal games these nobles played. It kept him employed.

"Is he willing now?" the man asked.

"That depends on what's required. He doesn't take just any job."

A wicked grin curled the corners of the man's mouth. "Oh, this isn't just any job. And once it's complete, he will not only receive restitution for what happened, but he will be rich enough to buy his own kingdom."

Bast narrowed his eyes, wondering just who he was dealing with here. Few Arithian noble houses had that kind of wealth. Even if this guy took over for Corinth, it would take him years to amass that kind of fortune.

"I don't think he has any interest in owning a kingdom or a crown," Bast mused.

"My point," the man said sharply, "is that I will pay him handsomely. More handsomely than he has ever dreamed. And to top it off, the crown would pardon all of his crimes."

Was this guy for real? Bast didn't care about pardons or crowns. And the *crown* had no true control over the emperor's men. Unless that crown was the emperor's, in which case...

"I'm listening." Bast couldn't curb his curiosity. What was worth so much?

The man glanced at the common room from the corner of his eyes before continuing. "The Jewel of Arithia."

Bast sank back in his chair, hand slipping off his mug of ale. Just the mention of the jewel made his heart beat a little faster.

A heist then. And not just any heist.

The Jewel of Arithia was gifted to the first king of Novavito by Terralibra, God of Balance. According to myths, the artifact offered strength and protection to the rulers of Novavito. What would this guy want with that jewel?

A similar artifact had been given to the king of Vorovesti. The Jewel of Mordelic, imbued with power by the Goddess of Light and Knowledge. That artifact had vanished more than a millennium ago, during the War of Two crowns, never to be seen again.

Bast had only seen the Jewel of Arithia once before, from a distance... Attached to a golden chain around the princess' neck just before she left in that carriage a week ago.

The Jewel of Arithia passed from ruler to heir when the heir came of age. It allegedly fused with their soul to ensure they maintained balance in the kingdom. Bast heard stories that the Jewel could not be stolen. It was impossible once it fused to the soul of the bearer. If Bast remembered correctly, the princess had come of age several years ago. That thing would be fused to her by ancient magic by now. There were only two ways to get his hands on the Jewel. Either the princess gave it to him of her own free will... or he killed her.

"You're mad," Bast said, a hint of respect bleeding into his voice. Because Bast's initial assessment of this man had been accurate.

The guy had balls of steel.

Bast didn't usually ask questions about the jobs. He simply did his research and filled his end of the deal. But to ask for this... A hundred questions thundered through his mind.

"If your friend can't complete this task, I will find someone else—"

"*No one* can complete this task," Bast interrupted. "Not even my friend." He lowered his voice leaning closer to them. "She has been wearing that thing for four years—"

"Five years." The man shook his head. "What I ask isn't impossible or I wouldn't ask it. And it isn't without extreme risk, which is why I'm willing to pay handsomely."

"You're asking him to kill the princess," Bast hissed lowly.

"I wasn't aware that he cared who he killed."

The two of them stared at one another. Steely determination dominated the man's entire form.

Bast could kill royals. That wasn't the problem. It was the fallout that scared him most. He would have to vanish for years—decades. Even with his skill, Bast would be hunted in every corner of the empire.

Not to mention the way she had peered *right at him* when he was wrapped in his shadows.

Bast shook his head and pushed back his chair. "Good luck in your quest."

"I cannot allow you to leave if you refuse," the man said firmly.

Bast froze. The statement would have made him laugh for its boldness were it not for the malicious glare in the man's gaze.

"I suggest you agree to my terms," he said.

Bast's lip curled in a snarl. "If you harm me—"

The laugh that cut him off chilled his bones. Who in the name of the lost gods was this guy?

"You have nowhere to hide, *friend*."

Oh, he knew. He knew *exactly* who Bast was, which meant he had to die.

"I see the calculation in your eyes." The man took a drink of his wine, wincing slightly at the bitterness of it. The air around him bled victory. "You're thinking if you kill me and flee the city, no one will ever know. Or maybe you can make it look like an accident." He cocked his head, smirking slightly. "But I have guards waiting for my return two blocks away, and guards all around the city at every exit on warning not to let *you* pass without my approval."

The way he leaned forward, sly as a fox, made Bast rue choosing this inn for the meeting. Like he had baited this particular slippery fox into his own den.

"You see, I know who you are. I know where you've been these past two weeks."

Two weeks? *Before* the assassination of Lord Corinth?

"And should anything happen to me after tonight, every royal in the realm will know your face. The Black Guard will hunt you without mercy. If you kill me, you sign your own death warrant." The man shrugged and leaned back in his chair. "I don't really see what choice you have. Because if you don't agree to take this job, I have men *everywhere* in the five kingdoms. Your face will be common knowledge. You will never be a *shadow* again."

Bast's pulse kicked up, adrenaline taking over. In every other circumstance, he would kill whoever knew who he was and what he looked like. But if this man had such wealth, no doubt he had connections everywhere.

No matter how hard Bast studied him, he detected no bluff.

Who in the fuck are you?

Bast glanced at Javon, who had remained perfectly still and silent throughout this conversation. Javon, the king's banker, who would sanction the murder of the princess. Javon, who betrayed no shock at what the man revealed about him. If anything, the banker appeared highly pleased with the outcome of this meeting.

Was Lord Corinth just a warmup? A way to test the waters with Bast's skills before bringing out this job?

His heart thundered against his chest. He had no choice. Not yet. For the moment, Bast just had to get out of the city. This guy probably had spies everywhere that would watch his every move and report back. Would they know who he was?

"No one else can know the truth," Bast said. "Or you are tying my hands, blindfolding me, and pushing me into a den of starving wolves. I need complete and utter anonymity in everything. A whisper that you've leaked this, and I vanish to the western continent. Maybe with your precious loot, and you'll never know when I might come for you."

The man grinned. "Delightful. I enjoy your games, friend."

Bast downed his ale. "We aren't friends."

Following the directions the man who called himself Platius gave him, Bast made his way to the north gate, keeping away from any city or Black Guards. The name was a cover. It had to be.

When he reached the gate, he found the guard Timon and introduced himself as Luca, as instructed. The guard led him through a secret passage in the wall by the north gate, to the stables where guards kept patrol mounts, then led him out into the mountain road beyond.

Bast mounted the black mare—had the horse been chosen specifically for the color?—and he didn't waste a moment in the mountain pass that spilled into the forest and plains to the north. The mare took off like a dark streak of lightning, and Bast used the shadows of night to mask her movements through the pass.

Javon and Platius would both have to die before this was all done. No one could know.

But he would have to find a way to keep them from talking before he had a chance to kill them.

CHAPTER 12

Warnings

Two weeks.

Two weeks of travel with Queen Giata, listening to her instruction on who would be whom among the suitors. Two weeks with no way to escape. Aslyn couldn't take much more of her mother.

Once they had passed through the northern gate at the Arithian Dam, the ship's crew members loaded the royal carriages onto ships to travel up the Great River toward Stormvalor.

Aslyn could count on one hand the number of times she had left Arithia in her young life, and this trip to Stormvalor—despite the reasons for it—felt like a grand adventure. That sense of adventure swiftly vanished the longer they traveled by ship up the Great River and Aslyn had nowhere to hide from her mother.

Her only reprieve came from the few minutes here and there Aslyn could wrestle above deck, watching the kingdom—*her* kingdom—pass. The lush green Aryth

Mountains cradled the river, and the king's road wound alongside a rocky cliff to the waters below. The colors of those mountains never ceased to amaze Aslyn, though she had spent a lifetime staring at them from her bedroom window.

When the route opened into the forest, then plains, Aslyn had marveled at the gently rolling hills and massive, ancient trees. A small town along the King's Road into the mountain pass bustled with life. Aslyn observed the people with a hint of envy as they moved freely, wishing she could also move so freely. But always, some guard or advisor or parent loomed in her presence. Aslyn would never move that freely.

By the time the ships passed into the kingdom of Umbr, jagged, treacherous mountains loomed on the left side of the river. Even the clouds over the mountains were a dark and dismal shade of gray and Aslyn swore the air reeked of decay. How could anyone live in such a place?

Every time she came above deck, Aslyn felt eyes on her as they passed by the shadow of those mountains. It was ridiculous, of course. No one watched her from the mountains. But she couldn't shake her fear that the emperor watched them from his castle high in the Umbr Mountains.

By the time their ships docked in a small fishing town just over the Vorovesti border, Aslyn yearned for solid ground.

The carriages unloaded with both Aslyn and her mother on board. They rode through the town to one of two inns where rooms had been reserved for them ahead of their arrival.

The streets of the town were so packed with people that the royal guards had to clear a path for the carriages. Aslyn mused that they looked like armored shepherds trying to move flocks of sheep.

Of course, the people craned their necks to try and peer into the windows of the carriage at the occupants.

"Stop gawking, Aslyn," Queen Giata hissed. "You are crown princess, not some common girl."

But Aslyn couldn't help herself. She tried to sit properly, but her gaze continued to fix itself outside the carriage at the teeming town. Where did all of these people sleep?

Their rooms at the Azure Valley Inn were... accommodating. Aslyn found they left something to be desired, and the mattress was far more lumpy than even her bed on the ship. Apparently, the entire town was bursting with visitors on their way to Stormvalor for the tournament. Residents even rented out rooms in their homes for a lofty price.

Celebration had already begun even two days from Stormvalor and days before the start of the tournament. People sang and ate late into the night. Aslyn, of course, could not leave her room, but she could hear the celebrating well enough regardless.

And all night long, Elisio stood guard outside her door. Aslyn wished he hadn't wormed his way into being her guard for this trip. It would only make things harder for both of them when the time came.

The last leg of the trip lasted only two days over land. Shortly before sunset, the carriages approached the ancient stone city.

Aslyn read all about the founding of Stormvalor. That Terralibra, the God of Earth and Balance, had hewn the stones in the city Themself as a gift to Justis and his most devout followers. But the stories paled compared to the true stark beauty of the city. Each building stood proudly, made of seamless gray stones adorned with colorful foliage. The scent of wisteria from the numerous vines climbing the walls coasted through the air.

While the wealth of the people and the merchandise on display as the carriages passed was not as grand as Arithia, it certainly put the prosperity of this most ancient city on parade.

And the celebrating! Citizens in colorful clothing sang and danced and moved through dense marketplaces. A group of dancers with ribbons that shimmered in the sunlight put on a show for a gathered crowd. The ribbons flashed like lightning with each movement—an homage to Justis, God of Storms.

Already, Aslyn plotted her escape from her room to partake in the festivities. Would she be able to convince Elisio to take her into the city? Probably not. Somehow, she would have to find her way to join this merriment. She had smuggled some simple clothes into her trunks, just in case.

All the way through the city, her mother spoke of Aslyn's responsibilities in the weeks to come, and once more reminded her of the men she was to meet during this visit. Aslyn tuned her out. She knew her duty and she would do her best to uphold that responsibility. But not at the expense of *living*.

"I've arranged for us to stay in the best suites available in the upper levels of the arena," her mother said as the carriage slipped into the darkness of a stone tunnel.

Aslyn nearly slumped in disappointment as the city vanished from sight but caught herself in time.

"You are not to leave your suite without your guard," her mother continued. "Or myself. Your safety during our stay is of the utmost importance. Tonight, we will settle into our rooms and get cleaned up from our travels. Tomorrow, the Gamemaster has arranged a tour of the arena for us."

The carriage broke out of the dark tunnel and into a stable yard filled with sunshine.

Aslyn accepted the footman's hand as she stepped out of the carriage, and the moment her feet hit the ground she tilted her head back to take in the monolithic status of the long-lost god of war, awed at the sight. Arithia was not without its gigantic statues, but this one made all the finest Arithian statues appear tiny.

A host of servants awaited the royal carriages, with an older man Aslyn assumed was the Gamemaster by his robes at the center. He offered them a genuinely warm smile and bowed deeply, but not as much so as the servants with him.

The royal guards formed an arc around the queen and princess.

"We are most honored to have you here, Your Majesties," the Gamemaster said. "Allow me to show you to your suites while the staff takes care of your trunks and horses."

Queen Giata inclined her head in respect. "We would be delighted. Thank you for making these arrangements for us."

After a few more platitudes, the Gamemaster guided the queen and princess along the stone corridors and up the spiraling staircases. Aslyn took everything in. The rich tapestries and stone edifices of Justis' famous battles, blue and black banners of the god and the emperor, and lamps designed to reflect off the glass and increase the light in the halls. Everything took her breath away. The arena was a city unto itself!

Aslyn couldn't help but wonder where the competitors all hid away. She had hoped to sneak a glimpse of some of them, but only servants and squires roamed the halls on important business.

"Where are all the competitors?" she asked, unable to contain her curiosity a moment longer. "I thought they stayed here during the tournament."

Queen Giata shot a warning look at her daughter.

The Gamemaster offered a knowing smile Aslyn wanted to smack off his face. "They do, Your Majesty. Their rooms are on the main level near the training grounds. The tournament begins in three days. All twenty-five men are busy with their training in preparation for the events."

"Of course." Aslyn smiled sweetly at him, then edged toward the stone rail overlooking the courtyard below. But all she saw were servants unloading their trunks onto carts to bring up.

The suite proved to be far more than simply rooms. The entryway gleamed with polished tiles leading to a grand staircase split to either side of the main living space. The upper level had only two doors—one on either side. A railing from those upper levels overlooked the main living space. Beneath those rooms on the main level, several other smaller rooms would provide sleeping space for the guards and servants.

Aslyn followed her mother into the main living space as the queen gave final instructions to their footman.

The sitting room shone with bright light through the glass windows. Rich furniture in various hues of green formed a conversation space. Aslyn strode through the room to the arched double doors and pushed them open.

An open-air balcony overlooked the arena and offered a premium view of the statue of Justis. Aslyn ran her fingers along the wisteria vines wrapped around the balcony columns, breathing in the sweet scent.

"Aslyn!" her mother called from the sitting room. "You need to get cleaned up before dinner!"

Aslyn sighed, but as the breeze shifted, she grudgingly admitted her mother had a point.

Kaiti led her up the grand staircase and back to her room, bowing deeply as she opened the door for the princess.

Aslyn's gaze swept over the room she would call her own for the next few weeks. She had her own private sitting room—though much smaller than the one downstairs—with a fireplace and green-hued furniture. She paused in the bedroom doorway to take in the large four-post bed. A moment later, she was running her fingers over the plush, white down comforter.

Like the main sitting room, Aslyn's rooms had a balcony. Aslyn asked her maid to draw a bath as she stepped onto her private balcony.

This stone balcony offered Aslyn a view of the arena below, and for a moment, she feared her mother wouldn't let her leave her room during the events. Would the queen make her watch from the safety of her balcony?

Solisina help me if she tries, Aslyn thought. Praying to the lost Goddess of Light seemed a pointless endeavor, but she couldn't help herself.

Sounds of distant cheering caught Aslyn's attention and she leaned against the cool stone rail and craned her neck.

From here, she could just barely see the edge of the training ground teeming with shirtless men. However, Aslyn couldn't get a clear look at what happened or even see the men well. Sighing in dismay, she retreated into her room in search of a bath.

Dinner proved to be a bore, and after dinner, her mother came to Aslyn's rooms to help organize the clothing. The entire ordeal had taken hours, her mother picking through everything and giving Aslyn an earful when she found the training leathers and simple dresses.

"Don't even think about training while we are here," had been one warning of many against putting those leathers on. Followed by, "You are not here to blend in, but to shine like the jewel you are," when the queen tossed the simple dresses aside carelessly.

Dresses and jewels, heeled shoes, and dress boots were all carefully arranged by day. The queen warned Aslyn not to wear the same clothing twice during their stay, and if for some reason she needed a new dress, one would be ordered for her.

Before Queen Giata finally left, she gave Aslyn one final warning. "You don't step foot outside these doors in anything but your best. If you want to catch the best prize, you need to *be* the best prize. At all times."

Aslyn heaved a sigh and rolled her eyes in exasperation at her maid. Kaiti fought off a smirk.

"I can handle getting ready for bed tonight, Kaiti. You need rest as much as me, but please return by sunrise," Aslyn said, smiling at the girl. Kaiti would likely be her only friend while she stayed here, aside from Elisio—assuming they were still friends at all. "My mother will have a heart attack if I'm not dressed and presentable by breakfast."

Kaiti curtsied deeply from the door. "Yes, Your Majesty."

A moment later, Aslyn stood alone for the first time since leaving home. In minutes, she changed into her night dress, unpinned her hair, and climbed into bed, sighing in delight at the softness of the mattress.

Dark shadows swirled around her, grasping her in a tight hold. Aslyn struggled, but the more she moved, the harder the shadows squeezed her. She opened her mouth to scream only to have that darkness slide down her throat and cut off all sounds.

Aslyn bolted upright, her blankets kicked off.

Elisio burst through the door, danger in his eyes. "You were screaming. Are you alright?"

Aslyn couldn't stop shaking, couldn't stop the terror rushing through her as she peered into the deepest shadows of her room. "I... It was just a nightmare."

In seconds, Elisio closed the distance between them. He pressed the back of his hand to her forehead, then his hand slid down her face, his thumb stroking her chin affectionately.

"Are you sure?" he asked, his deep voice concerned.

Aslyn swallowed and nodded. "Just... don't leave yet." She hated asking, but that nightmare left her shaken and she didn't want to be alone.

Elisio threw a glance at the open door, but he nodded. If any other guards heard her and were coming, they would be in the room already. His thumb traced over her lips.

Aslyn's already racing heart skipped, remembering the way it felt to lie with him. Weeks. It had been weeks since she had dared allow him into her bed.

He seemed to read her thoughts, because Elisio leaned closer, brushing a gentle kiss over her lips. Aslyn relaxed into the familiar feel of him, opening her mouth to his probing. The hand on her jaw slowly traced down her neck and her chest heaved in anticipation.

But as his palm roamed over her cleavage, Aslyn remembered herself, remembered what she told him in Arithia. Aslyn jerked back, nudging Elisio away.

She shook her head. "I told you we can't do this anymore."

Gods help her, she wanted to, though! Aslyn didn't love Elisio. But he made her feel things she had never experienced before. She appreciated him and everything he shared with her. But the wall around her heart couldn't allow him a crack to slip through. She could never marry a guard. Nor did she want to marry him.

Elisio flinched. "Aslyn—"

"Don't. Please. Don't say it." Aslyn pulled further back. "If you are to remain in my service," He grinned at that and she scowled, "then you need to remain on the other side of that door at all times."

Elisio's hand boldly slid up her thigh. Aslyn batted it away.

"No. I told you back in Arithia."

"But we work so well together." The hunger in his eyes made her pulse quicken. Space. She needed space.

"You weren't supposed to be here," Aslyn said. "We both knew how this would eventually end. Perform your duties as your commanding officer has instructed or I will find a new guard."

He withdrew his hand and stood, his face no longer hungry, but angry. Her declaration would result in his demotion should he ignore her warning, and he knew it. Elisio bowed deeply. "As Your Majesty commands," he said, his tone far too sharp.

The door thudded shut behind him, making Aslyn flinch.

She didn't want to be alone, but Seven Gods above and below, it was better this way.

Chapter 13

Glimpses

It only took Aethan one day to realize why his father had selected Roric as his squire. The boy showed remarkable intelligence for his age and proved invaluable at getting information without even trying.

Upon his arrival, Aethan had sent Roric on "tasks" around the competitor's quarters and free spaces. The boy vanished for hours, planting seeds about his assigned champion so causally Aethan wondered how the boy hadn't been part of the noble courts. Or how he had managed to go unnoticed, if he had been in those courts.

Meanwhile, Aethan had ventured into the competitor's courtyard to stretch his limbs and warm up with his weapon. He hadn't bothered to bathe or change, and as other competitors passed by—no doubt to learn what they could about him—Aethan misled all of them, letting them think his movements were a touch too slow and that he was afraid to get dirty.

That night at dinner, Aethan noted the way competitors stuck to the men from their own kingdom. He watched them all.

The five men from Oshon were all lithe limbs, but their arms showed just how much time they spent with rigging on ships, as did their tans. Henric, the pack leader, moved with a grace Aethan knew he would need to be wary of in the arena. Henric called the others by name like they were his underlings—Kern, Weylen, Ulric, and the smallest, Ryker—and the four men glared at him when he wasn't looking. The table offered him little more than a passing, curious glance as he moved toward his table with Trystain.

The Elpisian competitors varied in size and notable strength. Qin was a broad-shouldered mass. Gorim had a tattoo of the moon and stars on his left cheek. Von kept his head bent over his meal like he hadn't eaten in days. Yun ate more civilized, watching Von with disgust. Vinter was the only one who watched Aethan pass like he studied him.

When Aethan and Trystain joined the other Vorovesti competitors, Aethan heard one of the Novavito men mutter something about the "pretty man". If Aethan remembered correctly, his name was Cormic, and the man he whispered to was his twin brother Cavis. Their king had selected them for their brutal battle tactics, and Aethan knew to be more wary of the two of them. The other three at the Novavito table—Hardy, Lungen, and Seth—were arrogant as well, but not as much so as the twins.

But it was the Umbr men that truly worried Aethan. All five of them were massive men with such dark eyes they almost looked black. Aethan wondered if they had the strength to crush skulls in just one of those massive hands. The five of them seemed to work as a silent unit, observing the rest of the competitors, sharing knowing glances, smirking as if sharing unspoken jokes. They couldn't read minds. The emperor would never allow that kind of magic to survive.

Yet when one of the men, Bryse, met Aethan's curious gaze, his brows twitched up as if to say, *Are you sure he wouldn't allow us to keep such magic?* Bryse broke the silence at their table, but his deep voice was so low, Aethan couldn't tell what he said. Yet he could easily see how the other four—Eyton, Marek, Nixt, and Rett—reacted, chuckling and glancing as one... right at him.

Aethan's stomach twisted but he didn't show them his discomfort. Weakness against them would be deadly. Lorin, the last Vorovesti competitor from Murandy Hills, had paled. He wouldn't last long against them if he showed such weakness.

By the end of the first day, Aethan knew far more about each of his competitors than they would ever realize. Both from his own observations and the information Roric had brought back to him. Already, Roric had learned that Weylen from Oshon had a tendency to lock his squire and everyone else out of his room at night. What brought him to such fear of an unlocked door? After hearing that, Aethan observed the way Weylen stuck close to Ryker's side. The two seemed thick as thieves.

The next morning, *all* the competitors mocked him at breakfast, but Aethan let their comments roll off with a graceful, charming smile and self-deprecating laugh. At least people were talking across kingdom lines.

After a full week of training, no one laughed anymore. Aethan showed them just enough skill to hold his own in a fight, but kept his full capacity secret. They could learn the truth when they faced him in the arena. Not a moment before.

Trystain found Aethan's games amusing. He had tried to follow suit until he faced off against Bryse in the sparing ring with training swords. The weapon master observed their fight and picked apart each of their weaknesses. It had bothered Trystain enough that he let it get into his head. Then the true brutality of Trystain came out. Yet it still wasn't enough to do more than graze Bryse.

That had resulted in days of mocking from all the Umbr competitors. Mocking that only made Trystain angrier. Aethan had tried to calm his friend, but when it came to his pride, Trystain could be touchy.

In group bouts, Cormic and Cavis worked almost as effortlessly as a single unit as all the Umbr men did. The Oshon competitors knew how to follow Henric's orders, but occasionally Kern or Ulric would push back. Once, Ryker had taken a "killing blow" that Henric had called. It turned into a genuine fistfight between the two that the weapons master had been forced to break up.

The Elpisian competitors showed off their faith with prayers to Justis before each training session—faith that the Umbr men ripped to shreds without mercy. Even Aethan had a hard time keeping to himself at the blasphemy rolling off their tongues. He simply offered a witty retort about how, with or without Justis' presence during the tournament, they demonstrated their true colors.

Something about Aethan's tone made Bryse's face and neck turn red with rage. He took three long strides toward Aethan, hands in fists, before Eyton, Marek, Nixt, and Rett all jumped in front of Bryse and pushed him back without a word.

"You're either bold as shit, or you have a death wish," Cavis had told Aethan that night. A hint of respect shone in Cavis's eyes.

And so the days of training passed. Two weeks of brutal schedules and alphas asserting their dominance.

Tomorrow night the competitors would all attend the Tournament Open Mixer and brush shoulders with the social elite from all around Divica. Aethan knew what it truly was. A chance for the rich to get a better handle on where to place their bets. An opportunity for eligible women to meet the men.

A night to watch Iskra brush shoulders with someone other than him.

Aethan funneled that frustration into his training, moving smoothly through the motions with his practice sword.

He overheard Henric, Calvin and Von, along with a couple others, talking about the crown princess who apparently arrived the previous night. Aethan tried to ignore them.

Aslyn trailed along beside her mother as the Gamemaster personally escorted them through the arena hallways. They saw the commoner seating section, the noble boxes, and their own royal box. "Should you wish to watch here instead of from your balconies," he informed them, pointing up at the balconies another level up.

He pointed out the ballroom where the Tournament Open Mixer would be held, and the lush gardens beyond the ballroom. They passed private meeting rooms and refreshment centers. Yes, the arena truly was a city unto itself, as she first suspected. There was little need to leave at all.

Almost absently, the Gamemaster waved toward a long corridor teeming with squires and servants rushing from room to room. "The competitor's quarters are down that hall, though I imagine Your Majesties would not deign to visit there. We have meeting rooms so you can avoid that hallway for the entirety of your stay. Should you wish to meet with a competitor, just let one of the game wardens know and they will have the squire make arrangements."

Aslyn swore she heard Elisio stiffen behind her. Not that her future husband necessarily would be among the competitors. Noblemen would come out of the woodwork in the weeks ahead, and many of them would be suitable as well. Though she knew her mother wanted her to take interest in one of the competitors in particular.

"I would like to see the training ground," Aslyn said.

The Gamemaster choked on what he was about to say, hesitating as a young squire in a blue jacket bowed deeply and hurried past.

"Your Majesty, the men are training," he said.

Aslyn smiled brightly. "Perfect!"

Queen Giata glanced at her daughter before plastering a cordial smile on her face. "What I think my daughter means is that she would like to assess their skills for herself, before the tournament begins."

Well, that was not entirely wrong, though certainly not what she meant either.

The Gamemaster bowed in subservience before marching them right down the competitor's hallway.

Aslyn held her head high as she proudly followed, tempering her excitement. Honestly, she wanted to see if her own skills stacked up to these men in any way.

A squire pivoted the moment he saw them and bolted back the way he had come. A shirtless man with long dark hair tied back with leather stepped out of a room and his eyes widened upon seeing them. A moment later, he bowed deeply from the waist, his muscles rippling with the motion. Aslyn's gaze swept over him, looking for some clue as to who he was.

"Good luck to you, Master Cavis," Queen Giata said.

"Your Majesties," he replied, not rising from his bow.

Cavis. One of the Novavito twins her father had selected to compete this year. The brothers were supposed to be a vicious team.

The hallway turned along a covered gallery lined with stone columns covered in wisteria. And beyond the gallery, dozens of shirtless, sweating men trained. The Gamemaster didn't slow his step or bother with introductions to any of the men. He simply carried on as if they had not come just for this purpose.

But the men noticed *her*. As she followed along the outer edge of the training ground, more and more men found excuses to move to the far side of the training yard... closer to her. Aslyn knew she couldn't look directly at any of them or her mother would brutally dress her down for it later. But she did her best to note who watched her and how they looked at her, more like a toy to play with than like the queen she would one day become. One competitor—more mountain than man—leered openly, undressing her with his eyes. She had half a mind to march onto the ground and impale him with his own sword.

Beyond the main cluster, two men continued their archery practice, ignoring her completely. Both had light blond hair and lean forms. And gods help her if she didn't appreciate the way their muscles shifted beneath those thin shirts with each movement. Something deep inside of her heated watching them, and she was a little affronted that they hadn't cared in the least that she had walked past.

Behind her, Elisio cleared his throat. Aslyn ripped her gaze away to find her mother eyeing her down the hallway. Aslyn's face heated as she strolled over to join her mother, stepping out of the gallery into another hallway that would take them back up to the visitor's sector of the arena.

Not an hour later, Aethan heard a few others whispering, and some competitors moved to the far side of the training yard. By the time Aethan finished with archery and marched over to join them to ask why everyone congregated on that side of the yard, the crowd disbursed.

Aethan frowned, wiping sweat from his brow. The men made lewd jokes about a young woman. Then Bryse mentioned something about teaching the princess a few things.

Aethan swallowed, staring at the now empty hallway she had vanished through, and he hadn't even gotten a glimpse of her.

As training wound down for the day, Aethan entered the stable to see to his horse. Trystain followed hot on his heels.

"You've been holding back," Trystain said as he moved toward his own mount. "Don't think I haven't noticed."

Aethan swiped his arm across his sweaty forehead and shrugged. "Better that they don't know what I can do until it's too late. Surprise is a friend. Remember, this is as much about intelligence as it is about strength."

Trystain snorted. "That places Bryse out of contention."

Aethan chuckled. "Among a few others." He peered around to be sure no one else was around.

Roric ran in, breathless, and bent over, sucking down breaths as he pressed his hands into his knees.

"What's wrong?" Aethan stiffened, immediately on alarm.

Before Roric answered, Trystain cursed under his breath.

Aethan followed his gaze to see both of their fathers approaching. He groaned. These last couple of weeks had been hard, but at least he hadn't had to worry about his father hovering to correct every mistake.

"He must have hitched himself to your dad to get access back here," Trystain grumbled. Aethan knew Lord Cyrus had arrived two days ago and Trystain stuck to the competitor quarters, ignoring his father's summons. This would be just as bad for his friend as it would be for Aethan. Maybe worse. But his friend plastered a smile on his face when his father stepped into the stable. "Father, I'm glad you made it here. I've been so busy I couldn't—"

"With me," Lord Cyrus interrupted, flicking a finger toward the training grounds. "Now." Then he pivoted and marched back out the door, expecting his son to follow obediently.

Which Trystain did after a sympathetic smile with Aethan.

Lord Lux Starkling waited with his hands in his pockets, the very image of patience. Aethan continued brushing his horse.

"How has training been?" Lux Starkling asked. If Aethan didn't know better, he would have believed his father was attempting small talk. But Lux Starkling did nothing without purpose. The question was what his angle was this time?

"Good. I feel great, actually," Aethan admitted truthfully. He felt more fit than he ever had before.

"Have you met with the princess yet?"

Aethan inwardly sighed. And there it was.

"She passed by the training grounds today, but I've been a bit busy."

Lord Starkling's tone shifted dramatically. He was no longer casual, but all hard edges. "She's been here for an entire day. You need to get in front of her before the Tournament Open Mixer, before the others have a chance to sink their teeth in."

Aethan didn't want to get in front of her. And if the others sank their teeth in first, that would work out for the best as far as he was concerned. "Dad, I've been in training since the sun came up and only just finished."

"And last night?" Lord Starkling asked swiftly.

Aethan half turned toward his father, jaw slackened. Did he honestly think running into her path the moment she arrived would be of any help? His temper flared. He was sweaty and exhausted and couldn't hold his tongue.

"Has it ever occurred to you that maybe I'm not interested in her?" he snapped.

Lord Starkling's eyes darkened a shade in anger. His jaw twitched as he stalked closer. Too close. The warning in his dark eyes gave Aethan chills.

"Has it ever occurred to you that maybe this isn't about what you want, or what I want?" his father hissed.

Wait, what? Aethan blinked at that. He assumed his father wanted this because of the additional power and influence it would give the family. But if it wasn't that...

"Just do what I tell you, Aethan."

And something about the way his father said those words filled Aethan with both terror and curiosity.

CHAPTER 14

A Moment of Freedom

"I don't know about this, Your Majesty," Kaiti said, wringing her hands and glancing at the door to Aslyn's sitting room.

After dinner, Aslyn had told her mother she felt weak and wanted to get a good night of rest before tomorrow's mixer. Elisio had tried following her into her room, but Kaiti kindly encouraged him to wait in the hall outside the sitting room so the princess could rest in peace.

The moment Aslyn was sure she was alone, she had donned her training leathers for easier movement. Kaiti's only job was to ensure no one came into her bedroom while she "rested".

"I made a sport of sneaking out of the palace," Aslyn said with a grin. "These balconies are so much easier."

Kaiti protested only a little more as Aslyn slipped on her riding boots and stepped onto the balcony after checking that no one would spot her.

The sun was setting, which gave her just enough light to see without making her escape obvious. All she wanted was a moment of freedom without someone trailing along behind her, a chance to escape to fun in the city and become part of the pulse of the tournament she had witnessed from the carriage.

Aslyn swung each leg carefully over the balcony rail, peering at the balcony below. The column gave her something to shimmy down. Once her boots touched the rail, Aslyn glanced into the main sitting room. Her mother sat with a lord Aslyn didn't know, making some kind of apology. Another man stood with his back to Aslyn, half obscured by the grand staircase.

If she moved quickly, Aslyn could slip down to the spectator balconies, then stroll out into the hallway from there.

Aslyn gripped the rail, hanging precariously. Taking a steadying breath, she let go and dropped like a cat onto the next balcony.

When she stepped into the hallway, Aslyn breathed in the freedom. No guards, no mother. In training leathers instead of fancy gowns, none of the people in the halls seemed to recognize her as the princess.

Aslyn wandered the halls, trying to make heads or tails of where she was going just so she could escape the arena for an hour or two. Sadly, the place was a maze. No matter which way she turned, Aslyn ended up in another corridor.

Male voices caught her attention. Aslyn couldn't hear what they said, but they clearly argued. She slid her fingertips along the knife hidden in her belt. Not that she thought anyone would dare harm her here, but it didn't hurt to be prepared.

Aslyn waited for a minute after the voices stopped, then stepped out of her hiding place. Absorbed in her concern for those distant voices, Aslyn wasn't paying attention and smacked right into a rock-hard chest. Aslyn squealed as she stumbled back, but he caught her elbows and steadied her.

The most beautiful blue eyes she had ever seen peered down at her with... concern. But not recognition, thank the seven gods. He wore a nobleman suit of rich blues and golds. His pale blond hair rested in perfect order, and Aslyn caught herself examining the powerful lines of his face. Her face heated.

"Sorry. I suppose I should watch where I'm going," she said.

"Maybe." His blue eyes took in her clothes—the fighting leathers—and his brows rose. Gods he was beautiful. The most beautiful man she had ever seen...

"You can let go," Aslyn said sharply.

"You can be a little nicer," he replied, releasing her arms. "You're the one who ran into me."

"And I apologized." Aslyn stepped around him.

"You don't wanna go that way," he said, smirking. "The men are returning from... evening libations. A beautiful woman crossing their path would be a mistake."

Aslyn's heart hammered harder when he called her beautiful. "Are you implying I'm incapable of handling myself?"

He chuckled, shaking his head. "While I would hate to insult you, those are Stormvalor competitors. I'm not sure even the most fearsome woman could hold her own against some of them. Let's be honest, you're no Kieta the Strong, even in..." He once more looked down her body and her face heated. "In leathers."

So, he knew his legends to mention the warrior woman, Kieta the Strong. Aslyn shouldn't have been surprised based on the way he dressed as a highly ranked nobleman. Kieta the Strong had been instrumental in the battles during the War of Two Crowns. Whenever she took to the battlefield, thousands of Narcisse's soldiers fell. Some believed her to be graced by Justis himself—the original Stormvalor Champion chosen by the god himself.

Eager to get away from him, Aslyn turned and walked down the hallway... away from the returning men. She could be sensible if she wanted.

Boots scraped against the floor behind her and Aslyn paused, glancing back over her shoulder at Blue Eyes.

"You can stop following me," she snapped.

He shrugged. "I was already headed that way. That isn't my fault."

"You could at least walk with me instead of trailing me like a..." Aslyn cut off before she called him a guard. He didn't seem to know who she was, and she wanted to keep it that way.

He cocked his head as he studied her. "Like a what?"

Aslyn flushed. "Like a homeless dog."

He slid his hands into his pockets as he joined her. "Well, you certainly know how to charm a man. We love being compared to homeless dogs, you know."

"You're insufferable."

Blue Eyes glanced sidelong at her, his lips thinning. His patience for her attitude wore thin. Aslyn wanted to apologize but couldn't bring out the words. Before she could force herself to speak, he bid her goodnight and increased his stride, muttering about her trailing *him* like a dog instead. Aslyn hated that she enjoyed watching him walk away, then wondered if maybe he thought the same thing a minute ago.

He rounded the bend and Aslyn slowed her steps, hating how horribly that had gone. She hadn't even gotten his name. Seven Gods help her if she didn't want to see Blue Eyes again.

The disastrous encounter repeated on a loop in her mind as she wandered absently. How in the name of Justis did she get out of this place?

Aslyn didn't know if minutes or more had passed before he came around a bend in the hallway again, marching straight for her, his face set with determination. Something about the look in his blue eyes made her heart jump into her throat and Aslyn pulled her knife from the belt to defend herself.

Then she heard another, deeper voice, approaching. Several of them.

Blue Eyes murmured an apology as he seized her arm, ignoring her knife completely. Aslyn jerked back, unable to shake his grip.

"Let go," Aslyn demanded, thrusting the knife toward him. He batted it aside in a way that made her feel utterly helpless. She was *not* helpless.

The voices of the approaching men grew louder, closer.

"I need you to trust me for just a minute," he said, adding a belated, "please."

Aslyn wasn't sure why, but something about the way Blue Eyes seemed almost worried made her trust him. She gave a small nod. The voices were so close. They would come around the bend at any moment.

Blue Eyes pulled Aslyn into the doorway of a meeting room, pinning her against the wall as he leaned so close that his lean, muscular body brushed against hers. Aslyn's head spun, and her heart hammered. He pressed his arm against the doorframe so that it blocked her face—though she wasn't sure why that mattered—and he put a finger to his lips.

Aslyn just nodded. His face leaned so close to her neck she was certain he could see her erratic pulse. Fiara help her. He smelled so good—like wisteria and... and blackberry currant with musky undercurrents.

A second later, barely a heartbeat, the group of men passed, and judging by the lewd comments they made about—about *her!*—she was thankful Blue Eyes had rescued her from their path. They might have recognized her and who knew how that would have gone.

He remained fixed in place until their voices faded away.

"You can back away now," Aslyn mumbled. She placed her hands against his hard chest and pushed just enough to create a gap.

He stumbled half a step, catching his balance gracefully.

"I think I'll be going," Aslyn said, out of sorts when he looked at her like that. Like she was an interesting puzzle.

"Do you need me to escort you somewhere?" he asked.

The idea of strolling up to her suite with him made Aslyn's stomach writhe madly. Her mother would kill her for sneaking out, but returning with a man she didn't know...

"No."

Aethan had been headed back to his rooms after his father failed to get him in front of the apparently ailing princess. The harsh words his father threw at him before returning to his own suite had stoked Aethan's fury.

And then there was *her*. The mysterious woman in leather.

Aethan had never met a woman as stubborn or proud as this one. Her snappy remarks infuriated him in strange ways. He hated every word that came from her mouth, yet he wanted to encourage more of it. When he left her behind, angry that she had called him a homeless dog, Aethan had been happy to be rid of her. But the moment he saw Bryse and the other Umbr men headed in her direction and heard the comments they made about the princess, Aethan knew that woman would cross paths with a pack of starving wolves.

So he went back.

And she had the audacity to threaten him with a knife! He would have laughed at the pitiful weapon were it not being wielded in his direction. Instead, he deftly yet firmly pushed it away, letting her know she wouldn't land a blow on him if she tried. Thankfully, she was sensible enough not to try.

Begging her to trust him had taken a load of patience. But they didn't have the luxury of time. And curse him, but Aethan was drawn to that dark skin, fascinated by it, so smooth and richly bronze. While he did his best to shield her from the pack's sight, it had taken so much restraint to resist touching her skin. The rich scent of jasmine and roses filled his senses.

She had barely even thanked him, had refused further help, then stormed off.

Aethan let her go. He didn't like the way she made him angry. The way she made him want in ways he had reserved for Iskra.

Whoever she was, he hoped to never see her again.

CHAPTER 15

Mixing

Aethan couldn't be more grateful that his father hadn't been allowed into the competitor's hallway today. He needed as much time as he could steal to breathe before the day's events began.

Afternoon sunlight streamed through the high windows in his bedroom, illuminating the sapphire bedspread as he dressed in his best suit. The dress shirt had been carefully selected to match his light blue eyes, with a black jacket and matching vest. Even his black shoes shone in the sunlight thanks to Roric's thorough polishing the night before.

While none of the events started until tomorrow, Aethan understood that today truly kicked off the tournament. While some of his competitors may not realize it, Aethan knew that everything the competitors said and did, who they spoke to and who they ignored... The Gamemaster noticed everything.

As he finished getting ready and Roric brushed off the jacket to smooth out wrinkles, the two of them discussed the plan for the evening. While Aethan brushed shoulders with some of the more influential men and women at the mixer, Roric would remain near the other squires to learn what he could. Roric would also monitor Iskra for Aethan. If the wrong man approached her at the mixer, Aethan would be sure he never spoke to Iskra again.

Aethan understood why Iskra was at the tournament—he hated that he couldn't give her what she wanted until this was over and done—but he would not let her fall into the wrong hands. Iskra's intelligence would serve her well, but Aethan knew what some men could be like.

While Aethan donned the finishing touches to his suit, Roric slipped out of the room. By the time Aethan made his way to the door, Roric ducked back in.

"He's waiting," Roric confirmed.

Aethan drew in a breath and let it out through his nose. Of course his father would be waiting for him at the end of the hallway.

"And there's no other route to the ballroom?" Aethan asked again. "Not even across the courtyard?"

Roric shook his head ruefully.

Aethan grimaced, striding into the hallway. Better to get this over with.

Roric immediately vanished on his own mission.

Trystain emerged from his room and grinned at Aethan as he joined his friend. Together, they strode down the hallway.

"I feel like I've been waiting all my life for this moment," Trystain said, his excitement evident in the way his hands twitched. "We're a united front in all of this for as long as we can be. Remember that." He glanced sidelong at Aethan.

Aethan recalled the promise they made to one another at only thirteen, before Aethan fully realized just what this tournament would entail. But he knew he would need a friend at his side, so he nodded in agreement.

"Will Sybil be here?" Trystain asked, trying to sound casual, but a hint of a smile played on his lips.

"Yes, she arrived with my father," Aethan replied. It actually relieved him to hear his friend fret about Sybil. Aethan had been worried Trystain would toss her aside for something better. He should know better. Trystain has been entranced by Sybil for years now. The rest was talk and show.

"I wonder if we will see the Novavito princess," Trystain added.

Aethan just shrugged at that, his gaze fixed on his father at the end of the hall speaking with Trystain's father.

"They don't look happy with one another," Aethan noted, nodding at their father's.

The body language between the two men was tense, their faces serious.

Trystain groaned, mirroring the way Aethan felt. "Great. This should be fun."

Aethan paused, pulling Trystain to a halt while they were just out of earshot. "No matter what?"

Those three words invoked the old promise between the two of them. Trystain grinned at Aethan as he nodded. "No matter what."

Perhaps it was foolish or childish to invoke that old promise at this moment, but Aethan needed the reassurance. He needed to know he and Trystain remained on the same page. They clasped hands there in the hallway, the small scars from that blood promise touching as they had years ago, a gentle reminder of what those three words meant. *Against any friend or foe, from now until the end of their days, they would protect one another like brothers and remain a united front. Brothers by choice, if not by blood, no matter what may come.*

Aethan released his hand and heaved out a dramatic breath. "Well, time to face our first real challenge." His gaze flitted to their fathers, who now watched the two of them with equally stern faces.

United, they marched the last few steps, giving their fathers respectful acknowledgment as they continued together toward the ballroom.

"Aethan, I need a moment," Lord Starkling said, effectively stopping Aethan in his tracks.

Trystain shot him a look of understanding that said, *We'll meet up later.* Then his best friend carried on down the hallway with his father while Aethan paused, turning to face his father.

Lux Starkling's gaze roved over every detail of Aethan's suit, as if searching for something to pick him apart for. But Aethan had expected this and been meticulously careful about everything. Even his cufflinks were perfectly aligned with his sleeves to show off the family sigil.

"I know you and Trystain have a long friendship," Lord Starkling said. "But you need to remember that, in this place, he isn't your friend. You are both after the same thing."

Aethan fought the urge to roll his eyes at his father. His hands clenched as he stuffed them in his pockets so his father wouldn't notice. "We might have the same end goal, but that doesn't mean we aren't friends."

"I'm telling you, this tournament changes people," his father said firmly.

The two strolled side-by-side at a slower pace than other competitors who breezed past them on their way to the mixer—some with squires in tow.

"Trystain is no different from any of these other men," Lord Starkling continued. "He will remain your friend as long as it benefits him, and the moment he sees an opening, he will vault himself higher and use you as a hoist—even if it breaks you."

Aethan didn't believe a word of it. Trystain was his closest friend. Both of them knew there would come a point in the tournament when that friendship couldn't help them win, but it didn't mean Trystain would push him down like his father suggested.

The silence must have convinced Lord Starkling that he understood because his father shifted tactics.

"When we get to the event, I will introduce you to the more influential men in the five kingdoms," Lux Starkling said. "Your primary focus today is to charm them and the princess." He glanced at Aethan, the warning in his eyes. "I don't want to see you speaking with Lady Iskra. She and her family have accepted the situation and asked for space."

Aethan flinched as he heard the unspoken "from you" at the end of that sentence. Iskra wanted him to stay away?

They rounded a corner and Aethan heard the buzz of hundreds of voices from the ballroom and wide hallway outside.

"What if the princess decides she likes someone else more than me?" Aethan asked. The nerves and the pressure settled over him, pressing down and down and down.

"She won't." Those two words were spoken with such confidence, but Aethan couldn't stand the idea of losing Iskra for nothing.

"But what if she does?"

Lord Starkling rounded on Aethan, forcing him to stop short to avoid crashing into his father. "She won't." There was no room for failure in his father's countenance. "Because you will do whatever it takes to ensure she doesn't take a liking to anyone else."

Aethan had no desire to ensure the princess chose him, and it wasn't because he was the Starkling heir ready to take over stewardship of Stormvalor. Nor was it because he thought his sister wouldn't be up to the task. She was. If he ever trusted anyone to manage this city and their family fortune, it was Sybil—especially with Trystain at her side. He had complete faith in the two of them together. Aethan simply had no desire to leave his kingdom. Vorovesti pride pulsed through his veins. It was his very lifeblood. He didn't want to move to another kingdom to rule beneath his wife.

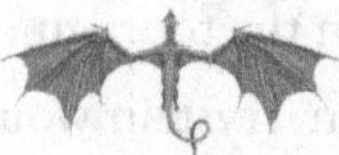

A slyn Kiernan glided through the massive Stormvalor ballroom for hours, making small talk with various lords who wanted their sons in front of the crown princess or competitors who leered at her a touch too openly.

Aslyn had chosen her most modest dress for this event, fully expecting the hungry eyes. But even the thick gold lace that crossed her chest, leaving the men little to stare at, had done nothing to keep those men from studying her cleavage, anyway. Seven Gods help her. She hated men sometimes.

The ballroom itself was lavish but paled compared to the white and gold ballroom in Arithia. Stormvalor's walls were stark gray stone. The pillars housed wrapped vines of colorful blooms, and brightly colored tapestries adorned the walls, depicting some of Justis's most famous battles.

The sheer number of people present was suffocating. Hundreds moved in and out of the garden, ballroom, and hallway. The din of conversation sometimes made it difficult for Aslyn to hear what anyone said while standing beside her.

Elegantly decorated tables mounded with food and drinks spotted the room, and servants milled around with trays as well. Aslyn attended a fair number of lavish galas in Arithia over the years, but those guest lists were limited to only two hundred people at the largest events.

Stormvalor must have overflowed with five to six hundred men and women, a village itself in this elegant ballroom.

Queen Giata remained vigilant at Aslyn's side, quickly but politely dismissing anyone she deemed unworthy of her daughter with brutal efficiency.

Aslyn watched for Blue Eyes. Once, she thought she spotted his pale blond hair only to realize it was a young woman and not a man at all. Another time, she thought she saw the back of his head moving through the crowd, but he vanished almost as quickly as he appeared.

She wasn't sure why she wanted to see him. He had been rude during their encounter. Yet she couldn't seem to forget that scent of fresh spring air or the way it felt to have him so close to her. All foolish, of course, because it didn't matter.

Only one competitor had been given permission to walk with Aslyn through the garden beside the ballroom without the queen at her side. Though Elisio still loomed on their heels.

Lord Marek Bloodstone hailed from Lemheller Gap in Umbr. His father served Emperor Oxon as Chief Military Advisor, which made him one of the highest-ranked competitors in the tournament. It was for that reason alone that Queen Giata had allowed them a private walk. If walking surrounded by hundreds of people with guards on your heels could be considered private.

Aslyn had not expected to like Lord Marek. Upon first impression, he was a massive man with arms as big as Aslyn's head and shoulders broad enough to pull a plow. Aslyn assumed he would be a brutish jerk.

But Lord Marek proved himself witty—almost charming. She supposed she could do worse. His eyes were hard black pits, but she caught glimpses of amusement whenever he made jokes.

Still, a lord from Umbr couldn't be the best choice for her. Aslyn wondered what Marek would gain from winning her hand—aside from the obvious position of power. She would ask, but not today.

When she returned to where her mother waited for her at the garden doors, Aslyn thanked Marek for his company. He kissed her hand as he bowed to her, and she spotted another man glaring at Marek's back. The man was nearly twice Marek's size and looked as deadly as they came.

By the time Marek straightened, Aslyn had plastered that warm smile on her face again.

She and her mother had hardly taken two steps before someone called for her mother's attention. Aslyn followed the sound to see the lord from the sitting room last night approaching. But it was the young man who strode alongside him that made Aslyn's mouth go dry. Her heart leaped into her throat.

At the same moment, Blue Eyes realized who she was, and his own eyes widened slightly in alarm.

Aethan rubbed shoulders with everyone his father introduced him to, as well as a few who simply wanted to meet him to find out if the stories stacked up to reality. Having spent years at court in Mordelic, Aethan knew how to turn on the charm and shmooze with the wealthy to win them over. He had learned what to say and not say, when to laugh or offer kind words, and who to flash his winning smile at. All of it was a game.

Iskra had crossed their path twice, hardly even casting him a glance as her parents towed her along. He tried not to stare after her, to respect her space, but it was hard when all he could imagine were the things she did to him and how he wanted her. Aethan would be eager to hear what Roric had to report about Iskra's companions later.

Lux kept a tight leash on Aethan all afternoon, refusing him to even follow Iskra for a step or move toward the wrong person. But for now, he focused on keeping his father happy. Even if he watched some of the other competitors mingling without an overbearing shadow, laughing, smiling, drinking... *free.*

Hundreds of people milled around, and it took them forever to find the Novavito queen and princess. When Lux muttered he had at last spotted them, Aethan's stomach began writhing madly. He wished his father would explain why this alliance was so critical. He might get on board if he knew the truth.

The moment Aethan spotted the princess, his breathing shortened. It had taken a moment to convince himself that the princess was the same woman from last night. After all, how could it be? What kind of princess snuck around an unknown location in fighting leathers with only a pitiful knife for protection? The way she looked at him made it clear she had made the same connection.

He tightened his jaw, remembering how she had dismissed him the night before, how cold-shouldered she had been. It made sense now, he supposed.

Lord Starkling made small talk with Queen Giata, but Aethan hardly noticed what his father said as he studied the princess. Rich, bronzed skin. Eyes of shining amber. Silken, curly black hair that hung loose around her shoulders unlike last night, when she had it tied back from her face like a commoner.

The princess cast a worried glance at her mother, then back at him. He knew why immediately. She feared he would say something about her adventure last night.

Hearing his father introduce him, Aethan remembered himself and resumed his usual charming façade, bowing to the two women respectfully.

"Princess, I'm pleased to finally meet you," Aethan said, taking her hand and kissing it. "And relieved to see you've recovered from last night's ailment."

Their eyes met once more as she picked up on what he didn't say. *I won't give away your secret.*

"I've heard a fair bit about you, Lord Aethan," Princess Aslyn said in a much more polite tone than she had used the night before. "But no one told me how blue your eyes are."

Queen Giata stiffened, and Aethan caught the worried glance she cast at his father.

Aethan took the comment in stride. "A blue sky to match the sun in your eyes," he said smoothly.

Princess Aslyn's cheeks colored. Just like they had last night. What was she thinking when she blushed like that?

"Queen Giata, can I offer you a drink?" Lux asked.

Aethan knew that was his cue. His father had drilled it into him earlier. "I would be happy to escort the princess around the garden while you are away." He offered his arm to Princess Aslyn. "If you will suffer my company, that is."

The princess's eyes widened ever so slightly at that.

Aethan's father hissed a warning at him.

But Princess Aslyn slid her arm through his. "I suppose I shall make do."

The two of them strolled away, leaving their parents behind. Aethan couldn't help a touch of relief. It was the first time he had shaken his father since they met up outside the competitor's hallway, and Lux Starkling's presence had been grating on him.

A shadow fell over the princess before they made it a few steps. Aethan glanced over his shoulder. A royal guard with even bronzer skin and dangerous eyes trailed the two of them.

"Is that your homeless dog?" he asked.

Aslyn clucked in irritation and shot him a warning glare. "That is Elisio, and he goes where I go."

"Can he turn invisible?"

She blinked in confusion. "What?"

"I didn't see him last night."

CHAPTER 16

A Fool's Bargain

Lord Aethan hadn't given Aslyn away in front of her mother, which she silently thanked him for, but the moment they were out of earshot he made it clear he remembered what she had said to him last night. And just mentioning it with Elisio so close at her back filled Aslyn with a new kind of dread. What would Elisio do if he found out she was sneaking out... to see Lord Aethan, another man, of all things?

Not that she had snuck out to *see* anyone, but Elisio wouldn't care.

Aslyn hissed at Aethan's comment about last night, fighting the urge to glance back at Elisio. She could practically feel his eyes burning a hole right through Aethan.

Aslyn spoke under her breath to keep Elisio from hearing. "Stop, or he will be worse than a homeless dog."

"Is that what you call all your guards?" Aethan teased without missing a beat.

"It's better than what I call my suitors," Aslyn retorted.

Aethan chuckled. "I beg to differ. You called me a homeless dog already."

"I will concede that I was incorrect about the homeless part, at the very least."

"How generous."

Aslyn couldn't explain why she *wanted* to dislike Aethan. Perhaps because her mother had been pushing so hard for him as a strong choice for her future husband. The trouble, it turned out, stemmed from the fact that she *did* like him. As they walked through the manicured garden, sticking to the main paths, Aethan displayed a sharp wit and intelligence that surprised Aslyn. She had expected him to be a slow brute. Instead, he made her laugh.

It turned out Aethan had an eye for court intrigue. He said nothing aloud to give it away, but the way he carried himself, how he watched everything around them, the general awareness he had for the eyes and ears on them, all made it obvious he was more than just muscles and a pretty face.

Aethan mentioned his sister fondly, stating that she was attending the tournaments to cheer for him. Aslyn wondered for a moment if his sister was the young woman she had spotted with the pale blond hair earlier in the afternoon.

"Your sister would take over if you left, then?" Aslyn asked casually, though genuinely curious.

Aethan tensed at her side as she finished her question. A ripple of worry coursed through Aslyn. Had she been too forward? She was far from making any decisions about her future, though Aethan certainly had proven himself at least easier to talk to than the others, if nothing else.

Aslyn stopped, and the suddenness of it jerked him to a halt. He turned to face her, those beautiful blue eyes fixed past her shoulder.

On Elisio.

"Do you not want to leave Vorovesti, Lord Aethan?" Aslyn asked evenly.

Better to find out now than later.

"I'm proud of where I come from," he said carefully, pulling his gaze away from Elisio. "And who I am."

Aslyn couldn't help but wonder what kind of expression her former lover must have on his face. If he caused her problems, she would have to have him reassigned.

"You should be," she said in all sincerity. "No one can take that away from you."

"Is that not what you would do?" The utter lack of hesitation in his response and the hint of sharpness in his tone startled Aslyn at first.

Then it sank in. Did he think he already secured this place?

Aslyn threw back her head and laughed an honest, rich laugh. "Oh Lord Starkling, you are quite amusing." He blinked in shock at her reaction. "Let's not get ahead of ourselves. You don't get one walk with me and that's that."

"I didn't mean—"

Anger flared in her belly that he would dare even think such a thing. "If I am to be some *prize*—"

"That's not the word I would choose."

His tone was again sharp, but Aslyn ignored that comment and pressed on, "Then I expect whomever aims to *win* me to work for it. Prizes are only given to winners, after all." She took a few steps closer to Aethan, and for a moment, she breathed in the scent of him, hating how it made her warm. "So work for it."

He raised a brow in a challenge. "If I don't want to?"

Fear and disappointment flared through her, but she refused to show him her weakness, or how much she wanted him to want to. "Then what was the point of this conversation?"

Aethan's gut writhed like mad. He made a grave error by asking her those questions. Somehow, he had to fix this before the princess walked away. Seven Gods help him. His father would tear him apart for this if he found out how poorly Aethan handled himself. But Aslyn had a way of getting under his skin.

He hefted out a sigh and scrubbed a hand over his face. "I'm sorry. But... can I be honest with you?"

Aslyn placed her hands on her hips and narrowed her eyes. "Please do."

No matter how he proceeded, Aethan couldn't mention Iskra. He couldn't even hint about her. That certainly wouldn't help matters.

"I just wanted to get my dad off my back," Aethan admitted. "He has been pushing me about this moment for weeks. And it isn't that you aren't perfectly... lovely."

Aslyn gave him a flat glare at that.

Aethan pushed on. "But I thought I had everything figured out. My future and my dreams..."

"And then your father heard my mother's announcement," Aslyn said. Sympathy shone in her eyes. Perhaps she understood his dilemma better than expected. "Shall I relieve you of your burden then, Lord Aethan?"

He chuckled, shaking his head. "Do you truly think that would do me any favors?"

Aslyn considered the question. Then she slid her arm around his again to continue their walk. "Perhaps you and I could do one another a few favors. I find myself in a bit of a bind." She glanced over her shoulder and Aethan knew she looked at the guard.

People bowed to the princess as they passed, and more than a few pairs of eyes observed their exchange. Aethan knew these people already gossiped about what this exchange might mean for the two kingdoms.

Aslyn must have sensed something as well. She stopped at a bench surrounded on three sides by a thick hedge, giving a quick command to her guard to keep others away. He took up position outside their hedge alcove, hand on his sword, but as he turned his dark eyes glared at Aethan. A warning, no doubt.

Aslyn settled on the bench, patting the space beside her. He acquiesced, unbuttoning the bottom button of his jacket as he sat to keep it from pulling too tight.

The princess leaned closer, lowering her voice so the guard wouldn't hear her. "I am told I have to find a husband before I return home. It's quite a big deal, actually."

Aethan stiffened at that, wondering where she was going with this, but she patted his hand reassuringly.

"Perhaps this is a fool's bargain," she continued, fidgeting with her necklace, "but worthwhile for both of us. You can get closer to these men in ways that I cannot."

Startled, Aethan watched her for signs of deception. "Surely your mother has prepared you."

"She has advised me."

"But you don't trust her judgment?"

Aslyn ran her hands over her skirt. He recognized that as a nervous habit. Sybil sometimes did it when she was uncomfortable.

"I trust my mother has the best interests of the kingdom in mind," Aslyn replied. She bit her lip, watching a couple saunter past, clinging to one another.

Ah. Yes, Aethan understood exactly what Aslyn meant. While her mother would do what was best for the kingdom, that might not necessarily be what is best for the princess.

"I need the truth, Lord Aethan," Aslyn said. "You are proof that what looks ideal on paper may not be the best for both parties."

Aethan nodded. "I understand."

Aslyn turned toward him, taking his hands. Her amber eyes glowed as she stared at him, imploring him. "Help me make the right choice, and I will spend enough time with you that your father will back off."

As tempting as the offer was, Aethan immediately found a glaring hole. "Do you really think that my failure will be seen as anything else when I leave here without you?" He could have Iskra, if he could work this out. In fact, he could *tell* Iskra as much before it was too late!

Aslyn chewed her lip a moment, then eyed him so coyly his stomach flipped. "Not if you win the tournament. Who could be angry with a Stormvalor Champion? You would be entitled to your own wealth… your own fate."

Aethan couldn't help a good-natured chuckle at that. "You make it sound so easy to become the Champion."

She leaned back, grinning at him and fluttering her lashes teasingly. "I thought you were favored to win this year?"

"Fine." Aethan grinned back at her. "You have a deal. Where shall we begin?"

The evening passed quickly with so many vying for Aethan's attention. He continued reflecting on his conversation with Princess Aslyn. She had not been what he expected. Aethan suspected he would enjoy the weeks of helping her find her husband.

Roric had been waiting when Aethan at last entered the suite.

"Anything good to report?" Aethan asked.

"A lot of things are probably not worthwhile, but I leave that for you to determine," Roric admitted. "And one thing I thought you might find interesting."

Aethan shrugged out of his suit jacket and laid it over the back of a chair before crossing for a drink of water from the pitcher on the table.

"I heard just a few minutes ago from Marek's squire that Bryse is furious with him," Roric said.

Aethan looked up and noticed the grin on Roric's face. Oh, he had something interesting to share, for certain. "Why?"

"Apparently, Bryse thought Marek stepped out of place by making a play for Princess Aslyn," Roric said, practically shaking with excitement. "They nearly came to blows in Marek's suite less than half an hour ago."

Interesting indeed. Considering the agreement he made with Aslyn, Aethan knew he had to be sure she stayed away from Bryse. If she preferred Marek, it could help him in the tournament as well. Marek and Bryse just might tear each other apart fighting over her. Not that he thought either of the Umbr men were good enough for a princess.

"What about Iskra?" Aethan asked, afraid of the answer.

"Hard to say at this point," Roric replied, retrieving Aethan's jacket to clean and put away. "Her parents led her around all night to meet quite a few potentials. I'll keep an ear to the ground as much as I can, though."

Aethan downed the water, then nodded his thanks. Iskra had meant what she said and he knew it. She would seriously consider anyone her parents found worthy.

But who would it be?

CHAPTER 17

The Truth of the World

Instinct warned Bast Blackblade to avoid the main roads north. The incident at the Slippery Fox Inn had been on his mind endlessly for days after leaving Arithia. Instead of heading straight north, Bast cut across Novavito and the Seoras Plains. He slept under the stars as much as possible, far off the worn roads of the plains.

A few times when rain fell in thick sheets, Bast paid farmers to allow him to sleep in the hayloft and keep his black horse in the stables below. Everyone was wary of a man in black, but once he flashed the right coins in front of them, that hesitation vanished.

The Seven Gods be damned. These farmers were not doing as well as they should be. Most of the animals were emaciated from rationed food while farmland yielded pitiful harvests. Coins couldn't fix their problems, but it would alleviate some of the burden of feeding themselves or paying their ruling lord rent for their dying land.

Seoras Plains were supposed to be the most bountiful in all the five kingdoms. If crops were so bleak even here, there was little hope for anyone anywhere.

No matter where Bast stopped, the situation remained the same. The poor remained poor. The land grew more and more untenable. Livestock died of starvation more often than a butcher's axe. More than half the meat that made its way to market had spoiled long before finding a home.

Having spent his teenage years in the streets of Elysia, Bast had watched Elysians worship gods that had long ago abandoned them all. He saw how worship was used as a weapon against the masses.

Were the gods still present, Divica would be much different. Those using the Seven Gods to wield power unjustly would have fallen to that god's wrath, as they had in the old days more than a millennium ago. The farmers would have fat livestock and bountiful harvests. The creatures fished out of the oceans would not cause wasting diseases.

Screw the whole of Divica and their lost gods. Bast Blackblade made his own way.

The packs provided for Bast on the horse didn't hold much more than a map of the five kingdoms of Divica—a map Bast didn't need—enough wealth to purchase a vast expanse of land anywhere in Divica, and food rations to get him buy for nearly two weeks. Apparently, his patron, Platius, wanted to ensure he wouldn't need to stop for supplies on the way north and had assumed he would head straight to Stormvalor.

It had taken Bast nearly a week to reach the first river crossing. The ferryman had charged him more than the crossing was worth—likely assuming Bast could afford to lose the coins.

The small fishing village on the other side had pitiful docks with rotting planks his horse nearly went through when they disembarked. Most of the fishing boats in the water were in even worse condition.

Bast approached the only inn, needing a bed for the night before he continued to Port Verix on the east Umbrian coast. The thatched roof needed to be replaced, and a fungus grew on the log walls of the inn. But there would be no other choice unless he wanted to sleep under the stars again.

He left his horse with a stable boy who eyed the mount like she was a feast. Bast gave the boy an extra coin to ensure his mount remained in the stable untouched all night. It seemed to do the trick.

The innkeeper didn't bother looking up from his record book on the counter as he grumbled upon Bast's entry. "Told you we ain't gonna serve you til you pay your tab, Jorgie."

Bast strolled straight up to the counter, placing his hands against the sticky surface within the innkeeper's line of sight.

Curious eyes lifted from the records, slowly drifting up Bast. No doubt he examined the well-cared-for leathers and expert stitching of the riding cloak. By the time he met Bast's gaze, his eyes were wide, eager for the coins about to land on his counter.

"Are you here for a meal or a bed?" the innkeeper asked, perking up. His moustache shook with each word, and the lines around his eyes smoothed out.

"Both."

"Name?" the innkeeper asked, pen poised over his record book.

One of the emperor's laws. No one could rent a room without taking down a name in case the Black Guard needed to check the registry against their wanted posters. That didn't prevent people from offering the wrong name.

Bast couldn't give his name. Not if Platius knew who he was. "Quade."

"Like the old hero of Novavito?" the innkeeper asked.

"I suppose." Bast produced enough coins for a room, a meal, and a hot bath. Coins which disappeared swiftly into the innkeeper's pocket. Bast then set a gold coin on the counter, his index finger pressed against it as he stared down the innkeeper.

Greed shone in the man's dark eyes as he stared at that gold coin.

"For discretion," Bast said firmly.

"Of course." The innkeeper reached for the coin, but Bast didn't let go.

"I like my privacy. This place doesn't strike me as a village used to visitors."

The innkeeper nodded vigorously, glancing at the black hilt of Bast's sword, Darkheart. The moment of clarity shone in the innkeeper's eyes. He knew betraying Bast would end badly for him. Bast lifted his finger, and the coin disappeared in a heartbeat.

"I'll take my meal in my room. None of that fish your people dredge up, either." Bast had no desire to fall ill while traveling north.

The stairs groaned as Bast followed the innkeeper up to his room. Or what passed for a room in this village. The slope of the roof made it hard to stand upright through most of the room. A couple of pots on tables had dirty rainwater, no doubt from the recent rain. Which meant the roof leaked.

Seeing the state of these villages and the people in them made Bast loathe the royals who lived in comfort, overtaxing and underserving their own people. Between the missing gods and the careless royals, these people were doomed to poverty.

Perhaps, once he reached Stormvalor, Bast would steal from more than just the princess.

Bast could rob all of those wealthy fools blind and give it all back to the people they refused to serve.

The notion had him plotting all through dinner and his bath.

CHAPTER 18

Shattered Lances and Desperate Moves

During the first week of the tournament, Aslyn watched from her family box alongside her mother. The thunder of the crowds would have made Justis proud, were any gods still around to witness the events. Aslyn swore at times the entire arena shook from the sound of the roaring, cheering, and stomping crowd.

It had been easy to find herself swept up in the spectacle of it all as the twenty-five competitors participated in a week-long jousting tournament. On the first day, each man had been randomly paired against another. Crowds had swiftly chosen their favorites judging by the thunderous noise they made when particular names were called.

When Aethan's turn had come, Aslyn found herself holding her breath as the horses charged toward one another, the Jewel of Arithia clenched tight in her anxious fist. The clash of lances created enough sound to be heard over the crowd, and Aslyn winced. It had taken her a moment to realize the Elpisian competitor—Gorim, the Gamemaster had called him—had been unseated.

Aethan's squire rushed over to retrieve his broken lance, and Aethan dismounted.

Despite herself, Aslyn surged to her feet along with the crowd and cheered for him as he slipped off his helmet and passed it off to his squire. But unlike the other competitors, Aethan strode over to Gorim and offered a hand to help the man up. The noble action earned him more fans from the crowd.

When Aslyn settled back into her seat, she caught her mother smiling at her in approval. None of the others had driven her out of her seat, and Aslyn was certain her mother took that as a good sign. Truthfully, she was just happy for her friend—assuming she could call Aethan a friend. He needed to win this tournament as much as she needed to find a husband. Naturally, she would cheer him on. But her mother didn't need to know the real reason behind her excitement.

Marek had won his match against Lorin, another Vorovesti competitor. Aslyn had cheered for him as well, but not with as much enthusiasm as she had shown Aethan. Another fact her mother no doubt read into.

That evening, Aslyn had dinner with one of the nobles attending the tournament. Lord Wilym poured on charm so thick Aslyn thought she might suffocate from it. She humored his bad jokes, but when the meal was over, Aslyn had been happy to part ways. Elisio trailed in her shadow, strutting like he knew her date had gone poorly and she had little remaining interest in Lord Wilym.

On the way to her suites, she crossed paths with Aethan's squire, Roric. He bowed deeply to her, and she asked after Aethan. He simply reported that his lord was well and eager for the next day of matches. The note in his hand caught her interest, and Aslyn dismissed him, then followed covertly, wondering who Aethan sent notes to. Elisio gave her a few questioning glances as they followed the squire, likely wondering what she was up to. Aslyn wasn't ready to answer that question just yet.

The squire knocked on one of the other noble suite doors. An older man opened, frowning at the sealed note. He didn't bother reading it as he ripped it in half and handed it back to Roric, then slammed the door in his face with a sharp, "See what your lord thinks of that."

Roric dipped away red-faced. Aslyn slipped out of sight, yanking Elisio back with her as Roric hurried past with the pieces of the note.

The next day, Aslyn guided her mother down that same hallway and casually asked who rented those rooms.

"The Lord and Lady Pridell, from Vorovesti," the queen replied, hardly glancing at the door. "Prudish and rude people, if you ask me."

A lord and lady from Vorovesti. Surely someone Aethan knew well, then. What made Lord Pridell so angry that he would insult his king's nephew?

As the jousting tournament continued, Aslyn once more found herself swept up in the excitement of the event. Only twelve competitors remained today, and those eliminated yesterday clustered in small groups in their own area of the arena floor, cheering on their friends and fellows.

Marek faced off early against an Elpisio man named Von. It took two passes. Lances shattered on the first, and squires swiftly rushed in with replacements for both before the men even turned their mounts. With the next pass, Marek unseated Von. Aslyn cheered loudly for him.

More men faced off, leaving only Bryse, Trystain, and Henric seated. When Cormic had his turn against Ryker, from Oshon, Aslyn's mother showed more enthusiasm than she had for any of the others. Cormic had been one of two competitors selected by Aslyn's father. It was no wonder her mother would cheer loudest of all for him. He, of course, won his match. Aslyn hadn't doubted he would. She had met him a few times and knew of his skills with a lance—not to mention a sword and shield.

As Aethan readied himself for his match against Kern, from Oshon, Aslyn watched as he turned his gaze up at the noble boxes before putting on his helmet. For a moment, Aslyn thought he looked for her. But when she followed his line of sight, she noticed a young woman seated with her parents in the noble box. Why was he looking at *her*?

Queen Giata noticed as well, frowning ever so slightly.

"Who is that?" Aslyn asked, unable to help her curiosity as she absently fiddled with the Jewel of Arithia at her throat.

"Those are the Pridells," her mother said, and judging by her tone, she was far from amused.

Aslyn swiftly made the connection. He had mentioned having his own hopes for the future when they met. Then he sent a note to them that the woman's father clearly rejected. Now he looked at her with…what? Hope?

She turned her attention back to Aethan to attempt gleaning more, but he already sat in the saddle in full armor, lance in hand. This time, when Aslyn held her breath, she wasn't entirely sure what she worried about. Him losing… or the young woman.

The crowd held their collective breath as the lances crashed into their targets. Kern tipped back in the saddle, but didn't fall. For a moment, he just dangled there like a leaf clinging to a branch in an autumn breeze. Then armor crashed against the dirt. The collective breaths released in a thunderous cheer as Aethan raised his lance in the air, victorious again.

That night, Aslyn just happened by the Pridell suite with Elisio in tow as Roric delivered another note. And again, Lord Pridell rejected it with curt words.

Aethan sank into the hot bath, enjoying the way the heat relaxed his sore and tense muscles. For all his victory on the arena floor, Aethan had failed spectacularly off the field. Iskra wasn't even getting his messages. Sometimes Lord Pridell sent back the message, and sometimes he ripped it up first. The intent was clear. Lord Pridell held a grudge against Aethan and intended to wed his daughter elsewhere.

The door to the bathroom whispered open as Roric tiptoed in with fresh clothes.

"Is the water warm enough?" Roric asked.

"Perfectly." Aethan opened his eyes and rolled his head to the side to eye the squire as he busied himself around the bathroom. "Do you have any good news for me yet?"

Roric gave a small shrug as he laid out a fresh towel. "I've heard from the Umbr squires that Bryse has been asserting his dominance over his fellow Umbrians. He still hasn't forgiven Marek for stepping in where he thought he had rights. The fact that the princess has hardly glanced at Bryse hasn't helped his temper."

The boy took a seat on a stool as he continued. "Bryse and Marek might look unified in public, but once they're alone, it's a whole other story."

Aethan smiled ever so slightly. Good. He hoped those two turned on each other and made his life easier. Marek acted perfectly respectable in public, but he had been deferring to Bryse more of late and it drove Aethan mad.

"Also…" Roric reached into his jacket and pulled out an envelope.

Aethan's letter to Iskra, once more rejected. He frowned.

"He said to stop sending the messages so that his daughter can move on," Roric said, a hint of regret in his voice. He didn't want to deliver the message. "Rumor has it she's taken a liking to someone, but I don't know who."

Aethan closed his eyes against the ache in his chest.

Silence fell over the bathroom as he soaked his aching muscles.

"Sire?" Roric's voice was muffled.

Aethan opened his eyes, surprised to find himself submerged up to his nose, as if some subconscious part of him would rather die than face the truth. He lifted his chin from the water.

"Make sure my armor is ready for tomorrow."

Roric frowned, but murmured agreement and left Aethan alone in the water.

The next morning, Aslyn couldn't handle not knowing. She rose early and instructed her mother's guard that she would meet her mother in the box for the matches, but she wanted to see Lord Aethan to wish him luck.

Elisio walked alongside Aslyn this time as they made their way down to the competitor's quarters.

"Lord Starkling, then?" Elisio said once they were well away from her suite doors.

"Is there a problem?" Aslyn asked sharply.

"He's not really your type, Your Majesty." Was that jealousy Aslyn detected in his voice?

"What would you know of my 'type'?"

"More than most, I would wager," Elisio said, and the boldness of his statement made Aslyn furious.

She stopped, planting her hands on her hips and rounding on him. "You forget yourself."

"Is it really so easy for you to brush aside the man who shared your bed for three years?" Elisio asked. His dark eyes burned into her.

"I tire of this same debate," Aslyn replied tersely. "Don't mistake this for me not caring, but a great burden rests on my shoulders that I wouldn't expect you to understand. You don't get to judge me for doing what must be done for all of Novavito. I warned you that coming on this trip would be a bad idea, but you went behind my back."

"You can't order me to stand down," he said, stepping close. "Not in this. You might command a lot of things because you were born with a crown on your head, princess, but there is one thing you can't control."

Aslyn hated how much taller he was than her, how she had to look up to glare down her nose at him—how at one time she had loved the way he towered over her. "What's that?"

His dark eyes drifted down to her lips. "My heart."

"You are too close to me, and far too bold, Elisio," Aslyn said, loathing that he made *her* step away to gain space and distance. "Do what you want with your heart, but I reject it."

Before he could say more or pin her with those dark eyes, Aslyn turned on her heel and strode away to the competitor's quarters. Elisio, of course, followed her, but this time he kept himself a few feet back.

Aslyn didn't want to hurt Elisio—she truly did care for him—but she couldn't allow him to continue like this. For a moment, she had been certain he was about to kiss her. In the hallway. Where *anyone* would have seen them. And Aslyn knew he didn't care.

They reached the hallway where commotion bustled along the passage. Doors opened and closed as squires rushed in and out to ready the competitors participating today. A few of the men visited friends to wish them luck.

All eyes fell on her as she proudly marched down the hall.

"Can we help you find something?" Bryse asked, smirking as he eyed her up and down. Aslyn recognized his voice from that night Aethan had shielded her from some of the men. He had said very unlordlike things about what he would do to her with just a few minutes alone.

Aslyn had never been more thankful to have Elisio guarding her back. He sensed the danger from Bryse as well, stepping closer to her and resting his hand on his sword. Something told Aslyn this wouldn't be a quick fight if it broke out.

"Your Majesty." Marek slipped out of his room, shooting a thankful look at his own squire as he closed his door. Had the boy warned him? He glared for just a moment at Bryse from the corner of his eyes before turning his charm fully on her. "Did you come all this way to wish me luck?"

"Of course," Aslyn replied, smiling sweetly at him. Marek was handsome with those black eyes and shaggy dark hair. But he was so *big*. Was *all* of him that big? "Though I doubt you need it."

Bryse lumbered closer and Elisio tensed. "He needs all the help he can get. Rumor has it he's facing off against the Starkling heir today."

Marek versus Aethan? Aslyn's heart clenched. She knew they would likely face off if they advanced far enough, but some foolish part of her had hoped they at least would both make it to the final round.

"I hear a kiss for luck is customary in Vorovesti," Bryse said, smirking at her.

Marek practically snarled at Bryse in warning, but Aslyn could handle herself.

"Well, if that's the case..." Aslyn strolled gracefully toward the Umbrian competitors.

Bryse straightened, his smirk growing and hands twitching. Marek tensed as if preparing for a fight.

Aslyn stepped around Bryse and marched right up to Marek, then popped up on her toes to kiss his cheek. He still had to lean down so she could get close enough. "Good luck, Lord Marek," she whispered.

Marek's face flushed and he grinned at her, a fiendishly charming smile.

Aslyn spun on her heel to find Aethan and Trystain watching her from a doorway, both as casual as large cats. It was Aslyn's turn to flush as Aethan's brows climbed. She licked her lips and glided toward him.

"Your Majesty," Trystain said with a graceful bow. "Your beauty far surpasses the claims."

Aethan bit the inside of his cheek and pressed his lips together as if smothering a laugh. "Indeed," he said, but the amusement at Trystain's expense was not lost on Aslyn.

"Thank you, Lord Trystain," Aslyn said graciously, dipping her head to him. "You are from Vorovesti as well, yes?"

Trystain agreed, but seemed a little put out that she had to ask. Yes, Aslyn heard of him. Her mother had told her that Trystain had grown up training with Aethan, and his family was well-positioned in Mordelic, but nowhere near as powerful as the Starklings.

"I was hoping to speak with Lord Aethan for a moment," Aslyn said, politely dismissing Trystain.

He picked up on the clue, shoulders slightly slumped as he walked away. Had he been hoping for one of those good luck kisses as well? He was from Vorovesti, after all. Aslyn let it go. She had questions Aethan needed to answer.

"Would it be improper to invite you inside?" Aethan asked, glancing at Elisio. "He would come along, I assume."

"I would," Elisio replied, warning in his tone.

Aethan nodded cordially, as if he had expected no less. "Well then, Your Majesty. Please." He stepped back, motioning into the room.

Aslyn nervously brushed her fingers over the Jewel of Arithia. She knew everyone in the hallway watched her. They would gossip about this, and word would likely reach her mother. But it would also reach Aethan's father, which might be a good thing for him.

"Close the door, Elisio," Aslyn commanded as he followed the two of them inside.

Elisio glared at her. "It might give others the wrong idea, Your Majesty."

"I'm sure with you in the room, that won't be the case." Would he really dig in his heels here in front of Aethan? Aslyn wouldn't stand for it.

Elisio must have known as much. His jaw twitched, but he did as commanded.

The room was much larger than Aslyn had expected, and furnished with fine sofas. Banners of sapphire blue with a flying dragon in gold hung from the rafters. His house banner. Aslyn had seen it all over the city upon arrival.

Aethan offered a glass of ice water to Elisio, which surprised the guard, but he took it with thanks. As Aethan joined her, Roric entered from the room to their left holding a tray of two mugs and a pot of coffee. Aethan thanked the squire and dismissed him, then poured a cup for himself and another for her.

Aslyn accepted, but didn't take a drink. She summoned the words for what her heart needed to know. Elisio would listen to every word and no doubt use it against her later.

"I hear you are facing Marek today," she said, breaking her own awkwardness. "Try not to be too hard on him."

Aethan leaned back against the sofa, resting an arm casually across the back. He cocked his head, considering her words, and narrowed his beautiful blue eyes. "Marek? Really?"

She stiffened, still irritated with Elisio. Now Aethan thought to know her mind as well? "Yes, Marek. Is that a problem?"

"He's Umbrian." He made a sour face as he took a drink, making it clear just what he thought of Umbrians.

"And you're Vorovesti. What is your point? If you have a suitable reason for me to reconsider, I would suggest something more substantial than telling me where he is from, as if it matters."

Aethan's eyes flared with anger. His silence stretched until, at last, he gritted his teeth. "They're all brutes. He's rumored to have a short fuse behind closed doors, and he lets Bryse walk all over him. That can't bode well for his ability to rule. Does that help?"

"Rumored?" Aslyn tempered her impatience at his tone. "Fine, I will take that into consideration, but it will not remove him from my list just yet. Some people are not who they seem on the surface."

"I suppose," he said slowly, unconvinced.

"For instance, my mother has not stopped talking my ear off about where you were looking before your match yesterday." Aslyn hadn't meant to throw this in his face in anger, but after how her morning had already gone, her patience for men assuming they knew her mind wore thin. And Seven Gods help her. She wanted to hurt him. "She believes you are interested in the young Lady Pridell."

Aethan froze, throwing a glance at Roric, who shrank back into another room without a word. Aethan took a careful drink of the coffee, then set it on the coffee table in front of them.

"And if I was?" he asked, lowering his voice so Elisio didn't hear him.

"From what I've gathered, Lord Pridell has no interest in you." She tried to keep her tone light, though she struggled. It didn't matter if Aethan's interests were elsewhere. They had an agreement. "You must have really done something to anger him."

Aethan grimaced, drawing in a breath through his nose and pushing it out just as violently. "It's not... entirely my fault." His bright blue eyes met hers, and despite herself, Aslyn's heart skipped. "He's not happy that my father has refused his daughter because..."

Aethan bit off the end of his sentence.

And the last piece clicked into place. "Because of me. And you tried to tell her about our agreement."

"My messages aren't even reaching her, and her father is shutting me out." Utter misery marred his face. Aethan tried to hide it from her, but Aslyn had seen that look before when Dorin lost Darma to Ned. The reality of Aethan's situation losing Lady Pridell devastated him.

Aslyn's suspicions had been right. "You love her." She barely spoke the words loud enough for Aethan to hear—and certainly not Elisio.

Agitated, Aethan surged to his feet so suddenly Elisio tensed. Aethan paced the floor. "It doesn't matter. I've been carved out like a rotting infection."

"It does matter." Aslyn stood and stepped closer, taking his hand to stop him in his tracks. "Maybe I can help."

"You've done enough."

She flinched.

"Sorry." His shoulders sagged. "But I don't see how."

Aslyn smirked. "I can invite her family to watch the matches with me. Who can refuse a future queen?"

He pulled back a little, studying her with skeptical eyes. "And do what? Tell Iskra the truth in front of her parents? In front of your mother?"

"I don't know if you've noticed, but that arena is very loud during matches." She released his hand and strolled toward the door. "I had better hurry if I plan to invite her to join me."

"Invite my sister, as well," Aethan called after her.

Aslyn paused, turning slowly beside Elisio.

"She will make a good buffer."

"And that brings along your father, doesn't it?" Aslyn wasn't sure about having Lord Lux Starkling in her private box so close to her. But she put all of her bravado on display. "You really like taking dangerous risks, Lord Aethan."

"Yes," he grinned. "I am known for being dangerous."

Aslyn laughed softly as she slipped out the door.

CHAPTER 19

The Real Prize

Aethan stood in the competitor's staging area beside the arena as Roric double-checked the horse's saddle and the weapons. In the center of the arena, Trystain mounted his horse and reached down for the lance his squire offered. At the other end of the jousting line, Cormic, the favored Novavito competitor, lowered his lance and adjusted his shield.

Aethan studied their techniques as he had everyone these past few days. The horses lurched into motion. Trystain commanded his horse with ease, but the lance moved too much as he rode. Aethan murmured over and over for Trystain to hug it tighter and firm his grip.

At the last moment, he realized Trystain had done it on purpose to throw Cormic off. While Cormic aimed his lance at an angle, Trystain's shield shifted into a better defensive position and he tightened his grip mere seconds before the tip of his lance connected with Cormic. It happened so fast anyone not watching closely would have missed the way Trystain's shield bucked Cormic's lance off to the side. The shield shattered, which would earn Cormic points for the strike, but the lance glanced off Trystain's shoulder as Trystain thrust his lance hard and true into Cormic's armor. It caught on the edge, allowing Trystain the advantage to hook Cormic for just a moment and push him out of the saddle.

Aethan roared with celebratory cheers for his best friend, slapping his palm against the stone wall with a couple of others cheering Trystain on.

Trystain dismounted the moment his horse halted, and he ripped off his helmet, holding it high and grinning brightly. The stands were packed with onlookers who roared in delight.

The loss didn't put Cormic out of the tournament. Of the six competitors today, four would advance to the next round tomorrow. The men who lost would have to joust for the final spot.

Trystain strolled over to Aethan as Bryse and Henric prepared for their match. It seemed the rumors were true. Aethan would face off against Marek.

"Easy as a Verixian whore," Trystain joked as he stopped in the competitor's staging area near Aethan. His squire rushed to help him remove the bulk of his armor.

"If you hadn't caught his armor, you would still be out there," Aethan teased.

Trystain rolled his eyes good-naturedly. "If you say so. Maybe tomorrow your sister will come down to offer me favors for my victory."

Aethan chuckled. "You're getting ahead of yourself, I think."

The arena erupted into thunderous cheers and stomping feet, cutting off Trystain's retort. Both men turned attention on the current match.

Henric and Bryse made their first passes at one another, and the resulting clash shattered Henric's lance and shield. His squire rushed over as he turned his mount to give him a fresh set. Bryse already charged down the line for a second pass. Henric would never get enough speed to unseat Bryse.

The horse lurched into motion, but Henric barely had time to lower his shield before Bryse struck. The shield served as little more than thin paper as the lance pushed through it. Henric's horse whinnied, slowing to a stop as the rider sagged in the saddle.

Aethan's breath caught as he leaned closer and saw the blood.

Then Henric slid from the saddle as limp as if he had no muscles or bones. As the crowd roared in delight, the Oshon competitors all cursed and hollered for healers.

It took several full-bodied men to rush out and pick up the armor-clad competitor and carry him off the arena floor.

Aethan's gaze slid from the blood in the dirt down the staging area wall and met Marek's as they both realized the same thing. This competition was far from a friendly bout.

And they were about to face off against one another. Would Marek be as brutal as his fellow Umbrian?

Aslyn's heart hammered viciously as Aethan and Marek prepared to joust one another. Her gaze continued drifting to the blood from Henric's horrible injury still fresh in the dirt. It was part of the risk. Everyone knew that. But knowing it and seeing it had very different effects on the audience.

Aslyn had asked Aethan to go easy on Marek, but she hadn't asked Marek the same. Now, she wasn't sure she could even breathe as the thump of their horses' hooves charged toward the inevitable collision. Despite wanting to see what happened, Aslyn found herself unable to watch. Instead, she picked at her nails, earning her a reprimand from her mother beside her.

The arena thundered in response to the clash of steel. It took immense strength of Aslyn to lift her gaze, terrified of what she might see.

The horses turned, preparing for a second pass. Then the race resumed.

"I can't watch this," Aslyn groused.

"Don't let anyone see you as too weak to stomach this," Queen Giata said.

Aslyn doubted anyone watched her when the jousting was underway, but she didn't look away this time.

The two men clashed. Shields cracked and broke. Marek moved in slow motion, leaning back, listing to the side. Aethan gripped his reins quickly as he nearly lost balance.

Aslyn surged to her feet, heart in her throat, and leaned against the rail. She breathed in deeper and deeper, terrified that something horrible had happened to either man.

Marek fell off his horse, and for the heartbeats it took for him to roll over and push himself up to his feet, Aslyn hardly dared to breathe.

The crowd already cheered Aethan's name, but he ignored them. Aslyn watched in fear and awe as he marched over to Marek and offered his hand to shake.

Marek threw his helmet in the dirt, said something to Aethan, and stomped away, ignoring Aethan's friendly gesture.

All of Aslyn's relief vanished in a puff of anger. Could Marek not even *pretend* to be a good sport?

Aethan refused to let Marek see how much his words had stung.

"I'm not your friend, Starkling," Marek had said. *"We are both after the same thing. You use that hand to jerk yourself off, princeling."*

As Aethan soaked in the bath, he couldn't shake the hate burning in Marek's eyes in that moment. That hate stung even more than the words, unjustified as it was. Obviously they both wanted to win the tournament. What was the point of being here otherwise? But that didn't mean they couldn't form friendships.

Lord Starkling's warning that these men would use him and climb over his corpse resurfaced. It couldn't be that grim.

Aethan dressed and headed to Trystain's room. He needed to talk to his friend.

But when he knocked he received no answer. He knocked again, glancing down the hallway as he waited.

Trystain's squire opened the door and his eyes widened. "Sorry, Lord Starkling. He isn't here. He's out to dinner."

Was Trystain meeting with Sybil? He sighed and reassured the squire it wasn't urgent, then strolled away.

For a while, Aethan wandered aimlessly. He couldn't shake what had happened today. Henric had survived, thank the Seven Gods, but he was in critical condition.

While he still lived, that could change at any moment. And Bryse had boasted about nearly killing one of them, as if it proved him superior to the rest of them. Worse, the other Umbrian competitors fed into Bryse's self-importance.

Including Marek.

Roric rushed over, breathless. Aethan frowned at his squire.

"What is it?"

Roric drew in a breath, then delivered the news. "Your father is waiting for you."

Aethan fought off a groan. That couldn't be good. He nodded and followed Roric back to his rooms.

Lord Lux Starkling waited at the dining table in the main room with a generous meal waiting. Aethan said nothing as he settled into a chair across from his father.

Lux Starkling held a glass of red Murandy Hills wine in his hand, eyeing the legs against the glass. "I'm a bit perplexed, Aethan. The princess invited your sister—and me by extension—to join her tomorrow for the event. Yet tonight, she dines with that Umbrian swill you ousted just this afternoon."

Aethan's stomach twisted. He piled food onto his plate to cover for his discomfort. Aslyn dined with Marek after the way he had acted today? Aethan knew she didn't care about the loss Marek suffered today. But Aethan had thought her a better judge of character. Marek rubbed him the wrong way.

"And?" He sliced a chunk of steak, acting as casual as possible. "You must know I'm not the only one she's considering."

Lord Starkling took a drink of his wine, then set the glass down and leaned forward as he grabbed his fork and knife. The move felt threatening. "You led me to believe things were progressing well, yet she has not had dinner with you."

Aethan cut him off before he could launch into a stream of belittling comments. "No, but she has invited my sister to join her for the match tomorrow, which means quite a bit, I would wager. And she did come visit me this morning to wish me luck before the matches. We are both very busy people right now."

Lord Starkling hammered his fist into the table as he snapped, "She should be busy with *you*."

Aethan jumped and hated himself the second it happened. He chewed his steak slowly to collect himself.

"I want an announcement by the Champion's Ball, public and unshakable," Lord Starkling demanded, glaring at Aethan.

The Champion's Ball happened before the announcement of who won the tournament and the illustrious title of Stormvalor Champion. Which meant he wouldn't be the Stormvalor Champion by then even if he performed perfectly. The weight of that reality smothered Aethan. He set down his silverware and folded his hands in his lap.

"She is clever, father," Aethan said carefully. "I can't just muscle my way into her heart and demand it. Trust me, that won't go well."

"Why not? That Umbrian garbage seems capable, and I know you come from better breeding than him. Don't tell me your charms are limited to that Pridell girl." Aethan flinched at that, and hated the way his father gloated, as if he prepared for a final killing stroke. "Princess Aslyn knows about your attachment to that girl. I don't know how she found out, but she invited the Pridells to her box tomorrow as well as your sister and me. I will attempt damage control, but if I find out you are sending any more messages to that girl, you will regret the day you crossed me. Because whether or not you win a future queen, you will *never* have that Pridell girl. Is that clear?"

He knew about the messages Aethan sent? Aethan's jaw tightened, but he nodded.

"I can't hear your head shake, boy. Speak like a man."

"I hear you loud and clear, father." The sharpness in his tone made his father glare at him.

"Now, let's talk about tomorrow and that Bryse fellow."

Nearly two hours passed before Aethan's father finally left to let Aethan rest. The moment the door was closed, and Aethan was certain his father wouldn't return, he turned and called for Roric. The boy rushed in from his own room to the left of the main living space.

"Sire?"

Aethan's jaw twitched. "What's the first thing I asked of you when I arrived?"

Roric's gaze darted back and forth as he sought the answer. Finally, he said, "Trust."

"How in the name of the Seven Gods did my father find out about those messages?" Aethan snapped.

Roric floundered, shaking his head as he slowly paled. "I... I don't know. But I will find out."

Aethan had been heartbroken when Roric had returned with the ripped, unread notes. But he had burned them in the fireplace. No one knew about them except for Roric and Lord Pridell... and the princess.

No. It couldn't be her.

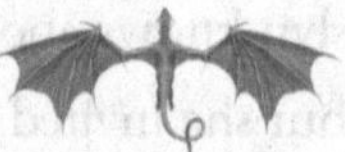

Aslyn had been furious with Marek when he arrived for dinner. She intended to give him an earful about his poor sportsmanship. But Queen Giata had lingered in the sitting room as Aslyn and Marek dined together. And by the end of the meal, he had smoothed out her ruffled feathers.

"I feel I should apologize for the way I behaved today," Marek said as they strolled toward the balcony. "The tension of the moment got to me, I think. My father has put a lot of pressure on me to win this tournament. I don't want to burden you with all of that, though."

Aslyn rested a hand on his arm and gently encouraged his gaze away from the arena floor below. "You can share your burdens with me, Marek. I would like to know you better."

He huffed out a self-deprecating chortle and shook his head. "I doubt that. My father might be powerful in Umbr, but I'm no Starkling. I'm not even sure I can compare to the likes of him. Not for someone like you."

Aslyn arched a brow. Did Marek think so little of himself? "You are one of only twenty-five men selected to compete in this tournament, and one of five from your kingdom. I think that compares just fine." She set her drink on the rail and forced him to meet her gaze as he attempted avoiding her. "Besides, I will decide for myself the sort of man I think you are."

He's rumored to have a short fuse behind closed doors, Aethan's warning crept into her mind. But she hadn't seen evidence of that for herself, except, perhaps, his frustration after losing to Aethan earlier today.

Aslyn cleared her throat and threw him a warm smile. "Let me guess. Your father expects you to win because you are *his* son, and he's the emperor's military advisor?"

Marek's mouth twitched up in the corner, but a sadness still lingered in his dark eyes. "You would think it's that simple. Unfortunately, if I don't win, I'm not worthy of being his heir."

Aslyn couldn't help it. Her jaw slackened at that as her eyes widened in shock.

Marek nodded bitterly. "Yeah. Now you get it. On top of that, now that I have the attention of a princess, so if I can't win her over, I'm doubly doomed. I don't have the heart to share his words with a lady such as yourself."

Despite herself, she stepped closer to him. "Marek, I'm so sorry."

He laughed at that. Not at her, but at his own situation. "Oh, don't worry about me, princess." He winked at her. "I have it on good authority that she's smitten with me."

It was Aslyn's turn to laugh, and it was a pure sound from her lips. She couldn't remember the last time anyone had done that—except Dorin... *And Aethan.* She banished that rogue thought. "What would someone like you stand to gain from winning the hand of a princess? Why her?"

Marek rested his forearms on the stone rail and gazed out at the arena. Even leaning as he was, Marek actually remained at eye-level with Aslyn. She had never considered herself small or short, but beside him, she felt tiny.

"I get a crown, obviously." He glanced at her, grinning, and she once again laughed at his playfulness. His dark eyes slid over her in a way Aslyn found she didn't mind at all. Then he added, "Come on. That answer is obvious. Forget the tournament. The real prize here is right beside me. Fierce and beautiful and funny. What's not to love?"

Love...? Aslyn swallowed. That wasn't a word she was anywhere near ready to use for anyone. *Perhaps he didn't mean it that way*, she thought.

"Then the tournament, the way things happened today... you aren't angry with Aethan for beating you?"

Marek gave half a shrug. A breeze ruffled at his wavy dark hair. "It's the nature of the tournament. I'll get him next time."

The absolute confidence in his own abilities endeared Marek even more to Aslyn's heart.

"Tell me about your home, in Arithia," Marek said wistfully as he gazed up at the sunset over the stone walls of the open-air arena.

"It's the most beautiful place in the realm," Aslyn said, resting her hip against the rail beside him. His gaze flicked momentarily at her body before returning to the sunset. "The Great River pours over a massive dam endlessly, then flows through the heart of the city until it meets the southern ocean. The Aryth Mountains are lush and green year-round, and waterfalls from the mountains feed into fountains all over the city." She bit her lip after taking a sip of wine. "But my favorite part is the way the air always seems to smell like flowers."

A little like Aethan smelled. Aslyn fought off that rogue thought. He made his interests very clear. Aslyn was both excited and terrified to meet the woman who stole his heart so completely.

Marek shifted, turning as he leaned on the rail, and the way he studied her made Aslyn wonder what he saw. He tucked her stray hair behind her ear with his free hand. Then his fingertips lingered along the edges of her face.

"You wanna know what I think?" Marek asked, his voice a rich timber that gave Aslyn gooseflesh. She bit her lip and raised her brows at him. "This is the most beautiful place in the realm." He leaned closer, and Aslyn's heart beat so hard she was sure it would burst from her chest. "*You* are the most beautiful thing in the realm."

His gaze dipped to her lips and Aslyn knew he would kiss her any moment.

But it felt wrong. Too soon. As he closed the distance, she turned her head so his lips met her cheek instead.

Aslyn slid back, putting a little more distance between them. "Marek, I like you."

"Uh-oh." Marek stood, bracing himself for rejection.

"No. I don't mean..." Aslyn chewed her lip anxiously, locked in his gaze. "I just mean I would like to take things just a little slower. Get to know you better before..." Her face flushed.

"The kiss was too much," he said as he understood her meaning.

"For now."

He shrugged, but there was something disheartening about it. "I can live with that. And I'm sorry if I overstepped. I just... I find you irresistible."

Those words sang to her heart, and she relaxed a little as they slid into more comfortable conversations.

They lingered there on the balcony for another half an hour before Marek grudgingly admitted he needed to head back to his rooms to rest. Having been eliminated, Marek had other training to see to in as much spare time as he could. If he lost this event, he needed to make up ground going forward.

They said goodnight, and Aslyn ventured into her room, sighing as she sank down onto her bed.

"That is a *lot* of man," Kaiti said with a smirk.

"Nothing I can't handle."

But instead of thinking of Marek as she readied for bed, Aslyn found herself wondering what Aethan was doing, and if he would be forced to compete against Bryse tomorrow in the final round.

Those thoughts gave way to nightmares where Bryse stood over Aethan, his lance pierced through Aethan's armor and chest, into the dirt beneath him. Bryse putting Aethan's eye out with an instant kill. Over and over, she saw the beast of a man killing Aethan in new ways.

And when she finally woke in the morning, Aslyn was covered in sweat.

CHAPTER 20

Broken Lances

Aethan checked the hook on his greave to make sure it wouldn't slip during his match. Near the back corner, Trystain readied himself, exchanging hushed words with his squire. Today, the four remaining men would not know who they faced until their names were called to the arena floor.

The odds of Trystain as his first opponent were slim. The Gamemaster would want to keep the playing field level for each kingdom remaining—Vorovesti, Umbr, and Novavito. The only way Aethan would face Trystain would be if they both won or lost their matches.

Which left one of the two of them to face Bryse. He remained utterly unapologetic for his treatment of Henric yesterday, even after they were informed Henric had slipped into a coma in the night.

Aethan didn't want to face Bryse, but he knew he stood a better chance than Trystain. For days, Aethan studied the way Bryse carried his lance and shield, how he rode the horse, where he struck. Aethan knew he didn't have Bryse's brute strength, but he was confident he stood a chance to outwit Bryse. Especially after his strategy session with his father last night.

Roric finished fastening Aethan's chest plate, and Aethan held up a hand to hold off on further preparation. He clomped toward his best friend in his armored boots.

They would begin soon, and the crowds filled the stands so thoroughly people nearly spilled over the walls around the arena floor. Today would end the jousting event. Everyone turned out to watch.

"Tryst," Aethan said, keeping his voice low in case Cormic or Bryse eavesdropped. "If you end up facing Bryse—"

"I can handle it, Aethan," Trystain said, rolling his neck as his squire adjusted the back of the armor.

"I know." He didn't know. He feared what would happen to his friend. "But just in case..."

Trystain smirked at him, placing an armored hand on his shoulder plates. "Oh, Aethan. If I could, I would choose you, too."

Aethan fought the urge to roll his eyes. "Keep your shield low. Bryse prefers striking low. Shift your neck aside *as* he strikes, or he will alter his trajectory to—"

Trystain's name boomed from the arena walls, cutting off the rest of Aethan's sentence. His friend picked up his helmet and marched out, waving proudly at the masses. His squire hurried behind with the horse, shield, and lance.

And Aethan's worst fears were confirmed when Bryse's name followed only seconds later.

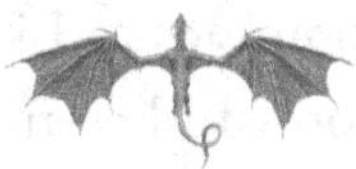

Even with twelve people in the royal box, everyone had room to spare and move around. Aslyn noted the extra men her mother put on guard, as if she expected one of their guests to turn hostile. Wisteria vines curled around the columns holding the roof over the box and dangled from above, swaying languidly in the gentle breeze.

Queen Giata had insisted on a few servants and a wealth of food. As if any of them would eat when people they cared for were fighting for their lives on the arena floor, but Aslyn hadn't argued.

The Pridells arrived first. Aslyn stood beside her mother to greet their guests. Lord Pridell and his wife offered them both gracious smiles, but Aslyn noticed the way both of them swiftly and shrewdly assessed her—the princess who stole their daughter's perfect match. If only Aslyn could tell them the truth, that Aethan still preferred their daughter.

The young woman who entered a moment after her parents caught Aslyn's breath. Iskra certainly was a stunning beauty. Her silky strawberry blonde hair hung in waves over her shoulders, pulled back from her face in elaborate braids that joined the lush cascade of silk. The red dress hugged her curves and flared out from her hips, showing off her perfect figure.

As they were introduced, Iskra Pridell's hazel eyes shone with envy despite the friendly openness of her smiling face. She offered Aslyn a polite curtsy, dipping her chin as was proper, and even that motion was graceful.

No wonder Aethan loves her, Aslyn thought. If Iskra's personality in any way mirrored her beauty and grace on the surface, she could steal any man's heart.

Already, Queen Giata had cornered Iskra's parents to talk politics and the tournament. She heard her mother ask who they favored, and their response was as anyone would expect—loyal Vorovesti to the core as they mentioned Aethan, Trystain, and Borin. Aslyn remembered the anger on Lord Pridell's face as he ripped that message from Aethan, though, and didn't believe they truly wanted him to win.

When Aslyn turned her attention back to Iskra to invite her to the section of balcony with the best view, she noticed Iskra studied her with scrutiny. What did she see when she looked at Aslyn?

"I would be thrilled if you would join me over here," Aslyn said, motioning to the seats to the left nearest the rail. She grinned and leaned closer to whisper conspiratorially. "Away from the stuffy, overbearing parents."

Iskra graced Aslyn with a smile that didn't meet her eyes. "Sounds perfect."

While Iskra settled in, choosing the chair she must have known Aslyn had been using every day up to this point, the guards announced Lord Lux Starkling and his daughter, Lady Sybil Starkling.

Queen Giata graciously greeted them, guiding Sybil over to join Iskra and Aslyn.

"We shall leave the girls to be girls," Queen Giata said to Lord Starkling with a wink, sliding her arm through his to pull him toward the Pridells.

The moment Aslyn laid eyes on Sybil the resemblance between the siblings was apparent. Sybil had the same pale blue eyes and ashen white hair, the same angular face and small nose. She even moved with the same kind of grace. The cut of her dress revealed an intriguing mark of a dragon over her heart. Aslyn didn't mean to stare at it, but she couldn't help noticing something about the lines. Before she could be caught gaping at it, Aslyn welcomed Sybil to join them.

Sybil moved toward the railing, peering down at the arena floor.

"You must be very proud of your brother," Aslyn said as she settled in her chair.

"There was never any doubt how well he would perform in the tournament," Sybil said. "But yes, I am. Him and Trystain both." A hint of adoration flashed in her eyes as Trystain's name was announced. Sybil's back straightened as she watched him.

"The two of them are all but promised to one another," Iskra provided.

But her proclamation was drowned out by Bryse's name. Sybil's hands gripped the railing so tight her fingers turned a mottled red-white. *She's aware of what Bryse did yesterday, then*, Aslyn noted.

A pulse of fear for Aethan's sister rushed through Aslyn. The fear she herself had felt yesterday when Aethan faced Marek surely paled in comparison to what Sybil felt now.

Aslyn rose and stopped beside Sybil, placing her hand over her new friend's, offering her strength. Sybil glanced at her, gratefulness in those blue eyes. They reminded Aslyn so much of Aethan that she had to look away.

The men mounted and readied the charge. Sybil's grip on the railing tightened as they raced toward one another. As Bryse's lance pushed toward his face, Trystain shifted just enough for the blow to glance off his shoulder. Still, the impact was enough to break Bryse's lance and throw Trystain off-balance. Sybil's lips parted like she wanted to cry out, but she restrained herself.

Trystain didn't waste time turning his mount and charging again. But what Bryse lacked in horseback speed, he made up for with brute strength as they clashed again. Both men swayed like they might fall, but neither did.

Sybil pressed a hand to her mouth, eyes wide. Aslyn squinted at the men and spotted the red blood blooming on Trystain's neck. Her gaze darted to the competitor's staging area where Aethan stood at the wall, shouting orders at Trystain, pounding his fist against the stone wall in front of him. It was clear he knew his friend was in danger and wanted to help.

The lance in Trystain's hand dipped as he adjusted his grip mid-run. He leaned close to the mount's neck, blood dripping from his wound, but his focus was singular. Yet he lost enough blood to weaken him on the third pass. His shield broke in two as Bryse's lance struck. Trystain fell off the back of his horse with enough force that his back slid across the dirt.

The crowd cheered as Bryse celebrated.

"Get up," Sybil muttered under her breath.

Aslyn watched Trystain. His legs shifted, but he didn't move to stand.

"Get up," Sybil said more forcefully.

Aslyn squeezed her hand and Sybil squeezed it back. Trystain slid his helmet off, gulping down breath while lying on his back.

Bryse stalked toward Trystain.

"Get up!" Sybil shouted. "Getupgetupgetup!"

Trystain rolled on his side as if her voice willed him to obey, and he pushed his hands under him.

Bryse stopped beside him, said something, then kicked him on his back again before striding right over Trystain's body.

Aslyn heard a shout from far below, deep and commanding, and it drew her attention toward Aethan. Several competitors wrapped their arms around him to hold him back as he shouted at Bryse, fighting to break free.

Bryse didn't even pause as he smugly strode past Aethan. Fury burned in Aethan's veins. Why did the Gamemaster allow such behavior? They were supposed to act with honor, and what Bryse had just done to Trystain was anything but honorable.

"Win your match, princeling, and I'll put you down next," Bryse said as his squire hurried to remove the armor.

Determination coursed through Aethan. Yes. Win his match and he would show Bryse exactly what he thought of him.

"Roric!" Aethan shouted.

Iskra clicked her tongue as Aslyn and Sybil finally settled in their seats once Trystain stood and staggered toward the competitor's staging area.

"That Umbrian brute knew exactly what he was doing," Iskra commented in irritation. "With one blow, he asserted his dominance over both Aethan and Trystain, eliminating one from the contest and infuriating the other."

Aslyn observed the way Aethan readied himself, the furious determination on his face Aslyn could see clearly even from the balcony.

"He's too angry," Aslyn noted to herself.

"Exactly as Bryse wants him to be." Iskra leaned forward as Aethan's name was called to uproarious applause. "If he is consumed with battle rage, he will make mistakes."

Cormic joined Aethan on the field, having earned the final spot after a joust-off with Marek yesterday.

Aslyn fidgeted with her necklace, then noticed the way Iskra watched Aethan. She glanced over at their parents, engrossed in their own conversations about the last match.

Aslyn lifted her chin as if studying the men below as well. "He chose you, you know," she said casually.

Sybil stiffened, glancing at the two from the corner of her eyes.

Iskra's jaw slackened and her hands clenched in her lap. "I'm not sure what you—"

"We have an agreement with one another," Aslyn interrupted. There was no time to play the innocence game. "He tried to tell you, but your father has rejected all of his messages."

Iskra fell utterly still, eyes glued to Aethan as he mounted his horse.

As Aslyn explained the agreement, and that Aethan had been trying to tell Iskra so that she knew he was still fighting for her, Iskra Pridell pulled her hands back and pressed her palms against her stomach. Tears lined her eyes, but she didn't let them fall. Aslyn had been so busy studying Iskra's reaction to the news that she had missed Aethan's match.

It wasn't until Sybil shot to her feet and cheered for her brother that Aslyn realized it was over. Aethan peeled off his helmet and turned his horse toward their box. Toward them. He pointed his lance at them.

At Iskra.

Not that anyone else would be able to tell who he pointed at.

Aslyn joined Sybil, cheering loudly for Aethan.

Iskra remained seated, stunned by what Aslyn had confessed.

"Aslyn, dear!" Queen Giata called from the other side of the box.

Aslyn turned. "Yes, mother?"

Queen Giata lifted a ring of stardrift flowers woven around a crown of vines.

A champion's favor.

Aslyn felt the color drain from her face as her mother's intentions sank in.

Before the final match—Aethan versus Bryse—women could approach the competitors on the arena floor and place that ring of flowers on the lance for luck.

It was as good as signaling to the world that she was interested in courtship with Aethan.

Beside Queen Giata, Lord Lux Starkling beamed with pride. Though whether for his son or what that ring of flowers would mean, Aslyn couldn't tell.

Iskra rose from her seat, unsteady on her feet for a moment.

Aslyn quickly stood as well. "Iskra—"

"After the final match, I would like you to deliver a message to Aethan," Iskra said.

Queen Giata frowned, fury slowly building in her eyes.

"Of course," Aslyn agreed, ignoring her mother's glare.

"He needn't worry," Iskra said evenly, emotion slipping out of each word. "I've secured my future."

Iskra gathered her skirt and made her way to the exit.

Aslyn hustled after Iskra, despite the obvious disapproval of her mother. "Iskra—"

"I apologize if I seem abrupt, Your Majesty," Iskra said. "I'm feeling a bit over-heated. I think I'll get some rest."

"But—"

Iskra shot Aslyn a dirty look from the doorway. "He's all yours. I don't want him any longer."

The words were a blow. Aslyn hated that she felt relief that Iskra had let go. She hated that *she* would have to deliver the brokenhearted news to Aethan.

Sybil had been too distracted by Trystain, rendering her utterly useless as a buffer as Aethan had promised.

"Aslyn!" Queen Giata snapped. The moment she did, the guards blocked the princess from leaving.

In a fury of her own, Aslyn stormed over to her mother and snatched the ring of flowers.

"A re you sure you're alright?" Aethan asked Trystain again.

His friend had stripped down to his undershirt, rubbing and wincing at the nasty bruise Bryse had given him. The wound wasn't deep. The bleeding had already stopped.

"I'm fine. Stop fussing like a mother hen and get on your dumb favors from the women."

Aethan scanned his friend one more time. Some of his anger had subsided after Roric walked him through a few breathing exercises. But it had not gone away completely.

As Trystain implied, a line of women, young and old, had lined up to offer their favors to the final two competitors. Aethan drew in a breath and let it out slowly.

Before he even left the competitor's staging area, Bryse had gathered a handful of his own favors. Why any of those women would be interested in him, Aethan couldn't understand. But they fawned over Bryse all the same, and none of his arrogant flaunting turned them away. A few looked more than pleased by it.

Aethan shook his head as he made his way onto the arena floor with his lance. He hated this part, but knew it was necessary. Winning over the crowd was a big part of winning the entire tournament.

Several dozen women waited for him. Aethan flashed a charming smile at them as he approached. *It's a show*, he reminded himself. His gaze darted up to Aslyn's royal box, but only Sybil stood at the railing. The queen and his father mingled in the box as well. No sign of the Pridells.

His father's gaze swept across the arena floor, and at the same time, a murmur broke out from the back of the crowd. The women waiting for him parted as guards cleared a path.

A vision in a cream dress trimmed in gold approached. Aethan's breath caught as he watched the way Aslyn glided over the dirt like her feet never touched the earth. A gentle breeze made her silky black hair wave behind her.

And in her hands, a ring of stardrift flowers.

Aethan struggled to swallow as she glided straight for him, confident in each movement.

Remembering himself, Aethan sank to a knee and lowered his lance. "Your Majesty," he said.

"Lord Aethan Starkling, you have earned the right to stand before me," Aslyn said.

He stood again, realizing that the crowd of thousands watched the two of them. The hum of excitement made his nerves tense. This woman was beautiful, but... Aethan's gaze slipped past her, seeking Iskra. Was she on Aslyn's heels?

No one followed the princess.

Aslyn slid her ring of flowers over the tip of the lance, then stepped close to him. "I believe a kiss for luck is a Vorovesti custom as well," she said.

Aethan's face heated, but he nodded.

Iskra hadn't come.

What did that mean?

Aslyn kissed his cheek.

"Iskra?" he asked quietly in her ear.

"Later," she replied just as quietly before pulling away.

Aethan blinked furiously to fight off the sorrow already ripping into him. Later.

Because she had rejected him, and Aslyn attempted to spare his feelings before facing off against Bryse. Why else would she not tell him?

He nodded. "I'm honored, princess."

"Keep a level head and strong spirit, win the final match, and you will be invited to a private dinner with me."

Where they could speak privately about what happened. "Anything for you," he said, as if saying *I understand.*

As Aslyn walked away, none of the women who had come to give him favors dared to place their ring of flowers on his lance. Not when the princess had shown him favor.

Once the final two men had a chance to rest and refresh, and the arena floor had been reset, Aethan and Bryse stepped out of the competitor's staging area—at opposite ends—to uproarious applause, cheers, and stomping feet that shook the area.

During his respite, a few competitors Bryse had rubbed the wrong way had come to Aethan offering tips for what they had noticed during his matches. Aethan took all the advice in and stored it away, but he would trust his own studies and instincts. He couldn't let anything else cloud his judgment.

But he hadn't forgotten the way Bryse treated Trystain, or what he had done to Henric.

Aethan blocked out the eyes on him, the noise all around—everything. As he mounted, his focus became singular. This match had to end quickly. The longer Bryse stayed in the saddle, the harder it would be for Aethan to unseat him. The man's monstrously thick legs would cling to the horse in a death grip to keep him in the saddle.

"Remember how Kieta the Strong took down the black dragon?" His father had instructed him last night.

And Aethan remembered. He knew that story by heart. He understood what those words meant.

Roric offered him good luck as he passed up the lance and shield, then swiftly moved out of the way. He would be at the other end of the line with a new set immediately, if needed.

Aethan hoped they weren't needed.

As the Gamemaster lifted the flag to ready the men, Aethan drew in a steadying breath. *Keep a level head*, Aslyn had said. She knew Bryse had worked him into a frenzy on purpose.

The sounds of the cheering faded as the flag dropped. Aethan spurred his horse forward. Though he knew the world continued around him, Aethan's focus fixed solely on Bryse. The way the horse beneath him moved, how he held his lance, where his eyes went. Aethan took it all in, lowering his own lance.

The corners of Bryse's eyes crinkled.

A smile.

Aethan couldn't see the smile behind the face mask, but he did see the way those eyes reacted to it.

The yards closed between them until the point of impact approached.

Bryse lowered the tip of his lance.

At Aethan's horse.

At the last second, Aethan braced his lance high, lifted his shield, and sharply turned his mount out of harm's way. The tip of Bryse's lance scraped against the horse's hindquarters armor loud enough to hurt Aethan's ears. The horse whinnied and bucked, but Aethan kept in the saddle, spinning the horse as it came down.

If he didn't unseat Bryse on this next pass, the match would be lost. Aethan adjusted his grip as the horse surged toward his foe. The lance braced against his ribs. The impact might break a rib or two, but the extra force would be enough to knock Bryse off.

But his foe couldn't know what he planned. Aethan kept his eyes on Bryse's, studying the massive man.

Kieta the Strong defeated the dragon when she was the smallest thing on the battlefield. She had done it through sacrifice and risk. She had been willing to take a near fatal blow to land the killing blow.

Aethan didn't want to kill Bryse, but he wanted to punish him for what he had done.

Using his eyes and the tip of his lance, Aethan faked his move. Their weapons struck. Aethan dug his heels and thighs, gritting his teeth against the impact of his lance against his ribs.

Both lances buckled and shattered.

Aethan immediately dropped the broken end to grab the saddle as pain raged in his ribcage.

It wasn't until he turned his mount to thunderous applause that he spotted Bryse no longer on his horse, but most certainly on his feet. He picked up the broken end of his lance tip and hefted it like a lightweight javelin straight at Aethan.

Aethan threw himself from the saddle to avoid the deadly strike. He already won. Losing his seat no longer mattered.

The impact with the ground made blinding pain steal his breath from his lungs. His ribs hollered in fury, and it was all he could do to clear his vision.

And when he did, Bryse stood over him, the broken wooden shaft of the lance poised over Aethan's chest.

Time slowed.

The crowd thundered with noise. Aethan wasn't sure if they were booing Bryse or cheering him on.

Screams ripped through the air.

Aethan couldn't gather the breath or strength to move and save himself.

Bryse raised the shaft over his head, preparing to strike. Trystain, Kern, and Ryker barreled into Bryse as he plunged the shaft downward, tackling him to the ground. The shaft flipped in the air, falling helplessly to the ground.

Cavis and Cormic each offered Aethan a hand, hauling him to his feet. Aethan screamed in pain, blinded by it for a moment as he fell against something large and solid.

Lorin, the final Vorovesti competitor, held Aethan upright.

Wincing, gasping for breath, Aethan ripped off his helmet and tossed it aside.

The noise crashed against him.

The crowd cheered.

For him.

CHAPTER 21

Lord of the Harbor

Port Verix teemed with sweaty bodies, gull calls, shouts from the harbormen, and beckoning whores. Once a part of Vorovesti, the harbor city had long ago been the home of wealthy merchants. It still was, but the city had been corrupted by men and women grappling for wealth and power under the rule of the emperor.

Someone like Bast Blackblade should be able to thrive in a cutthroat harbor city like Port Verix. The games these people played with one another played to his own skill sets. Pirates strolled along the packed streets careless of the wanted posters of their faces plastered to walls. Dirty deeds went down out in the open where anyone could witness the exchange.

Bast Blackblade liked his privacy when conducting business.

During his search for a decently reputable inn, Bast strolled past half a dozen such deals and no less than two wanted pirate crews drinking and laughing and gambling at tables outside taverns.

If a cesspool of crime existed in all of Divica, it was here in Port Verix.

Emperor Oxon had Black Guards in the city, of course, as well as a lord appointed for his shrewdness and exorbitant wealth. The Black Guards were easily bought off by the wealthy so only the poor crowded the city prisons. The Lord of the Harbor ignored crimes as long as that ignorance lined his pockets.

Bast Blackblade only visited Port Verix when he needed information and never took on jobs in the city. These patrons were as likely to entrap him as pay him, and he wasn't willing to take on the risk. The brokers he had in the city were innkeepers and well-liked barmaids. They brokered for information and nothing more.

Unfortunately, it meant that more people knew him in Port Verix as well. Not as Blackblade—that information was well-guarded. No, these people knew him only as Sebastian, a traveling informant to the most powerful kingdom in Divica. None of them would be able to agree which kingdom that happened to be, should they ever discuss it, but it didn't matter.

All that mattered to these people was coin. As long as he had coin to share, they would tell him anything.

Bast settled on an inn close to the north gate, in case he needed to make a swift escape.

It had been several years since Bast set foot inside Loam and Fiddle. The lively chatter and music washed over him the moment he stepped inside. The delicious scent of freshly baked bread made his mouth water. Spending so much time on the road, eating only meager, half-spoiled food had left his appetite wanting.

Bast settled on a stool at the bar, motioning to the innkeeper.

Porrige finished serving a drink, then made his way over. Bast knew Porrige and his barmaid well enough that the man recognized Bast after a moment studying his face.

"Well, Coravita bless me," Porrige said cordially, invoking the Goddess of the Sea and Life, "if it isn't Sebastian." He uncorked his finest rum and slid a glass of it to Bast. "How long should we expect you this time?"

"I'm not sure yet. I just stepped into the city." Bast took a sip of the rum, savoring the delicious hint of honey. "You're busier than I remember."

Bast nodded to the crowded tables.

"Aye," Porrige leaned against the bar. "We've had a lot of folks passing through on the way to the Stormvalor Tournament. Word has it the Novavito princess is there this time. And looking for a husband, to boot."

"Poor sap," Bast muttered into his glass.

Porrige chuckled. "You talking about the princess or the unfortunate soul who marries her? Pretty as she is, I can't imagine enjoying that kind of pressure."

Bast shrugged it off. A crown was a crown. They all ended up the same in the end. Greedy, ignorant, then dead.

Bast downed his drink. "I'll take a bowl of stew if it's fresh, with bread and a room for the week." Bast glanced over his shoulder as a group burst into a lewdly altered chorus of a song venerating Solisina, Goddess of Light. "As far from the riffraff as you can get me would be good."

Porrige chuckled and nodded, accepting the payment. "Should I contact Selia? She's got a fresh crop of pretty girls."

Bast considered saying yes. It had been weeks now since he enjoyed the company of a woman, but he had work to do. Besides, a fresh crop of girls likely meant the girls were either slaves, girls too poor and alone to care for themselves, or they were kidnapped from homes somewhere across the ocean. Bast liked women as much as the next guy, but he had more discerning tastes than that. So, he begrudgingly shook his head with a grimace.

Porrige didn't press further. A few minutes later, he returned with the food and an Umbrian black and tan stout.

Bast kept to himself as he ate and drank, listening to the conversations for any hints about the princess or the tournament. Everything he learned would help him once he arrived. Bast still hadn't entirely decided how he would approach this particular job, and soon he would need an answer.

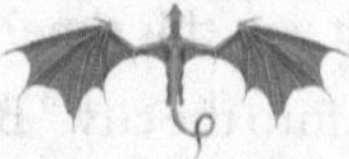

Over the next few days, Bast visited various parts of the city with his ear to the ground for any information that would be helpful. The first major event of the tournament ended with the Starkling heir winning in what the men called a brutal victory. A few other events were underway to mixed results.

The most interesting pieces of information Bast had gleaned from random conversations were that an Umbrian named Bryse had nearly killed a couple of guys, and the princess was rumored to have shown interest in another Umbrian lord, Marek. Bast recognized that name after the story expanded slightly. Bloodstone, son of Emperor Oxon's military advisor.

But rumor also spread that the princess had given the Starkling a favor and a kiss in front of the entire arena before the final jousting match.

It was at that moment, as the news sank in, that Bast knew what he had to do next. But first, he needed an identity no one would question.

Which meant he needed to make friends with the Lord of the Harbor to obtain false credentials. There would be no other way to get in front of the princess for this job. He needed her trust to take the jewel.

CHAPTER 22

Time to Heal

Thankfully, Aethan's ribs weren't broken. He wasn't sure who to thank for that small miracle. However, the internal bruising had turned the entire left side of his torso an ugly shade of purple so dark it nearly looked black. Every morning and every night, Roric brought a healing salve and a cold compress. Aethan loved the way the cold felt against his skin, and the soothing sensation from the healing salve.

Yet he also hated them, because he knew that the compression wrap came after.

The bruising was painful, but the words Aslyn delivered from Iskra were even more painful than any physical wound.

Three days after the jousting event, the bruise began to lighten. After five days, it had turned an ugly shade of greenish yellow.

Healing took longer than normal because Aethan couldn't afford to rest. Not if he wanted to remain competitive. Training couldn't be skipped, and he gritted his teeth every day to avoid showing his fellow competitors just how much pain he was in.

Aethan spent his days training and participating in events, and his nights either having dinner with his father and sister or conspiring with Roric to give him an edge in the next day's event.

Roric proved himself adept at being a spy, even if the boy refused to admit that's what he was. The other squires had begun following his lead. Whether that was because he was the Starkling squire or simply because Roric had a lighthearted, magnetic personality, Aethan wasn't certain. It didn't matter. All that mattered was how free with information the other boys were to gain Roric's favor or trust.

Ryker often disappeared at night for hours. Even his squire had no idea where he vanished off to. Sometimes, the Oshon squires would meet to chat and play games, which was how they spotted Ryker leaving Weylen's rooms in the middle of the night. No one knew what the two were up to, and Aethan was determined to find out. Especially if it cost him odds on the arena floor.

Roric has been particularly excited about the hushed conversation amongst the Elpisian competitors. "They say the Saints of the Seven are coming. That the signs are everywhere."

Aethan gritted his teeth at that. The Saints of the Seven were a fairytale told to children to make them hopeful that the dying world might bounce back. But no chosen saints were coming to restore order. If anything could heal the dying world, it was magic, and the Imperial Seat was determined to extinguish all traces of that, just as it had wiped out the elves.

Roric also reported that Bryse had begun beating his squire. The boy never complained about it, but Roric and others heard Bryse's anger and saw the evidence on the boy. Aethan wanted to teach Bryse a lesson, but knew the arena floor would be a better place for it.

Bryse hadn't been ejected from the tournament for his actions, despite Aethan's father fighting with the Gamemaster over the attempted murder. The display of dishonor would count against Bryse, but everyone who entered the tournament understood the risks, according to the Gamemaster. Aethan Starkling was no exception to the rules. Aethan's father was fairly certain Bryse had the power of Emperor

Oxon backing him in the tournament, and the Gamemaster would never go against the emperor's wishes.

How far their honor had fallen from Justis.

The Umbrian competitors had taken to traveling in packs. None were ever alone, and each defended their countrymen when slurs were hurled their way. Aethan had attempted befriending Marek, but the man had responded curtly.

"I told you we aren't friends, and we never will be, Starkling," Marek had hissed. "One way or another, I will win the princess. And if I had been in your place in that jousting match, that favor would have been mine. Don't think it means anything."

Aslyn had brushed the behavior off as expected. "You're overreacting," she told him during one of her regular visits. "As far as he's concerned, the two of you are fighting for the same thing. The Champion title and the princess's hand. Of course he wouldn't want to be your friend."

"He seems to think you would have given him the favor over me if it had been us out there," Aethan said, trying to sound amused and certain he failed at it.

"He's right."

Aslyn said it so plainly, so matter-of-fact, that anger burned through his veins. Didn't she understand what she was getting herself into? How had Marek pulled the wool so thoroughly over her eyes?

"Aslyn…"

"Don't sound so high and mighty," Aslyn snapped. "You see the competitor fighting you for what you both want. I see the man beneath that."

"But you don't know—"

"Dare to tell me what I think, Aethan Starkling, and see how that goes for you," she hissed. Her sharp tone had Elisio tensing near the door.

"You *asked* for my help," he argued. "And I don't want to see you get hurt."

Aslyn softened just a little. "I appreciate your concern, and I hear you, but I need you to accept that ultimately I will make this choice for myself."

He didn't argue the point further. He wasn't in the mood to fight with her.

Archery had followed the jousting after two days for the competitors to rest—aside from training. Every pull of the bowstring sent searing heat along Aethan's bruises, but at least he knew nothing could hurt him. While his final placement in the archery tournament had been respectable—he finished in fifth place—Aethan knew that he could have done better at full strength.

Instead, Ryker, from Oshon, had won. That night, over dinner with some of his friends and fellow competitors, Aethan learned that Ryker was a captain of the archery squad in Lago, the capital of Oshon. Even among his own people, Weylen had said Ryker was considered an expert marksman.

At least Bryse had placed tenth. Archery was certainly not one of his strengths.

Hand-to-hand combat matches had been a different matter altogether. While Aethan's bruises were still healing, his competitors still used that weakness to their advantage, forcing him to defend that side or use it to strike over his right side. More than once, a punch or kick had aggravated the injury and caused blinding pain. Aethan did his best to fight through it, barely winning his first matches. Yet when he was forced to face off against the broad-shouldered, muscular Qin, Aethan hadn't been quick enough.

Qin moved quick as lightning, using a martial art style Aethan had only heard about—the ocea'mele dance of the Pal Ka'iko islands. Between his injuries and Qin's skill, Aethan lost handily. A fact which had turned his father very surly over dinner that night.

Qin faced off against Bryse in the final match. It had been quite a spectacle. Between Qin's speed and skill and Bryse's brute strength, the two fought for nearly ten minutes before Bryse caught Qin's leg and brought him down with a resounding crack of bone.

Just as Henric recovered enough to join them in training, Qin ended up in the healer's wing instead. He wouldn't heal in time to finish the tournament, though. Not with a broken leg.

Some evenings, Aethan and Aslyn would meet to update one another when she was not courting someone else. The princess had insisted they talk in Aethan's sitting room so he could rest. When he remained standing, leaning casually against the back of a chair but firmly upright, Aslyn commanded him to sit. His pride took a blow when he grudgingly admitted sitting hurt.

Aslyn had forced him to lie on the sofa, propping his head up with pillows before settling into an armchair.

After a week, they began walking together. First, just up and down the hallway as she fussed over his healing, then eventually they moved on to the arena garden—always with Elisio following a few yards behind.

The suitors Aslyn currently took a liking to hailed from every corner of the five kingdoms of Divica. She gave him names. He gave her whatever he and Roric could learn about each.

None of them were good enough for her. Aethan had been sure to point out clearly exactly why each of them failed to meet acceptable standards for a future queen so often Aslyn grew irritated and announced, "If you will not help me find a suitable match, I don't know what we are doing... unless you have decided to throw your own name in the running."

Aethan denied interest. But the more time he spent around Aslyn, the more he wanted to spend time around her. Her spirit was wild and fierce despite her upbringing, and Aslyn was quick with her wits—something Aethan often found lacking in others. Sometimes, watching her leave had been painful and he found himself eager to see her face or catch the scent of jasmine and roses.

But she deserved better than him, too.

Because he couldn't quite let go of Iskra, no matter what Iskra had said.

Aslyn had delivered Iskra's message, but he couldn't accept that she had found herself a match already. Nor that she could love whoever this guy was nearly as much as she had loved him. He had sent Roric to hunt down the name of whoever Iskra had chosen to replace him. It hadn't taken Roric long.

And when he heard who it was, betrayal stabbed through Aethan's heart.

Cavis.

Aethan had eaten and joked with Cavis. They had trained together. He liked the man and considered him a friend these past weeks. Cavis never said a word about it. He never even hinted that a woman had caught his interest like most of the others had. Did Iskra tell him about her past with Aethan?

At first, Aethan had denied the truth. Roric must have misunderstood.

On the eve of the sword fighting tournament, Aslyn sent an invitation for Aethan to join her in the garden. The green had faded from his bruise to a light yellow-brown and most of the tenderness was gone, thank the Seven Gods. He would need better range of motion for tomorrow's sword fighting event.

As with any other evening, Aethan and Aslyn strolled arm-in-arm along the gravel garden paths. Elisio remained far enough behind that they could speak privately as long as their voices weren't too loud.

They discussed tomorrow, Qin's condition, Bryse's abhorrent behavior, as well as a few of Aslyn's suitors. The two had grown comfortable with one another these past weeks, and both laughed and teased one another freely. He now considered her a close friend.

The hushed voices of another couple drifted through the hedgerow. Then a silky laugh that drew Aethan up short. He knew that laugh as well as his own.

"Aethan?" Aslyn asked softly as she realized they had stopped.

He didn't know what his face must have looked like to her, but it must have given something away, because Aslyn let go of his arm and reached for his hand.

Aethan twisted away from her touch and slipped past, marching on jealous instinct toward the bend in the hedgerow to where Iskra's voice emanated.

Aslyn hurried after him, hiking up her skirt to hasten her steps.

But he stopped short as he turned the corner and spotted Iskra's strawberry blond hair. The way she rested her hands against Cavis' chest and stepped closer, how her long fingers curled around the lapels of Cavis' jacket, the tilt of her chin as she gazed up at him.

She used to look at me like that.

It wasn't just Aethan's steps that halted. His heart stopped beating. His mind refused to accept what his eyes clearly showed him.

Neither of them noticed him or Aslyn, completely taken with one another. Cavis leaned closer to Iskra and she closed the gap.

As they kissed in familiar ways reserved for Aethan, the world dropped out from beneath him. Everything stilled. His hands trembled at his sides, curling into fists.

"Don't," Aslyn said softly, taking one of Aethan's hands, easing the fist open, and gently tugging him back around the corner.

But Aethan couldn't look away. Nothing about the way Cavis and Iskra kissed was chaste. The truth of what he witnessed made something deep inside of him whither up and die.

Aslyn pulled harder. Aethan stumbled after her, too stunned to think for himself.

"Elisio, we need a few minutes alone," Aslyn told her guard.

Aethan sank onto a bench in a hedge alcove. His gaze dropped to his hands and he studied them, wondering how he had made such a mess of this. Why was it that everything he touched shined like the sun yet burned him?

Aslyn hiked her skirt again and kneeled in the gravel in front of him, taking his hands. "Aethan, I'm so sorry."

"Did she ever love me?" he asked in abject misery.

"I'm sure she did at some point."

"How...?" He choked on his own breath and swallowed thickly. "If she did, how could she have moved on like that so quickly? It hasn't been that long."

Aslyn pulled in her lips and chewed on them in sympathy. The corners of her amber eyes scrunched as she reflected that sympathy back at him.

"I have nothing," he muttered.

"It might feel like that right now, but I assure you that isn't true. You could have your choice of any woman you wanted."

Any woman. Except the one he wanted. Aethan's anger burned bright in his blue eyes. "I don't—!" But he cut himself off as Aslyn winced, and he realized he was shouting at her. Aethan took another deep breath. When he spoke again, his anger burned in each growled word. "I don't want *any* woman."

Aslyn's heart cracked in two for Aethan's obvious heartbreak. He didn't cry. Aslyn wasn't certain he did that often. Yet the misery etched into his face, creasing otherwise smooth features. She wanted to fix this for him, make it all better, but there was nothing she could do.

He had entered this agreement with her so that he could win Iskra back. Judging by what Iskra had said in the royal box a week ago, and the way she had been so obviously enraptured with Cavis, Aslyn knew Aethan had lost her just as certainly as he did.

But to hear Aethan Starkling give up...

"You are helping me," Aslyn said gently, "allow me to help you."

Aethan lifted those beautiful blue eyes so full of defeat and she wanted to pull him close.

But he instead pulled away and stood so suddenly she would have fallen on her backside had he not grabbed her arm and pulled her up as well. Aslyn stumbled into him, her own traitorous heart skipping as he steadied her in his arms. Then Aethan retreated.

"I need to be alone," he announced, shoulders slumped and head hanging.

Aslyn worried that this would affect his performance tomorrow and she whirled around as he strolled away, hands in his pockets.

"Aethan, you can't let this defeat you," Aslyn said, hustling a few steps toward him.

Aethan stopped, glancing over his shoulder. "Winning is all I have. I won't throw that away."

Encouraged, she shuffled closer and reached for his shoulder as she spoke. "Maybe we—"

Aethan again pulled away. "Goodnight, Aslyn."

CHAPTER 23

Lessons and Swords

Aethan Starkling kept his comments to himself over breakfast, and it required the strength of Justis to keep from glaring at Cavis. Every time he glanced at the other man, all he saw was the way Cavis held Iskra, touched her... kissed her. He left breakfast early, unable to stomach sitting at the same table with Cavis while the man smiled and joked and acted chummy.

Trystain picked up on Aethan's mood and followed on his heels.

"Care to tell me what has you so upset?" Trystain asked, matching Aethan's stride as he chewed up the rug on the way to get himself ready for the events of the day.

"No."

"Is it that Umbrian brute Bryse?" Trystain asked.

Silence.

"Marek?"

Silence.

Trystain sighed. "Maybe it will help to get it off your chest, Aethan. Whatever it is."

They reached Aethan's door, and he considered turning his friend away. But Trystain was the only person here he trusted—aside from Aslyn and Sybil. Maybe Trystain had a point. Telling him the truth might help him focus better during the matches today.

He motioned Trystain into the room, then closed the door behind them. Roric had left before breakfast to ready Aethan's equipment for the day. The two men were alone.

Aethan let it all out. What happened with his father and Iskra before leaving Mordelic, the details of his agreement with the princess, what he saw last night. Everything poured out.

When Aethan stopped, Trystain blew out a breath, leaning back on the sofa. He studied Aethan, who paced the floor in agitation.

"That sucks," Trystain finally admitted. "I know you love her. I ... I can't even imagine what it would be like finding Sybil like that with someone else. I might consider killing him, so you're already a few rungs better than me."

Aethan relaxed a little. It had felt good to have his friend commiserate. "I don't know what I'll do if I have to face him in these matches. Especially today."

Trystain nodded thoughtfully. "You'll do exactly as you always do, because it's who you are. You'll face him in a fair fight and conduct yourself honorably." Trystain leaned forward and winked. "Just don't lose to him."

Aethan couldn't help but chuckle and shake his head at his friend.

"I'm serious," Trystain said, but he grinned jokingly. "If you lose to him, *someone* will have to pick up the pieces, and I intend to be busy with your sister. Maybe the princess will decide to step in."

For all his joking, Trystain wasn't wrong. Aethan knew Aslyn well enough now to understand she would be at his side to hold him together. Somehow, that made him feel a little better.

The mood shifted, and the two of them headed toward the staging area to prepare for the day.

Bast Blackblade arrived in Stormvalor the night before the sword fighting matches with far less gold than he would have liked. He took a room at an inn near the arena under his new name—Zayne Khrahar—and chatted with other men and women about the events so far.

Becoming Zayne Khrahar meant packing away his usual leathers and hiding his sword. He visited the best tailor in the city to get measured for suits "appropriate for his station at the events in the arena." He also had to hire a maid and a guard to truly adopt his new persona. Of course, his new employees had no clue he was not Zayne Khrahar. Only the Lord of the Harbor knew.

Bast learned the truth of what had happened since the start of the tournament—the weak, the vicious, the favored—as well as the odds for or against each of the competitors in the next part of the tournament. Official standings were guarded by the Gamemaster, but several bookies all over Stormvalor had unofficial records. The top five names were all Bast needed for the next day.

Bryse, Marek, Aethan, Ryker, and Cormic. Though a few other names crept close to their ranks.

Those were the men he would watch to place his bets today and increase his coin reserves. Bast also bet on an underdog from Novavito named Cavis. His odds of winning each round of the event were slim, but a few people Bast had chatted with from Novavito insisted they knew of Cavis' skills, and that he should be a top competitor for the event. He placed a fairly moderate bet on Cavis, hoping it would pay off.

Once he had his winnings, Zayne Khrahar would make his grand entrance into high society in the arena itself with a very generous bet on the event winner.

Bast also heard rumors from some of the Elpisian visitors. Dumb rumors that made his irritation rise to new heights. The Saints of the Seven were coming. The prophecy was already being fulfilled. Sadly, they thought Starkling was one of the signs. A bunch of fanatic garbage as far as Bast was concerned, and they were feeding off the excitement of the events to draw more believers to their cause.

Spectators pressed into the stands in droves. Bast slid easily into the crowd as he made his way into the arena. All along the walkways, merchants set up shops for each of the competitors, selling pennants, kingdom flags, wooden swords carved with names.

Bast judged how well-loved competitors were by how busy those merchant shops were. The mass crowding the Starkling shop was by far the largest. No doubt the merchant would sell out before the event began.

The difference between the people who waited at the Starkling shop versus that of the Umbrian Beast, as Bryse was called by the people, showed a wide difference between the two men themselves. Where the Umbrian Beast fans were large and crass with those around them, the Starkling fans were more reserved—though no less loud in their devotion.

None of this made sense to Bast. He wasn't the sort to buy into a spectacle. Nor did he harbor illusions that waving a flag would get someone's attention in a crowd full of flags. Were it not for this job—and the threat of exposure—he wouldn't have come at all.

If Bast thought the noise outside the arena had been riotous, it was nothing compared to the thunder of voices he heard as he stepped into the spectator stands.

One by one, competitors strode onto the arena floor as their names were called, waving at the crowd.

Bast lifted his gaze to the private viewing boxes above, seeking out the princess and positioning himself across from her box so he could study her reactions to the matches. Knowing how she felt about certain competitors would be easier to discern by observing than by trusting the word of strangers.

From so far away, Bast couldn't see much more than her dark hair and richly bronze skin, but the princess was unmistakable as she stood in her box, cheering for Aethan, Trystain, and Marek when they stepped forward.

The first round of matches comprised twelve rings on the arena floor. Each competitor was paired off and put in a ring, and all twelve matches happened at the same time. Bast watched Cavis closest. If Cavis made it to the final six, Bast would quadruple his bet. If he made it to the last match, that would double again. And if he won, that would double again. But just to be safe, Bast had also placed money on Aethan, who everyone called an "expert swordsman".

In Bast's experience, few men were anywhere near skilled enough to be true experts. They often died quickly and easily to his own blade.

Curious about their skills regardless, Bast observed each fight carefully. The competitors certainly were more highly trained than most. Some were more graceful, smooth, and swift while others struck blade against blade with brutal strength. And one-by-one, the matches ended. Thankfully, both of Bast's bets remained in the event.

The winners were given a brief break to cool down and get refreshment brought by their squires.

The second round lasted a little longer than the first as skilled swordsmen fought for the upper hand. Blood dripped from the weapons, but so far no one had fallen from serious injuries. Gorim won his match first, making quick work of his opponent. Next was Trystain over Vinter, then Aethan over Rett.

But three battles continued to rage. Cavis and Ryker appeared nearly evenly matched, but Bast noted the way Ryker favored his right leg. If Cavis was smart, he would see it and use that to his advantage. Bast almost wanted to shout it at the man—he would gain a small fortune if Cavis won, after all. But his voice would never be heard over the thunder of other voices all around the arena.

In another ring, Marek launched a vicious attack on Cormic, driving the man back step after step. Cormic's heel stepped out of the ring, naming Marek the winner.

A moment later, Cavis had Ryker on the ground with the match-ending swing that would have been lethal had the man not slowed his swing to mearly kiss the skin of Ryker's neck instead.

Only one match remained. Competitors circled the ring to cheer the two men on, and Bast watched the way Aethan called out to Borin, pointing out the way Bryse's heel shifted as he recovered from a swing.

But it was all Borin could do to keep Bryse from impaling him. The Umbrian Beast struck again and again, and though his movements were slow, the strength behind each blow forced Borin to take just as much time to recover before blocking another strike.

Aethan shouted something at Borin, pointing. Cavis joined Aethan, encouraging Borin as well.

Borin caught on just as Bryse's sword swiped for his neck. He ducked and threw his shoulder into Bryse, pushing the big man back. Bryse's sword awkwardly swung downward across Borin's back, but too low to do any damage. Before Bryse could recover, Borin shoved him back. The Umbrian Beast stumbled and landed flat on his back. Borin's blade tipped Bryse's neck.

For a moment, it looked like the match was over, but Bast knew what would come next before Bryse even moved. The Umbrian Beast wrapped his legs around Borin's, throwing him to the ground in one smooth, vicious motion.

And then he was over Borin, sword swinging down. A few of the competitors lunged forward to stop him, but someone at their backs spoke a word that froze them in place.

Borin's head rolled across the arena floor.

Bryse raised his bloodied sword high in victory.

And people cheered.

Bast had a stomach for death, without a doubt, but this was nothing more than bloodsport.

What were these people cheering for?

Aslyn nearly vomited on her box floor as she watched Borin's head roll. He had won the match. Or should have. She hadn't met Borin herself, but knew Aethan had traveled with him. They both hailed from Mordelic.

By the time she had recovered, the body had already been removed and workers combed the dirt as if it could make the puddle of blood disappear. Aslyn swallowed hard, pressing her palms against her stomach as if that would stop it from churning madly.

"Do you need to return to your room?" Queen Giata asked, sincerely concerned for her daughter's wellbeing.

Aslyn shook her head. With Aethan and Marek still in the running to win, she couldn't leave. Aethan needed her support. She couldn't stop seeing the utter devastation on his face last night.

Bryse had been escorted to one side of the competitor's staging area, where the Gamemaster and a few other officials spoke with him.

On the other side of the space, Aethan sat with the other Vorovesti competitors. She had expected him to be a mess, but instead found him offering comfort and what could only be words of encouragement to his countrymen. One of their own had fallen, and whatever Aethan said must have inspired some kind of courage, because they all now looked at him in grim determination. And Trystain's grip on the hilt of his sword tightened.

Aslyn chewed her lip, wishing she knew what they said to one another.

Most of the others crowded around the Vorovesti men—around Aethan.

All but the Umbr competitors. Aslyn watched Marek, lingering between the two groups like he wanted to go to the Vorovesti, but the tether of loyalty to his own countrymen kept him away. As activity began anew in the staging area, preparing for the next round, Marek broke away and walked over to Aethan.

They exchanged a few words and nods, then parted ways as Marek's name was called for the first of three matches.

Marek won against Trystain, though it had been a good fight. As the next two competitors were announced, Aslyn thought she might be sick all over again.

It only left Aethan with one competitor...

Bryse.

Aethan had never hated anyone before. Dislike, certainly, but never hate. It was such a powerful emotion it could overcome all logic.

But Aethan hated Bryse. He had half a mind to return the favor Bryse had paid Borin when they faced off.

And they *would* face off. They were the only unmatched men remaining.

Marek had attempted offering condolences and apologies. Aethan accepted the words, but deep down, he wasn't certain he had it in him to truly feel like Marek cared. The man followed Bryse's orders and threw hateful words Aethan's way. It had taken great willpower to refrain from reminding Marek they would never be friends.

As Cavis defeated Gorim with mountains more honor than Bryse would have, Aethan turned to find Roric already at his shoulder. The boy offered the freshly cleaned sword and shield.

Aethan took his sword but waved off the shield. It would only slow him down.

Roric paled, glancing past Aethan at Bryse as he readied himself, but the boy didn't argue.

The ring for this match was significantly larger than his first match, which was good. It gave him more room to move around. His speed would be his ally.

The Gamemaster waited for the two of them in the center of the ring—which was little more than a line drawn in the dirt. Bryse grinned viciously at Aethan as he strolled closer.

"I expect a *clean* fight, gentlemen," the Gamemaster warned, glaring at Bryse as he stepped back to give them space.

Aethan almost laughed. Bryse wasn't capable of fighting clean, and if Aethan allowed himself to doubt that for a second, he would join Borin in the afterlife.

"No shield, princeling?" Bryse taunted. "Give up already?"

"I won't need it against you."

Bryse's grin transformed into a sneer. "I'll have fun with your princess once I've handed you defeat."

Aethan laughed this time, never taking his eyes from Bryse's. He wanted to distract Aethan for a hard, unexpected blow. But Aethan wasn't born yesterday.

"Something funny, prick?" Bryse hissed.

"If you think the princess belongs to anyone, you're a fool. Besides, Aslyn would never degrade herself with gutter trash like you. You're so far beneath her you couldn't even touch her boots."

Bryse snarled, swinging his sword to loosen his wrist. "I'm going to enjoy this."

"I doubt it." Aethan shifted his feet without breaking eye contact. "I won't even break a sweat."

As Aethan hoped, Bryse growled and surged forward. But his swing was predictable. Aethan simply spun out of the way, tapping the flat of his blade against Bryse's back. The crowd roared with cheers as the fight began.

Bryse recovered, executing several practiced maneuvers in a row. Aethan easily dodged and parried, and as they pulled away from one another again, blood dripped from Aethan's sword.

Bryse's eyes widened in rage as he realized that blood belonged to him.

"You're slow and your moves are predictable," Aethan said, arcing his sword to fling the blood away. "Try again, but this time, watch where your feet are going as you swing, or you leave yourself open to another strike."

The beast roared and surged toward Aethan.

Bast watched the fight in rapt fascination. Perhaps Aethan deserved a little more credit than Bast had initially given him. The man handled himself like a trainer teaching a student. And the Umbrian Beast truly became his namesake as he roared and charged and fought like a wild animal.

Having been in more than his share of sword fights, Bast knew when an opponent was pushing his advantage, as well as which strikes would deal the most damage. But Aethan remained composed, utterly unflapped and uninterested as he continually sidestepped.

The crowd didn't like this fight. It didn't stack up to their expectations as Aethan toyed with the beast. But as Bast watched Bryse's blood drop into the dirt, he knew where Aethan struck. The injuries wouldn't kill Bryse if they were treated soon. Nor would they do long-term damage.

But the beast had slowed because of them.

Aethan tucked a hand behind his back and held his sword ready, taunting the beast.

Bryse stepped back, listing slightly to the side. And when he moved forward again, not only could he not lift his sword, but he crashed to his knees.

Bast smirked as Aethan kicked the sword out of Bryse's weakened grip. Then he spun toward Bryse's back, used his boot to push the beast to his hands, and pressed the edge of his blade to Bryse's neck.

Bast admired the man's skill.

Aethan leaned toward Bryse, knowing the man wouldn't be able to move quickly enough to do much of anything. But just in case he tried...

"Try anything before they announce my name, and my blade will repay Borin's debt," Aethan hissed.

Bryse froze.

Aslyn held her breath as Aethan fought Bryse—or schooled him in sword fighting, more accurately. It made her heart hammer harder as she watched him move with calm, practiced ease, landing strikes no one noticed until the blood started dripping from his sword.

And then the match was over. The Gamemaster called Aethan's name.

Before pulling away, Aethan shoved his boot down on Bryse's back as he withdrew his sword.

Then he turned straight for her, offering a bow.

Aslyn giggled in a way that made her mother beam.

CHAPTER 24

A Dance of Blades and Feet

The final match would be a true test. All three men would face one another all at once. Aethan knew that after the way he had put on a show against Bryse, Cavis and Marek would probably gang up on him.

Thankfully, Aethan had experience with that kind of fighting.

Roric cleaned the sword without a word, but the awe on the boy's face when he handed the sword over had been hard to mask.

Admittedly, it felt good to show Bryse just how inconsequential he was in this event, but Aethan knew he would pay for it later. Bryse might target Aslyn to get back at Aethan.

As with the other events, women were allowed to come and offer favors to the final contenders. Aslyn hadn't come down since the joust, but with both Aethan and Marek on the arena floor, it didn't shock him when she emerged with her guard close on her heels.

He and Marek both straightened as she emerged.

Aslyn's gaze flicked over at Cavis. Aethan followed her gaze just as Iskra stepped forward and gave Cavis the favor, as well as a kiss on the cheek.

He swallowed his anger for the moment and returned his attention to Aslyn. She studied both Aethan and Marek for a moment. If her mother had her way, Aethan would get the favor again. But he knew Aslyn well enough to know that she would give it where she wanted—not where her mother ordered. In fact, she might just give it to Marek to defy her mother if the mood struck her.

Not that Aethan truly wanted it. Yes, it would keep his father happy a little longer, but he knew Aslyn took her quest to find a husband seriously—even if he thought Marek was a terrible choice.

"Gentlemen," Aslyn said, and they both dropped to a knee and bowed their heads to her. "You certainly haven't made this moment easy on me."

Even the spectators had fallen silent, as if they, too, wanted to hear what the princess said.

"Aethan."

As she said his name, he raised his gaze. The sun shone in her amber eyes, making them glow. He held his breath as he waited to see what she would say or do next.

"I'm quite proud of how you performed today." The unspoken words rang clearly to him. He knew what she wanted to say. That his struggle last night had worried her, but he performed admirably as promised. None of those words could be said aloud or people would wonder what had happened.

"Marek, you showed integrity when you offered condolences to the Vorovesti competitors," she said.

Marek raised his gaze to meet hers.

Aslyn stepped forward, and Aethan's heart drummed louder than the crowd.

She slipped the ring of flowers around Marek's sword, then kissed his cheek. No matter that Aethan had expected her to do as much, his blood still thrummed with wild energy as his breathing shortened.

Especially as the crowd reacted in shock and Aethan realized this would hurt.

Because his father would be certain to call him in to exchange words about losing his grip on the princess. And it only proved what Marek had said to him correct.

Aslyn would have chosen Marek in that jousting match. Aethan hated that feeling.

But not nearly as much as the gloating look Marek shot at him the moment Aslyn turned and walked away.

"Ouch," Cavis muttered.

"I don't need your sympathy," Aethan snapped as he stood.

"Touchy."

Marek snickered.

Aethan rounded on Cavis, trying to maintain as much as a calm, confident front as possible in front of the packed arena, but fury burned in his eyes. "Were you planning to tell me about Iskra?"

Cavis blanched. "It isn't... I mean, I hadn't intended..."

Aethan edged closer, smiling for the crowd but glaring at Cavis. "Don't tell me what you intended. I saw you last night."

Cavis worked his jaw as he struggled for words.

Aethan stopped close to his chest. "Nothing to say for yourself?"

"She approached me," Cavis said quickly. "And Seven Gods help us all, but I ... I didn't find out about you until a few days ago."

Marek perked up as he adjusted his sword belt, like he thought he might gain some further advantage against Aethan.

Aethan deflated as the truth hit him. Iskra hadn't even mentioned him?

"Why?" Aethan asked, suddenly breathless. Though he wasn't sure what exactly he was asking. Why didn't she mention him?... Or why Cavis?

"I... I love her. And I'm sorry. I really am." He meant it. He really was sorry. "By the time she told me, I thought you and the princess..."

Aethan nearly laughed.

Marek snorted, bringing them back to the moment. He lifted his sword and slid Aslyn's favor off the blade, holding it out to his squire like a prized trophy. *Arrogant prick.*

"Poor sap," Marek said as he strolled out into the open arena floor. "You lost both of them."

The words punched the last of the air from Aethan's lungs as he shuffled after the two of them.

Iskra chose Cavis.

Aslyn chose Marek.

He *had* lost them both.

Or maybe he never had them in the first place.

As the match between the three of them began, Aethan moved slowly, watching Cavis and Marek both for signs of movement in his direction. In these kinds of bouts, offensive moves usually signaled some kind of alliance. But none of these three were allied.

Aethan fought to keep his breath even and block out all his failures. Not a half an hour ago, he had toyed with Bryse until he was on the ground. Aethan could handle this. Neither of these men had the training he did. Marek's father was a military leader for the emperor, so that might not be entirely true. He supposed it made sense that Marek might actually have received better training. And Cavis was hand-selected by his king. What made him stand out?

Marek moved in a flash, forcing Cavis back with one stroke of his sword while pivoting to attack Aethan on the backswing. Aethan easily deflected the attack, then stepped in closer to force Marek back.

In a matter of seconds, the fight between the three turned into a dance of blades and feet. Any time one of them found an opening to attack another, they struck hard and swift before backing off.

All of Aethan's taunting against Bryse worked against him. Now these two knew what he was capable of and wouldn't make the same mistakes. They respected his space, striking fast and darting out of the way.

Sweat dripped down Marek's face and into his eyes, forcing him into defensive maneuvers. The sun burned bright in a cloudless gray sky overhead and cast shadows just long enough for Aethan to see the shadows moving more dramatically than his opponents.

Marek lunged while Aethan's back was turned, and Cavis shouted, thrusting his blade between the two of them. Aethan had just enough time to recover from a stumbling step and turn with his sword raised before Marek landed the blow that eliminated Cavis from the fight.

Had Cavis just sacrificed himself for Aethan? Was it an act of guilt?

Aethan shuffled backward to create space, then wiped the sweat from his own brow as Marek turned his attention fully on him.

"I believe they call this *nal'kali*," Aethan mused.

"What's that mean?" Marek asked, taking the moment to recover himself.

"Ancient elvish for a fate that's meant to be. You and me. Here. Facing off. *Nal'kali.*"

Marek snorted, assuming a defensive stance. "Brains won't save you from this, Starkling."

"Tell me why you follow Bryse," Aethan demanded as he circled the other man.

Marek narrowed his eyes. "Why?"

"You outrank him back home, I assume," Aethan said casually. "What does he have on you?"

Marek gritted his teeth and lunged. Aethan parried and struck Marek's side. But the blade came down at an odd angle to block his attack. Determination twisted Marek's face, and he recovered and launched a series of vicious attacks that made Aethan wonder just how closely he had struck to some truth.

Did Bryse have some kind of blackmail against Marek? Was that why Marek constantly glanced his way before speaking to anyone not from Umbr? What did Marek have to hide?

And how would it affect Aslyn?

"He's going to hurt her, Marek," Aethan said as he defended against the vicious assault. "You know it just as well as me. If you care about her, protect her from him."

Marek snarled.

Marek's feet finally gave him away the moment before he launched another attack.

Aethan sidestepped, deflected, then sliced the winning blow into Marek's leather-covered stomach. He gave a final shove with his free hand to be sure he kept his opponent off-balance enough to risk a counterattack that would keep the match going.

Marek stumbled sideways and fell to a knee.

Aethan struck quickly, tipping his blade to Marek's throat.

As much as he wanted more answers, he didn't dare ask now. Marek probably never would speak of it. Instead, he simply said, "Help me protect her from him."

The crowd thundered with delight as Aethan was named victor.

Aethan reached out to help Marek up.

The other man glared at him but took the hand and rose. Something gleamed in those dark eyes. Resolve. Understanding, perhaps.

And as they stared one another down, warning in both of their gazes, Aethan knew he would have to get to the bottom of whatever secret Marek held. But he also knew Marek would protect her. It was to his own benefit if he did.

CHAPTER 25

Haunted and Hunted

Aslyn's dark red dress whispered over the stone floor of the arena corridors as she glided to meet with Marek. Elisio dogged her heels, making his dislike for the Umbr man known. But he was worse than Aethan, assuming that because he had shared her bed, he knew the first thing about what she wanted or needed in a partner. Just like Aethan assumed he knew because he was of royal birth. Neither of them saw the pieces Marek revealed to her. They didn't truly know him as she did.

The number of Black Guards patrolling the corridors increased significantly. Aslyn didn't like it. What brought these deadly shadows out of the darkness and into the light?

She swallowed as she entered the private garden. Elisio took up position near the entrance, hand on his sword and eyes on her.

The space had been transformed. Glittering lights strung along tree branches, creating a miniature patio around a table and chairs in the center of the small space. Wisteria fluttered from vines and trees as if a wind called them to dance around her.

Marek stood beside the table, a white rose in his hand. Aslyn couldn't help but smile. She adored white roses. The purity of the delicate flower always reminded her of the innocence of her youth and the potential for a better future.

When she reached him, the smile on his face was forced. He held out the flower to her, and she graciously accepted.

"Sit," he said, motioning toward her chair. But the way he said the word sounded more like a command than a request for her company.

Still, Aslyn eased into the seat, sweeping her skirt around her legs as she did.

The table played host to a miniature feast. Roasted duck with steamed vegetables and smashed potatoes. Marek poured each of them a glass of red wine from Murandy Hills—the finest wines in the realm.

"I'm glad we could meet tonight," she said sweetly as she sniffed the delicate bouquet from her wine glass. "I was worried you wouldn't be up to dinner after..."

Marek's jaw twitched. "Yes. Thank you for reminding me I once more lost to Starkling." There was no humor in his tone.

Aslyn frowned. "I'm sorry. I didn't mean to upset you. I just—"

"You know, it would be nice if we could get through a conversation without you bringing him up." Marek took a generous drink of his wine, then sliced viciously into his duck.

Aslyn tensed and sensed Elisio watching them like a hawk from the side of the small garden. "I won't apologize, if that's what you want. I'm not sure I appreciate your attitude."

Marek snorted, stuffing a forkful of meat into his mouth. He chewed with as much anger as he had cut the meat. After he swallowed, he finally met her gaze. And something dark and dangerous burned his eyes. "What's his deal, anyway? He was talking about Cavis's woman, too."

Iskra. She had given Cavis her favor and not even spared Aethan a glance.

"Excuse me, what do you mean, *too*?" she asked as his words fully sank in. Was he implying that Aslyn belonged to him now?

"I mean he got in Cavis's face for stealing away that blonde chick like he was after her *and* you," Marek said sharply.

Aslyn folded her hands in her lap, her plate untouched. "That's *not* what I was asking, Marek. Are you trying to say I'm yours?"

Marek took another drink and resumed eating as he said sharply, "I don't know *what* you are."

What was wrong with him tonight, commanding her to sit, snapping at her with every statement? And now what? Was he angry because she hadn't strictly defined whatever was happening between them?

Aethan's warning rang out in her mind. Up until tonight, Marek had never raised his voice with her and had kept his temper in check.

She needed time and space to process this change in him. Aslyn tossed her napkin on the table and stood. "We're done here."

"What?" Marek hissed.

"I don't have to sit here and take this. I'm leaving." Aslyn made it two steps before Marek was on her, his grip on her arm painful as he pulled her back around. She tugged at it to wrench herself free, but his grasp was too tight for her to shake.

Elisio's boots thumped against the ground, chewing up space between the two of them as swiftly as he could.

"Let go," Aslyn growled.

"Please, don't go." Something in Marek cracked open and his eyes turned desperate, worn out, sorry. "Please."

Steel sang against a scabbard as Elisio began drawing his blade.

Aslyn held out her free hand to stop Elisio before it was too late. "Let go, Marek. I won't be manhandled like this."

He immediately released her, bowing his head. "I'm sorry. I shouldn't have..." His voice trembled.

Aslyn waved Elisio back. Marek wouldn't do anything more. Not in this state.

"Please forgive me," he whispered, sorrow bleeding from every word.

Aslyn cupped his face and forced his gaze up to hers. Were those tears in his eyes? "What happened, Marek?"

He drew in a deep breath, pressing his cheek into her palm. "My father arrived today." He sounded beaten. "Just in time to watch."

Recalling what Marek had said about his father's expectations, Aslyn's heart broke for him. No doubt their interaction had not gone well. She stroked his cheek. "I'm sorry. And I'm sure I didn't help matters."

Marek hung his hands limp at his sides, and his shoulders sagged. "It isn't your fault. I shouldn't have acted that way. He has this way of getting under my skin."

"How about we sit back down, and you tell me all the ways you would like to teach your father a few things about family and manners?" Aslyn smirked at him.

Marek forced a small smile and nodded.

The rest of dinner went better. Marek let loose a string of horrific ways he would teach his father a few lessons. The specificity made her wonder just what Marek's childhood had been like. Eventually, he lightened up and started joking again, the way she was used to him acting.

The entire time they ate and talked and held hands, Elisio glared at Marek like he wanted nothing more than to run him through with that sword. Aslyn was just thankful they had averted a fight between the two men.

At the end of the night, Marek walked Aslyn back to her suite, stopping down the hall, just away from the sight of the other guards posted outside the door. His hand tightened on hers. Not possessively, but affectionately.

Aslyn turned to face him.

"Thank you, Aslyn."

"For what?"

"For letting me vent. For listening... For not running away." Marek edged closer, and she liked the way his body heat warmed her skin.

He reached up, tenderly touching her face. "I want to kiss you so badly."

Aslyn remembered how she rejected his first attempt. Marek had been respectful of her wishes since then, but she could see how hard that struggle had become for him. She was also very aware of Elisio watching everything they did.

Still, she licked her lips and leaned into Marek's massive chest, standing on her toes. He leaned closer.

"This is permission, in case you haven't noticed," she whispered.

Aslyn barely finished her sentence before his lips brushed over hers with so much heartbreaking tenderness. It wasn't a greedy or hungry kiss, but more of a show of how deeply he cared for her.

What made the moment worse for Aslyn was the realization that, as his lips brushed against hers, she thought of someone else. Someone she couldn't have. Someone who didn't want her.

Aethan.

After Marek showed how vulnerable he was tonight, Aslyn wasn't about to give him any hints of this. Instead, she gently broke away from the kiss and smiled at him. "Goodnight, Marek."

He grinned at her. "Goodnight, beautiful."

CHAPTER 26

Their Idol and Champion

Bast Blackblade stood on the balcony overlooking the city, examining the dark storm clouds that rolled in. Last night, he had met with the Gamemaster after some persuasion. By the end of the conversation, he had been given a luxurious suite inside the arena with promises that his requests would be carefully fulfilled.

Of course, the ridiculous amount of gold Bast had given the man had made a difference. Thankfully, both of his bets on the sword fighting had paid out handsomely.

During his stay in Port Verix, Bast had persuaded the Lord of the Harbor to create a new wealthy identity for him. Flashing all his wealth in the man's face helped, though he had lied that it was just a drop in the bucket. The Lord of the Harbor had greedily eyed the gold and jewels, instantly forgetting to ask *why* Bast would need his help or a new identity.

The papers the Lord of the Harbor had provided not only helped Bast find the "help" he would need during his stay, but it had made the Gamemaster see gold every time he looked at Bast.

"Your things are all settled in your room, Lord Khrahar," Esterly said, dipping into a curtsy so deep he could see right down her dress. Not that he wanted to stare. She was homely looking. "And I've confirmed the tailor will be here with your requests by dinner."

Lord Zayne Khrahar. His new name for the duration of his stay. After his mission was completed, Zayne would mysteriously die, leaving behind only gossip about who he was and what had happened to him.

"Thank you, Esterly," he said. "I've left a list of supplies I will need during my stay. See to that, will you?"

"Of course, my lord."

He needed a maid and a guard at the very least to keep up appearances. Esterly had been the first hire. Delvin, the guard, had been the second. Esterly hired a chef as well, insisting that Lord Zayne Khrahar needed to eat well during his stay and have a reputable chef in case he invited visitors.

The only visitor he would even consider allowing into his suite would be the princess. He had to earn her trust.

But first, he had to get in front of her. Thankfully, that was well in hand, too.

The atmosphere over dinner put Aethan Starkling on edge. He joined his father and sister in the Starkling suite, a set of rooms not too unlike his own, except for the view from the balcony of the city of Stormvalor. Vines of wisteria climbed the columns outside.

Dark clouds over the city reflected the mood at the Starkling table, like a pending storm waiting to break. Those clouds had grown closer since the previous evening, now shrouding the entire city of Stormvalor.

Sybil picked delicately at her food across from Aethan, hardly speaking and only casting him empathetic glances. He wanted to speak to his sister alone, but his father seemed determined to dominate his time.

Already, his father had harassed him about Princess Aslyn giving "that Umbrian trash" her favor instead of Aethan. Then he proceeded to pick apart every way Aethan was failing at his task. Nevermind that Aethan already festered in a foul mood because of Cavis and Iskra.

All morning long, the competitors were confined to their hallway, not even allowed onto the training ground. No one explained why. Even Roric had been unable to leave their hall to learn more. But something about the way the Umbr competitors smirked at everyone else and whispered to one another made Aethan's skin crawl.

By the time they were given free rein to move again, Lord Starkling had sent the invitation for Aethan to come see his family—though calling it an invitation was more than generous. Aethan had known if he didn't come, his father would have hunted him down.

Lord Starkling had also been less than pleased with the way Aethan had toyed with Bryse. Apparently, it made him look arrogant and unsympathetic to the spectators. Aethan gritted his teeth through that, snapping about showing Bryse he wasn't as special as he thought he was, that he deserved far worse for what he had done to Borin. Not that Lord Starkling had cared. Oh, it had mattered to him that an Umbrian had killed a Vorovestian, but that was as far as it mattered to his father.

"The next event has been delayed a few days," Lord Starkling said, either oblivious to his children's tension or just not caring at all. "The Gamemaster and I have spoken at great length just this morning. Two new suitors for the princess arrived today. He wouldn't tell me who they were no matter how I pressed, but he informed me that one of them holds enough sway to force the Gamemaster to host another ball... tomorrow."

Sybil's eyes snapped up from her plate, widening at that.

Aethan's shoulders tightened. Did his father expect him to speed things along and get a promise from Aslyn earlier? "Why?"

Lord Starkling picked the meat off the bone on his plate, and his mouth set in a grim line. "There will still be a Champion's Ball, but that event will now take place after the final event, where the winner will be announced. This other ball has been added at the insistence of one of these new arrivals. I'm dying to know who this is if even *I* couldn't hold sway with the Gamemaster."

Tomorrow? Aethan didn't mind attending galas. He enjoyed the drinks and food and dancing. Yet this one filled him with dread. Iskra would be there.

With Cavis.

"Obviously the attire you brought along for Champion's Ball cannot be worn twice, so I've had a tailor create a new suit for tomorrow," Lord Starkling continued. "But we all need a strategy for the next twenty-four hours."

Aethan settled back in his seat, no longer hungry. Sybil seemed put off her appetite as well. In fact, her face had gone slightly paler. Did she already know what was about to happen? Perhaps that explained her strangely silent behavior tonight. Had she Seen something about this ball?

"I've taken the liberty of inviting the princess to visit you tonight," Lord Starkling informed Aethan. "Whatever you have done to turn her favor toward that Umbr man, undo it. Fix whatever you broke before the ball."

Fix it. There was nothing to fix. He and Aslyn had an agreement, but his father couldn't know that. "I assume I'm to monopolize the princess' time at the ball," Aethan said flatly.

"That will hardly be enough," his father said. "If this new suitor has gone to such trouble with the Gamemaster, it's safe to assume he won't allow you to horde Princess Aslyn's time." His gaze flicked to Sybil. "Which is where you come in, dear. Your job tomorrow night is to keep these two men busy and charm them both. I want them so busy fawning over you they forget about the princess."

Sybil swallowed hard, flicking a glance at Aethan. Worry shone in her eyes.

"What about Trystain?" Sybil asked, her voice meeker than usual.

"What about him?" Lord Starkling didn't even have the courtesy to look at his daughter, despite the obvious distress in her voice. It made Aethan angry. "His performance has been lacking. I can't say I've been impressed."

Aethan clenched the arms of his chair to mask his anger, but it grew hotter, in danger of bubbling up. Trystain was a top ten competitor, knocking on the top five door. His performance had been anything *but* lacking.

"Daddy, I—"

"Don't, Sybil," Lord Starkling said lowly. The warning cast in her direction silenced her protest. "I haven't promised Trystain Cyrus anything. If he finishes in the top five, we can return to this discussion and review your best options, and I will give a marriage contract to whoever you choose from those options, but not a moment before. Meanwhile, you will do as you're told. And right now, I am telling you to put on your best simpering charm and keep these men away from the princess."

Sybil muttered her agreement.

Aethan ground his teeth. Would he become like his father one day, ignoring the desires of his own children in favor of power and position? *Morumbris take me if I end up like him*, Aethan thought bitterly. He would welcome the god of death.

Trystain would be furious when he learned of this conversation, and Aethan couldn't say he blamed him. Sybil had been all but promised to Trystain for years. They loved one another. If Aethan's happiness had been shattered, he would do everything he could to preserve his sister's.

"What kind of honor does this family have if we continue offering something and taking it away when it's no longer beneficial to us?" Aethan asked darkly.

Lord Starkling jaw ticked. "If you understood the situation—"

"But I don't. Because you only tell me anything when it benefits *you*. You were perfectly pleased with the idea of me marrying Iskra until you caught wind of something better."

"Better for you!"

"According to you," Aethan hissed. "I have half a mind to win the princess over not to give you what you want, but to get away from you."

Silence fell. None of them moved. Sybil didn't even breathe as father and son stared one another down.

Lux hadn't competed in the Stormvalor tournament in his youth. He was too young the first time it rolled around, and too old the next.

His father broke the silence first. "Do you have any idea what you stand to gain even at this moment, Aethan?" Lord Starkling set down his wine glass gruffly, then pushed back his chair and stood. "Come with me."

Aethan leaned back and crossed his arms. "No."

Lord Starkling waved a hand toward the open balcony doors. "You're acting childish. I only want you to step out there."

Aethan snorted, glancing at his sister before grudging standing. He would pick the rest of this fight carefully for her. He tossed his cloth napkin on his plate and marched toward the balcony.

The evening breeze cooled his flaming face, and Aethan breathed in the familiar scent of the flowers to try and calm his temper. Lamps flamed brightly on the balcony, making the gold on Aethan's jacket glow.

Below, people moved along the city streets, free to live their lives however they saw fit. Aethan envied them. He was trapped in this arena for the duration of the tournament, but worse, he was trapped under his father's thumb forever.

"I have acted as steward to this city for nearly twenty years," Lord Starkling said. "But our family, the Starklings, have controlled it for longer than we've had an emperor. During the War of Two Crowns, our ancestors barely held on to this place. I refuse to fail our people here. But when they look up at this balcony, do you know what they see?"

Aethan rested his hands on the rail, leaning against it. He shook his head.

"Watch them for a minute and you will," Lord Starkling said almost sadly.

So Aethan observed, curious where his father was going with this and what it had to do with the princess or their family.

Starkling banners hung from the balcony rails, proudly showing off who resided here. Aethan watched them flutter on the breeze, their sapphire blue swaying gently. The setting sun glinted off the golden family sigil. The same one tattooed over his heart from birth.

Stormvalor bustled with teeming life. Aethan could see it all even from this distance. People milled around the arena imbibing drinks and dinner, sharing songs and gossip. Coins traded hands as bets were placed.

Then gazes began turning upward to the balcony where he stood with his father.

More and more gazes, accompanied by voices cheering and chanting "Starkling".

"They don't look up here and see me, their lord and steward," Lux said. "They see you. Their idol and champion."

The truth of those words settled over Aethan, a weight pressing down on him. He knew he had fans, but he had never considered the implication of a Stormvalor lord competing... and winning.

"None of this is about me, Aethan." Lux motioned toward the crowd cheering for his son. "It goes beyond my name, beyond a stewardship or a crown."

Aethan eyed his father curiously, knowing the truth lingered just a few words from his father's lips.

"Aethan," Lux lowered his voice, stepping closer to his son. "I don't push you out of greed for myself, but for your future. Emperor Oxon is losing power. His son will take over soon. Rumor has it Prince Valen is in search of a new wife. His last, it seems, died of an unexpected illness. The future of the realm is... hazy."

Those seven words made Aethan's stomach flip. Was the emperor's reign in danger? He had been loyal to the realm, though maybe not as much as to Vorovesti. He wasn't sure how to feel about the possible implications of a threat to the empire. Did his father want this union to solidify support for the empire then?

Aethan turned toward his father to ask, but his father spoke first.

"You're starting to understand. Imagine what you, a Stormvalor Champion, could do when allied through marriage to one of the most powerful kingdoms in the realm with the full backing of the King of Vorovesti?" The somberness on his father's face made Aethan's heartbeat increase. "I'm not doing this for me, or for power, Aethan. I'm doing it for you. For *everyone*."

He waved his hand out at the crowd on the street below.

"But it won't matter if you don't *try*."

Try winning Aslyn over. Try getting her to understand the potential dangers ahead of them. If his marriage to Aslyn could truly do so much, Aethan would only go against his own moral compass to refuse. The people wanted, *needed* a figurehead they could look up to; someone they admired and who adhered to codes of honor and valor to protect the realm. His life—his pride—was not worth more than the safety of the five kingdoms of Divica.

"Can you do that, son?"

Aethan nodded grimly.

Lux Starkling patted his son on the shoulder and left Aethan on the balcony to consider his words.

The future he wanted was gone.

But the future of the realm could be in his hands.

Winning the tournament was no longer for pride, glory, or prestige.

A slyn eyed the ominous clouds over the arena—the city of Stormvalor as a whole—with much discomfort. Though she walked the corridors of the God of Storms revered home, something about those dark clouds left her uneasy. Storms broke over the Aryth Mountains back home often enough, but they had never looked so dangerous.

She couldn't even chalk these clouds up to the god himself. Where one time this could have been interpreted as a sign that Justis watched the tournament, Aslyn felt no such reassurance.

The invitation to visit Aethan had been a surprise. She assumed he would want time and space after learning the truth about Iskra and Cavis. Perhaps he needed friendship more than space.

As she strolled down the competitor's corridor with Elisio in her shadow, Aslyn overheard bits of a conversation between two of the Elpisian competitors.

"Perhaps the god has not gone," Von said to Yun. "It's possible he's just been waiting for a worthy champion to make his reappearance."

"And you think that's Aethan?" Yun asked, doubt threaded thickly in his voice.

Aslyn slowed her pace and subtly shifted closer to their open door.

"He's winning," Von replied. "So far, anyway. And the people were chanting his name tonight. And his family has ruled over Stormvalor, Justis' home, for longer than we've had emperors."

Their voices began fading as Aslyn continued. She couldn't stop and listen without someone noticing, and Elisio was certainly watching her every move. But one series of clipped words drifted to her, and it made her breath catch high in her chest.

"...Slumbering Hero ... Saints of the Seven ... Cavern of Lost Souls... Champion..."

Did the Elpisian competitors believe Aethan to be the legendary Slumbering Hero? Of all kingdoms tied more closely to lore and prophecies and the gods, Elpisio won by a long shot. Their entire ruling class based themselves on such things.

But the stories Aslyn heard of the Slumbering Hero could never be Aethan. Not as she was taught. The Hero was a child of a human and an elf, cast into eternal slumber until the time came to fight against the growing darkness. A Martnarving heir, now long gone, the line extinguished by ancient emperors.

Once more, she glanced at the ominous darkness overhead.

No. She couldn't allow herself to buy into such rumors and myths. The storm simply rattled her nerves.

As for the Cavern of Lost Souls, that was another myth, a cave in the southern ocean no man could find, let alone enter. According to legends, the Isles of Storm protected the immeasurable power collected in that cavern from unworthy souls. One day, a worthy champion would arrive to harness that power to use...

...against the growing darkness.

Aslyn paused outside of Aethan's door, closing her eyes and taking a breath to center herself. She couldn't let children's tales rattle her. She was a future queen.

Aslyn raised her hand to knock, but the door opened and Roric, Aethan's squire, squeaked in alarm before opening the door wide and bowing out of her way.

"He's waiting, Your Majesty," Roric said.

"Thank you, Roric." Aslyn offered the boy a smile that lit up his face with pleasure. Then she eased around him and into the main living room, Elisio steps in behind her.

Aethan stood with his back to Aslyn, facing the closed doors leading into the competitor's courtyard beyond. His hands were buried deep in his pockets. It seemed heavy thoughts plagued him just as surely as her.

"Aethan?" Aslyn motioned for Elisio to take up position near the hallway, then crossed the room, sidling around furniture to join him. "How are you doing?"

"I have no idea how to answer that," Aethan said softly. The sincerity in his voice touched Aslyn's heart. "You first. How is Marek?"

She stopped beside him at the doors, peering into the dark courtyard. An eerie hue of gray fell over everything outside. She studied Aethan's profile, the determined set of his jaw and sharpness of those blue eyes as he peered into the darkness as if searching for something.

Something about him had changed. Aslyn couldn't place what, but she could see plainly he was not the same man he had been before the last event.

"You don't really care about him, do you," she said, not bothering to ask. "He was surly over dinner last night. I didn't appreciate his attitude and when I said as much and tried to leave, he grabbed my arm and begged me to forgive him."

Anger flashed in Aethan's eyes as he met her gaze. His jaw twitched. "He did *what?*"

"You are all emotionally wrung out," Aslyn said, trying to placate that anger. "He saw his mistake swiftly and let go, but..." She sighed, turning her own gaze out the glass doors. "I'm a bit worried that his behavior does him little credit under harsh circumstances. Something I cannot afford to have at my side while ruling my kingdom."

Something like relief softened his face. "So you've eliminated him from the running."

She bit her lip and shook her head. "Not yet. As I said, you've all been through a lot, and yesterday was a stressful day for everyone." Aslyn turned toward him, placing her hand on his arm. "Which makes me wonder how you are truly doing, Aethan. Between what happened with Iskra and being forced to watch Bryse kill Borin, I'm worried about you."

Aethan's eyes searched her own, and Aslyn saw the uncertainty in him, the fear, but also the determination. She could get lost in those bright blue eyes, and not for the first time she lamented his disinterest in her. But she also respected his decision.

"Is that the first time you've seen death?" Aslyn asked softly.

Aethan shook his head but swallowed so hard she heard the sound. "I saw my mother die... but that was different. She..."

He dipped his gaze away and stepped back from her. Aslyn took his hand and edged closer, offering comfort. For a moment, he just stared at her, and when he spoke, Aslyn's heart broke for him.

"She simply grew weak over time," he said quietly. "She just withered up like something sucked the life-force right out of her until... Until there was nothing. Emperor Oxon came to see her and speak with my father and uncle before the funeral. They performed the Flames of Inspiration and burned her body." He shook his head.

Aslyn knew the ceremony. With the disappearance of the gods, Fiara's funeral rite had become the most popular choice—committing the body to flames in honor of the goddess of flame. Many believed the Goddess of Fire and Sin was the only one who remained. Long ago, when people had stopped worshipping her, Mt. Fjaroe had erupted, belching dark clouds and spilling lava as if in warning. Judging by the way Aethan's face twisted slightly, Fiara's funeral rite had not been his mother's plan.

"Aethan, I'm so sorry," Aslyn murmured, squeezing his hand.

"It never made sense to me," he whispered, breaking just a little more over each word. "Anyway, yes. I've seen death. But what Bryse did was murder, plain and simple, and the Gamemaster doesn't seem to care. Apparently, it's part of the risk."

"That's horrible."

Aethan snorted in disdain. "Can we talk about something else?"

"Sure." Aslyn let go of his hand, missing the warmth of his touch, and leaned against the back of the sofa. "Why you invited me here would be a good place to start."

"Right." Aethan straightened, forcing a smile for her that she knew he didn't feel. "I hear there is a ball tomorrow. I was hoping you would allow me the honor of escorting you."

Aslyn's breath caught. Escorting her was as close to a date as any of these suitors could hope for, and it would formally put him in front of everyone quite publicly as her main choice. But he hadn't wanted this, or her, or a crown before. Had something changed?

Aslyn wanted to say yes. Instead, she settled for, "Is that a question, Lord Starkling?" Then she offered him a coy smile.

Aethan chuckled, but even that sound was forced as he struggled with his own emotions. He took her hand and brought it to his lips. Aslyn's heart skipped. No, it was in her throat. No, it had stopped completely. "Your Majesty Aslyn Kiernan, Crown Princess of Novavito, would you allow me the honor of escorting you tomorrow?"

Aslyn swallowed down the immediate yes that leaped to her throat. She teasingly peered down her nose at him. "I will have to think on it."

His face fell slightly.

She smirked. "I'm sure I will have an answer for you by lunch tomorrow." She gave him a humored curtsy, then glided toward the door, refusing to look back.

But she could feel his gaze burning into her as she went. At the door, she paused and gave him a sultry smile. "I have a feeling my answer may be a positive one."

And before slipping out, she caught him smiling.

CHAPTER 27

A Terrible Trap

By lunch, Aslyn had sent a message stating when and where they should meet to enter the ball together. Aethan eagerly made his way to meet with her, excited to spend some time with her.

The arena corridors were crawling with Black Guards as Aethan made his way to meet Aslyn. He hadn't seen so many in years, since his mother's funeral. Aethan was dying to know what could have caught the Black Guards' interest. Was it simply because of the tournament ball, or was there more to it?

"The future of the realm is... hazy."

Perhaps this increased guard presence had something to do with what his father had hinted at last night. He wished he had been allowed to carry a blade for protection. Not for himself, but for Aslyn. Would she be in danger tonight?

Lost in his worry, Aethan had absently found his way to where he was to meet with the princess. A hushed argument up the corridor drew Aethan to a halt.

Elisio faced the princess in formal guard attire. At least *he* had a sword on his hip, small and ceremonial as it was. That sword was better than nothing, which was all Aethan had to offer.

The anger on Elisio's face intrigued Aethan. The guard's neck had tensed with suppressed rage. His shoulders were tight, as if fighting the urge to keep himself in line.

Aslyn stood before Elisio, hands on her hips, chin high.

Seven Gods help him. She was stunning even with her back to him! Her hair had been swept up off her neck, yet a few black curls brushed her skin. Sparkling stones hung from her hair, reflecting nearby lights with each subtle movement. The back of her dress hung in silken folds down to the middle of her back, while the short sleeves hung precariously at the edge of her shoulders. And the way the shimmering golden silk clung to each curve of her body...

Aethan had always been aware of Aslyn's beauty, but tonight, even the stars in the sky didn't sparkle and shine with as much ethereal grace as the princess. In fact, Aethan had never seen anything so utterly perfect.

Aethan swallowed, momentarily forgetting himself.

After only a few steps toward the princess and her guard, their argument stopped dead with a cutting glare from Aslyn to Elisio. The guard eased a step back, hand resting on the hilt of his short sword. And the look Elisio gave Aethan made pieces click into place, though he didn't yet see the full image.

Aslyn turned toward Aethan, giving him a full view of her perfection.

The dress hung in silken folds perfectly over her chest. Up close, Aethan noticed the fine needlework roses stitched over the bodice in matching gold. Yet when the light caught those roses, they popped with life.

A diadem rested high on her forehead before vanishing into the twists and folds of her hair. At her throat, a glittering diamond-studded necklace displayed a locket of fine golden vines wrapped around a sterling silver book and latch. In the center of the locket, a large, brilliant emerald stone.

Aethan heard stories about that locket—the locket that doesn't open. The Jewel of Arithia, said to bind itself to the soul of the Novavito royal in possession of it. A symbol of hope and birthright.

More than the dress—which only made her more stunning—or the necklace, above the perfectly styled hair and manicured fingernails, beyond the way her golden dress made her deep, rich bronze skin glow, was the way her eyes lit the moment she studied him.

Glowing eyes of sun-kissed amber left Aethan hopelessly breathless.

He was in trouble tonight. Not because he had decided to take his father's request seriously—that part he was certain he would enjoy.

No, Aethan Starkling would find himself unable to relinquish the princess to another for a moment all night. And if one of her suitors persisted, Aethan grew increasingly worried about how he might react.

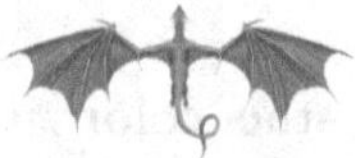

The moment Aslyn laid eyes on Aethan, all the anger she had felt toward Elisio a moment ago vanished. Everything about his suit made his carefully styled blond hair and sky blue eyes so pronounced Aslyn momentarily lost her own thoughts.

Seven Gods help her. He was the most beautiful man she had ever seen.

The various deep shades of blue in his suit complimented him perfectly. The ascot that spilled from the lapels on his gold-embroidered jacket was such a deep shade of blue it reminded Aslyn of the night sky. The golden dragon sigil of House Starkling danced along the dark ocean blue of his jacket lapels and cuffs.

"I hope I haven't kept you waiting long," Aethan said, offering his arm.

Aslyn swallowed as she slid her arm through his. He hugged her arm a little closer to his side, and the warmth of his body made her own skin heat.

"No, you haven't." Aslyn heard the quiver in her voice and prayed he didn't notice.

"I assumed you prefer to make an entrance," Aethan said as they turned and headed toward the nearby hall singing with festivity. Aethan's gaze slide along her dress, and his eyes danced in a way that made her heartbeat increase. "Though in that dress, you could make an entrance no matter when you arrived."

A flush crept across her cheeks. "Will you be slathering me with compliments and thick charm all evening?"

He chuckled, and Aslyn hated the way it made her body respond. "Yes. I've heard I have two new suitors to contend with tonight. Wouldn't want you slipping off with one of them instead."

All the excitement slid out of Aslyn and she sighed. "I've heard the same, but my mother doesn't know who one of them is yet, and she's never heard of the other. Apparently, he comes from new money. A lot of it."

They entered the main corridor and were met with a host of attendees milling about. The décor spilled into the massive foyer outside the ballroom, along with a slew of people in rich dresses and tailored suits. They glittered with wealth from all five kingdoms in Divica.

Everywhere, hints of blue—the color associated with Justis, God of Storms—hung from rafters or adorned tables. Stardrift and wisteria floral arrangements added a breath of sweet air to what would soon be a mass of sweating wealthy attendees.

Aslyn clung to Aethan's arm tighter, pulling him to a stop before they could venture into the belly of the festivities. Already, curious gazes turned toward them, whispering about the favored competitor accompanying the princess.

"Are you feeling unwell?" Aethan asked, placing a hand over the one she rested on his arm.

"No, it isn't that," Aslyn said. Aethan deserved the truth before they ventured much further. "My mother was thrilled when I told her you asked to accompany me tonight. Beyond thrilled, actually."

Aethan seemed to understand there was more. "But?"

"I was strongly advised that I should be sure to make some time to learn what I can from these new suitors." Aslyn's heartbeat drummed against her ribs as she peered into his beautiful sky blue eyes. "I can't do that if you are with me."

Something flashed in his eyes. "Do I at least get the honor of walking you through the door?"

"Yes, of course. I didn't mean it had to be right this moment." Aslyn couldn't bear to see that look in his eyes. Disappointment. But she knew him well enough now to know he wouldn't complain. "I just don't want you to be alarmed."

Aethan smirked and gave her arm a gentle tug toward the massive arching ballroom doorway. "That's funny, because my father was explicit about preventing exactly that. Give me an hour of your time before you abandon me, will you?"

Aslyn flinched. "That's not fair."

"I was teasing, Aslyn," Aethan said, patting her hand as they reached the doors. "Relax. An hour. That's all I ask."

Aslyn nodded. She could give him one hour before parting ways. And she would find her way back to him, because she wanted everyone to see her leaving with him.

Lux Starkling would be furious. Aethan knew it for certain, but if Aethan wanted any chance at fulfilling his father's wishes, he had to respect those of the princess as well. Hopefully, if Aethan could dominate an hour of Aslyn's time, surely that would help alleviate some of his father's anger. It also gave Aethan a chance to do what he could to charm Aslyn before they parted ways.

From the moment everyone saw him arriving with the princess on his arm, whispers began. The more time they spent together as the evening wore on, the louder those whispers became.

Marek had glowered furiously at Aethan every time they crossed paths, but his exchanges with Aslyn were suave. Far too suave for Aethan's liking. Marek didn't bother hiding his overt interest, touching Aslyn's arm every time he thought he could get away with it. When Aslyn told Aethan she wanted to introduce him to someone, Marek had kissed Aslyn's hand and asked her for a dance before the evening was over. Thankfully, she hadn't given him a promise to follow through.

The two of them moved around the massive ballroom, eating, drinking, and dancing. Aslyn's face opened up the longer they spent time together. All of his jokes and charm had softened her to him in ways he hadn't seen her soften to anyone else all evening. Despite how he felt about her upon arriving in Stormvalor, and how much of a fight he had put up in the weeks following about allowing her in, he found himself softening to her as well.

They laughed and told one another about their upbringing as they danced, and the march toward the end of his hour loomed so close it made Aethan ache to consider parting ways.

When she spoke of her brother Dorin, Aethan could tell Aslyn loved her brother as he did his own sister. The way her face lit up as she told stories of their childhood made something inside of him light up as well.

"So he climbed the wall because he was afraid Captain Shino would catch him," Aslyn finished her story, pure amusement making her eyes water. She laughed and Aethan laughed with her.

"Why didn't he just put his hood up and slip out with the other guards like he planned?" Aethan asked, bemused.

Aslyn shook her head, grinning. "Dorin has always been terrified of Captain Shino. Ever since he was a boy and the captain caught him trying to sneak out of the castle during the Ember's Blaze Festival. Captain Shino forced him to run laps around the training ground until he collapsed to 'work off his youthful energy'. And then the captain told our father, and he was forced to spend the next month shadowing our father everywhere."

Aethan chuckled. That sounded like something his own father would do.

Aslyn pressed on, telling more stories about her youth. Her most recent story made something deep within him stir to life. Apparently, her father understood she would need to know how to wield a sword in defense of her kingdom, so for several years, Aslyn had been trained by the best Master-at-Arms in all Novavito. She had befriended many of the guards during that training, and now she could outmatch many of them. Aethan realized she knew her guard Elisio better than most. They likely had trained together growing up.

"The guards even gave me a nickname," Aslyn said, like it was a badge of pride.

"And that would be what?" Aethan guided them through the steps of their dance without a thought. Even after nearly an hour, he was still undeniably drawn to her.

Aslyn's cheeks flushed at his question, and she dipped her gaze away. He adored this shy, reserved side of her. "No, it sounds stupid."

"Now I have to know," he teased.

For a moment, she said nothing as she gathered the courage or dignity to reveal her secret. When she spoke, her words sounded as pained as she looked. No, not pained. Horrified. "Princess of the Sword."

Aethan bit his lip to keep from laughing out loud, but his shoulder shook just enough for her to notice with her hand on his arm. Aslyn's amber gaze snapped to him.

"Do not mock me!" Her eyes widened as she made her firm declaration. "I could put up a good fight against even you, Aethan Starkling."

"Should I shudder for my status as future Stormvalor champion?" he asked in amusement.

"Maybe you should," Aslyn said, lifting her chin arrogantly. But the amusement shone on her face as well.

Aethan spun Aslyn out away from him, then pulled her close against him. "What a dangerous pair we would make, then."

The air between them instantly thickened as Aslyn's startlement shone. All humor vanished, replaced by a charged energy. But the look she gave him was not one of mutual affection. It was uncertainty and fear. He kept his hand on the small of her back, absently moving his thumb over the silken barrier. It required every ounce of his willpower not to stare at her lips and imagine what they felt like. And he certainly couldn't kiss her for the first time here, in a ballroom full of witnesses.

Has she kissed anyone else? He wondered. No. He didn't want to know. Marek likely had kissed her, or at least tried to.

Her voice assumed a serious gentleness he didn't like as she said his name like she was about to say more, to reject the very notion of them. He couldn't have it. Not tonight.

Before she could say more, Umbr horns sounded and the music cut out. Black Guards marched into the ballroom in perfect formation. Attendees voiced their fear and alarm at the intrusion as the guards edged everyone out of the way, headed straight toward the two of them.

Aethan's heart jumped into his throat. He spun Aslyn beside him, wrapping a protective arm around her.

The crier in the doorway announced the newest arrival. "All hail and make way for Heir to the Imperial Throne, His Imperial Majesty, Prince Valen the Exalted, First of His Name, Future Emperor of Divica."

And as Prince Valen strode into the ballroom to hushed whispers and thousands of watching eyes, Aethan realized in horror who one of these new suitors would be.

A small entourage trailed the prince, their gazes sweeping over several of those in attendance, as if picking apart every piece of them in an instant. But it was the prince Aethan couldn't look away from.

Prince Valen was only a couple years older than Aethan and blisteringly handsome, from his pale white hair to the chiseled cut of his features and those depthless pools of darkness in his eyes. His black suit was as dark as a void. Even his fine boots bore no scuffs—nor any reflection of light.

A small retinue followed near his heels. A woman with black hair and a man who reminded Aethan of the Vorovesti ambassador, Zambul.

Each step drew Prince Valen closer and closer to Aslyn.

Aethan's grip on her waist tightened, and he realized she trembled. But he couldn't tuck her behind him. Not only would it not stop the prince, but Aslyn would undoubtedly resent him for making her—a future queen—appear weaker in front of so many.

Lord Starkling materialized at Aethan's shoulder away from the princess, hissing in his ear. "Do not allow her time alone with Prince Valen."

Aethan startled, not expecting his father to come out of nowhere. When he glanced back, Lux's eyes were on Prince Valen as he drew closer.

Aethan held his breath as the prince neared, muscles coiling tight. He wasn't sure why instinct told him Valen was dangerous, but with Aslyn huddled close to him, Aethan couldn't help but worry.

Hardly a whisper passed through the room as everyone watched Prince Valen stroll through the corridor across the ballroom floor that his Black Guards had created for him.

Aethan's heart hammered all the way up his throat. Aslyn placed a hand over his on her waist, grasping his hand tightly.

Prince Valen strolled right past with hardly a glance at the princess. Aethan frowned at the prince's back, wondering who could have his attention if not the princess.

Then he saw Sybil with Trystain not twenty paces ahead of the prince's path.

Sybil had gone ghostly white.

Lux hissed softly in anger.

Prince Valen stopped dead in his tracks, depthless eyes locked on Sybil.

"Lady Sybil," Prince Valen said, his commanding voice carrying to every corner of the ballroom and beyond. "I've traveled a long way to meet you."

"No…" Lux's protest was little more than a breath across Aethan's shoulder, but he felt the anguish and tension in that one breath, regardless.

Now it was Aethan's turn to tremble as Prince Valen held his hand out to Sybil. Aethan couldn't breathe. Everything moved so slowly. Trystain gripped Sybil's hand and arm in both of his own hands as if ready to whisk her away from the prince.

All eyes were on the two of them.

Sybil licked her lips nervously, completely drained of color, and slid her free hand into Prince Valen's offered hand despite Trystain's murmured protests.

Prince Valen bowed and kissed Sybil's hand.

Trystain gave her a gentle tug, so subtle anyone could have missed it were they not looking directly at him.

"Could I have a few moments of your time, Lady Sybil?" Prince Valen asked.

Behind Aethan, Lux had gone as still as death. Aethan was certain he had as well.

Sybil licked her lips again and said in a shaky yet sweet voice, "Of course, Your Imperial Highness."

"No, Sybil, no." Trystain's protests were dark and muted, but hadn't missed the prince's notice.

Prince Valen turned back to the woman in his entourage, whispering something to her. She nodded, her black hair shifting like muted red flames with the movement. A trick of the light, no doubt.

Sybil politely recused herself from Trystain's grasp, stepping closer to the prince. The mysterious woman with the prince stepped toward Trystain. He tensed, shuffling back a step like readying for a fight. But the woman simply smiled at him and said something Aethan couldn't hear. Trystain relaxed ever so slightly, nodding at her.

What just happened?

Sybil held Prince Valen's hand as he marched her to the center of the ballroom. Something told Aethan he had to stop this, whatever *this* was.

When the prince stopped and pulled Sybil close to him, Aethan took half a step forward, but his father's hand fell hard on his shoulder, squeezing painfully tight.

Music began anew, and Prince Valen whisked Sybil around the dance floor, her sapphire skirt swirling.

When Aethan looked for his best friend, Trystain had vanished along with the prince's female companion.

What had he and his father discussed just last night? That Prince Valen's wife had died... and he was on the hunt for a new one. He traveled a long way to meet Sybil, that's what he said. And just like that the pieces fit snuggly, perfectly, together.

No. Not Sybil. Not my sister...

Aslyn said something to Aethan's father, then took Aethan's hand and gently tugged him away toward the garden doors and the evening beyond. Aethan resisted at first, but didn't want to draw attention to himself.

"Fresh air will help," Aslyn cooed as she guided him along.

With the emperor's heir in the room, fewer people took notice of Aethan and Aslyn. Prince Valen *never* made appearances.

As the two of them walked out together, Marek caught Aethan's eye. And he was grinning like he had just won a match.

Aslyn didn't stop until they were far enough from the ballroom that the music faded to a distant hum.

The cool air filled Aethan's lungs but did little for the burning in his heart. Freshly bloomed weeping willows lined one side of the gravel path, surrounded by flower buds far from bloom. Overhead, that ominous sky remained as if understanding his mood and the atmosphere inside.

"Aethan..."

"He didn't even look at you," Aethan said, too stunned to respond appropriately.

"I'm not surprised." She stepped closer.

Aethan shook his head. "He can't have her. Not my sister!"

"Hush," Aslyn hissed urgently.

"We all have a path to walk, Aethan." Sybil had spoken those words back in their family temple in Mordelic. And then she drew a promise from him. *"Stay the course. No matter what. For me. Carry on with strength, honor, and valor."*

Aethan thought he might be sick. Had Sybil known then what would happen tonight? Surely Prince Valen traveling all the way from the Umbr Palace to Stormvalor couldn't be for anything but what he suspected. And that look on her face tonight. The utter fear and defeat... and acceptance.

Aethan gritted his teeth as red-hot fury rushed through him like fire. He clenched his fists. "He can't have her."

Pivoting on his heel, Aethan marched back toward the ballroom. Lightning crackled through the dark clouds overhead, but no thunder sounded.

The storm, it seemed, would finally break.

"Aethan stop," Aslyn called after him, her elegant boots scraping against the gravel in her haste. She rushed around and pressed her hands against his chest.

He veered to sidestep around her.

Aslyn grabbed his lapels and yanked him back. "Stop! Listen to me. Please. You cannot interfere. It doesn't matter how many people adore you right now, Prince Valen will have you killed if you interfere."

Aethan scoffed. "He wouldn't go that far."

Aslyn's eyes shone brightly, urgent and certain in the moonlight. "He would!" Aslyn stepped closer, smoothing out the lapels now that she was certain he wouldn't flee immediately. Her voice lowered so no one nearby might overhear. "I don't know what Emperor Oxon is up to, but before I left Arithia, my father warned me about the emperor's ambassador. He was worried Umbogo would try to trick me into giving away the crown with an Ambassador's Promise. That's why I must find a husband before returning. I can't give him an inch to seize."

Aethan tried to connect Aslyn's reasoning, but the fury in his veins clouded his thoughts.

"If what you suspect is true, and the prince is here for your sister, they are playing a bigger game," she continued. "If his ambassador cannot trick me into marriage, he has to keep us apart."

"Why?" But even as Aethan asked, he knew the answer. His father had given it to him just last night. The power of their kingdoms united through marriage. Aethan groaned. "But my sister—?"

"Prince Valen cannot court me," Aslyn said. "My brother is fair game to any other kingdom's heir, but not me. An heir cannot marry an heir."

Aethan knew this rule. It was the reason King Orrin had wanted Aethan to be in this position instead of his own son. Gannon and Aslyn couldn't marry under current empirical rules. None of the other kingdoms had a daughter for the prince—or at least not one eligible for marriage. Elpisio had no heirs at all. Vorovesti had a crown prince but no princess. Novavito had a crown princess and a prince, but no spare daughters. Oshon... They had already given their daughter to the prince, and she had died.

Sybil was the next closest thing to a royal—their mother had been a princess. And if Sybil left Vorovesti...

"A Starkling must always rule over Stormvalor," Aethan muttered. Another fact his father had reminded him of just last night. Did he truly not know that Prince Valen had arrived at the time? And it didn't fully make sense. There was no law stating Aethan couldn't rule Stormvalor from elsewhere. His father ruled over the city largely from the capital. What did Prince Valen really want with his sister? "But she's in love with Trystain."

"I know." The sympathy in Aslyn's voice made some of Aethan's fury dissolve. "But your king cannot refuse the match. Nor can your father. Not without committing treason against the empire."

Aethan hated these rules he had spent a lifetime fighting to obey. Prince Valen couldn't just walk in and claim his sister like that. She should have *some* say in what happened to her!

"We all have a path to walk, Aethan."

That truth brought tears to his eyes. Sybil somehow had known what fate had in store for her, and if she was given a choice, she would choose her path with the prince. But *why*? Why would she sacrifice her own happiness, her love?

Aslyn held Aethan's face in her tender palms. He deflated, resting his forehead against hers. "What can I do to help you, Aethan?"

Aethan closed his eyes and breathed her in. "Don't let go of me just yet."

Aslyn's thumb stroked his cheek. "I wasn't aware I had a hold of you in the first place."

He opened his eyes again, peering into her brilliant ambers. "Yes, you are." His lips inched closer to hers. "You've had hold of me for longer than even I realized."

Aslyn's head spun with heady excitement as Aethan's confession settled over her, his lips inching slowly toward her own as if waiting for her to close the sliver of distance between them. The scent of wisteria and blackberry currant filled her senses. A smell so sweet and gloriously, wonderfully Aethan. Willow leaves rustled on the breeze, and a song of love and triumph hummed from the distant ballroom.

Seven Gods, Aslyn was falling for him.

"Your Majesty," Elisio's voice shattered the spell.

Aethan pulled back, but only a little, and he continued holding her against him.

"Not now, Elisio," Aslyn called over her shoulder. Where had he come from? How long had he been listening and watching them?

"Her Majesty Queen Giata has summoned you," Elisio said evenly.

Aslyn sighed heavily, overwhelmingly disappointed that this moment had been stolen from her. If she found her mother and had not been summoned, but instead had been interrupted by a jealous Elisio, Aslyn would end him.

Aethan eased his hold and pressed her hand to his soft lips. Her heart skipped and disappointment writhed in her stomach. She wanted those lips on her own, not on her hand. She had craved it since Marek had kissed her. Perhaps even before that.

"It's fine," he reassured her. "I should find Trystain. Besides, my hour is up. You still have a suitor to meet."

He tucked his hands into his pockets as he turned down a garden path away from her.

"Aethan?"

He paused, turning back to her.

A hundred statements ran through her head, all the things she wanted to say but just couldn't find the words for. The way this night had changed something inside of her. The way *he* had changed something inside of her. That she no longer knew if she even wanted to meet the other suitor. But none of the words came to her lips.

Aethan smiled softly. "Goodnight, princess."

Then he was gone down the paths. Aslyn turned and marched past Elisio toward the ballroom. "This had better be good, for your sake."

Elisio said nothing as he trailed on her heels.

CHAPTER 28

A New Suitor

Bast Blackblade hadn't even recognized himself when he looked in the mirror earlier in the evening. His black hair had been trimmed and styled in traditional Verixian wealth style. The suit he received just that morning from the tailor was the lightest, finest thing he had ever worn in his life. The cut formed to his figure, making it hard to hide his strength. But the dark hues of gray and burgundy complimented one another strikingly well.

The fine silver embroidery seemed a bit much, but the moment Bast entered the ballroom, he was glad for it. Every man in the room had some kind of embroidery on their jackets. The more elaborate, the higher their social rank, apparently.

Bast mingled with caution, changing the register of his voice so no one would recognize it after all of this was over. After all, he recognized a few former clients in the crowd.

No one batted an eye at Lord Zayne Khrahar. Not even the wealthy men from Port Verix who introduced him to Bryse and Marek—though it was possible the

Lord of the Harbor had bought them all off. Bryse spoke with just as much brutality as he fought. His wounds from the match against Aethan Starkling had healed swiftly, further confirming for Bast what he already suspected. That young lord knew exactly what he was doing when he incapacitated the beast. And Bryse held a grudge as pure as death itself. Aethan's trouncing of the beast had put an inevitable death sentence on his head.

Marek was a large man as well, but nowhere near as large as Bryse. He carried himself with a lethal grace that reflected his sword fighting skills. When Bryse had joked about teaching Aethan a lesson, Bast noticed the way Marek's eyes gleamed. Particularly as he glanced through the crowd at Aethan dancing with the Novavito princess. Bast stored that jealousy away for later use.

For the better part of an hour, Bast observed the princess spending all her time on Aethan Starkling's arm. The two of them laughed and mingled and ate and danced as if being in one another's company were the most natural thing in the world. That closeness would cause Bast problems. Not because he wanted the princess for himself—he certainly had no interest in her or marriage—but because Aethan would be whispering in her ear and watching Bast like a hawk the moment he thought the other man was a threat to his chances, and Bast had already seen how cunning Aethan could be.

Bast would have to wedge them apart as well, which would likely be more of a challenge than Marek.

When the Black Guards marched into the ballroom, Bast melted into the background, keeping as far from them as possible. The handsome, pale-haired, black-eyed man who trailed them created a ripple of shock as he entered. Bast silently cursed his poor luck as Prince Valen strolled in like he already ruled the world. Bast watched the prince stride right past the princess and relaxed slightly. At least there was that stroke of luck. Marek and Aethan he could handle. The Imperial Heir was another matter.

After the prince selected his dance partner and they stepped onto the dance floor together, Bast once more sought the princess, who had vanished—along with Aethan Starkling.

Cautious of the Black Guards, Bast made his way around the ballroom, peering through hundreds of heads for his target. He ventured into the garden, nodding politely to those he passed as he searched. Where had they gone?

Far out in the garden, Bast heard the hushed voices and inched closer to listen. He always had superior hearing, and it proved useful more times than he could count.

Aethan and the princess exchanged quiet, urgent words that smacked of treason against the imperial throne.

The princess is opposed to the emperor? Bast found this nugget of information immensely useful, if not shocking. And for some reason, deeply satisfying.

The frankness with which the two spoke reinforced the connection Bast suspected between them. He would have to tread carefully where Aethan Starkling was concerned. Aethan's moral compass would be his greatest weakness.

Before he could be caught eavesdropping, Bast silently made his way back into the ballroom to find Queen Giata. If he could not accidentally bump into the princess on his own, he would need to recruit the help of her mother.

And then he would worm his way into the princess' good graces.

Aslyn practically floated as she returned to the ballroom where her mother waited. The evening with Aethan had been more than Aslyn could have dreamed, and she couldn't stop wondering what it would be like to kiss him. He certainly had wanted to kiss *her*. That knowledge alone lifted her spirits.

Queen Giata held a small court near to the garden doors where fresh air could keep the smell of the sweating bodies inside away. A few lords and ladies crowded around, all of them ringed by the queen's guards.

Elisio joined that circle of guards as Aslyn stepped into the fire.

"Ah, here she is!" Queen Giata held out a hand.

Aslyn took it as she stepped toward her mother. "Sorry if I kept you waiting. I was just saying goodnight to Lord Aethan." She kissed her mother's ring before letting go.

"Has he left the party, then?" one of the young women asked, peering over heads in search of him.

A flash of jealousy made Aslyn's cheeks heat, but she smiled sweetly. "Yes, he and his friend Trystain have gone to train, I think." Aslyn was not about to reveal a hint of what truly chased Aethan away, nor his distress over his sister in Prince Valen's company. Were they still together in the ballroom somewhere? She wanted to look but now was not the time.

Watching the hope on that woman's face transform into disappointment filled Aslyn with satisfaction.

"No doubt he plans to put up a good fight in the next event," one man said. His stone-gray eyes shone as he eyed her. Aslyn wasn't sure she liked that look in his eyes—not after what nearly happened with Aethan—but he certainly was ruggedly handsome with a square jawline, broad shoulders, and a striking dark gray suit that screamed new wealth. His carefully styled hair was as black as the night sky. The way his suit clung to his form made it clear he was in peak physical condition. "I've only seen one other as adept with a sword as him. It's clear why he's a fan favorite. He's certainly *my* favorite."

A few of the women in the small court eyed this man like starving animals. He either didn't notice or didn't care.

"Aslyn, this is Lord Zayne Khrahar," Queen Giata said, motioning to the gray-eyed man.

This was Lord Khrahar? Aslyn had expected him to be... older. Men of new money tended to be more her father's age, if not older. How had Lord Khrahar come into such wealth at his age?

"He was hoping for a few minutes of your time tonight," Queen Giata added.

Lord Khrahar's gaze dipped to Aslyn's chest just for a moment with greed in his stone-gray eyes, and she swore the Jewel of Arithia warmed against her skin. Her imagination, no doubt. He barely cast his gaze downward long enough for Aslyn to notice.

The moment he realized Queen Giata had given him an opening, he smiled at Aslyn, and Seven Gods help her if that smile wasn't one of the most disarming ones she had ever seen.

"A dance, Your Majesty," he amended. "And if after that you decide my company is not to your taste, I won't horde your time a moment longer. I will respectfully bow out."

Something about the way he said that made Aslyn's hackles rise. Was that a backhanded comment about how much time she had spent with Aethan tonight?

He bowed formally, offering his hand. "If you would do me the honor?"

Aslyn glanced at her mother, who already glared at her with disapproval for how long it took her to respond.

Let's get this over with, she thought with a sigh.

"I would be delighted," Aslyn said, sliding her hand into his.

His skin was warm, hand calloused. He knew how to use these hands, unlike most of the lords in attendance. In Aslyn's experience, only men used to a hard day of work had such calloused hands, whether that be training or labor. She couldn't help but wonder which had earned him the callouses. Judging by his physical condition, she guessed the former.

Lord Khrahar escorted Aslyn to the dance floor where other couples moved through the rehearsed steps. Despite his rough hands, Lord Khrahar's touch gently rested against her waist and her hand. New wealth or not, within a few steps his grace became apparent.

"You're light on your feet, Lord Khrahar," Aslyn said, attempting to make light conversation.

"Despite what you probably think, this isn't my first ball," he said. "And please, call me Zayne."

"Zayne." Aslyn repeated the name with a small nod of acquiescence. "Are you not used to being a lord yet, then?"

They moved in nearly perfect rhythm around the dance floor almost by second nature. Zayne led so naturally he could have been born of this life.

"I try not to put labels on things," he said with a small shrug. "In my experience, such things can sometimes attract unwanted attention."

"Yet you are perfectly happy to flaunt your new lordship for the world to see here tonight," she noted, watching the way his eyes peered down at her—*into* her. It made her stomach twist uncomfortably.

"Whether or not I desire the attention, sometimes necessity dictates matters for me."

Aslyn smirked. "You mean so you could win a dance with me."

The way his face shifted as he smiled enhanced his rugged charm. "Well, who wouldn't want to win a dance with the most beautiful woman in the room?"

Aslyn laughed. "Calling a woman beautiful proves nothing of your intent."

Zayne didn't even hesitate to respond, and his words struck her to her core. "There are numerous ways to prove intent, but few would be appropriate in a crowded room."

Aslyn's face heated, and she hated that she had to look away from those intense stone-gray eyes as his meaning became abundantly clear. Her gaze landed on Marek, sharing a drink with a pretty young woman, but his dark eyes were locked on the two of them on the dance floor. She quickly returned her attention to Zayne.

"I think you are confusing beauty and desire," Aslyn said. Just saying the word desire to him made her heart race. Not because she wanted him—*certainly not!*—but because her mother would be horrified to hear what they said to one another.

"I will admit that the two are not always tethered to one another," Zayne admitted. "One can find beauty in the sunset but not desire it." He spun her, then pulled her close against him. The man was all hard muscle. Why was he not competing? The thought did little to help her already racing heart. "But in this instance, they are most certainly one and the same. However, we hardly know one another. I would presume nothing. Nor would I dare tarnish my hard-earned reputation... or yours. Still, desire is what it is."

Who *was* this guy? The way his words slid into her skin and made her imagine what he implied took Aslyn by surprise. She fought off the images of what he might be capable of as she remembered what had already happened tonight. No, she wanted Aethan. And not just because of a few slick words, but because of his beautiful soul.

It filled Aslyn with shame that she had even considered Zayne when she had been in Aethan's arms only minutes before. Aethan who wanted her and knew her.

"I've seen that look before," Zayne said, breaking her momentary spell.

Aslyn found him peering into her soul again.

"You've already given your heart to another," he said.

"I don't know if I would go quite that far," she replied, refusing the idea that she had done so. She wasn't ready to jump off that cliff yet. First, she needed to be absolutely certain Aethan wasn't choosing her because Iskra was no longer an option.

The way Zayne studied her made Aslyn uneasy, as if he truly could see her heart and soul. They continued dancing in silence for a minute—apart, together, spin, apart, twirl, together, spin. Every movement he made was far more fluid than anyone she had danced with before, including Aethan.

"If he didn't recognize the jewel in front of him from the first moment he saw you, he's a fool," Zayne said at last. "You deserve someone who will lie down everything to put the world at your feet. If he has given signs he is willing to do that, I apologize."

But Aethan hadn't. Not once. As much as Aslyn hated to admit it, Zayne had a point. Aethan had dismissed her immediately when they were introduced. He wanted Iskra. Was Aslyn his backup plan? She fought back the sorrow that thought brought to her heart.

"I am a future queen," Aslyn teased, unwilling to show Zayne her doubts. "I don't need the world when I already have it."

Zayne grinned and shook his head. "You have a kingdom. But imagine how much more you could have beside a man who would bring your enemies to their knees for you."

"I have no enemies."

"Everyone has enemies, princess."

Those words brought the emperor's threat to the forefront, and her grin froze. She did have enemies—foes more powerful than her. Umbogo, for starters. Prince Valen, perhaps. Emperor Oxon...

Zayne noticed. "Information and connections, princess. Those are the two most powerful tools in the whole of Divica. And the right man would use those tools for the woman he loved."

"And is that you?" Aslyn nearly laughed and couldn't hide that from Zayne. "Do you speak of love when we've only just met?"

"I cannot speak for love, but I *can* tell you that I saw the jewel in front of me."

Her heart thudded harder.

The song ended, but neither of them stepped back or let go. Aslyn tried to read him, as Zayne did to her. After a moment of staring at one another, Zayne lifted her hand to his lips. The way his lips caressed her skin promised what else he might be capable of. And those beautiful, rare stone-gray eyes never broke from hers.

"I hope I haven't turned you from me completely, Your Majesty," he said lowly.

"No." The word rushed out a touch too quickly.

Zayne smirked and nodded, then released her and stepped back, bowing. As Aslyn remained stunned in place for a moment, he moved to step around her.

"Zayne." Aslyn spun around. He paused, those sharp eyes locked on her. "You may call me Aslyn. And I believe I'm quite thirsty after that dance."

A ghost of a smile curled his lips. "An honor, Aslyn. Let's get you something to drink."

Aethan hadn't expected Trystain to wander too far from the ballroom. Not with the threat of Prince Valen looming over Sybil. As he made his way through the corridors near the ballroom searching for his friend, he was caught up in numerous minor conversations from which he had to politely interact before slipping away from his fans and well-wishers. Several young women had requested a dance, from which he politely declined, saying he needed to prepare for the next event. Each one had pouted in disappointment.

Trystain, meanwhile, had been nowhere near the ballroom. The longer Aethan searched for his friend, the more concerned he became. He had openly defied the will of the imperial heir by clinging to Sybil in front of hundreds of witnesses. What if Trystain had been quietly escorted away for punishment—or execution?

Worry lodged itself in Aethan's heart, growing stronger and more overwhelming the longer he searched. The training grounds. The competitor's courtyard. The meeting rooms. The arena. Trystain's private suite.

Nothing.

Panic took root in place of worry.

The best way for Prince Valen to eliminate his competition for Sybil's attention was to actually eliminate him. And no one but his own father could stop him.

Stormvalor's arena had numerous ancient dungeons, few of which Aethan had been permitted to explore in his youth. But he knew the way. If Trystain had been locked up for punishment, the prince would want him to vanish below the arena until he could be dealt with.

Aethan strolled past a meeting room, and the hushed, urgent voice within drew his attention. Was one of the Trystain? Aethan stalked toward the partially closed door, peering cautiously inside.

Within the room, Aethan recognized two of the men—Bryse and Marek. Bryse stood beside an older man who bore a striking resemblance to Marek. Bryse's arms were crossed over his massive chest and a glint of triumph shone in his black eyes as he stared down his fellow competitor. Marek's back was to Aethan as he faced the older man, probably his father.

"But it's going well," Marek quietly protested. "I would rather not risk that."

"I didn't ask what you wanted," Lord Bloodstone growled at his son. "I gave you an order and I expect you to obey me, boy."

Marek's shoulders sagged slightly and he held his hand out. Lord Bloodstone pressed something dark into Marek's palm. Aethan squinted to try and see what it was. A black stone of some kind. Before he could truly see more, Marek slipped it into his pocket.

"Be careful with that," Lord Bloodstone warned his son. "It's highly dangerous, understand?"

"Yes, sir," Marek said. "I promise to be careful with it."

Aethan knew he had to go before he was caught eavesdropping. He quietly slipped away to find a dungeon entrance and continue his search for Trystain. But as he walked away, he wondered what, exactly, Lord Bloodstone had given Marek.

As Aethan approached a secret passage he had discovered during one of his many visits as a boy, a call drew him up short. Aethan turned to find Cavis jogging toward him alongside Cormic.

Aethan hesitated. "Shouldn't you be busy with Iskra?" He couldn't help the biting tone.

Cavis flinched. "She seemed to think *you* needed me more." His gaze slid past Aethan toward the secret passage entrance. "As usual, she appears to be right."

"I'm fine. Just looking for Trystain."

Cormic's face set in grim lines. "Yeah, we worried about him, too. He's been flapping his mouth about Sybil since arriving. We figured this probably isn't going over too well. Prince Valen hasn't released her from his company yet."

Cavis snorted. "I think it's pretty clear he won't."

Aethan felt the blood drain from his face, and Cavis flushed. "Sorry. I forget sometimes that she's your sister."

Aethan shook his head, brushing off the apology. He couldn't tell them what he and Aslyn suspected. He wasn't even sure where their loyalties lay. "I appreciate your concern, but I think I'll just finish up my search alone then head to bed."

The brothers exchanged a glance that clearly spoke some unknown language between them. Then Cavis sighed. "If we allowed you to search alone and, Seven Gods forbid, something happened to you, Princess Aslyn would likely have us flayed for sport."

Cormic nodded in grim agreement. "We're coming with you."

CHAPTER 29

Welcoming Change

As a child, Aethan Starkling had never been allowed into the underbelly of the arena. Lux Starkling insisted it was sacred ground and no place for a child. As a teenager, he had managed to sneak as far as the dungeons with Gannon and Trystain before they were caught. Aethan, of course, bore the brunt of his father's wrath—putting his friend in danger and the Crown Prince of Vorovesti at risk had been his own fault.

But those adventurous moments had given Aethan some idea what to expect when they descended the winding staircase. The steps slowly bent around the outer wall as if following the curve of the arena itself, hewn from smooth stone, before reaching the dungeons below.

The stench of the dungeons hit Aethan before his torchlight could reveal anything along the cell doors below. Piss and crap and vomit and sweat formed a toxic cloud that permeated the air so thoroughly he could taste it as he breathed.

Cavis gagged behind him, and Cormic patted his brother on the back but didn't utter a word.

All three lifted their torches high to bounce light off the low stone ceiling.

Iron cell doors with matching iron bars for windows lined one wall of the narrow hallway.

"Trystain?" Aethan called. But he doubted he would find his friend down here. There were no Black Guards.

No guards of any kind.

Their footsteps slowed and Aethan strained his ears to hear something—anything at all—in the cells, ahead, or behind them.

Silence filled the space unnaturally, penetrating so deep it made his bones tense.

"I don't like this," Cormic muttered. "He's not down here. We should go back."

He was probably right, but Aethan needed to check each cell first, in case his friend had been knocked out when they threw him in a cell. Maybe there were no guards because no one would hear Trystain scream for help. Maybe he was unconscious in one of these cells.

Aethan moved toward the first door, noting a strange rune scrawled in white chalk over the entryway. He peered through the light of the torch to the darkness beyond the door. A form shifted and hissed at the light. Aethan squinted for a better look. Its shape was unnatural, not entirely human. What did they keep down here?

As curious as he was, Aethan came here with one objective—to find Trystain—so he moved on to the next cell, and the next.

Every cell had the same white chalk rune over the door, and each held a creature cloaked in shadows. All of them hissed at the torchlight. One grew violent, throwing itself at the cell door with a rattling thud that rang in Aethan's ears. Cavis and Cormic cursed behind him, steadying him when he stumbled backward. Then as one, they edge cautiously closer.

The creature formed of shadow itself, pulling away from the light of their torches. This one appeared more human, standing on two bowed legs, clawing spindly arms and nails against the iron door.

"What the fuck is that thing?" Cormic breathed.

Aethan only shook his head.

The creature opened its mouth and screamed at them—an unnatural sound that echoed in the silence—and bared its rows of long, razor-sharp teeth. Those teeth could easily slice through flesh and pierce bone. Aethan shuddered at the thought. Why *were* they here, and for how long had they been down here already? Did his father know of this?

Cormic reached up toward the white chalked rune. Aethan pulled his hand back.

"Don't," Aethan said. Some instinct told him those runes helped contain these creatures.

Cormic frowned as he lowered his arm.

"Aethan, let's head back up," Cavis said.

Aethan nodded in agreement and turned to go.

But at the end of the long hall, Aethan spied another iron door—this one solid and seemingly impenetrable. He had never noticed that door in his youth. As he moved with cautious steps close to the door, Cormic and Cavis called to him quietly, urging him to come back. A soft light emanated from the door.

"Thousands of years ago," Aethan said to his companions as he watched the door, "the god Terralibra created this arena on the bones of Justis palace. The dark god Morumbris razed Justis's palace to the ground with his powerful dark minions during his bid for power."

The brothers muttered their discontent with where this was headed.

"And you think these things are those creatures?" Cavis asked.

"No. Not those." He didn't know what those things were. Aethan pressed on as he reached the door. "According to myths about the ancient days, Justis and Terralibra worked together to create a prison that only the gods could open. A prison to hold back Morumbris' minions." The door pulsed with soft blue light. "Many believe that prison to be beneath the Umbr Mountains, but no one can be certain where that prison truly lies."

The two fell utterly silent at his back. Aethan didn't bother looking at them as he reached toward the door.

"What are you doing, Aethan?" Cavis hissed.

"He's lost it," Cormic grumbled.

Aethan pressed his palm to the cool iron door and blue light rippled outward in waves from his palm. "What if this is the door?"

Cormic snorted. "Right. Thousands of years of searching, and a Starkling finds it not fifty feet below the arena behind a solid wall?"

Wall? "You don't see the door?"

He glanced back in time to catch the nervous glance the brothers exchanged.

"My hand is on it. It's rippling with light."

Cavis shook his head. "Sorry, Aethan. You're seeing things."

Aethan frowned and returned his attention to the door. How did they not see it? Determination to prove them wrong coursed through his veins. He pushed against the iron door.

It made no sound. It didn't even slide open.

But a moment later, Aethan stood on the other side.

Before him, a stairway spilled wider and wider into the depths below. At his back, Cormic and Cavis' voices were muffled as they shouted at him through the door. He hadn't teleported. He had simply passed through. A fist hammered against the door as Cormic shouted his name. Cavis said something about going for help.

No, my father can't know we were down here!

Aethan put his hand against the door again and pushed, and he once more stood before the brothers. Their eyes were wild with panic, both reaching for the knives in their belts. None of them carried a sword. This time, he truly had led his friends into danger.

Yet his curiosity took the better of him. Aethan grabbed Cormic by the hand and pulled him through the door.

Cormic shouted profanities, panting heavily as he realized where he now stood. He turned slowly, running the torch over the doorway to inspect it for seams.

Aethan grinned at him and moved through again to find Cavis in a panic. He held out his hand. "Come with me."

Cavis shook his head, but when he heard Cormic calling for them on the other side of the wall, he relented. And as his sweating palm slid into Aethan's, Cavis, the fierce Stormvalor competitor, trembled.

Both brothers stumbled away from Aethan the moment they were together again, eyeing him like a disease.

"Magic." Cavis breathed the word with a mixture of awe and disgust.

"What did you do to us, Starkling?" Cormic growled.

Aethan stepped back, holding up his hands in supplication. "Nothing. I swear. I don't know why it responds to me and no one else. But I intend to go further to find out more, if you are willing to tag along."

Neither responded. They gave him the same calculating stare as he passed, stepping out of his way in unison and giving him a wide berth. He gave them each a reassuring smile as he passed.

Then Aethan raised his torch and descended.

The moment Bast Blackblade looked into Aslyn's eyes, he understood the depth of the danger they were both in. Those sun-kissed amber eyes struck him as familiar up close. The way she spoke was as well. Less arrogant and cold, but just as commanding and prideful. The horrible truth fell over him like a blanket as they took to the dance floor.

He couldn't kill her to steal the Jewel of Arithia, currently nestled at the apex of her breasts. Completing this job quickly was out of the question now. Aslyn's death wouldn't leave the kingdom of Novavito without an heir. It *would* change the course of not only her kingdom, but possibly all of them.

Especially if that jewel fell into the wrong hands. He sensed the power pulsing from it several times as they danced. It called to him like a siren's song, tempting him to touch it, take it, use it. Did she feel that power as well? If so, she hid the effects exceptionally well.

He wanted to tell her, but there was no way Aslyn would believe him when they had only just met. Zayne Khrahar had to earn the unwavering trust of the princess.

When the dance ended, Bast was ready to head out in search of answers or evidence. The truth about his patron and that jewel and this place had to exist somewhere in this gods-cursed city.

Yet Aslyn clearly hinted she was not done with his company, and he needed her trust.

They acquired drinks and walked along the promenade just outside the ballroom doors beside the garden. Aslyn's questions were relentless. She wanted to know everything about him.

Despite his desire to lie to her, something compelled Bast to tell her the truth. Or as much of the truth as he dared to share.

"I've moved a lot," he admitted, evading the truth. "I was born in Crowtown, but moved to Elysia as a young teen."

"So you aren't from Port Verix at all," Aslyn noted with keen interest. That news seemed to be a relief to her.

"I'm from everywhere," he admitted, once more sharing a morsel of the truth. "I started working as soon as I was old enough and have built up my reputation." Another veiled truth.

"What about your parents?" Aslyn asked.

Bast paused, peering at a host of budding rosebushes. "I'm not sure that's a conversation I'm ready to have just yet."

When he turned his attention back to her, the sympathy in her amber eyes and heartbreak creasing the corners of her lips surprised him. But she didn't press, as if sensing something tragic lay beneath the surface. Bast couldn't help admiring the way she so easily read his pain and respected his need for time.

If she looked into him too closely, Aslyn might spot the cracks in his stories. Hopefully, no one would think highly enough of him to dive too deep into his past. The Lord of the Harbor had done quite a bit to build some truth around him.

"Where do you see your future?" Aslyn asked, settling on a white painted iron bench. Her amber eyes sparkled in the lamplight with keen interest.

"I try not to think too far into the future," Bast replied. He glanced at the bench beside her, asking permission without words. Aslyn nodded once and he settled beside her, glancing at her guard nearby.

The jewel at her throat once more called to him. Bast tensed his muscles in response.

"Who doesn't think about their future?" she tittered.

"I've told you a bit about myself already," Bast replied, smirking despite the war for self-control within. "I assumed you would understand. Planning for the future is folly for a man like me when so much can change so quickly."

Aslyn hummed thoughtfully at that. "Fair enough. I guess I assumed you had plans of some kind."

"Oh, loads of them." Bast leaned back, resting his arm across the back of the bench. His fingers itched to touch the back of her necklace. If he leaned in at the right time, maybe he could lift the jewel without her noticing. *Stop being a fool*, he admonished himself. "I find being flexible with my future a much better avenue."

"So you are not averse to change."

"I welcome it."

A small smile curled the corners of Aslyn's lips and she flushed slightly, looking away. What was that all about?

"I assume I am not the only man who has shown you interest," Bast said casually. He shifted his attention to the ground, hoping to appear vulnerable to her. "Actually, I would be shocked if I were. I noticed you and Aethan Starkling have a quite comfortable relationship with one another. Would I be wrong to accept that I have an uphill battle for your attention?"

Aslyn drew in a deep breath and let it out slowly as she folded her hands in her lap. "My relationship with Aethan is... complicated. He's a good man."

Bast gazed sideways at her. "But?"

A small smile played on her lips. "It might not be as much of an uphill battle as you assume."

Bast smiled back at her. "Well, that's a bit of a relief. I actually quite respect his skills. The way he handled a sword was amazing. I wouldn't want to go toe-to-toe with him." Mostly because Bast knew he could kill Aethan, no matter how skilled the man was.

"Something tells me you would do okay against him," Aslyn remarked.

Bast chuckled. "You honor me, princess." He ran a hand over his pant leg as a show of nerves, then shifted slightly to face her more on the bench. "Is there anyone else I should worry about?"

"Shall I reveal all my secrets in our first conversation?" she teased. "Perhaps a little mystery is a good thing. It keeps you on your toes."

The shine in her eyes dimmed as a flash of anger crossed her face. Bast followed her line of sight.

Right to her guard.

The man gave them proper, respectful distance, but his hand clutched at his sword like he wanted to draw it. His dark eyes gleamed with jealousy.

Ah, so he was in love with the princess. Pity the poor fool had no chance. He must have known as much. Bast would need to learn more about the guard and keep a closer eye on him. He would be a danger to Bast's plans. Jealousy made men dangerous and impulsive.

The guard's gaze shifted away at the approaching man the same moment Bast heard the crunch of boots against the gravel-flecked brick walkway.

Not just any man.

Marek Bloodstone strode toward Aslyn with unhurried confidence. His expression reflected his admiration for the princess. Bast had noticed Marek watching the two of them for a couple of minutes before he approached, likely trying to get a grasp on his competition.

"Aslyn, I was hoping to get at least one dance tonight," Marek said in humor. "You've been so busy all night."

The devotion in Marek's eyes flickered. The moment passed swiftly, but Bast caught it. Hunger, dominance, and possessive brutality shined through.

"By all means, I don't mean to keep you all night," Bast said, standing swiftly. He took Aslyn's hand as she stood and kissed it again. "I hope we can talk again soon, Aslyn."

Aslyn licked her lips. "I'm sure that can be arranged, Zayne."

Aslyn excused herself and accepted Marek's invitation. Bast watched them go warily. Marek cast a furtive, warning glare over his shoulder as if to say, *This is mine, back the fuck off or I'll kill you.*

Bast simply smiled cordially after them. *Try to kill me, asshole, and see where it gets you.*

CHAPTER 30

Lost Tomb

The stairway tunneled down and down forever. Or at least, it felt like forever to Aethan and his companions. None of them spoke more than a hushed mutter of discontent, as if afraid something would jump out at them.

As the stairwell began widening dramatically, Aethan noticed the pillars of stone in the wall encased as if the arena had grown up around them. Each spanned wider than the three men combined, reaching up into the ceiling. Overhead, curved arches poked through the stone as if they, too, had been overgrown by the arena above.

Aethan's boot hit the ground at the bottom and he paused, peering into the expanse of darkness beyond. Trystain wouldn't be down here. He should look for his friend. But curiosity gnawed at him. Aethan had to know what was hidden so far beneath the Stormvalor arena.

Cavis moved around the edge of the wall, running his hand cautiously over the stone. He lowered his torch. It kissed a recess in the wall that ran horizontally along the stone. Nothing happened.

"I hoped that would light it," Cavis informed them as he turned back to Aethan.

He joined Cavis, with Cormic shuffling along on his heels. It did appear to be an ancient fire trough in the wall to light the massive chamber. Aethan touched his finger to the stones in the trough.

"I don't like this," Cormic grumbled. "First you talk about an ancient prison filled with dark minions from nightmares, now we're dozens of meters below the earth in the dark where anything could be hiding in the shadows."

Cavis grinned at his brother. "Scared?"

"Anyone in their right mind would be!"

"Stop," Aethan whispered.

Near the fire trough, ancient runes were embedded in the stone wall. Aethan traced his finger over them, trying to remember something about them from his studies. Few could truly understand the language of ancient runes anymore. The knowledge had been largely lost to time. But something about this felt... familiar. He ran his finger over the runes.

"Do you know what they mean?" Cavis asked as if he honestly expected Aethan to have the answer.

"No. Not... not really." Aethan dug deep into his lessons for some kind of answer. "I know a couple of scattered fragments. Something about catacombs, gods, and..." Aethan's breath caught as he recognized three of the runes as clearly as he would recognize his own face. Three runes he had seen every day since his birth.

Three runes tattooed over his own heart within the wings of the dragon there.

Strength. Honor. Valor.

His family motto.

He traced those three far more intimately than the others.

"What is it?" Cavis asked, sensing some shift in Aethan. "Tell me nothing again and I'll knock your head into the wall."

Before Aethan could answer, the trough sparked with light. Not flames, as he had expected, but blue-white light that shot around the massive chamber, igniting the trough embedded in the wall in dazzling, flashing light.

Cavis and Cormic both cursed, drawing weapons and readying for a fight.

The moment passed quickly as they all gaped at the sight before them.

The ancient catacombs lay within a massive underground chamber, a testament to the grandeur of ages past. Every surface reflected the gleam of iron and bronze, intricately wrought into elaborate swirls and ornate decor that adorned the walls and ceiling. Even the floor was a marvel, a mosaic of polished stone interwoven with veins of iron and bronze that shimmered in the flickering torchlight.

"Seven Gods..." Cormic breathed in awe. "Is this...?"

Aethan's own pulse quickened in reverence. He had never seen such a place in all his life. This was a place of myths and legends, a story he heard hundreds of times in his childhood. A place lost to time.

This was the Hall of Champions, where the God of War's most revered champions found their eternal rest.

"Yes, I think so," Aethan whispered reverently.

The air was thick with the weight of history and the solemn reverence of countless generations of fallen warriors who rested here. Only the most loyal and favored to Justis, God of War, were given a place along the main chamber floor. Their tombs, fashioned from the same gleaming materials, stood in stately rows, each one a masterpiece of craftsmanship and devotion.

As Aethan meandered through the hallowed chamber, the sense of awe was palpable. The legends of these mighty champions seemed to whisper from the walls, their deeds immortalized in the very fabric of this sacred place. It was a sanctuary of honor and remembrance, a place where the echoes of valor would resonate for eternity. How many were his own ancestors?

The air was cool and carried a faint metallic tang. The gleam of iron and bronze adorned every surface. Elaborate swirls and intricate decorations danced along the walls, their craftsmanship so exquisite that they seemed almost alive, twisting and turning in the flickering light.

Columns rose like titans from the ground, their surfaces adorned with runes and carvings that told the tales of legendary battles and heroic deeds of these fallen champions. Each alcove and niche held the resting place of a fallen champion, their sarcophagi adorned with the symbols of their valor and prowess in battle. Weapons and armor, still gleaming as if newly forged, were placed reverently beside each warrior.

Aethan slowly made his way toward the opposite end of the massive chamber where Cavis and Cormic already pushed and pulled together on the giant, arching bronze doors. The Hall of Champions had to be at least as large as the arena—if not larger.

"They must be locked," Cavis said to Cormic as they once more failed to even budge the doors.

Aethan tipped his head back to gaze up at the intricately carved bronze arch around the double doors—those doors must have been at least a dozen meters tall! Climbing up each door, matching blue-painted bronze reliefs of a dragon in flight, its mouth open in attack, faced one another. Not just any dragon.

Storm, Justis' mount and companion. The legendary blue dragon.

"What do you think is on the other side?" Cormic asked Cavis.

Aethan suspected the lost Shrine of Justis. His immortal lair. Just like the Hall of Champions, the Shrine of Justis had been lost long, long ago. He calculated they must be directly beneath the giant statue of Justis that loomed over Stormvalor.

He wrapped a hand around each handle, a sneaking suspicion crawling through him, and pushed with all his might. Cavis and Cormic snorted at his efforts—after all, if they couldn't open the doors together, he certainly couldn't do it alone.

"Let's head back up and keep looking for Trystain," Cavis said as if coaxing an agitated child away from danger. "Leave everything here untouched."

Cormic made a sound of disappointment, but he didn't argue with his brother. The wealth of fine weapons alone could supply an army.

If no one else had found this place in at least a century, it would remain here, undisturbed, waiting for him.

As the trio took to the stairs once more, Aethan glanced back over his shoulder at the doors to the shrine. Something beyond called to him.

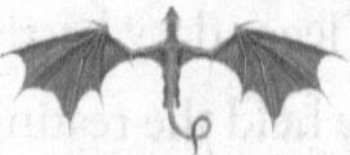

Marek guided Aslyn through the steps of their dance, but his movements were more blocky and not nearly as smooth as Zayne or Aethan had been. Not that dancing truly indicated anything about his worth. He pulled her close to him, and she could smell him as she had before—like campfire and metal—but something else not swirled around him. *Is that sulfur?* She wondered as they danced.

His large hand splayed across her lower back, thumb caressing through the thin fabric of her gold silk dress. Warm breath rolled down her exposed neck as he leaned close. Much closer than was proper.

"My father is here, watching us," he whispered. His deep voice sent a ripple down her spine.

"Then we should give him a show," she replied.

Marek pulled back and their gazes met. He smiled. It was nowhere near as charming as Aethan's, nor as disarming as Zayne's, but something about the sincerity of it was so utterly Marek.

"Just how good of a dancer are you, Marek Bloodstone?" Aslyn asked.

"Good enough." He immediately stepped back, holding her hand and spinning her in wide, dramatic fashion before him. Aslyn's skirt flared, brushing nearby bodies forced to make way for the two of them as they consumed more of the dance floor.

Marek twirled, spun, dipped, and rocked Aslyn through the motions until both of them were laughing. He wasn't light on his feet, but he was graceful enough not to step on her feet as they moved together.

It wasn't long before other couples on the dance floor joined their twirling waltz, with the two of them in the center.

By the time the song ended, Aslyn needed a break to breathe. Marek offered his arm, and they made their way off the dance floor to retrieve drinks, then stepped into the open air of the garden doors.

As they crossed the room, Aslyn tried to catch a glimpse of Sybil, just to see how she was faring with Prince Valen. The two sat in a private booth near another set of open doors, surrounded by Black Guards. Sybil seemed fairly relaxed. In fact, it almost appeared as if she were flirting back with the Imperial Heir.

Marek noticed where her gaze had drifted. "I've only seen him once before," he said, leaning casually against the doorframe.

Aslyn half turned to keep her gaze on Sybil without being obvious about it.

"It was just after his wife died and they burned her body," he continued, lowering his voice. "He looked like he was carved from stone, and I swear he looks younger now. Memory is a strange thing."

She simply nodded in agreement. But something about Prince Valen was off. She could just feel it.

Despite her curiosity, she refused to allow it to distract her from Marek's company.

CHAPTER 31

No Matter What

Aethan took up the rear as the trio left the tomb. Cormic practically raced for the stairs once they passed through the door of iron and light into the dungeon hall. Cavis didn't rush as quickly as his brother, but the haste in his steps made it clear he was also eager to put this place behind them.

"Wait!" Aethan called after them from the bottom of the steps that led them out into the arena halls once more.

Both men stopped when they realized Aethan didn't follow.

"Your king hand-selected the two of you for this tournament, yes?" Aethan asked. He already knew the answer, but waited for both of them to nod. "I'm trusting your loyalty to the Novavito crown is strong, then." Again, they nodded, though this time with a touch more suspicion. "And the princess?"

Cavis grimaced. "I know where you're heading, but she hasn't chosen you yet."

"True. But would you want to risk my displeasure if she does?"

"Just say it," Cavis snapped.

"I need your vow that you will keep all of this secret." When Cormic appeared ready to protest, Aethan held up a hand. "I will talk to Aslyn about this myself when the time is right. I wouldn't ask you to commit treason against your crown, but I will ask that you allow me time to approach her first."

Cavis scowled. "You want us to not tell our future queen that we just unearthed the lost Hall of Champions?"

"You owe me."

"Why do you owe him anything, Cavis?" Cormic asked darkly.

But Aethan and Cavis eyed one another, a battle of wills waging between the two men.

"It makes you angry, doesn't it?" Cavis asked at last. "That she chose me."

"It did." Aethan shook his head. "It doesn't any longer." He climbed closer to the two men. "A vow. Before we leave here."

Cormic appeared ready to protest, but his jaw slackened as Cavis said, "I give you my vow never to speak of what we discovered tonight unless it becomes detrimental to my king or future queen's crown."

"Cavis!" Cormic hissed.

Cavis turned to face his brother. "It could be dangerous if word of this gets out anyway. Better that we are all on the same page. And Aethan won't tell anyone. Not when this secret hides beneath the city his father rules over."

Cormic considered his brother's words, grimaced, then repeated his brother's vow, though with much less conviction.

"Thank you," Aethan said. "I swear to you that your faith in me will not be misplaced, and your loyalty will not be forgotten."

They continued their climb up the stairs, and Aethan heard Cavis say to his brother, "Besides, it can't hurt to have a Starkling on our side."

Not long after the three emerged from the dungeon entrance, Roric ran up to Aethan, panting, relief all over his young face.

"There you are! Thank the gods. Trystain has had me tearing this place apart looking for you."

Aethan's heart skipped. "Where is he?"

Aslyn's exhaustion became absolute by the time she returned to her room. Kaiti helped her out of her dress and took her hair down, running the brush through it as they discussed the events of the evening.

After spending that time with Aethan, she thought she knew what she wanted. But Zayne had left a lasting impression she couldn't shake, and a lot of what he said made her question Aethan's true desires. Zayne hadn't meant to do it on purpose. How could he possibly know? Still, a seed of doubt had planted in Aslyn's mind and she couldn't ignore it.

Not only would a match between Sybil Starkling and Prince Valen change things for Aslyn's friends, but it would change her own future as well.

"A Starkling must always rule over Stormvalor." Aethan's words haunted Aslyn as she set her bracelet on the vanity. Did that mean Aethan would not leave his family legacy or the city of Stormvalor? His code of honor might bind him to this place no matter what either of them wanted. And if there were true, Aslyn knew her hopes with him were already fading.

Not that it truly mattered. She didn't even know if this was what he wanted. Not really.

And Marek... Just when Aslyn thought she was certain she was ready to let him go, he changed her mind. Tonight, once he had her full attention, Marek had been far more charming than ever before.

Behind her, Kaiti bit her lip as if fighting off some urge to put her nose in Aslyn's business.

She sighed. "What is it?"

"Well... it's just... Lord Starkling is so..." Kaiti sighed dreamily.

Yes. Aslyn understood exactly what Kaiti meant.

"If only matters were so simple," Aslyn agreed.

"You would choose him?" Kaiti flushed as soon as she asked. "I'm sorry, Your Majesty. It's not my business. I just like to live vicariously."

Aslyn wondered what it would be like to be in Kaiti's place. "I don't know. This decision before me is no small task. I want love. I need trust and a partner capable of supporting me and my people. Maybe even someone who understands them."

Like Zayne. He seemed to have a better understanding of what the common person went through based on everything she learned about him tonight. "Lord Khrahar is also a good choice, and ruggedly handsome." Aslyn almost sighed recalling her time with him. No man had ever stirred so much desire in her so quickly before. But this was not about desire. It was about the future of her kingdom, and she didn't really know Zayne. Not yet. "And Marek remains quite charming and could offer our people protection from the emperor."

Her fingers traced over the Jewel of Arithia at her neck. It had warmed in Zayne's presence. Aslyn couldn't understand why, or how that mattered. But somehow it felt important.

"While I do envy the attention those men give you," Kaiti said as she set the hairbrush down, "I don't envy the choice you have to make. Are you any closer?"

Aslyn heaved out a sigh. "I wish I could say yes, but every time I think I've decided, I doubt myself again. I just need more time."

And more time to get to know Zayne Khrahar.

Trystain relaxed on the sapphire sofa as Aethan burst in on Roric's heels. The light from the nearby lamp made Trystain's strawberry blond hair shine. He straightened, but didn't rise when Aethan appeared.

Aethan's irritation flared. He had been searching for his friend, thinking the worst had happened, and Trystain appeared fine. Better than fine. Despite all that happened in that ballroom, Trystain practically glowed with newfound confidence.

"Are you harmed?" Aethan asked as he crossed the living room in a few long strides. His gaze swept over Trystain, but he couldn't spot any obvious signs of harm. Nothing at all, actually. "Where were you?"

Trystain grinned that boyish, charming grin. "I could ask the same of you. Your poor squire was beside himself when he couldn't find you. You gave him quite a fright. Leaving the arena, Aethan?"

Aethan shook his head, sinking into the chair across from Trystain. "I was looking everywhere inside the arena for you. Cavis and Cormic were with me."

Trystain nodded as if Aethan had just told him some unsurprising secret. "You had quite a night with their future queen. I'm not surprised at all that they jumped at a chance to help you."

Aethan flinched, remembering his evening with Aslyn... and how it had ended. Seven Gods, he had never wanted to kiss and hold someone so badly in all his life. Not even Iskra. It terrified him to his core. It had been some stroke of luck that her overbearing guard had interrupted.

"Forget about all of that," Aethan said, leaning his elbows on his knees. "What happened to you? You opposed the Imperial Heir in front of a ballroom full of people, then his assistant pulled you away and you vanished. I thought..." Aethan sighed. "I thought something horrible happened to you."

Trystain waved off Aethan's concern. "No. Lady Fia was quite gentle and reassuring. She accompanied me back to the Imperial suite. We had a few drinks and spoke openly with one another."

"About Sybil?" Aethan asked, tensing as he worried about his sister's future.

"Among other things." Trystain shrugged and leaned back, laying his arm across the back of the sofa.

A million questions burst into Aethan's mind, but only one escaped. "What are his plans with my sister?"

A look of pure regret crossed Trystain's face, and Aethan couldn't breathe as his friend answered, bracing for the worst like one would brace for a punch. "I can't tell you."

Dark fury rolled through Aethan. "What?" he growled in disbelief. There was no way he heard that right.

Trystain's brows drew together like he wanted to say something, but the agony of his silence appeared a physical pain to him. "I'm sorry, Aethan. I would if I could. You know I would. But... The only way to get Lady Fia to agree to tell me anything, to calm me down, was to get my vow of silence. I didn't mean to give it, but it happened anyway."

Aethan gasped. An Ambassador's Promise. She must have tricked Trystain into saying something that would bind him to the vow without him realizing it. The dark anger pulsed and grew. Aethan surged to his feet, unable to remain seated a moment longer, and he paced the floor between them.

The only reason Aethan could think of for such a tricky vow would be the prince's true intentions. Prince Valen fully intended to take Sybil—with or without permission. If everything Aslyn said tonight had been true, the emperor was making very calculated, subtle moves against the kingdoms. A Starkling had to remain in Stormvalor. If Sybil went with Prince Valen, Aethan couldn't marry Aslyn.

Am I seriously considering this marriage now? Aethan pondered, shocked by the truth of it. Yes. He was. Because his father saw it as necessary. But Lux Starkling warned that it could strengthen the empire. So why would the emperor want to keep him and Aslyn apart?

Marek...

What part did Novavito play in all of this that the emperor wanted his own chosen man at the future queen's side?

Aethan stopped, turning toward Marek's rooms down the hall. Every time Marek made a misstep with Aslyn, somehow he won her over again. Was he part of the emperor's game? She had mentioned Ambassador Umbogo being suspected of trying to trick her into marriage. But that had failed. Or it would, if she chose another first. Her father sent her here to find a husband and avoid that fate. Would he approve of her choosing an Umbrian husband?

More than that, Marek was no common Umbr lord. He was a Bloodstone. His father was in charge of the emperor's armies. That connection couldn't be coincidence.

Why did Prince Valen want Sybil? And why did the emperor want Aslyn's crown?

Aethan stopped pacing and cursed sharply enough to make Roric jump from where he sat off to the side. Trystain simply eyed Aethan with curiosity shining in his eyes.

"Care to share with the rest of us?" Trystain asked.

Could he share with Trystain? Aethan eyed his best friend, who knew him better than most and often had been described as inseparable from him. But all of this was so much bigger than either of them. Aethan had to proceed cautiously. "What exactly did Lady Fia want with you?"

"At first, to calm me down. Once she did that, she worked hard to reassure me that my future would be safe, just maybe not what I had thought." Trystain stood, striding over to Aethan in the center of the room. He placed his hand on Aethan's shoulder. "Listen to me very carefully, Aethan. This is not a burden for you to bear. All will be well. Sybil's future is full of promise. Just focus on the tournament and that princess of yours. Everything else is in hand."

Aethan opened his mouth but couldn't come up with a response. Everything Trystain said was so loaded. And *nothing* was in hand.

Trystain squeezed Aethan's shoulder. "No matter what."

Their blood vow. Aethan nodded. "No matter what."

With a few parting words, Trystain left Aethan and Roric alone. Aethan waited a few breaths before turning to his squire.

"Did you learn anything useful tonight?" Aethan asked.

Roric chewed his lower lip, clasping his hands anxiously in front of himself. "There were a lot of rumors about your sister and the Imperial Heir. He wants to marry her. He wants to be her ally. He's simply trying to make friends with the next Stormvalor steward. Honestly, the rumors were all over the place and I couldn't pin anything down." He shifted feet. "Princess Aslyn seemed very taken with her new suitor, Lord Zayne Khrahar. He's new money in Umbr. I'll try to dig up more about him, but so far, all I know is that he owns a lot of ships in Port Verix. I overheard Ryker telling Weylen that he wasn't sure how the princess would resist Lord Khrahar for long."

Roric fidgeted with his fingers in front of him, like he was afraid of telling Aethan the next part. "I got a good look at him. He's... Well, he's got the rugged, tall, dark, and handsome thing going for him for sure. And she smiled at him a *lot*."

Aethan fought off a groan. Just when he thought he had made progress with her...

Was Zayne another Umbrian plant in his path? Another way for the emperor to increase his odds of successfully getting his own man in Aslyn's bed? Just the thought of her with either Marek or this Lord Khrahar made Aethan's jaw tighten so hard it ached.

Roric glanced at the closed suite door and lowered his voice, edging closer to Aethan. "Sire, the Black Guards are up to something in the arena as well. Their movements tonight were... strange. I don't think Prince Valen came for your sister—at least not for that reason alone. I think he's helping his father with something much bigger."

Aethan crossed his arms. "Tell me everything."

Roric rattled off the entire tale. How the servants shied away and the other squires avoided certain hallways. Where the Black Guards turned corners and vanished by the time he could follow. How they blocked off the arena floor completely for nearly an hour.

Aethan wasn't sure what any of it meant, but Roric had been right to suspect something.

CHAPTER 32

Out of the Gilded Cage

Aslyn couldn't help fussing over her dress and her hair as she waited for her mother to call her down. Kaiti fought her own smile, clearly able to read Aslyn's excitement.

Zayne had sent a request for her company, promising to pick her up at the suite and take her out. Did he mean out of the arena? That was one thing she had not been permitted to do since their arrival and the corridors became stifling.

Kaiti fastened the Jewel of Arithia around her neck and Aslyn dismissed her to watch for Zayne.

Once alone, Aslyn took a few measured breaths to control her racing pulse, staring at her reflection in the polished mirror. She was Aslyn Kiernan, Crown Princess of Novavito, which meant she needed to handle this date with careful consideration and not the impish excitement that took control of her.

A few minutes later, Kaiti knocked softly, smirking despite her attempts to remain professional. "He's here." The girl practically swooned.

Aslyn swallowed and rose, slipping on her boots quickly before tossing her shoulders back, raising her chin, and stepping onto the balcony overlooking the main living area.

Zayne sat on one of the plush sofas across the main space from her mother, his back to Aslyn's railing and doorway. He acted perfectly casual and comfortable even with her mother, as if she were anyone and not a powerful queen. One ankle rested on his knee and his hand sat atop it, making his fat golden ring catch in the light.

Aslyn schooled herself to remain composed as she descended, listening to the rich timber of his voice as he spoke to her mother.

"—just over ten ships in the harbor," he said, clearly answering one of Queen Giata's questions. "Four more are currently at sea."

"It's very daring and brave of you to attempt crossing the ocean to the western continent," Queen Giata said smoothly. "I'm not sure when the last time we successfully crossed that expanse was. Long before any of our times, I'm sure."

"And far overdue," he replied.

"Daring and brave indeed to send others in your place," Aslyn remarked as she rounded the bottom of the grand stairs and joined them.

Zayne immediately rose to his feet and turned toward her, bowing politely.

"He could lose a small fortune if it fails, Aslyn," her mother said sweetly, but there was an admonishment in her tone Aslyn knew far too well. "I applaud his daring."

"I meant no offense, Zayne," Aslyn said politely.

"None taken." He flashed that disarming smile that made her insides melt. "I appreciate bold honesty." Zayne turned to Queen Giata. "Your Majesty, thank you for offering such polite conversation."

"You two enjoy your walk," her mother said.

Zayne strode toward Aslyn, and the way he moved with such cat-like grace made her once more think of things she ought not to think. Seven Gods help her, but this man did something to her she couldn't fully understand. He offered his arm, and Aslyn felt a jolt of electricity surge through her as she slid her hand over his arm.

As they stepped out the door, Elisio fell in step behind them, no doubt glaring at Zayne's back. She didn't dare glance back to find out.

"Where are we going?" she asked anxiously.

"It's a surprise," Zayne said, grinning sidelong at her.

Making small talk with Queen Giata had grated on Bast's nerves, and he was more than happy to sweep the princess out of that stuffy suite the moment she arrived. Thankfully, neither Aslyn nor the queen seemed inclined to hold him up.

With the guard looming in their shadow, Bast couldn't take her out of the arena. It seemed the queen had set boundaries for her daughter.

Instead, Bast led Aslyn to a small stone courtyard he had stumbled across during one of his recon missions yesterday.

There was something sacred about the space, little more than a fifty by fifty square with a bubbling fountain in the center. But the stone whispered to him, secrets from ancient tongues he didn't understand but felt all the same.

Why he wanted to bring Aslyn here, Bast wasn't sure. Perhaps he hoped she would sense what he sensed in this place, and maybe he wanted to have that connection with her.

The sky shone gray but bright overhead, casting noon light straight down on the water bubbling in the center of the courtyard. Stone reliefs of soaring dragons climbed the columns around the square, cresting along the archways between each column.

The moment they stopped in the courtyard and Bast turned to Aslyn, his bubble of hope burst.

She didn't seem awed by this place. In fact, disappointment shone in her glowing amber eyes. "A courtyard. How... original."

Bast clenched his jaw in irritation as the stone once more whispered in that ancient tone. "Not just any courtyard. Do you not feel it? The ancient weight of this space? It's unlike anything else in this city."

Aslyn's shoulders sagged. "I wouldn't know." She pulled away and glided toward the fountain, perching on the edge.

Bast watched as she held out her palm. He held his breath, expecting something to happen, though he didn't know what.

Nothing. Water splashed over her palm and down into the base of the fountain.

Then her hand came up, and the tips of her fingers brushed over the Jewel of Arithia fastened at her throat. Her sharp gaze darted to him once more, studying him like she knew why he had truly come, like she knew he needed that ancient jewel.

Bast joined her on the fountain's edge, sliding his fingertips across the surface of the fountain base. "Your mother doesn't allow you out into the city, does she?"

Aslyn shook her head, dropping the hand into her lap. "Apparently even with our guards it's not safe enough for me."

Bast chuckled. "Yes, a true den of heathens resides beyond these stone walls."

"Don't mock me. I'm a bird trapped in a gilded cage."

"I wouldn't call this place gilded."

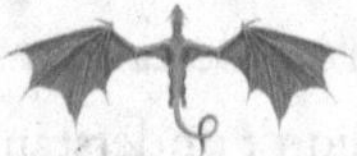

Aslyn watched the way those dark strands of hair slid along Zayne's strong features as he peered into the fountain as if searching for answers. He was so mysterious, yet remarkably frank. Aslyn found it refreshing. And the way his gaze tilted up to her as the corner of his mouth tipped upward made her throat tighten.

The conversation to this courtyard had been light and casual, comfortable, even. But the moment she realized this was their destination, something inside of her fractured. She had deep down been hoping that he would slip her out of the arena walls. Instead, he brought her here.

Aslyn fiddled with her necklace. It warmed around him. Again.

"I've heard rumors about that jewel," Zayne said, gazing at the Jewel of Arithia at her throat. "That it binds to the soul of the royal wearing it and they can feel its presence at all times."

Aslyn shrugged. "I think that's a legend. I don't usually feel anything from it." *Except around you.* Aslyn did not know what that meant and she was not prepared to unpack it today. Instead, she changed the subject. "Now that we are better acquainted, perhaps you will tell me more about your parents."

Zayne's face twisted in disgust and he looked away. "Aslyn..."

She reached out and took his hand. "I'm tougher than you think. I can handle it. Share the burden with someone, Zayne."

Once again, he stared at her, trying to read something inside of her, perhaps trying to judge if she was sincere. How bad could it be?

"They must be proud of the man you've become," she added.

Zayne winced. "I wouldn't know." He glanced sideways.

Aslyn followed his gaze to Elisio lingering far too closely. "Give us a little privacy, Elisio."

The guard's jaw twitched. "I don't think—"

"Know your place! Twenty paces and no less." Aslyn's tone harbored no room for argument. "Now."

If looks could kill, Elisio would have flayed Zayne. But he obeyed even as red crept up his neck.

"When you're ready, I make a great listener," Aslyn offered.

A haunted look filled Zayne's gray eyes. "My mother died when I was only eight."

"What happened to her?"

He swallowed, looking down at the hand she held in her own. "She slipped and hit her head."

Aslyn blinked. Such a random way to die, without purpose. "And your father? He is alive?"

Zayne shrugged. "I wouldn't know. I haven't seen him since I left."

"I'm sure he misses you," she said, squeezing his hand.

Zayne snorted. "I doubt it. Look, it isn't a nice story. I didn't have the privilege of growing up with loving parents. It's not a story I want to share." He straightened and leaned closer to her. Aslyn's heart thundered in her chest as he placed her palm over his own heart. "This is what matters. It's the only thing that matters."

Aslyn felt it in her fingertips, her palm, the steady and strong beat of his heart. "And yet you would give it away?" she asked, breathless.

"I haven't given anything. My heart is my own. If you want a place in it, you have to fight for that spot." His lips inched closer, and his free hand slid delicately along her jaw. "You cannot steal my heart, but you can possess it all the same."

His fingers trailed along her throat. Aslyn's entire body relaxed into his touch as if by some unknown magic.

Then his lips slipped past her face, and he whispered in her ear. "Leave your balcony doors open tonight, princess, if you want to be freed of this gilded cage for a while."

Aslyn's pulse beat so hard she could barely hear his words. He wasn't inviting himself into her room. He was inviting her out of the arena. She closed her eyes and inhaled this moment.

Zayne smelled like cedar and leather and musk—just as mysterious and intoxicating as he was.

Then he pulled back, lingering for a moment to stare into her eyes, before releasing his hold on her and springing to his feet.

Aslyn blinked at the quick withdrawal, her head spinning. Then she saw what drew Zayne's attention.

Marek and Rett entered the courtyard, both staring Zayne down.

Aslyn swallowed and schooled her body into a calm before rising.

"Aslyn," Marek said, but his black eyes were locked on Zayne, dark and dangerous. "I had the afternoon off and was looking for you. I thought we could spend some more time together."

Zayne took Aslyn's hand and brought it to his lips. "It's alright. We can continue this another time." His gray eyes shone with hidden meaning she fully understood. Later.

Tonight.

Aslyn's fingers tightened around Zayne's refusing to allow him to let go. No. She would not leave him for Marek. Not only had she promised this time to him, but he was the only one willing to set her free instead of caging her.

"It is not alright," she said firmly. "This is our time, Zayne. I'm sure Marek can wait his turn."

Aslyn didn't appreciate the way Marek's jaw clenched and his muscles coiled as if preparing for a fight. As if she were his and he would teach them both a lesson.

With a gentle tug, Aslyn pulled Zayne along with her as she made her way out of the courtyard. Elisio, as always, trailed in their shadows.

Marek growled lowly at Zayne as they passed, which only angered Aslyn more.

M arek had fallen squarely into Bast's trap. He had watched where the Umbr man went when not in training, knew that he had this afternoon off and that he often passed by this courtyard.

Bast had come far too close to telling Aslyn the truth about his childhood. Getting her to drop the subject proved harder than he thought it would be. Instead, he distracted her at the moment he knew Marek would pass by, leaning in to make it seem as if he would kiss her. No doubt it appeared far less innocent to Marek than it had been.

And Aslyn had reacted to Marek's demand for her time exactly as Bast had hoped. It revealed Marek's jealousy plainly enough that Bast could feel it.

She noticed.

She noticed and she didn't like it at all.

As they vanished from Marek's sight, Bast glanced over his shoulder at her guard, Elisio. "Do you go anywhere without him?"

Aslyn sighed. "Sadly no. He trails me the moment I step out my bedroom door."

"Well, it's good to know there's one place he doesn't follow." It meant using her balcony to sneak her out would be the best way to earn her trust. Bast filed that information away. If he could slip into her room through the balcony, maybe he could lift the jewel and disappear. Assuming it hadn't fused to her soul. What would she say if she knew who hired him to steal that jewel from her neck—at any cost?

T hat evening, Bast perched on a balcony in the shadows and watched Aslyn's door. It wasn't long before he was met with his reward. Still, he hesitated.

What am I doing sneaking her out?

It was foolish, letting himself get close to her. Despite his best laid plans, he had come terribly close to kissing her beside that fountain. This entire outing was folly. Would it earn her trust? Yes.

But what scared him most was what she might earn in return.

Aslyn retired to her room soon after dinner, telling her mother she was tired and asking Kaiti to leave her to rest. Then she swiftly changed into her training leathers, the only thing she had to wear that wasn't a gown since her mother confiscated the commoner clothing she tried to bring along. For her own peace of mind, Aslyn tucked her knife in her belt.

After braiding her hair away from her face as she had seen most of the common women at the tournament do, Aslyn opened her balcony door just enough for Zayne to see the signal.

Then she waited.

They hadn't set a time, but surely shortly after sundown would be ideal.

And she waited.

Maybe I misunderstood and he didn't mean tonight but tomorrow...

Aslyn spun around and examined her bed. Untouched. That wouldn't do. She busied herself rumpling the blankets and tucking pillows in to make it look like her form beneath the covers in case anyone peeked in on her. Upon close examination, it would be obvious. Aslyn counted on the maids and guards respecting her space.

When she spun around to check the door, Aslyn's heart jumped into her throat and she nearly cried out in alarm.

Zayne leaned against the open door, watching her with his arms over his chest. Instead of his nice suits, he wore common clothing. His gaze swept over her and he raised a brow, but when she opened her mouth to defend her choice of wardrobe, he held a finger to his lips and nodded toward the closed bedroom door.

Without a sound, the two of them slipped out, leaving the door only slightly cracked so she could quietly slip back in later. As they approached the rail, Zayne peered over toward the main balcony. Satisfied, he edged so close to her Aslyn caught that cedar, leather, musky scent on the breeze.

"I'll help you down," he whispered in her ear.

Aslyn nudged him away and swung herself over the rail before he could stop her. Zayne raised his brows and reached for her, but she knew what she was doing. Aslyn deftly dropped herself down as she had done before.

Last time she snuck out like this had been when she first met Aethan. Funny that she now snuck out with Zayne instead.

Zayne silently dropped down beside her, not even a whisper of air or boots in his wake. How did he do that? The calculating look he gave her made Aslyn preen. He hadn't expected a princess to know how to jump balconies. Good. She wanted to keep him on his toes.

They repeated the process until they reached the stands, then Zayne took her hand and pulled her along through the shadows of the corridors. Twice they ducked into an alcove when someone passed by, and he covered her with his body. Aslyn didn't protest a single time.

At last, he guided her down a dark tunnel, holding tight to her hand, and out into the streets surrounding the Stormvalor arena.

Aslyn paused, taking a moment to enjoy the freedom.

Zayne waited patiently, watching her, slightly bemused. She was beginning to like that look on his face.

Neither of them said a word until they plunged into the mass of bodies moving along the streets in every direction.

And the celebrating! Music poured out of every tavern and from several street corners. People drank and ate and danced in the streetlights. Friends laughed and played gambling games. Children and young teens raced freely along the streets pretending to be a competitor. Aslyn heard Aethan's name invoked several times as people claimed to be him amidst the games. A couple times, she heard Bryse's name and she tensed.

Zayne gave her hand reassuring squeeze and tugged her toward a street-side tavern. The doors to the inside were propped open and the patrons sang along to "Heroes Abide", one of the songs touting the strength of Justis, God of War. People stacked crates in the street to use as seats or tables where wooden picnic tables were not available. Barmaids flitted around tables with practiced ease.

Aslyn had never been a part of such a thing in her life.

"Let's get a drink," Zayne said.

A table of men and women outside the tavern raised their glasses as the two of them approached. "Zayne!" They cheered in unison.

He grinned at them.

"Come back to buy more drinks?" a woman with thick black curls asked. Her gaze swept over Aslyn. "Oh, you brought something pretty this time. Good. I was tiring of your stoic face."

"Stoic?" Aslyn chortled. She couldn't say he ever looked stoic around her.

"Aye, but only if you make space for us at the table," Zayne said. "Move your fat asses aside for a lady."

Aslyn tried not to show her shock at the candid way they all spoke to one another.

"Doesn't look much like a lady to me," a man with thick eyebrows said as he studied Aslyn. "But those are nice leathers she's wearing. Nice indeed." He smirked wickedly at her, revealing a few missing teeth.

"Hey, eyes to yourself, Butch, or I carve them out," Zayne said.

They made space on the bench and Aslyn seated herself so close to Zayne she was nearly sitting on him. He leaned his lips toward her ear and said, "You want to know me, this is the best way to learn."

A barmaid brought a fresh round of drinks, eyeing Zayne in a way that made Aslyn want to stab the girl's eyes, as Zayne had threatened to do to Butch.

"You are a pretty thing, for fact," the woman said. "Just like Zayne." She winked at him.

He snorted and took a drink from his mug with a chuckle.

Aslyn eyed the drink suspiciously. She had never seen a drink like this before. But she also didn't want to stand out, so she took a drink just as the woman said, "Reminds me of what they say the princess looks like. A raven-haired, amber-eyed beauty."

Aslyn almost choked on her drink.

Zayne slid his arm around her and she found she liked the feel of it.

But before he could once again defend her, Aslyn spoke up, "Like that entitled brat would ever leave those stone walls." She waved toward the arena dismissively.

The table broke out in laughter, but Zayne raised another of those bemused brows at her.

Yes, she liked that look on him very much.

For the next hour, they drank and Aslyn listened to the four tell stories about Zayne. How he showed up now and again to buy them drinks. How he saved one of them from an assassin. The more Aslyn learned about him, the more she found she liked him.

He truly was a man of these people and not just a lord over them. He knew so many of them by name—even passersby who called out and waved at him—that it made her head spin.

After drinks, Aslyn's head felt light and her body even lighter. She took Zayne's hand and dragged him into the street to dance to a lewd version of a song venerating Fiara, Goddess of Flame. Aslyn allowed the music to wash over her, forgetting courtly dances and letting her body move as freely as it chose. Zayne danced as well, but mostly he swayed and held her hand to keep her close as she lost herself in the music.

And the stoic look Gladys, the curly-headed woman, mentioned burned itself into his features. His gray eyes remained focused solely on her, as if she were the only thing in the world.

When she stumbled, Zayne deftly caught her and pulled her to him. Aslyn laughed and righted herself, dancing once more out of his arms. But when the rhythm slowed, the pulse of the music heating as if the Goddess of Flame stood among them, Zayne held Aslyn tight against his body, his arms folded around her waist.

At some point, Aslyn lost track of time, Zayne bid his friends farewell and escorted her along the streets once more.

"Thank you, Zayne," Aslyn mumbled, surprised by her slurred speech.

"For what?"

"For setting me free. For letting me just be without trying to control how I acted." Aslyn curled tighter against his side as his grip on her firmed. "No one lets me just be. There's so much... so many rules. Etiquette. Duty." The last word was a breath from her lips.

They stopped outside the tunnel leading back into Stormvalor's arena. Zayne brushed stray hairs from her face, holding her upright against him. He studied her, his gaze firm, unyielding, but hungry.

"We're all born into cages, Aslyn," he said softly, "and no two are molded the same way."

Aslyn leaned in for a kiss, wondering what if his lips tasted anything like he smelled.

Zayne turned his head away and leaned back, still holding her steady. "Not like this. You're drunk, *Sol'ami*."

"Free."

"Drunk."

Aslyn brushed her fingers over his lips and moved his mouth as she said, "Free." But darkness swept in around her and her body felt so heavy.

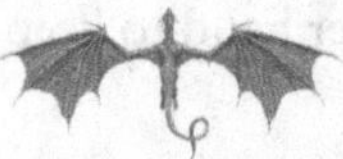

Bast had been left with no choice but to use his shadow magic to put her under. Aslyn had drunk too much. There would be no way she would get herself back up to her room, let alone how loud she was in this state. Everyone would see them sneaking back in or hear her confess things she shouldn't say aloud.

Some part of his armor had cracked beneath her relentless assault on his emotions tonight. When given free space to speak and act as she wanted, Aslyn was sharp-tongued, quick-witted, and gloriously enticing. Bast had subtly dispatched a few men who had gotten too close to her for his comfort, stuffing shadows down their throats or sweeping feet out from the drunks.

But Aslyn had fit in far better with the riffraff of Stormvalor than Bast had anticipated. He actually caught himself laughing with her. And when she danced... some dormant part of his soul had come alive.

Were she any other woman, Bast wouldn't have had any hesitation finding abandoned corners to steal away to. Yet he found himself unable to take advantage of her drunkenness and generous interest. Seven Gods help him, but she was beautiful. So fucking—

Nothing can happen between us.

Ever.

Calling the princess *Sol'ami* had been a slip of the tongue, a term of endearment, even if she didn't yet know what it meant. He wasn't sure why he chose that name, exactly. Only that it seemed to fit her in that moment.

Bast knew a few elfin words, having picked them up here and there. Speaking the words could result in the emperor hunting him down. Anything elfin had been outlawed over a millennium ago, after Emperor Narcisse had exterminated the Kruos elves and chased the Luthian elves off the continent.

Instead of going to sleep after he dropped her off in her bed, Bast returned to the streets of Stormvalor to dole out coins for those who played their parts. Oh, he knew some of them, casually. But the promise of coins for some made-up stories that made him look better would make anyone eager to make him into a prince.

And they had more than earned their payday.

CHAPTER 33

Know Your Place

Aslyn couldn't remember how she got back into her bed, but she had woken there, tucked under the blankets with her fighting leathers still on. Kaiti had been appalled to find her in such attire when she woke Aslyn, but the girl wouldn't tell. Nor would she ask questions.

Some parts of the evening were still a blur. Some of the memories of dancing with Zayne surfaced as she bathed, and Aslyn's humiliation toward her behavior made her flush even alone.

By the time Aslyn emerged from the bath, Kaiti had food and a tonic waiting. The girl understood something, at least. Aslyn downed the tonic. It would help alleviate some of the pressure in her head.

Had she tried to kiss Zayne? Seven Gods, she needed to apologize for her crass behavior.

And she needed to see Aethan. So much had happened since they last spoke.

Aslyn walked with her guards to the competitor training ground, where she sat on a shaded bench beneath the gallery overhang. The men trained hard with various weapons, fists, and feet. The tension in the air was palpable as Aslyn observed every movement, comparing it to her own training. Her gaze continually shifted to Aethan, who had not seemed to notice her presence.

Cormic and Cavis joked with Aethan and Trystain, and Aslyn's heart warmed as their laughter rang out loud enough to hear from her distant bench. Aethan fit so naturally with her own people—with everyone. *So does Zayne...* He had fit in so easily last night. Thinking about him at this moment proved quite unexpected.

Aslyn watched Marek boxing with Bryse. While she wasn't certain she had genuine interest in Marek any longer, she couldn't discount his usefulness. The wealth of information he could provide for her was abundant.

But her gaze continued drifting back to Aethan.

Her breath caught.

Aethan stripped off his shirt, using it to mop up sweat. Despite his lithe frame, his chest rippled with muscles. His arms were thicker than she had expected as well. Seven Gods, that would certainly influence her dreams tonight. No, she couldn't really consider Marek when she might be able to have Aethan after all.

Aethan said something, grinning, and slapped Cormic on the back. The other man appeared unimpressed, but Cavis broke out in cackling laughter.

Aslyn noticed the dragon tattooed over his heart. Once more, she found herself breathless, fingers clinging to her skirt.

Elisio moved closer to Aslyn, and she was about to call him out for it when she noticed why.

Zayne leaned against the gallery half-wall, peering out at the competitors as if searching for something. He watched Marek, and his lips drew in a tight line. He studied Aethan, as if gazing at an idol.

She rose from her bench and strolled toward Zayne. "Are you envious that you cannot compete?"

Zayne peered over his shoulder at her, and that hard expression softened. "Morning, Princess." He straightened and studied her as if seeking some weakness in her as well. "Hardly. I know my worth. No need to prove it."

"Why come to Stormvalor if you feel so strongly about this sort of contest?" Aslyn asked, crossing her arms. Why was she acting like this after how well they got along last night?

"I may have come into considerable wealth recently, but I'm no fool," Zayne said. "With the right bets, I could double down. Pride doesn't offer security. Money does."

Aslyn supposed he had a point. "Is that why you look like you're ready to pick these men apart? Because you're searching for the best odds?"

Zayne's mouth quirked up in the corner and Aslyn's heart skipped a beat. "Something like that." He stuffed his hands into his pockets and lifted his chin, a subtle move that only made him even more ruggedly dashing. Did he know that? "Though I would much prefer a walk with you, if you would give me the honor."

Part of her wanted to say no so she could watch Aethan train just a little longer. Especially shirtless. And she wanted to speak with Aethan. But if she lingered here too long, the competitors would notice. They would talk. In fact, leaving with Zayne likely offered her the best opportunity to escape such gossip.

She agreed, and they moved away from the training grounds.

Zayne kept his hands in his pockets, not even offering her his arm. Hadn't last night gone well? "Tell me, *Sol'ami*, do you come here to see the men without their shirts on?"

Sol'ami. The word rolled off his tongue so gentle and smooth it made Aslyn's skin heat. Some part of her remembered him calling her that last night as well. Why did he keep calling her that? What did it mean? And why did it make her entire body react?

Instead of demanding an answer, Aslyn defended herself. "Is it relevant that they wear no shirts? Can I not watch to learn about them as you do simply because I'm a woman?"

Zayne chuckled, shaking his head. "I would believe you if your face wasn't burning red."

"That's anger."

"My apologies then," Zayne said, but he didn't sound like he believed her at all.

Not that he should. She had come to observe their fighting styles and learn, but had easily been distracted the moment Aethan stripped that shirt off. Despite herself, Aslyn glanced back over her shoulder before they disappeared from the training grounds.

Aethan watched her. He stood frozen in place on the training grounds, those piercing blue eyes locked on her and Zayne, utterly defeated. And she hated that she made him feel that way even for a moment.

The sun burned so hot Aethan sweat right through his shirt. How could it be so hot with so much darkness in the sky? He stripped it off because the material kept getting in the way as he practiced group combat with Trystain, Cormic, Cavis, and Calvin. The next events would be a test of endurance. No one had been given clues about what that meant or how they would be tested, but pushing past their reasonable limits in training had seemed the best way to prepare.

Cormic and Cavis had gravitated toward Aethan as he, Trystain, and Calvin prepared to start. The brothers clicked into place in the group quickly and naturally.

Solisina help him, but if the sun didn't relent, Aethan was certain his skin would burn.

As they paused for a brief break, Cavis elbowed Aethan in the ribs and nodded toward the gallery around the training grounds, a cup of water already at his lips.

Aethan followed Cavis's nod.

The earth dropped out from beneath his feet. Time stopped.

Aslyn walked away alongside a man Aethan had not seen before. He knew everything there was to know about her suitors, but this guy... He could only be the new one Aslyn had mentioned. Aethan cursed silently as the guy smiled at Aslyn, oozing charm and good looks.

The air punched from Aethan's lungs as surely as if someone had thrown a fist into him. Aslyn peered back at Aethan over her shoulder, and he saw the words in her shining amber eyes. *I'm sorry.*

"Who's that ratbag?" Trystain asked.

"Lord Khrahar," Cavis said, glancing sidelong at Aethan as Aslyn turned the corner with Lord Khrahar and disappeared.

That was Zayne Khrahar? Aethan muttered a curse that drew a few startled glances from his friends. He had seen Zayne around and knew that Aslyn was considering him, but he hadn't connected the man with the name. And Fiara burn him if Roric hadn't been right about the tall, dark, handsomeness of Khrahar.

"Go," Cavis said as if reading his mind. "We'll cover for you."

Roric had better dig up as much information as he could about that guy. Quickly. Because Aethan was not about to lose Aslyn now. Not when he finally realized he had genuine feelings for her.

He would teach Zayne Khrahar his place.

The ploy had been far too easy to execute. Bast arrived at the training grounds after learning that the princess had gone down there to watch the men practice. He placed himself just within her line of sight, but far enough away that she would believe he hadn't noticed her making eyes at a shirtless Starkling—and tried to ignore how it filled him with fury.

He hadn't waited long—using the time to study the way Aethan and his friends moved, just in case he needed the information later—before Aslyn approached him.

The conversation had not opened as smoothly as he would have hoped. Bast thought that, after how open she had been last night, something had changed between them. Apparently, he had been wrong. She reverted to the princess she had been before, much to his disappointment.

"I feel I'm the one who should apologize to you," Aslyn admitted with a sigh, keeping her voice low so Elisio couldn't hear from his twenty-pace distance. "I did not act like myself last night. My behavior was—"

"Free?" Bast offered, remembering her insistence on using that word last night.

"That's one thing to call it."

"That's what you called it, actually," he said, smirking at her. "Repeatedly."

Aslyn's face turned red, and she swiftly averted her gaze as they entered the dimly lit corridor.

Some primal part of Bast recalled how it had felt with her last night, and he wanted to press now that she was sober to see if any of those feelings had been real.

But it didn't matter because she was off limits.

"I did enjoy last night, even if I made a fool of myself." She glanced at him, vulnerable and beautiful. "Did I... I mean... did we...?"

Bast chuckled lowly even as his blood heated at the prospect of anything—anything at all—with this woman. "No. You tried to kiss me, but it didn't feel like the right moment." He stuffed his hands deeper into his pockets and shrugged as she turned scarlet. "Then you promptly passed out in my arms."

"How did I get back into my room then?" she asked. For a moment she peered back at her guard, then seemed satisfied their conversation remained quiet and private enough.

Bast winked at her. "I'll keep that secret to myself." Because he was not about to tell her he used shadow magic to get them up there.

They continued at a slow, casual pace up the winding stairs and along to corridors until eventually stopping outside her door.

"What does it mean?" Aslyn asked. Her question took him by surprise.

"What?" he asked, unable to look away. Her eyes pulled him in and held him hostage.

"*Sol'ami*, the name you called me earlier."

Bast shook his head, smoothly correcting her pronunciation of the elvish word. "Perhaps I will tell you when we are better acquainted."

Her brows lifted. "Better than this?"

Bast felt the heat of a thousand suns burning into him—and not from the princess.

Aethan rounded the bend, approaching at a fairly swift clip. Bast fought off the urge to grin. Marek had already fallen. Aethan was about to be next. Somehow he cleaned himself up at least a little and put on fresh clothes. Had they moved through the halls at such a slow pace?

Aslyn turned when she noticed Bast's gaze had moved past her, and her brows climbed when she saw Aethan.

"Sorry to interrupt," Aethan said politely, hardly even winded as he addressed the princess. "I've been trying to catch up with you since the ball. You're busy, but if you have a few minutes today, I would love to steal them."

Bast pretended to be much like many other Starkling fans, wide-eyed and in awe. "No, that's quite alright. Please." He stepped back. "I have some business to attend to anyway."

Aethan held up a hand to stop him. "Are you sure?"

Well played, Starkling. He was good at this game.

"Yes, yes." Bast bowed to Aslyn. "I hope we can spare a few minutes for one another again soon, though."

"Thank you again, Zayne."

Bast made a quick escape before they could stop him, then moved as quickly as he dared through the shadows once he was out of sight.

By the time Bast reached his room, his heart was hammering like never before. He dropped into a crouch and grabbed a fistful of hair in each hand.

That woman would be the end of him.

CHAPTER 34

Blood and Roses

"I really didn't mean to intrude," Aethan said sincerely as Aslyn strolled into the royal suite with him following on her heels.

A few of the servants were busy making the next meal. Most of the guards were gone, which meant Aslyn's mother was out as well. Good. She would rather not have her mother around while she talked to Aethan.

Then Aslyn froze, her eyes falling on the massive vase of white roses. Her hand trembled as she recalled how Marek had acted yesterday. He was no longer an option now, obviously. Not when she had Zayne and Aethan to choose from… or at least Zayne, whose interest seemed singularly on her and not also another woman.

Which brought her to the brutal truth she needed from Aethan.

Aslyn stepped toward the flowers, Aethan only a few steps behind her. "Kaiti?"

Her maid materialized from the kitchen a moment later. "Oh, Your Majesty! Those are beautiful, aren't they?"

"Who are they from?" Aslyn asked, trying not to tremble. Was Marek trying to apologize? She couldn't forgive him. Not again.

"I didn't dare read your note, Your Majesty," Kaiti said. "But they arrived shortly after you left."

Aslyn plucked the note from the flowers and peeled it open. The writing was sharp, but clear and intelligently composed.

Aslyn,

Thank you for humoring me yesterday. Your gracious spirit is a boon to us all, Sol'ami.

Zayne

Aslyn bit her lip and tucked the note away in the folds of her dress. She turned to Kaiti, trying to ignore the pain on Aethan's face as she spoke. "They are from Zayne. Can you see they are brought to my room?"

Kaiti murmured in agreement and took hold of the massive vase of flowers, disappearing up the stairs.

"Things are going well with him, I take it," Aethan said diplomatically.

"I suppose they are."

"Better than with Marek, I hope." Aethan straightened, sticking his hands in his pockets and lifting his chin almost in defiance.

"Don't start, Aethan."

"It's an innocent comment."

"Is it?" Aslyn snapped. "Stop sidestepping. We both know you came up here because you saw me with Zayne. You've never skirted from being honest with me before. Please, don't start now."

"Fine." Aethan edged deeper into the sitting room where Aslyn stood with her arms crossed over her chest. His jaw twitched. "I don't like Zayne. I don't trust Zayne. I don't *know* Zayne. Nor does anyone else."

"Plenty of people know him," Aslyn argued.

"Who?" He crossed his arms and stared her down.

But Aslyn couldn't tell him the truth because it meant admitting she left the arena with Zayne, unaccompanied. That she spent an evening drinking with lowborns and dancing freely in the street. Her mother would lock her up and throw away the key.

Aethan's lips twisted as if he had just won the argument, only fueling her anger. "Exactly. Aslyn, I've talked to everyone who will share information, as has Roric and a host of others—including your own countrymen! No one heard of Zayne Khrahar before he showed up here to sweep you off your feet."

Aslyn threw back her head and laughed.

"Nothing about this is funny," Aethan said.

"You're jealous."

"So what if I am?" He threw his arms up.

"Zayne is kind and considerate and honorable, not unlike someone else I know," Aslyn snapped.

"He is *nothing* like me," Aethan growled.

Aslyn eyed his hands as they curled into fists. She had never seen Aethan so angry before. He wouldn't hurt her, would he? Surely not.

"Your Majesty," Elisio said darkly from the door, as if asking permission to toss Aethan out on his ass.

"Stay out of this, Elisio!" Aslyn snapped.

His jaw twitched, but he stepped back, hand on his sword, eyes locked on Aethan.

"Zayne idolizes you, you know," she said, attempting to cool her temper and speak evenly. "He talks about you, how much he admires you. Did you even see that look on his face in the hallway? Like he couldn't believe he was sharing the same air as you. Like he was in the presence of a god." Aslyn shook her head. "But you are no god, Aethan Starkling."

All the anger in his face washed away, replaced by a stoic façade. "I never claimed to be anything of the sort. I also don't care what he thinks of me. I made you a promise, Aslyn. And I take my promises very seriously. He is not who you think he is. I'm looking out for your future."

Aslyn's gut writhed madly as she sensed the end approaching and she wasn't prepared to face it. The words formed slowly, coalescing into what she was certain would be a big mistake, yet she needed to say them aloud.

"At least I'm his first choice, not his last."

Aethan flinched. Dead silence settled over the suite as the two of them simply stared at one another as if frozen in time. Despite his stoic façade, Aslyn saw the agony in his eyes and knew her words had hit just as hard as she feared they would.

Why did I say that? But deep down, she knew the answer, even if she denied it to herself. All of this would be much easier if he just walked away. Then she wouldn't have to choose. Or worse, she wouldn't have to worry about Emperor Oxon forcing them apart. Aslyn wasn't sure she could handle the pain if she gave herself to Aethan only to lose him.

He broke the silence first, swallowing first. "That's not fair. I've only ever looked out for your best interests."

"Tell me I'm wrong, then," Aslyn said, her voice cracking over the words. She wanted him to say she was wrong, desperately, yet at the same time, she didn't. "Tell me I'm wrong and you wouldn't have chosen her first in a heartbeat. Tell me you would have even considered me for a moment."

"A lot has changed," he said softly.

"Like her interest in you."

"Like my feelings for you!" Aethan's tense shoulders coiled tight, rising and falling with angry breaths.

No, don't say that. Tears burned in the back of Aslyn's eyes, but she refused to cry in front of him. It was better this way.

"I won't be your last option, Aethan Starkling. And if you can't tell me I'm wrong..."

"Zayne is playing a game with you, Aslyn." The cold calm in Aethan's voice was somehow worse than his anger. "Don't come crawling to me crying about it when he makes his move."

Then he turned and marched out the door.

Elisio didn't bother getting in his way.

It rattled in the frame like thunder when Aethan slammed it shut behind him. Aslyn's knees gave out and she sank to the sofa, burying her face in her hands to cover her tears.

"Your Majesty?" Elisio's gentle voice grated on Aslyn's nerves.

She pushed herself to her feet and stomped up the stairs, slamming her bedroom door and startling Kaiti as she stormed through the sitting room into the bedroom.

Then she let out a scream of anguish so long and loud it hurt her throat and stole all the air from her lungs.

Aethan marched to Zayne Khrahar's suite, ready for blood. If Aslyn wouldn't listen to him, he would get the truth right from the source.

When he arrived at the suite and knocked on the door, an older woman in a servant uniform opened the door. Her eyes widened in shock upon seeing him. "Lord Starkling!"

Aethan eased past her into the small suite. "I'm here to speak with Zayne."

"He isn't here, m'lord, but you are welcome to wait. Would you like a drink?"

He shook his head and marched to the sofa, sinking down to wait as anger burned in his veins. As he waited, that anger slowly transformed into regret. Any hope he had with Aslyn had been shattered.

Because she was right, and he couldn't tell her otherwise.

He would have chosen Iskra back then. He *did* choose her then.

But now...

Seven Gods have mercy. I screwed up again.

Bast had listened to the argument with Aethan from the balcony, pleased that she hadn't listened to Aethan's arguments against Zayne. But hearing her scream of agony after the fight had been more than Bast could bear. He went into the city to drink.

When he returned to the suite, only slightly buzzed from the alcohol, he was shocked to find Aethan Starkling sitting on his sofa, blue eyes locked on him.

Bast instinctively dropped a knife into his hand, just in case.

"You must be a very busy man," Aethan said coldly. "I've been waiting a while." He cocked his head, and something dangerous shone in his eyes. "Funny, you don't look like you idolize me. You look ready to cut my throat."

Bast dropped his jacket on a nearby chair and dismissed Esterly, who watched from the kitchen doorway.

"I'm a little shocked to find you in my suite," Bast said evenly, thankful he hadn't gotten trashed. Starkling would chew him up and spit him out if he didn't have at least some of his wits about him.

"I initially came here to force you to confess the truth to me, by any means necessary," Aethan said, still unmoved, calm, and cold. "But after having some time to think, I realized you aren't worth sacrificing my principles."

Bast nearly laughed at Aethan. As if the Starkling heir could have touched him!

"So why are you still here?" Bast asked, sinking down on the chair across the room, the knife still in his palm.

"For her. You see, I made her a promise. To protect her best interests."

"Which means you, I suppose," Bast replied snidely.

"No. I've made my own mistakes, and she knows all about them. What concerns me is why you are after her in the first place." Aethan's gaze slowly moved over Bast, sizing him up in ways few ever dared. "Your money is a lie. I can't prove it, but I know it. Maybe you are trying to climb out of a hole. Maybe the emperor offered you a hefty reward to win her over so he could steal her crown."

Bast blinked at that bold-faced treason from Starkling's lips. And then he realized what Aethan meant.

He thought Bast was bought off by the empire as a puppet. A low, deep chuckle rumbled up his throat, slowly transforming into a full-on laugh. Aethan scowled at the reaction.

"There is so much wrong with your argument," Bast said through his laughter. He took a few breaths to calm himself. "First of all, do I look like a puppet? No. If anyone is, it's that Marek bastard. As for money, I have more than enough to get by on my own. I don't need blood money from the Imperial Seat." Bast leaned forward, resting his elbows on his knees and all amusement gone. "I would sooner steal the imperial seat for her than give her crown to those worthless sacks of meat."

Aethan absorbed the words, chewing on them thoughtfully. The fury in his eyes shifted to intrigue. He scrubbed his hands casually as he put his thoughts together.

At long last, he broke the silence. "She has no idea the kind of man you are. There is blood on those roses you sent to her. I just don't know whose yet."

If only he knew how close to the truth that statement truly was.

Aethan stood, and Bast mirrored the motion. But the Starkling heir didn't make a move toward him. Instead, he turned his back like an idiot and marched toward the door. He paused before leaving and turned to Bast.

"I hope you mean what you said." Aethan's blue eyes turned stormy and Bast swore he heard thunder beyond the windows. "About her crown."

Then he closed the door.

CHAPTER 35

Fight Dirty

After leaving Kharhar's suite, he had cleaned up and gone straight to the Starkling suite, relieved to find Sybil there and not abducted somewhere by the Imperial Heir. Lux Starkling, however, had been strangely absent. He had hoped to speak to his father about the creatures locked in the dungeon, but he was also glad for the absence.

The Starkling suite shone bright with late afternoon light despite the overcast sky. Sybil lounged on a chaise near where Aethan sat.

Unlike his sister, he sat on the edge of the armchair, his composure just as on-edge as his insatiable need for answers.

Aethan listened to his sister talk about Prince Valen for more than half an hour. Aethan envied his sister's cautious optimism about Prince Valen. Her voice didn't bleed with excitement like other women might, but she did sound somewhat hopeful about what the prince wanted from her. Apparently, the two of them spent a great deal of time together at the ball, and Prince Valen had been charming, if a bit cool.

"He spoke of the future in terms of centuries instead of years," Sybil said. A soft smile graced her face. "There's something appealing about that. The intensity of it…"

Aethan's face scrunched. How could that be appealing? It wasn't as if any of them would be alive that long.

"Did he say why he was interested in you?" Aethan didn't want to stomp on his sister's fragile hope, nor did he want to assume this was about him. But no one seemed capable of giving any direct answers, and his curiosity couldn't take it.

"Am I not tempting enough?" Sybil teased. Her sky-blue eyes danced in delight.

Aethan bit his retort back. "Sybil… does he know?"

He hated asking, but a prospect like Sybil would be tempting to the Imperial Heir for more than one reason. Sybil sometimes caught glimpses of the future. Her visions were often hazy and hard to accurately read, but with the right training, that could be a dangerous tool in the emperor's hands.

"If he does, he has not said as much." She waved off his concern. "As for why he came all this way to meet me, apparently he believes my position in the empire will be critical in the years to come. I suppose if you run off to marry your princess, that could be true." She smirked mischievously at him, but something in her eyes was veiled in deception. Aethan couldn't make sense of it. Sybil had never knowingly deceived him.

"Are you trying to change the subject?" he asked.

"I saw the two of you at the ball together, as natural as if you were made for one another," Sybil replied. She shifted onto her side, resting her chin on her arm over the arm of the chaise. "I probably shouldn't tell you this, but your fates are intertwined. Don't ask how. I don't really know how to explain it. Like the sun needs the blue sky."

The words created a vicious maelstrom of angst and anger in his gut. It must have shown on his face, because Sybil said, "What happened?"

And he spilled everything, lamenting his argument with Aslyn, wishing he hadn't ruined yet another relationship. He didn't dare tell her about his conversation with Zayne. Not with her growing closer to the Imperial Heir.

"Lord Khrahar has nothing compared to you. And I saw the way she looked at you with hope and hunger."

Aethan sank back and shook his head. He had seen that hope that night, too, but the hunger? Besides, he had made a horrible mess of things.

"I saw her with him today. And the look she sent to me... It was almost like she was sorry, like she was letting go. And then I dumbly went after them and made an ass of myself. She won't forgive me for what I said."

Sybil laughed. "Aethan Starkling! Since when do you ever concede? Do you have feelings for her?"

Aethan swallowed the lump that suddenly lodged in his throat, unable to meet his sister's gaze. Instead, he studied his hands.

"You love her."

He shook his head but couldn't force himself to deny it aloud. "It doesn't matter. I screwed it all up. Again."

Sybil crouched in front of him, taking his hands and forcing him to match her blue eyes.

"It's not too late yet. If you truly want her, it's time to fight dirty, Aethan. Surely you've learned something about her by this point that no one else would know. Or at least few others. Use that."

Aethan flinched. "Against her?"

"No, genius." Sybil giggled. "Use it to endear yourself to her in ways the others cannot. Grovel. Then expose something vulnerable to her. And for the love of the Seven Gods, kiss her if you haven't done it yet. Because I promise you, men like Marek and Zayne Khrahar are doing the same thing. Your honor is a beautiful virtue, but sometimes you have to fight dirty."

Fight dirty...

Aethan grinned suddenly, seizing his sister's face and kissing her forehead. "You're brilliant."

She giggled. "I'm aware."

After changing into practice leathers, Aethan swiftly climbed the stairs to the Novavito suite. Two very dutiful guards regarded him with suspicion, but he simply smiled warmly at them and asked to see the princess.

Aslyn appeared at the door a minute later. Anger radiated off her, pure and righteous.

"Before you tell me to go to the underworld, let me apologize," he blurted. "You were right, and that shouldn't shock me. To make it up to you, I am offering you a chance to take your anger out on me."

She raised a brow, crossing her arms.

"With a sword."

Aslyn's lips parted, momentarily stunned. Her amber eyes swept over his practice leathers.

His own gaze slowly took in her gauzy dress. "Though I suggest you change. Perhaps something more like what you wore when we first met?"

Her eyes narrowed, then widened as it dawned on her what he meant. "You're serious?"

"I could stand to learn a thing or two from the Princess of the Sword."

The guards at the door choked, obviously surprised that Aethan knew of her nickname.

Watching Aethan walk out the door had crushed Aslyn's soul. By the time she recovered, she fell into a fit of anger, wishing for a chance to fight him. Now, he had given her exactly what she wanted. It was hard not to be excited, even if she was still mad at him.

They entered the training grounds together, and it was clear he had sent his squire ahead to clear the grounds so they could be alone. Elisio stationed himself in the gallery where he could watch and quickly move to protect her. With each passing day, Elisio grew quieter, and his tension increased.

The sun slowly sank toward the horizon. Sunset would be upon them soon, offering some relief from the heat of the day.

"I have been intensely curious just how skilled the Princess of the Sword is," Aethan said, holding out a hand. Roric swiftly handed over a practice sword to Aethan, then brought one to Aslyn, bowing as he offered it.

"Thank you, Roric," she said graciously. The practice sword had a different balance and weight than she was used to, but it only took her a few practiced swings to get the feel of it. A smirk played across her lips as she eyed Aethan. Aslyn fully intended to fight dirty to punish him for being an ass earlier. "Are you sure your pride can handle this?"

Aethan chuckled lowly. "I suppose we will find out."

Aslyn had watched the way he moved in combat more times than she could count since this tournament began. She had been alarmed by how easily he had defeated Bryse. As she moved into a defensive position, Aslyn knew she was outmatched. Aethan had already proven himself more skilled with a blade than anyone else she had fought. She had expected that cockiness to shine through as they set into position to spar.

But Aethan's eyes studied her with wary caution. He didn't assume he would beat her—even if he probably would. No, he prepared for the worst.

The first strike had been fast as an asp to her right. Aslyn deftly blocked as she had been taught, aware that he tested her defenses. Over and over, they struck, testing one another, never breaking through guard.

"You have good defense, but your left foot gives away your moves when you counterattack," Aethan said as he pulled back. "Your feet should deceive your opponent into making a mistake. Make them think you are moving one way only to counter with another before they can react."

Aslyn had been studying the way Aethan moved each time he struck and wondered how he could control his body like that. When he struck out again, Aslyn followed his instruction, moving as swiftly as she could swing the practice sword. To her delight, she drove him back a few steps.

"Like that?" she asked with a vicious grin.

He returned it.

A heartbeat later, those tentative tests were replaced by a series of attacks. Aslyn's pulse hummed with electric energy as their movements became a dance far more intimate than any they had shared on the ballroom floor. Every breath, every shift of feet, every movement of their arms. All of it made her excitement increase.

He advanced on her, and she deflected. Then she advanced on him. The two of them moved around the training ground in a waltz of swords. Yet she knew Aethan held himself back. More than once, she mistakenly attacked or defended, and his movements shifted with her.

Aethan shifted his body to the side, swinging the sword in an upstroke. Aslyn ducked and spun around it, shuffling a few more steps back as she adjusted her grip.

"Stop going easy on me, Starkling."

Aethan spun his blade dramatically. "I'm not sure you're ready for all of me."

Aslyn made a chortling sound in the back of her throat. "How about you let me be the judge of that?"

His brows lifted and he shook his head in amusement. The setting sun created a halo of light behind him that made her heart stop. *No distractions, Aslyn!* She admonished herself.

"As you wish," he said.

Before he finished speaking, Aethan struck.

Aslyn's breath came in quick, measured bursts, her heart hammering beneath her fighting leathers. The training ground echoed with the rhythmic clash of steel as she parried another of Aethan's swift strikes. His movements were a blur of expert precision, each attack a fluid extension of his body, leaving her scrambling to keep up.

"Focus, Princess," Aethan's voice was calm, a sharp contrast to the intensity of his strikes. He wasn't even winded! His piercing blue eyes never left hers, scrutinizing her every movement.

Aslyn gritted her teeth, determined not to let frustration cloud her judgment. She had asked for this, taunted him into this. She shifted her stance, trying to mimic the fluidity of his movements, but Aethan was already a step ahead, his sword flicking out to tap her shoulder lightly.

"Too slow," he said, a small smile tugging at the corner of his lips.

She bit back a retort, channeling her energy into a flurry of strikes, hoping to catch him off guard. But Aethan parried each blow effortlessly, his sword a shimmering blur between them. She realized then just how immensely outmatched she was, the gap between their skills was a chasm she couldn't hope to bridge even with her years of training.

"Remember your form," Aethan advised, deflecting her sword with a graceful twist of his wrist. "Strength isn't everything."

Aslyn nodded, sweat dripping down her forehead, stinging her eyes. She adjusted her grip, trying to recall the lessons drilled into her since childhood. With renewed focus, she launched another attack, this time more controlled, more precise.

Aethan's smile widened, a glint of approval in his eyes. "Better," he said, his voice carrying a note of genuine praise.

Aslyn drank it up.

Their swords met again, and for a brief moment, Aslyn felt a surge of triumph as she held her ground against his onslaught. But then Aethan shifted his stance, and with a swift, almost effortless motion, disarmed her, sending her sword clattering to the ground.

She stared at him, breathless and wide-eyed.

"You're improving," he said, his tone warm.

Aslyn rolled to the side, her hand snatching up her fallen sword just in time to block Aethan's sudden, swift strike. The clang of their blades reverberated through the courtyard, and she pushed herself up, her eyes locking onto his with renewed determination.

"Not bad," Aethan remarked, a glint of amusement in his eyes. He didn't give her a moment to recover, pressing the attack with a series of quick, precise blows. Aslyn struggled to keep up, her muscles burning with exertion.

Their swords clashed again and again, the rhythm of their combat a deadly dance. Aethan's expertise was undeniable, his movements almost a blur as he forced her back. Aslyn's steps faltered, each retreat more desperate than the last. She tried to anticipate his strikes, but he was always a step ahead, his blade an extension of his will.

With a final, powerful thrust, Aethan disarmed her once more. Aslyn's sword flew from her grasp, skittering across the cobblestones as her back collided with a pillar along the gallery wall. She gasped, the breath knocked out of her, and before she could react, Aethan's blade was at her neck. She felt the cool metal press against the pulse of her racing heartbeat. The blades were dull. He wouldn't actually hurt her, and she trusted him completely.

Seven Gods help her, Aethan stood so close, those beautiful blue eyes boring into hers, a mixture of pride and raw, intense heat in his gaze. "Yield, Princess," he said, his voice low and steady.

Aslyn's heart raced, her pulse thrumming in her ears. She was pinned, utterly at his mercy. And mother forgive her, she loved it. His demand felt weighted with deeper meaning. The setting sun shone behind him, making him even more deadly beautiful. Oh, she wanted him. Wanted those lips on hers. The heat from his body pressed into her. That glorious scent of a wisteria and blackberry currant mingled with sweat, and she remembered what he had looked like earlier in the day, shirtless and shimmering with sweat. All thoughts of their argument vanished as desperate need took hold of her.

"I yield," she breathed, her voice steady despite her racing heart.

Aethan lost his senses the moment Aslyn spoke those two words. The setting sun shone in her eyes, making the amber blaze as she stared up at him. He struggled with restraint as her body pressed against him.

"I told you that you weren't ready for all of me," he said, his voice deepening as his gaze dipped to those beautiful, full lips.

"And I told you to let me be the judge," Aslyn retorted breathlessly.

The sword clattered to the ground as he let it drop, his hand instead sliding into her black curls as their lips clashed as fiercely as their swords had. Aslyn's lips parted, granting him permission, and he seized it, lost in a deep animal hunger for more. His tongue delved deep, reveling in the taste of her and the small sounds she made as his hand moved down her body. Aslyn arched into the touch, pressing her body harder against him.

As her tongue brushed up against his, teasing at it, curling around it, Aslyn's hands deftly unfastened the buckles on the vest of his practice leathers until it hung loose. Aethan didn't even think as he shook it off his shoulders, leaving him in his white undershirt. His own hands began to explore a bit more freely, groping at her chest, creeping along the tight leather covering her ass.

Aethan was on the brink of losing control completely. His mouth roved over her jaw and neck with voracious hunger.

When her fingers curled into his hair and she breathed his name, Aethan shuddered. He nipped at her earlobe.

Some sensible part of him screamed to stop. They were on the training grounds where anyone would see them. Her guard no doubt watched every second of this with his own dangerous fury.

His lips found their way back to hers, softer this time despite her attempts to pull him into more.

"We need to stop," Aethan said, hardly recognizing his own animalistic voice.

Aslyn whimpered in dismay as he eased back, her fingers digging into his back beneath his shirt. When had she gotten her hands there? "I said I would be the judge," she said, her own voice heated with desire.

Aethan brushed a thumb over her swollen lips. The glittering of her eyes was like the sun, and the husky look in them made him wish they were somewhere private and alone. Then he knew he wouldn't stop himself. He would absolutely let her be the judge, let her take control and guide this however far she was willing to go. Aethan was certain he would slowly implode the moment he was alone just thinking about this kiss.

The flush of her skin and heat in her eyes... Aethan had once compared Iskra to the sun, but he had been wrong. So very wrong. Iskra was a candle next to the blazing light that shone from Aslyn. If the Goddess of Beauty stood beside Aslyn, Aethan wasn't sure he would even notice. "Seven Gods, you are beautiful. Like a golden sunset."

"Keep saying things like that and I will make you take me back to your rooms," Aslyn teased breathlessly.

"I'm sorely tempted." Aethan leaned his face closer just to feel the soft brush of her skin against his own. His lips once more came dangerously close to her neck, just below her ear. "But when this does happen, I need to know it's because you want me."

Aslyn leaned back and licked those glorious lips. "I do want you." Those four words sent a thrill to his core.

But that wasn't what he meant.

Aethan shook his head as he stepped back. "No, Aslyn. I need you to choose me."

"If that's your idea of a proposal, it could use work," Aslyn replied.

Aethan's heart stopped dead in his chest. It hadn't been meant that way, but... would it be so terrible? If they were engaged before Prince Valen made his move for Sybil known, would that supersede the rules?

The problem was, Aethan didn't know that Aslyn would say yes if he did ask.

"No, princess," Aethan said, retreating another step. He smirked at her. "Not yet." He picked up the practice sword, seeking a distraction from what they had just done—from this entire conversation. "I hope you can forgive me for earlier. It won't happen again. And thank you for humoring me with this sparring session, but I think it's time we part ways for the night." He bowed to her, then strode away before she could stop him.

Roric would have to put away the swords and retrieve his leathers. Aethan didn't trust himself near Aslyn much longer.

Bast had followed Aethan, worried what he might say to Aslyn when they spoke again. Bast kept to the shadows. No one could know what he was up to.

As he inched up on the training grounds, the sounds of practice swords clashing hadn't shocked him.

What had shocked him was the sight of the princess fighting Aethan Starkling. Bast's gaze darted around the edge of the training grounds to find the guard, Elisio, glaring at the princess and the young lordling. The man's hand mottled as he gripped the hilt of his sword tight, not because he worried for the princess' life, but because he clearly wanted to draw that sword and cut Aethan down.

A sword clattered against stone, drawing Bast's studious gaze from the guard back to the training ground.

Aethan had Aslyn pinned against a pillar, his sword against her neck. The moment she yielded, the intensity of their fight transformed into something else entirely. The passion and desperate need of that kiss created a surge of rage in Bast that he couldn't wholly explain. Princess Aslyn Kiernan was free to do what she wished with whomever she wished. Bast certainly had no actual interest in courting her. It was just a ploy for that jewel still chained around her neck.

Yet as Aslyn stripped off Aethan's leather training vest, then slid her fingers into his hair, Bast's fingers itched. A knife had slipped into his palm, and he seriously considered throwing it into the back of Aethan's skull with enough force to kill the lordling instantly.

Before he could do anything to reveal his true identity—or his presence—to anyone, Bast turned and vanished into the shadows once more. Screw this. He would slip into her room tonight while she slept, take that jewel, and do whatever needed to be done to sever her connection to it.

*N*ot yet.

Aslyn's steps were light as she made her way back to her suite. That kiss had been everything she had hoped for and more. And when Aethan kissed her, Aslyn had lost all sense of herself. All that existed was his body hard against her, his lips and tongue hungry for her, and a deep ache within her, the likes of which she had never felt before.

Elisio miraculously said nothing. Yet somehow, his utter silence was far worse than anything he could have said. The thump of his boots was heavy, and his entire body was rigid with tension, like the smallest thing would make him snap. He didn't even say goodnight as usual when she stepped into her bedroom.

After she closed her door, thankful that Kaiti was not waiting for her, Aslyn held her breath and closed her eyes, reliving that glorious kiss. Marek had kissed her a few nights ago, but it hadn't been anything like that. It never would.

And Zayne... Aslyn couldn't deny being drawn to him, nor that he would be a good man and a good match.

But it was Aethan.

It always had been.

Aethan Starkling, her beautiful Stormvalor Champion.

Tomorrow, she would tell her mother, then pray that Aethan felt the same way about her.

CHAPTER 36

Moving Shadows

Bast waited until late at night to don his black leathers and climb the arena boxes and balconies. The lower level lamps glowed softly in the royal suite, as they did every night. Bast had been studying it since he arrived for guard watches, evening movement, and any lurking dangers.

He peered into the main living space of the suite, confirming only two guards on duty. One outside the queen's suite. The other outside the princess' suite. Elisio was not on duty at night any longer. Bast wasn't certain if he was promoted or demoted, but he was thankful not to have the jealous swordsman nearby tonight.

With a leap into the shadows and a heave on the rail, he silently hauled himself up to the princess' balcony.

The doors were closed and curtained. The lamps glowed brightly inside.

Bast frowned, easing toward the door at an angle so he could peer inside. Instantly, he dipped back as Aslyn climbed out of bed, her skin flushed and utterly exposed. She walked away from the balcony doors, deeper into her bedroom. Bast's pulse quickened as his gaze swept over her nude form, the perfect curves and smooth, rich bronze skin.

Aslyn was not the first woman Bast had accidentally spied on in this state, but something about her made his heart thunder.

She could see me in the shadows back at the palace, Bast recalled. He must have subconsciously worried that she would do it again. And if she did, his cover was blown.

Aslyn vanished into another room. A minute later, Bast heard her splashing in water.

Bathing.

Maybe she had taken the jewel off. He could lift it while she bathed and be far from the city by sunrise.

Without evening shadows, he would be more exposed, but this could be a best-case scenario.

Bast pushed his shadow magic into the balcony door latch and hinges, then wrapped it around his boots to silence his steps. He eased the door open just enough to slip in and out.

The princess' suite boasted a massive bed with rumpled luxury sheets, a night-stand on either side without drawers, and a vanity. Bast's gaze swept over the night-stands. Nothing there but a knife. He hurried to the vanity, checking the jewelry boxes and drawers, pushing aside letters from home and from eager young men without a prayer to snag a princess.

Nothing.

He hadn't noticed it around her neck when she left for the bathroom. The necklace had to be somewhere in this room.

He quickly set to work checking for hidden storage spaces in the floorboards, loose stones in the wall, anything that might make a good hiding place, using tendrils of his shadows to expedite the process.

Nothing.

A splash from the bathroom was followed by the slap of wet, bare feet on tile.

Bast silently cursed his luck and slipped back out before she returned to the room. As the door closed, he spied her through the curtains, now wrapped in a thin silk robe.

The necklace dangled from her fist.

Aslyn's gaze swept the bedroom as if she knew he had been there. After a moment, she frowned, placing the necklace in her palm and running her finger over it. *She feels something from it!* Just like she could see into his shadows at the palace.

Bast needed to leave. Now.

Aslyn hadn't meant to wake in the night as she had, but the dreams of Aethan had been so vivid she couldn't fall back asleep until she quelled the fire burning in her core. The slickness and sweat would be uncomfortable to fall back asleep, so she had instead opted for a bath, setting the necklace on the stool beside her.

When she emerged, the green stone in the Jewel of Arithia glowed ever so faintly. Aslyn picked it up, alarmed at the warmth of the locket. It had only ever done that a few times recently. And each was when Zayne was near.

Aslyn put on her robe, afraid to find him waiting in her bedroom. A ludicrous notion, but she couldn't shake the sense that she wasn't alone, and that Zayne was near.

But no one was there. Aslyn remained utterly alone, and her room was as she had left it before her bath.

With a frown, she placed the locket in her palm, marveling at the warmth of it and wondering what that meant.

She made her way to the balcony doors. It was another ludicrous thought that he would be there on the balcony, but Aslyn knew she wouldn't rest again without being certain.

Aslyn pulled her knife from the sheath on her bedside table, then opened the balcony doors.

Cool night air blew in, and it smelled so much like Aethan—like wisteria and blackberry currant—that she ached for him again. Muttering to herself, Aslyn closed and locked the balcony doors, fastened the necklace around her neck, and settled in bed.

But she couldn't sleep, watching the moving shadows, thinking of the heated light in Aethan's eyes after he kissed her.

Bast watched the princess from a nearby balcony for some time. But it was clear she had no intention of sleeping any time soon.

Angry that he had failed, Bast hopped down from one balcony to the next until he reached the shadows of the arena stands.

Tomorrow, he would have to charm her into bed, then he could steal it right from her sleeping form and vanish before she woke.

Chapter 37

To Restore Balance

Aethan hardly slept, consumed by thoughts of Aslyn and the future. He rose with the sun, dressing quickly in his fighting leathers for the day, then he gave Roric a few final instructions to prepare for the day's event.

The journey to the Starkling suite made anxious butterflies flutter wildly in his stomach the closer he came to the door. He doubted his father would disapprove of his decision, nor would he be likely to reject it, but Aethan couldn't help being nervous all the same.

It didn't fail to strike him that when he arrived at Stormvalor, his plans for the future had been so vastly different. Aslyn had taken everything he thought he wanted and turned it on its head. Now, all he wanted was to prove himself worthy of her, to be her partner and her shield against any who would dare bring her harm. She was his sun and moon and stars, his hope and strength and heart. The feelings he had for Iskra had been real, but a pale reflection of his love for Aslyn.

Aethan paused outside the door to the Starkling suite, taking a deep, steadying breath, before stepping inside.

A servant greeted Aethan with wide, startled eyes. No doubt she was alarmed to see anyone so early in the morning.

"M'lord," she said with a curtsy.

"Is my father up?" Aethan asked. He didn't have a lot of time before he needed to report for the event.

"Just a moment ago, m'lord," she replied. "Shall I tell him you are here?"

"Please do." Aethan strolled over to the balcony to wait, peering out at the city of Stormvalor.

The overcast sun pressed against the horizon, casting long shadows along the streets, but also making the rooftops of some buildings glitter. Ominous dark clouds hovered overhead in that perpetual gray sky. Aethan prayed it wouldn't rain today. Completing the gauntlet in the rain would be quite a challenge.

"Aethan, what brings you here so early?" Lux Starkling asked, lingering near the doors in clothes he clearly donned in haste. He hadn't even bothered to brush his hair.

Dark circles made Lux's eyes appear haunted.

Aethan's stomach did somersaults. His nerves got the better of him and he leaned back against the balustrade, wrapping his fingers around the cool stone. Seven Gods, his hands were hot! Was he sweating? *Get a grip, Aethan.*

He knew what scared him. Not the fear that his father would reject the proposal. No, he was quite certain his father would heartily approve. What scared Aethan was the knowledge that the emperor's heir could still drive a wedge between him and Aslyn. A Starkling must always rule over Stormvalor, and if Prince Valen claimed Sybil for his future wife, Aethan would be forced to stay in Vorovesti.

"I come seeking your blessing," Aethan said.

Lux's brows lifted curiously.

Aethan couldn't help but smile despite the writhing mess of nerves in his stomach. "I would like to propose to Aslyn tonight, if she will choose me."

Lux Starkling froze. He didn't even blink as he studied Aethan. For some reason, this utter stillness made Aethan worried he had miscalculated his father's desire for this match.

Then his father crossed the balcony and pulled Aethan into a fierce hug. Aethan's arms hung limply at his sides, alarmed by the reaction. His father so rarely hugged him. Slowly, Aethan raised his arms and hugged his father back.

"My boy, you already know you have it," Lux said as he hugged Aethan.

They released and Lux stepped back, holding Aethan's shoulders. "The realm will be all the better for this match."

"Yeah, about that…" Aethan ran his fingers through his hair. "We actually think the *realm* may not be so happy with this match. In fact, she's convinced the emperor and his heir are actively trying to match her to one of their own."

Lux grimaced. "Marek Bloodstone."

Aethan nodded. "I suspect as much. Or Lord Khrahar."

Lux made a sound of disgust. "Yes, the new money suitor. He certainly came out of nowhere. Do you think he is a danger to her accepting your proposal?"

Aethan didn't want to admit it. He had hoped that last night had solidified him in her heart, but he couldn't shake the memory of how she had smiled at Lord Khrahar or how she had praised him during their argument. It pained him to say the words, but they fell from his lips. "Maybe."

"If you do this, you had better be certain she will accept," Lux said, leaning against the doorframe.

"Has Prince Valen indicated to you his intentions toward Sybil?" Aethan asked, the next part of his fear manifesting. "Because if he does, then Aslyn and I…" He trailed off, feeling the tremor climbing up his throat into his words. "There must always be a Starkling ruling over Stormvalor."

Lux considered his words, crossing his arms and tapping his finger against his lips thoughtfully. "I was going to wait to say anything. I didn't want to influence your decision with the princess."

That mess of nerves in his gut made Aethan sick to his stomach. "What is it?"

"Your uncle and I have already spoken about this possibility," Lux said at last. "We suspected Prince Valen might come for Sybil for a while now."

"Why?"

"Your sister doesn't just have royal blood, Aethan, nor do you."

Aethan blinked. What did that mean?

"You know of your sister's visions?" Aethan nodded, and Lux pressed on. "We tried to keep it secret, but Orrin believes Emperor Oxon found out. About a year ago, Sybil had a vision in public. We tried to cover it up, but it couldn't be coincidence that Prince Valen's Oshon wife died not long after. Just as we don't believe your mother's death was a coincidence of fate."

Aethan reeled from this news. Was his father saying the emperor had a hand in his mother's illness and death?

"Your mother received a gift from Emperor Oxon, an emerald necklace," Lux said, sadness darkening his bright blue eyes. "I couldn't get her to take that thing off once it was around her neck. She insisted it would insult the emperor should he find out."

Aethan remembered that necklace. The largest emerald he had ever seen in his life, wrapped in leaves of gold on a delicate gold chain.

"Her health slowly faded," Lux continued, his voice tightening in sorrow. "I didn't connect the pieces together until it was too late. It took two years, but... well you remember how she slowly faded."

Aethan's eyes pricked with tears as he remembered watching his mother die slowly while he was helpless to do anything about it. "You think... you think the emperor gave her a necklace that would kill her?"

Lux shook his head. "I think he didn't *care* if it killed her. It served another purpose, something I still don't understand. Do you remember Emperor Oxon coming to her funeral?"

Again, Aethan nodded, his heart twisting with betrayal. He had been loyal to the empire all his life. Could the emperor truly have been responsible for what happened to his mother?

"That necklace vanished by the time he left," Lux said. "I tore the house apart searching for it." Lux swallowed the lump in his throat and stared down at the floor.

Aethan remembered his father's mad rampage and rambling after the funeral. He had dismissed it as mad grief.

"I think that necklace somehow stole her life, that it stored the power inside," Lux Starkling admitted. "A force the emperor needed for whatever reason."

The floor tilted. Aethan's head spun. "Why? Why her?"

Lux drew in a breath, then let it out slowly. "Aethan, we never told you because... well because magic has been outlawed for so long by the Imperial Seat."

Aethan braced himself for a blow.

"Your mother was a healer. And a powerful one, at that. We did our best to protect Olivya from harm, to shield her secret, but your mother had a huge heart and drive to protect the people of Vorovesti."

"The plague..." Aethan's eyes widened. Not a year before his mother received that necklace, a plague hit Mordelic. The city was in danger of catastrophic loss of life. Nothing could stop the plague from sweeping through the streets. And then one day, it was just gone. "That was her, wasn't it?"

Lux grimaced, and a tear slipped down his cheek as he nodded. He quickly wiped it away. "I begged her not to use so much of her magic, but the agony of watching her people suffer when she could help them had been too much for her heart to bear. She said she would rather risk her own death than see her people suffer and die."

Then the emperor found out. Instead of letting them know and killing her outright, he had given her that necklace. The very item that slowly sucked the life from her.

And Prince Valen now took an interest in Aethan's sister for the very same reason Emperor Oxon took interest in his mother.

"You cannot allow Prince Valen to claim Sybil," Aethan said, straightening as determination rushed through him.

"You know as well as I do that I'm helpless to stop him." Lux's voice trembled. "I could try, and his Black Guards would kill me and take her anyway."

Curse the empire! He couldn't stand by and watch his sister be taken to her death.

"Before you do anything foolish," Lux continued, his voice hardening, "you should know that your sister has already seen what comes next." Aethan waited for his father to elaborate, but he didn't.

"Are you suggesting we just sit back and let her be used and killed?" Aethan's fists clenched at his sides.

"I'm telling you that your sister knows that the future of everyone in Divica depends on her going," Lux replied, and his own frustration and helplessness were clear in his sharp tone. "We have talked at length about all of this. If she doesn't go, the Imperial Seat will seek newer, stronger power to use, and then all will be lost. She has made her choice, Aethan, and she needs you to make yours."

Sybil told Aethan that his fate was tethered to Aslyn. Did that include the whole of Divica? If he aligned with Aslyn, could they have the power to protect the people of all five kingdoms? His father had already tried to tell him all of this, weeks ago when they stood on this very balcony.

At the time, Aethan assumed his father meant he and Aslyn could help strengthen the emperor's rule once more. But that hadn't been it at all. A Stormvalor Champion and the future queen of Novavito allied through marriage, with the full backing of Vorovesti would have enough power to topple a weakening emperor's power.

Had Lord Starkling known that night what lay ahead of Aethan, what Sybil had seen of their future?

"You are worried about a Starkling remaining in Stormvalor," Lux said. "And I'm telling you there will be. For now. I just yesterday proposed to a wonderful woman from Murandy Hills. Sybil will go with Prince Valen to keep him from seeking something stronger than her. You will marry Princess Aslyn and consolidate your power. And I will work diligently with my new wife to create a new worthy heir to this place should you fail."

Aethan flinched. "Fail?"

"To restore balance."

"To the empire?"

Lux shook his head. "The world, Aethan. Because the only thing stronger than your sister is you."

Aethan scoffed, shaking his head. "I don't have magic."

Lux raised his palms in supplication. "I can only relay what your sister has said. Go win the day. Win the tournament and win the princess."

CHAPTER 38

Captive

Aslyn hadn't been able to fall asleep for hours after her bath, and the sound of construction woke her with the sun. Grumpy and irritable, she marched out onto the balcony and gaped.

The entire arena floor was covered with a maze of equipment at various levels. One of the platforms—accessible only by a series of steps set so far apart one would have to jump to get from one step to the next—nearly reached the same level as her balcony! It reminded her of the training gauntlet in the Arithian guard barracks, but on a massive scale. Was this today's challenge?

Aslyn had hoped to see Aethan before the event, but she now doubted that would happen. It had probably been a foolish hope anyway. Competitors were kept busy the morning of events, preparing for what was to come.

Since there was no way she would get a moment more sleep with the noise below, Aslyn pulled the cloth rope that was attached to a bell in Kaiti's room. She hadn't even finished choosing her dress for the day before her maid entered.

"Your Majesty is up early today," Kaiti commented. Her own eyes were rimmed with dark circles. It seemed Aslyn was not the only one who hadn't slept well.

"It's hard to sleep with the noise below," Aslyn said as she covered a yawn that bled into her speech. "I need a lot of help this morning, Kaiti. I'm so tired that I can't think straight. Should I go purple or amber today?" She ran her fingers along the two dresses.

Kaiti strolled over, reaching into the closet. When she pulled out a pale blue dress, the smile on her face made Aslyn wonder what she knew.

"I have a feeling blue will be your color today."

Aslyn eyed the blue dress. She hadn't worn the dress yet, and she wasn't really sure why she had been saving it. But wearing it certainly felt like making a statement.

A statement she was prepared to make.

An hour later, her hair and makeup were in place. Aslyn removed the Jewel of Arithia, unable to shake the way it had warmed against her skin and made her think Zayne was creeping in the shadows. Better to leave it behind for now. Aslyn instructed Kaiti to see it tucked away in the safe, then dismissed Kaiti to her duties with the rest of the afternoon off to watch the event. She wouldn't need Kaiti again until evening if the day went as she hoped.

Queen Giata sat at the table by the closed balcony doors in the main living space, reading a note.

"Is that from father?" Aslyn asked as she joined her mother.

Queen Giata hummed, then folded the note and turned her sharp gaze up at her daughter. Aslyn hated that look. Nothing good ever followed that look. How was it that she, a future ruler of one of the most powerful kingdoms in Divica, could feel so small under that gaze?

"Well?" Queen Giata asked sharply.

Aslyn had been placing fresh fruit and a muffin on her plate, but that tone made her freeze and stare at her mother. "Well, what?"

"Time is almost up, Aslyn. Surely, you must have some idea who you prefer as a match by now."

Aslyn wiped her fingers on her cloth napkin and straightened in her chair. "Actually, I have. I was hoping to talk to you about it."

Queen Giata raised a sharp eyebrow and Aslyn knew what that meant. Her mother was waiting.

Aslyn took a drink of water to ease her suddenly dry throat. "I choose Aethan Starkling."

Her mother made a small sound in the back of her throat. Aslyn wasn't sure what that meant. "And how does he feel about this?"

Aslyn bit her lip as his words slid to the forefront of her mind again. *Not yet.* "He has not asked yet, but last night, he hinted pretty heavily that it was possible."

"Was this before or after he stuck his tongue down your throat and put his hands all over you?" Queen Giata asked sharply.

Aslyn flushed. How did she...? *Elisio!* She would murder him for this. Cold fury ran through her veins like ice. Aslyn folded her hands in her lap so her mother couldn't see how tightly she clasped them together.

"Does it matter?" she replied, attempting to sound nonchalant about it.

"It does when I hear this isn't the first time you've allowed one of these men to put their hands on you!" The queen leaned forward, staring down Aslyn, daring her to deny it. "I've heard all about your escapades with the Starkling heir, and Lords Marek and Zayne as well."

"I've done nothing of the sort with Lord Khrahar!" Aslyn snapped. "Marek was only a kiss, and it didn't spark anything in me. Certainly nothing like the way Aethan makes me feel."

"I'm sure it's easy to make a naïve girl believe that if you treat her the way Aethan Starkling treated you last night."

"I am not naïve," Aslyn replied darkly.

"Could have fooled me, child."

Aslyn took a deep breath to center herself.

"I'm glad someone had the sense to tell me what you've been up to before you give away our kingdom," the queen said.

The words were as good as a slap in Aslyn's face. She was doing this to *avoid* that fate!

"I thought this was what you wanted, *who* you wanted! Why are you angry that I've made the choice you pushed for in the first place?"

"Because you are not acting like a princess and future queen."

"So when a man behaves this way, it's acceptable, but when a woman acts the exact same way, it makes her loose in character?" Aslyn knew her anger was beyond control now.

"Among other places." The iciness of those three words slid over Aslyn's spine.

Her mother made it sound as if she had slept with all these men when she hadn't slept with any of them. Now relief that Aethan had the sense to stop them last night rolled through Aslyn. Without his restraint, she wouldn't have had a leg to stand on in this fight.

"For your information, my relationship with Aethan has born from friendship first," Aslyn said, her voice like a calm before the storm. "Neither of us took this courtship seriously. But I've fallen for him all the same. And I know he feels the same."

Queen Giata's hard eyes studied every inch of Aslyn for deception. She would find none here.

"What of the other woman?"

Aslyn flinched. She swallowed hard, then said, "Iskra has fallen in love with someone else. Cavis, of all people."

Her mother's eyes narrowed in suspicion. "That's convenient. These former lovers somehow end up in the same city, among the same social circles."

"It isn't like that." But Aslyn's heart wasn't in those words.

"You don't sound so certain."

Aslyn had enough. She pushed back her chair and stood as she said her peace. "You brought me here to choose a husband. I've made my choice. You can either accept it or not. But we are done here."

"We need Lord Khrahar's ships."

Aslyn didn't make it more than halfway across the room before her mother's words stopped her dead in her tracks. Slowly, she turned to face her mother. "Why?"

At last, the queen relayed the message from home. But it wasn't from her father. It was from Dorin. A band of rebels kidnapped the king, sank the Arithia fleet, and fled out to sea. Aslyn's knees shook.

The rebels her father had been so worried about had finally struck. What were they after? Why kidnap him?

"Is he... Is father alive?"

"Dorin isn't certain, but he's confident your father lives." Tears welled in the queen's eyes and Aslyn realized this wasn't just her father, it was the queen's husband. The news must have been a blow. "They will likely try to use your father to bargain for something."

Aslyn sank down on the sofa behind her, her face in her hands. But she couldn't afford to cry. Not now. Not yet. As next in line for the throne, Aslyn needed to keep herself together to guide everyone through this.

"Have the rebels made a demand? They must want something if they kidnapped him and didn't kill him." Aslyn wasn't sure what their aim was. All she knew was that they were unhappy with the current hierarchy in Arithia.

When her mother gave no answer, Aslyn lifted her face, heart aching to see the tears silently rolling down her mother's face. "I will speak with Zayne," Aslyn said softly. "He's smart and reasonable."

"He's also Umbrian," the queen said, her voice thick with worry. "He won't just hand over his fleet without getting something in return."

Her. Zayne would want her. But he wasn't truly Umbrian either.

"Has Dorin reached out to the king of Oshon?"

"He has. And you can probably guess what he wants as well."

Her. Or the crown she had to offer her future husband. Aslyn closed her eyes. "Who?"

"Ryker."

Aslyn huffed. Ryker was not her type, and he hadn't even seemed interested in her.

Once more, Aslyn had to consider the benefits of choosing Marek. His father was close to the emperor. She could use that kind of leverage to her benefit.

"I will deal with this. I will take care of everything. This is what I've trained for all my life. But I need you to know where my heart lies at the end of all of this."

Perhaps it was time for Aslyn to sit down and chat with Prince Valen. Aslyn rose as a plan began forming. Ryker, Aethan, and Marek were all beyond her reach at the moment, but Zayne and Valen were not. While she needed more information than what little her brother had provided, Aslyn couldn't afford to wait around for answers. She needed to prepare for action.

The moment Aslyn stepped out the door and closed it behind her, Elisio took his usual position. Aslyn spun and stabbed a finger at him. "You stay here."

"I cannot allow you to go alone, Your Majesty," Elisio said, and his eyes burned with defiance and satisfaction. Did he think he won? She would still choose Aethan or Zayne if she had to. Not him. *Never* him.

Aslyn stalked toward Elisio, fists clenched at her sides. The glare she shot up at him as she came toe to toe with him made Elisio flinch back. "Any guard who wishes to continue in my employment absolutely *must* be one hundred percent trustworthy. I have warned you time and again, yet you still betrayed my trust. How *dare* you speak my secrets to anyone else?"

"With all due respect, Your Majesty, you were not behaving in ways appropriate for a future queen," Elisio replied with utter cocky confidence.

"Regardless of what you think of my actions, it is not your place to decide what is best for me or the future of *my* kingdom," Aslyn snapped. "It is your job to protect me from attack and nothing more. If I cannot trust my personal guard to maintain discretion, he will no longer be my personal guard. What I do or don't do with my future husband is no business of yours."

"Starkling isn't—"

"I would warn you not to finish that sentence," Aslyn growled.

He flinched.

"Elisio, I strip you of your rank."

He balked. "You can't do that."

Aslyn didn't back down. "At this moment, I outrank *everyone* else in our kingdom. Do not dare tell me what I can and cannot do. You may stay with the guards until we return home, but you are not allowed in the royal suite for any reason, nor do I want to see your face for the remainder of our time here in Stormvalor. If I do, I will consider it treason against the crown. You are relieved, Elisio."

The other guards posted at the door gaped at her. Aslyn didn't care. They had better get used to taking her orders.

"You." She pointed at the younger of the two guards. "Fray, yes?"

"Yes, Your Majesty," Fray replied.

"With me." Aslyn didn't wait for confirmation. She had a lot to do and not a lot of time to do it.

It had taken nearly an hour to get permission to speak with Prince Valen. By the time she stepped foot in the Imperial Suite—a massive two-story apartment that dwarfed even her own in both size and luxury—the crowds swelled for the event. It would begin soon. Aslyn's time ran short. She likely wouldn't find Zayne before the event started now.

Prince Valen stood on his private balcony with a few of his companions, a coffee mug steaming in his hand. The doors out to the balcony were made of arching clear glass, allowing light into the colossal living space. Still, something dark loomed in the air. Aslyn hated the way it felt on her skin, as if a void of nothing reached for her.

A butler left Aslyn in the entryway alongside two huge Black Guards who would put Marek to shame. Aslyn could hardly breathe in their presence. She had been forced to leave Fray waiting in the hall.

The butler bowed his way onto the balcony, murmuring her arrival. Prince Valen didn't even glance inside. His gaze remained fixed on the gauntlet below.

Only Lady Fia responded. The woman swayed into the entryway, her curves accentuated by her stunning, hip-hugging red dress. It flickered like live fire with each step Lady Fia took. A slit in the skirt revealed sleek but strong legs beneath. That strange void of darkness seemed to part around her as if afraid to touch her. Her black hair shimmered red like some mysterious light reflected from it.

"Princess Aslyn Kiernan," Lady Fia said, offering a slight bow of respect, but hardly enough to be deferential. "To what do we owe the pleasure of your visit?"

"I have been waiting an hour to speak with His Imperial Highness, Prince Valen," Aslyn said, coating her voice in as much sweetness as she could muster. "I apologize if it's inconvenient, but I'm afraid it's a bit time sensitive. Can I speak with him now?" She peered over Lady Fia's shoulder as one of Valen's companions chuckled boisterously, but the prince remained unmoved, fixated on the arena below.

"I'm afraid he's busy today, Your Majesty," Lady Fia responded, and the fake, dismissive tone set Aslyn's teeth on edge.

"I will only need a minute."

"I'm sorry."

Irritation flared in Aslyn's skin, no doubt turning her red. "He doesn't appear busy."

All gentleness in Lady Fia's fake expression instantly vanished, replaced by a hard woman. "I think it's time for you to leave, Aslyn."

The Black Guards seized Aslyn by the arms before she could even register Lady Fia's words. In seconds, she was dragged backward toward the door like trash.

"Is this how our emperor and his heir treat their most loyal subjects and rulers of the five kingdoms?" Aslyn called out loud enough to be heard even on the balcony. "Perhaps they would prefer to hide in their castle and in this suite while those kingdoms crumble around them!"

An invisible gag rammed so far down Aslyn's throat she choked on it. She tugged at the guards holding her arms, knowing her efforts were futile but unwilling to go without some fight.

All sound fled in an instant, swallowing Aslyn in utter silence.

"Bring her to me." Prince Valen's voice was the only sound to penetrate the unnatural quiet. It lacked any of the charisma or charm she heard from him when he spoke to Sybil at the ball. This Valen was empty.

CHAPTER 39

The Price of Aid

Bast couldn't have cared less about the event today. His failure last night to steal the jewel only served to further infuriate his already dangerous temper. What Aslyn did with whom bore no consequence. He had a job to do. And when it was done, he would vanish, perhaps travel to another continent for a few years.

Some part of him had been tempted to slip into Aethan Starkling's bedroom last night and slit that entitled prat's throat. When Bast had tried to sleep, it had been fitful, filled with images of Aslyn and Aethan on that training ground. But in the nightmare, they hadn't stopped, and he had been forced to watch. Bast woke in a fury like he had never felt before.

Esterly approached as Bast emerged from his bedroom, an envelope in her hand. Why had he hired a hag for this position? Were she younger, more attractive, he could charm her into his bed and relieve some of this tension.

"What is it? I'm in a foul mood today," Bast snapped.

Esterly didn't even flinch, though she did frown. Fool woman. Didn't she know how easily he could kill her? "This arrived early this morning for you. With the Novavito royal seal."

Aslyn. Curse that woman! The image of her naked in her bedroom last night pushed into his mind. Bast gritted his teeth and snatched the letter from Esterly. Yes, tonight he would put an end to this tension, finish the job, and leave.

The paper was fine—expensive, even. And just as Esterly said, the envelop was closed with the royal seal. Why would Aslyn send him this? Surely she had better things to do, better men to...

Stop it, you idiot! He would make her forget Starkling existed tonight.

Bast broke the seal and opened the letter. His already hot temper blazed. This was not from Aslyn. It was from his *patron*.

I grow impatient. Finish the job.

Bast crumpled the letter in a fist, barely keeping from punching the wall.

He was done being used as a pawn. If Platius wanted this finished, Bast would return to finish it. After all, if Platius and Javon were dead, they couldn't talk. Sadly, to protect his identity, he would likely need Aslyn.

Bast quickly dressed and stormed out of his suite. As soon as the event ended, Bast would seduce the princess.

Aethan couldn't remember ever being this happy before. His father had reassured him that this was the best any of them could hope for and given this blessing.

First, he had to face the gauntlet, a series of swinging pendulums, post hopping, climbing a sheer rock face, dodging moving wooden arms, and another final hopping climb to the top of the tower to reach the finish line. But the moment that was done, he would find Aslyn and offer to lay the world at her feet if she chose him.

To finish the event, and finish well, he couldn't afford to be distracted by anything. All twenty-three remaining competitors would be on the course at the same time. The Gamemaster made it clear there were no rules against pushing competitors out of the way to complete the challenge. And the first to reach the top of tower platform would win the event. Once again, Aethan lamented how far the rules had fallen from the original values of strength and honor. He could only credit this corrupt bastardization to the fall of the gods.

As he readied for the event, Aethan couldn't stop grinning and his friends had noticed.

"What's gotten into you this morning?" Cormic asked, smirking fiendishly at Aethan as his own squire helped him ready.

"Maybe a better question is what he got into," Trystain teased.

Aethan couldn't help but chuckle. "Stop. It wasn't like that." Though it had come terribly close. His face heated just remembering how hard it had been to back away. But it had been the right thing to do. Aethan meant what he said to Aslyn. He needed her to choose him first. And if all went well, that would happen today.

"I don't know," Ryker said, joining in the teasing. "Looked like something got into you last night, didn't it, Weylen?" He turned to his fellow Oshon competitor.

Aethan's flush deepened. They saw him with Aslyn? Now he was even more thankful the two of them had stopped. Aethan averted his gaze from the others, knowing nothing he said would redeem him now.

But he found Marek and Bryse just within earshot getting themselves ready, too. And Marek was glaring death at him. Great.

"Undoubtedly," Weylen agreed, nodding sagely. "Did she choose you over those other chumps, then?"

Aethan nearly winced. That wouldn't endear any of them to Marek's mercy in the event to come. "Not yet," he muttered so Marek couldn't hear.

A resounding slap reverberated through the air in the competitor's staging area. All eyes turned toward the Umbr men. Marek's squire rubbed at his face, tears in his eyes, as Marek laid into him about his incompetence. A surge of both fury and fear rushed through Aethan. That anger was not truly directed at the squire and he knew it. Marek would be out for blood today.

Marek stomped away, the other Umbr competitors on his heels.

"All you need to do is beat that asshole, and you'll win the tournament," Cavis said lowly, watching the other men stalk away.

Bryse put a hand on Marek's shoulder and leaned close, whispering something. They both nodded. That couldn't be good.

"Who could say no to the Stormvalor Champion?" Cavis finished.

Aethan nodded, but it wasn't going to be so simple. He already knew the Umbrian men would have it out for him during the gauntlet.

"I know what you're thinking," Cavis added. "We have your back."

Aethan gave the Novavito man a small smile. "Thanks."

As Aethan listened to the Gamemaster explain the rules of the gauntlet to the audience, Aethan adjusted the buckles on his fighting leathers, trying to ignore the memory of how easily Aslyn had stripped it off him just last night. He checked his leather armguard and pulled on the gloves. He couldn't have his hands sliced open by rocks or ropes, but he also couldn't risk his grip, so he had Roric removed the fingers from the gloves early in the morning, as soon as he heard what they would be doing.

Roric helped Aethan strap on a small assortment of knives and daggers—a sword would be unwieldy and in the way for this event. "Keep your distance from the Umbrians while you're up there, sire," Roric said in a low voice as they worked. "Rumor has it Prince Valen met with them last night to offer them advice that will give them a leg up. I suspect your relationship with the princess has concentrated their focus on you."

Aethan said nothing in response, but he did give a small nod. The news wasn't exactly a shock, but it still felt good to hear Roric reinforce it with rumors he heard from other squires and servants.

"What about Lord Khrahar?" Aethan asked. "Anything new?"

"Rumors, mostly," Roric replied quietly. "They are saying some of his documents are forgeries and he may not be who he says he is."

Aethan's heart thudded, yet he couldn't say he was shocked. Aslyn spent so much time alone with Lord Khrahar. What might she have said that he could use against her?

It didn't matter. By the end of this day if all went according to Aethan's plans, Aslyn would choose him.

"Find out where he is while I'm up there," Aethan ordered. "And do whatever you can to keep him away from Aslyn until I can speak with her."

Roric nodded. "Yes, sire."

The young squire attached a small grappling hook to Aethan's belt within quick, easy reach. Aethan hoped he wouldn't need it, but the hook would keep him from falling to the ground if he slipped or was pushed off the course.

According to the rules, any competitor who fell from the course and touched the ground was disqualified. Final ranks were determined by the order in which they crossed the finish line, how far they got before falling, and how long they lasted.

Aethan had no intention of falling off.

All twenty-three men were positioned around the base of the massive course. Aethan took a deep breath to steady his nerves, then glanced to his left to find Marek smirking fiendishly at him from only two spots away. Aethan nodded to the man politely, putting on his game face. When he glanced the other way, he spotted Bryse three spaces to his right. Their positions couldn't be coincidence. Not so close to him. At least he had Cavis and Ryker at his sides.

The signal dropped, and all twenty-three men sprinted for their ladders onto the course.

The Black Guards half walked, half dragged Aslyn across the massive living room and out onto the large balcony. Even the scuff of her shoes against the tiles made no sound. They forced her down into one of the empty patio chairs, a hand on each shoulder. She tried to tell them it wasn't necessary, but no sound came from her.

No one else spoke. All eyes were on Aslyn. Dozens of them. One of the men had the same sharp chin and broad build as Marek. Was this his father? And another, seated primly in an armchair on the other side of Prince Valen with that familiar pale blond hair. *What is Sybil doing here?* The girl barely gave Aslyn more than a sidelong glance.

"I've heard you can be quite wild and biting when the mood strikes you," Prince Valen said.

Aslyn studied each of his companions, realizing that even the sounds of the crowd were gone. The only sound came from her thundering heartbeat and the Imperial Heir.

"You will make some man very happy one day…" He raised a pale brow. "Soon, I hear."

Aslyn's jaw twitched.

"Speak, girl," Prince Valen commanded, his voice deepening not in tone, but in forceful command.

Prince Valen gave Aslyn chills in a way no one else ever had—not like a cold or dread, but instead, a suppressing darkness that could suffocate her in a moment. Aslyn had once considered using her wiles to sway him into an alliance. Now, she was nearly certain that would be impossible.

The invisible gag slipped out of her mouth. Aslyn coughed, moving a hand to cover her mouth, but a massive black gloved hand pressed down on her wrist. She shot a glare at the guard.

"Is this how emperors rule?" Aslyn asked sharply.

A wicked smile curled the corner of Prince Valen's pale lips. "Perhaps it would serve you better to remember why you came in the first place, and to whom you speak. Or we can gag you and keep you here in silence."

The hairs on Aslyn's arms rose. Prince Valen made no idle threats. He would keep her prisoner here in his suite and no one would be able to stop him. She swallowed her angry retorts, eyeing Sybil beseechingly. The other woman didn't even look at her. Aslyn clenched her jaw. It wouldn't help her father to anger the Imperial Heir.

"Apologizes, your Imperial Highness," Aslyn said, forcing her tone into sweetness once more. "I'm not accustomed to being manhandled. It's a bit of a shock."

Prince Valen looked up at the guards and flicked one finger. Their grip on her instantly lifted and they took several steps back in perfect unison. "Better?"

Aslyn rubbed her sore wrist. "Yes, thank you."

Lady Fia settled on a lounger beside Prince Valen, her long legs peeking through the slit in her skirt as she leaned back and put her feet up. The prince stood beside her, utterly oblivious to her womanly wiles, unlike every other man on that balcony who ogled Lady Fia with covetous intentions.

Prince Valen simply took a sip of his coffee, studying Aslyn over his cup.

"I come hoping you will speak with your father about helping mine," Aslyn said bluntly. "He has been loyal to the empire his entire life, as have all of my ancestors."

"Has he?" Prince Valen sounded amused. "Is that why he sent you here to find a husband—a Starkling—without even considering the man the emperor sent directly to him for just that purpose?"

Aslyn blanched. Did her father know that was *why* Umbogo was sent? He must have.

"Let me guess, something has happened to your father, and you want us to bail him out of danger simply because he is the Novavito king," Prince Valen crooned. "I'm not certain it's in the empire's best interest to save him. Perhaps it's time for someone new to wear the crown." His black eyes swept over Aslyn pointedly.

She swallowed under that dark gaze. "Please. He's not just the king. He's my father."

"Family is important," Prince Valen said in affable agreement, yet something about it rang hollow. Then his gaze slid to the man Aslyn suspected to be Marek's father. "Is it not, Lord Bloodstone?"

A cruel smirk spread unnaturally wide across Lord Bloodstone's face. Marek Bloodstone. Yes. This was his father. What a hideous man. He made Marek look like a saint.

"Yes, I would do anything for my family," Lord Bloodstone replied. "It's just too bad you aren't part of my family, Princess Aslyn."

And there it was. Just like all those other men, he thought he could bribe her into marriage to his son.

"Just to be clear, I can only accept one proposal," Aslyn said, mustering all the courage she had. "The Oshon king wants me to marry Ryker in exchange for aid. Lord Bloodstone would exchange aid for a marriage to his son Marek. Lord Khrahar would ask for my hand in exchange for his ships. I'm sure you can see the dilemma. Especially when I've already promised myself to Aethan Starkling."

The last bit was a bit of a stretch. Aslyn had promised herself to him. Not aloud or officially, but all the same, as far as she was concerned, she was his and he was hers. If he would have her. Knowing that an alliance with Marek could go a long way to getting her more information, Aslyn mentally kicked herself for all but claiming herself already promised to Aethan.

For the first time since she sat down, Aslyn noticed Sybil eyeing her subtly, as if afraid someone would notice their friendship. Relief and hope flashed in her sky blue eyes, the first sign of emotion Aslyn saw from Sybil since her arrival today.

"Ah yes," Prince Valen's voice darkened with dangerous intent, oblivious to the exchange between the two women. "Who is this Lord Zayne Khrahar, anyway? No one seems to have met him before he arrived here in Stormvalor. Perhaps you could enlighten me."

Surely someone must have at least heard of Zayne before. New money or not, he didn't just appear out of thin air. Aslyn would have dismissed the prince's question as paranoid, except Aethan had asked Aslyn something similar. He couldn't find anything about Zayne.

Maybe Zayne wasn't a proper ship merchant after all. Maybe he was a pirate lord who would benefit from the fall of the empire? Could it be possible that Zayne had a different reason for being here? Perhaps this was all about vengeance for him, and the less people knew about him the better. He hadn't exactly been forthcoming about his past.

"I'm not sure my information would be terribly enlightening," Aslyn responded cooly.

"I've heard you spend a fair amount of time speaking with him," Prince Valen said. "Surely you've learned something useful we have not."

Aslyn couldn't tell them about Zayne's past—what little she knew. But she would have to tell them something to deflect suspicion.

"I can tell you that he worked hard for every coin he's earned, trading goods all along the coast and with Oshon," she said. "He's intelligent, a good dancer, and very charming in a bit of a roguishly free way. He also cares about the common people, sharing his wealth wherever he can with the poor because he remembers what it was like to have nothing."

Prince Valen crossed his arms and tapped a finger to his lips, considering every breath of what Aslyn confessed. "And yet my men cannot seem to unearth his fleet, his trade routes or trade contacts, and the tax records were—what did you call them, Fia?" He peered down at her.

Lady Fia's attention had been beyond the balcony. She didn't even break eye contact with whatever caught her interest as she answered bluntly. "Forged."

Aslyn's skin prickled. Her heart thundered even harder as she considered everything Prince Valen said. If anyone had the sources to unearth any of those things, it would be the Imperial Heir and his father.

Forged... If Zayne was a fraud, how much of what he told her bore any truth?

Prince Valen clicked his tongue in distaste. "You fell for his act, I see. Poor thing. Some women are just so gullible."

Gullible! Aslyn fought with her anger. She was not gullible any more than anyone else in Stormvalor had been about Zayne's past. He was not the reason she came here. Aslyn needed to focus on her true task. She could deal with Zayne later.

"Princess," Prince Valen said smoothly, "perhaps you would like to watch the event with us today. I think you will find it could change your mind about a few things."

Focus, Aslyn. Remember why you came here. She raised her chin. "One of your heirs is calling for aid," Aslyn said, not bothering to accept the invitation. "Would you ignore her request?"

"Come here and join me," Prince Valen said, crooking a finger at her. "I deeply desire sharing this with you."

The sounds from the arena returned as if someone slowly turned up the sound. Not just the hum of an anticipatory crowd, but the thunderous cheers she had grown accustomed to these past weeks. Aslyn's skin crawled, but she stood, moving to stand beside him, close to Sybil.

And when she looked out at the arena, the gauntlet event was already underway.

CHAPTER 40

The Gauntlet

Aethan paused for a moment to steady his breath as he teetered on one of the thick posts between him and the next level of the gauntlet. He scanned the lower level on all sides. The grueling obstacle course was designed to test every ounce of a competitor's stamina, agility, and willpower. The air was thick with tension as the other men navigated the same brutal trial. Each of them fought to reach the next inner layer of the course, where the challenges would only become more daunting.

He couldn't see Trystain, who had been placed on the opposite side of the course from him. A plot to alienate him from his friend in this trial, no doubt.

The poles before him were narrow, rising like spindly fingers from the ground. They swayed slightly with the weight of each man who leaped from one to another. Aethan knew one misstep could send him plummeting into the pit below, ending his journey in the gauntlet.

To his right, Cavis was already on the move, his form a blur of precision and power. They had trained together for days now, pushing each other to the brink to prepare for this moment. Now, Cavis was just another competitor. Aethan couldn't afford to be sentimental. Still, it was reassuring to have him close.

A rustling on his left caught his attention. Marek was closing in, his eyes locked on Aethan with a predatory gleam. On his right, Bryse approached with the same determined intent. They weren't here to win; they were here to eliminate him. Aethan's pulse quickened, adrenaline surging through his veins. He had to act. And fast.

Aethan launched himself forward, his legs propelling him to the next pole. It wobbled slightly under his weight, but he quickly found his balance. From there, he eyed the next pole, calculating the distance and his trajectory. With a deep breath, he sprang forward.

To the sides, he could hear Marek and Bryse gaining ground. Their footfalls echoed in his ears, a reminder of the danger closing in. He had to stay ahead, had to keep moving.

Cavis was a few poles ahead, his progress steady and confident. Aethan wished he could match his friend's pace, but he knew he had to be cautious. Each leap was a risk, and one wrong move would be his undoing.

Aethan pushed off again, his body sailing through the air toward the next pole. He landed with a grunt, teetering slightly. The pole swayed beneath him, and for a heart-stopping moment, he thought he might fall.

Marek was relentless, his advances growing bolder with each leap alongside Aethan, moving in Cavis' wake. Each time Marek leaped, he grunted with exertion when he landed. Bryse had given up his chase, instead following Marek's lead and heading for the inner sanctum and the next part of the course. They had likely accepted they wouldn't catch him on the poles without risking their own positions. Instead, they would try to cut him off from the platform on the other side.

Determination burned in Aethan's chest. He had come too far, trained too hard to be eliminated like this. With renewed focus, he fixed his gaze on the next pole, his mind shutting out everything but the task at hand.

He leaped again, his body moving with practiced grace. He landed firmly, his legs absorbing the impact. One more leap, he told himself, just one more to reach the next inner layer. He could see the platform ahead, the narrow bridge that would take him to safety—at least for now.

Aethan gathered his strength, every muscle coiled and ready. With a final, powerful jump, he soared through the air, arms outstretched. His heels missed the edge of the platform and he threw his body forward onto his toes before he could fall. Triumph surged through him. Aethan took a moment to catch his breath, his chest heaving with exertion.

Marek and Bryse thumped in unison onto the platform. Neither had come as close to the edge as him. Aethan had a heartbeat to meet their gazes. All three seemed to understand the same thing at the same time.

If Aethan started the climb up the rock wall first, they might not catch him.

It passed in a heartbeat, then Aethan sprinted for the rock wall as they sprinted for him.

From the Imperial balcony, Aslyn had a clear view of the entire gauntlet. And on their side of the course, Aethan climbed the slick rock wall painfully slowly. On his heels, Bryse and Marek both climbed almost close enough to reach Aethan. Aslyn held her breath as she watched, unable to think of anything but Aethan's safety. It was clear to anyone watching that the two Umbr men were targeting Aethan.

Aslyn gripped the cold stone balustrade, hardly able to think, to move as she watched Aethan climb. Marek gained on Aethan gradually to his left. Bryse was slower than Marek, and he shouted something up at Aethan. Aslyn strained to hear but knew it would be impossible over the roar of the crowd.

They were halfway up the wall when Marek pulled ahead. Aethan reached for his next handhold only to find Marek's boot in the way. Marek paused, grinning down at Aethan. His lips moved as he taunted Aethan, but Aslyn couldn't read what he said. Before Aethan could react, Marek's boot pushed down on Aethan's shoulder.

Aslyn cried out, slapping both hands over her mouth as Aethan's body swung awkwardly away from the wall when a hand came free. The rest of the crowd cried out with Aslyn, then roared with approval when Aethan's hand wrapped around Marek's booted ankle and pulled. Marek slid a few feet down the wall before catching himself.

Aethan launched himself upward as quickly as he could, trying to put more distance between himself and the Umbrians.

Like a giant building his own path up, Bryse punched fist after fist into the wall, making rock break and creating crevices for better grips for his massive hands. Again and again, he climbed relentlessly after Aethan.

"Why is he not doing as I advised?" Lord Bloodstone snarled.

Aslyn jumped in alarm. He stood so close that his broad chest brushed her shoulder and the heat from his body increased her own temperature. Had they told Marek and Bryse what to do to win today? Or maybe how to eliminate Aethan from the event…?

Bryse seized Aethan's entire calf in one massive hand and heaved.

Aethan fell.

The world stopped.

Aethan flailed in the air, reaching for the rock wall. His back hit the platform with a thump that sent a ripple of silence through the crowd. Aslyn's heart jumped into her throat. She couldn't blink or breathe as she waited for him to move.

Aethan coughed, rolling over to push himself to his feet. Aslyn nearly screamed encouragement at him before remembering who stood in her presence.

Get up. Get up and climb, Aethan…

Aethan wasn't the only man to fall from the wall. Three others fell as well. Two of them rolled off the platform at the bottom and onto the ground, eliminating them from the contest.

Bryse roared at Marek loud enough Aslyn just caught it from their balcony. "Go!"

The platform thundered and trembled as Bryse dropped down near Aethan. Marek watched only for a second before resuming his climb.

Bryse lumbered toward Aethan, grinning viciously as Aethan stumbled to his feet, clearly dazed from the fall.

Aethan's head spun as he pulled himself to his feet. Adrenaline surged through him, the only thing keeping him on his feet as the edges of his vision blurred and his limbs felt heavy. He took a deep breath, trying to steady himself, then coughed up blood. That wasn't a good sign.

A thud echoed from behind, and Aethan turned to see Bryse landing on the platform nearby. The wood shook under Bryse's weight. The Umbrian Beast straightened to his full, imposing height. Bryse's eyes gleamed with malevolent intent as he locked onto Aethan, a predatory grin spreading across his face.

"Well, well, if it isn't Aethan, the little hero," Bryse taunted, his voice a deep rumble. "People are already calling you the Stormvalor Champion." He spit on the platform to show just what he thought of that assessment. "I wonder what they're gonna say when I'm through with you, bug."

Aethan clenched his fists, his mind racing. He knew Bryse's intent was to throw him off the platform, to eliminate him from the contest for good. And if there was a way to eliminate him from the tournament as he had done to Borin or Qin, Aethan knew Bryse would seize it.

But this was about more than just the competition. If Bryse and Marek succeeded, if he died here, Aslyn would be dependent on Zayne for protection, and if he was a fraud... Aethan blinked, clenching his jaw and tensing his muscles for a fight.

"I've been waiting some time for this moment, ever since your arrogant display in that sword fighting contest." Bryse advanced slowly, savoring the moment. Aethan took the opportunity to collect himself and seek an advantage. "Once I'm done with you, Aethan, I'll find the lovely princess. I'll have my fun, and then I'll hand her over to Marek. He's been eager for a taste of royalty."

Rage surged through Aethan, burning away the haze of his daze. This fight was for Aslyn's safety, for her freedom. He couldn't let Bryse win. He couldn't let that monster touch her.

Aethan dropped into a fighting stance, ready to defend himself. Bryse lunged, swinging a massive fist aimed at Aethan's head. Aethan ducked just in time, feeling the rush of air as the blow missed by inches. He retaliated with a quick jab to Bryse's ribs, but it was like hitting a wall. Bryse barely flinched.

"Is that all you've got?" Bryse laughed, swinging again. Aethan dodged to the side, his mind racing for a strategy. He was faster, but Bryse had the advantage of strength. He needed to be smart, to use Bryse's bulk against him.

Bryse's next punch was a wild swing, and Aethan seized the opportunity. He ducked low and swept Bryse's legs, but the Umbrian's sheer size made it difficult to topple him. Bryse stumbled but regained his footing quickly, his grin fading into a snarl of anger.

Aethan had no choice. He reached for the knives strapped to his sides, the blades flashing in the sunlight. Bryse's eyes narrowed.

"Oh, the little hero has claws," Bryse mocked. "Think those toys will save you? It isn't a sword. You have to get close enough to me to strike."

Aethan didn't respond. He lunged forward, slashing at Bryse's arm. The blade bit into flesh, and Bryse roared in pain and fury. Aethan danced back, but Bryse's retaliatory swipe grazed Aethan's cheek hard enough to momentarily darken his vision. It instantly began bleeding, and Aethan knew he would have a nasty bruise there.

Bryse came at him like a bull, charging with reckless abandon. Aethan side-stepped, slashing again. He aimed for weak spots, trying to wear Bryse down. The platform was narrow, and they both knew one misstep could be the end of the fight.

The crowd roared with delight, but Aethan blocked them out. He couldn't afford the distraction.

Bryse's rage made him sloppy, but his sheer strength kept him dangerous. He grabbed Aethan by the arm, lifting him off the ground with ease. Aethan struggled, slashing at Bryse's hand. The blade cut deep through tissue and muscle to scrape at bone. Bryse dropped him with a howl.

Aethan landed hard, rolling to his feet just in time to avoid a crushing stomp. He slashed at Bryse's leg, the knife sinking deep. Bryse growled, his balance faltering. But Aethan didn't release the handle of the knife, yanking it out as Bryse moved a step away.

Desperation fueled Aethan's movements. He ducked under another wild swing, driving his knife into Bryse's side. The Umbrian staggered, blood streaming from multiple wounds.

With a final, desperate effort, Aethan shoved Bryse toward the edge of the platform. Bryse teetered, his eyes wide with shock and rage. Aethan braced himself and kicked with all his might.

Bryse fell, his massive form disappearing over the edge.

Aethan only allowed himself a second to put the knives away, panting. The threat was gone, but the fight wasn't over. Marek was still up there somewhere.

With trembling limbs fueled by adrenaline, Aethan climbed faster than he had climbed before.

If Aslyn hadn't made her choice last night, Marek's dishonorable behavior in this event would have certainly made it for her. The way he tried to eliminate Aethan from the contest was disgusting, dirty, and cheap.

Aethan fought against Bryse on the platform so valiantly she couldn't help but admire everything about him. He was so deadly and graceful. Where Bryse would have done anything—anything at all—to eliminate Aethan, Aslyn knew Aethan's only objective was to get him off the platform so he couldn't be a problem in the gauntlet any longer.

But their fight was not the only one.

At the top of the rock wall, Cavis and Cormic came together to try and fasten a rope for Aethan to climb. Marek charged at them, kicking the rope into the abyss. In a matter of seconds, Marek led the remaining Umbrian competitors in a vicious fist and knife fight against the Novavito brothers.

Others joined Cavis and Cormic. Henric, Ryker, and Von joined the fray. Trystain rallied the rest of the Vorovesti competitors to him. The remaining competitors ignored the fight, continuing their ascent up the gauntlet in the hopes of boosting their overall rank in the tournament.

Aslyn couldn't decide which fight to watch. Below, Aethan struggled against Bryse. Above, the other competitors tried to slow Marek down for him. For Aethan. It warmed her heart that he had inspired such dedication from so many of these men.

A future king, indeed. Aslyn would be beyond honored to share her rule with him. He was already a king without a crown.

When Aethan kicked Bryse off the platform, Aslyn squeaked before checking herself.

"Worthless brute," Lord Bloodstone sneered in disgust, glaring at Bryse bleeding on the ground.

Aslyn needed to get out of this suite somehow. Soon. Preferably with Sybil. She glanced at the other woman, but Sybil hadn't blinked as she watched her brother fight for his life.

Aslyn gazed at the fight atop the stone wall. Four of the competitors had vanished. Cormic pulled Cavis back from danger as Cavis's arm hung at his side. Trystain covered their retreat alongside Ryker as Rett covered Marek's back.

Marek abandoned the fight and now sprinted across the first beam of pendulums trying to knock him off. Henric blocked Marek's path, holding his arms out to steady himself on the wobbling beam, a knife in his outstretched hand. Marek tensed his body.

"Go, boy," Lord Bloodstone commanded, as if his son would hear him.

Marek sprinted past a pendulum, shoving Henric off the beam before barreling to the small platform on the other side, just before the next set of pendulums that looked more like giant's maces.

Ryker pushed past Rett as Trystain kept the Umbr man engaged in a fistfight. A knife appeared in Ryker's hand and he whipped it at Marek while Cormic hauled Aethan over the edge of the rock wall. The knife sank into Marek's shoulder-blade right near the armpit.

Marek ripped the knife from his shoulder and hurled it at Ryker. The response was so lighting quick, no one in the crowd seemed to realize what happened until Ryker's body fell from the rock wall, limp and lifeless, his own knife lodged deep in his eye.

Aethan and his allies rallied together for a moment as Marek pressed onward.

The crowd roared at the bloodsport, and the men in the suite cheered Marek on. Everyone except Sybil and Aslyn.

Aslyn's gaze was locked on Aethan as he wiped his forearm over his brow, adjusted his knife in his belt, and exchanged a few words with his allies. As one, they moved toward the pendulum beams.

"Marek is performing impressively, Lord Bloodstone," Prince Valen said in that silky smooth, yet commanding voice. "So far, he's proving his mettle."

Aslyn bristled, unable to hold her tongue a moment longer. "He is conducting himself without honor."

A ripple of soft, condescending chuckles swept over the balcony as they all laughed at her. Aslyn glared at Prince Valen. "I would like to leave now."

"When the fun is only beginning, princess?" Prince Valen shook his head and edged closer to her. His movement forced Lord Bloodstone away, which was something to be thankful for, but he put his arm around her, hand on the railing at her other side as he leaned closer. "I think you should stay. I do so enjoy your fiery temper."

Aslyn tensed, wanting to push him off, knowing that if she laid a finger on him, his Black Guards would be on her in seconds. His arms were a prison around her. Why had she come here? Had she honestly expected him to help her?

Aethan's body screamed with pain as he moved forward, the cuts and bruises from his confrontation with Bryse making each step a struggle. His breath came in ragged gasps, and he could feel the warmth of his own blood seeping through his clothes. But he couldn't stop now. Marek wasn't far ahead.

The next section of the gauntlet loomed before him: the pendulum beams. Massive, swinging beams hung from above, each one capable of knocking a man off balance and sending him plummeting to the ground below. Aethan watched as a few of his allies attempted to navigate the beams, only to be swept away by their powerful arcs.

It was all about timing.

Aethan steadied himself, watching the rhythm of the beams. They swung back and forth with relentless precision, a deadly dance he had to master. He took a deep breath, counting the seconds in his head, and then he moved.

His first step was tentative, but as he found the rhythm, his confidence grew. He darted forward, slipping between the beams with a nimbleness born of desperation. The beams whooshed past him, close enough to ruffle his hair, but he stayed just ahead of their deadly swings.

One step, two steps, three—he was halfway through. Aethan paused for a split second, recalculating the timing. He could see the end of the beam section, the platform just beyond. He watched the next beam swing past and then sprinted the remaining distance, leaping to safety just as the beam whistled through the space he had occupied a heartbeat before.

He landed on the next platform, rolling to absorb the impact. His body protested, every muscle screaming in agony, but he forced himself to his feet. Ahead of him were the wooden dummies, their rotating arms a constant threat. The only place to step was directly in their path. Far below, a net hung suspended in the air to catch whomever fell—or was knocked off.

Marek darted toward the ladder just beyond them, attempting to create more distance. But Aethan was determined, hot on his heels.

The dummies were designed to force competitors to use their duck and dodge skills. Their wooden arms spun unpredictably, ready to knock anyone who faltered off the platform. Aethan's mind cleared, focusing on the movements of the dummies.

You've trained for all of this, he reminded himself. *You can do this*.

He approached the first dummy, ducking under a swinging arm. The second arm came at him from the side, and he twisted his body to avoid it. His movements were fluid, instinctive, each dodge and weave a testament to his training. He slipped past one dummy after another, the spinning arms missing him by inches—often less. One even scraped against his leather vest.

Aethan's focus was absolute. He could hear the thud and swish of the wooden arms and feel the rush of air as they passed close by. His world narrowed to the rhythm of his movements; the precise timing needed to navigate the gauntlet of dummies.

He reached the final dummy and ducked low, feeling the arm brush the top of his head as he slid past. Ahead of him was the ladder, leading up to the next level of the course. Without hesitation, he grabbed the rungs and climbed, his muscles straining with the effort.

He reached the top of the ladder, pulling himself onto the next platform. His body ached, and his wounds throbbed, but he stood tall.

Ahead, a series of steps embedded in the wall, the gap between hardly close enough to step from one to the other without jumping. Marek stood on one of the wooden steps about halfway up the wall, his gaze turned up away from the course.

Aethan couldn't help his curiosity. He turned his attention to the balcony not twenty feet up the arena wall. His heart stopped dead in his chest.

Aslyn stood at the balustrade, clutching it as she gazed down at him. She was a vision, utter perfection to rival the myths of the beauty of the goddesses Solisina and Fiara. The sight took his breath away as her black curls swayed over her shoulders.

But at her back, Prince Valen spoke into her ear, his arm wrapped around her, gripping the balustrade beside her own hand. And on his other side, Sybil. The two women Aethan cared for most deeply were firmly in the clutches of the Imperial Heir.

Marek chuckled, a deep rumble that sent a surge of fury down Aethan's spine. "I am only meters from sealing the deal, Starkling. I beat you, and the princess is mine. Complete with the blessing of the emperor. Not even she can refuse that."

Aethan stalked toward the first step. "You can't win, Marek. Weylen is already at the top. He won."

Marek shrugged. "I only have to make sure you don't cross the finish line."

Determination spread through Aethan's limbs as he hopped onto the first step. Marek couldn't stop him at this point. Not without risking his own position. He shielded his eyes from the sun and peered straight up the wall. He could scale this before Marek managed the rest of the steps.

"Good luck, Marek," Aethan said, turning his attention away from the other man.

The Gamemaster was clear about the rules. It didn't matter how you got to the top. As long as you got there. Aethan's lip twitched and he silently thanked Roric for his forward thinking as he unhooked the grappling hook from his belt, wound up, then launched it to the top of the wall. He couldn't pass Marek on the steps without one or both of them falling. But he could climb.

The hook caught on rocks and wood above. Aethan gave it an experimental heave to ensure it would hold his weight.

At the bottom of the stairs, Cavis had knives out, chuckling and shaking his head. Aethan eyed him warily.

"Bold," Cavis said, then he grinned like a court jester. "I like it. Go and I'll slow Marek down."

Aethan swiftly knotted the rope around his waist, then he leaned back, gripping the rope, and began the climb.

From the balcony, Aethan heard a man shouting insults and commands at Marek.

Aethan gripped the rope tightly, thankful for his gloves protecting his palms. Each pull sent a jolt of pain through his tired muscles, but he pushed the discomfort aside. The wall was high and daunting. The rope swayed slightly with every movement, no doubt slowly cutting through the fibers. He had to be cautious yet swift, not only to beat Marek, but to avoid the rope snapping. There was no room for error.

Below him, he could hear the commotion on the open staircase. Cavis, Cormic, and Trystain were making their stand, hopping from one step to the next in a desperate attempt to slow Marek down or knock him off balance. Their shouts echoed around the arena, blending with the roar of the crowd.

Aethan glanced up, the top of the wall coming into view. *Just a little further*, he told himself, gritting his teeth. All he had to do was reach the top before Marek.

The crowd thundered with approval, their cheers growing louder with each upward pull. They were with him, willing him to succeed.

A chant slowly broke out and spread. "Stark-ling! Stark-ling!"

You are their idol and champion. Lux Starkling's words sang to Aethan's soul. If beating Marek had not been motivation enough, the will of the crowd certainly encouraged him to pull harder.

As he neared the top, the rope jostled more violently. Aethan's heart pounded as he noticed how frayed the rope had become. If that snapped... No, he refused to look down.

A few more pulls and he reached up, fingers brushing the edge of the platform. With a final, determined effort, he pulled himself up and over, collapsing onto the solid surface.

Aethan lay there for a moment, breathing hard, his body trembling with exhaustion and relief. He made it. He was at the top.

Aethan rose to his feet, standing tall and victorious, his fist held high. The crowd erupted into deafening cheers, their approval washing over him like a wave. Weylen and Vinter were already at the top, whistling for him as well. Third. He had taken third. That was good enough to keep him in first place overall. Especially with Bryse not finishing the event at all.

As he reveled in his triumph, Aslyn screamed his name. He turned toward her. But Aslyn pointed at the platform behind him.

Aethan turned as Marek's hand reached the top, his face a mask of determination and fury. Aethan's eyes met Marek's, and for a brief moment, the world seemed to pause. Win or lose, Marek would not accept this without a fight.

Marek climbed over the edge, his eyes blazing, never leaving Aethan. He straightened, and the two men stood face to face, the tension between them palpable. The crowd's roar faded to a distant background noise, their attention focused entirely on the two competitors.

Aethan's mind raced, considering his next move. It was over. They both reached the top. They both placed high in the event. But that fury radiating from Marek was not something to be ignored.

Marek took a step forward, and Aethan mirrored him, both men ready for the final battle. The gauntlet had tested their strength, their endurance, and their will. Now it would test their resolve.

The platform was narrow, the space limited. Already, five others crowded the space with the two of them. If a fight broke out, Aethan had to be wary of how he moved. A fall from this height could be deadly if he missed the nets below. Every movement would have to be precise, every strike calculated. Aethan's eyes narrowed, his body tense but ready. He would not back down. Not now, not ever.

Cavis and Trystain had reached the top, and they both took a step toward Marek's back. Aethan shook his head at them.

He had to face this alone.

"I don't want to fight, Marek."

Marek's lip twitched in a sneer.

Aethan held up his hands in supplication. "We both finished in the top five. Just let the rest go. It doesn't have to end like this."

Marek cracked his neck to one side, then the other. His hands curled into fists and the muscles in his arms strained against his fighting leathers.

Aethan sighed to himself. Marek was out for blood. Nothing else would do.

Aethan and Marek circled each other on the narrow platform, their fists raised and eyes locked in a deadly stare.

"I wonder what she tastes like," Marek taunted. "Not her mouth. I've already sampled that. But those other lips…"

Fury burned through Aethan. The storm clouds overhead were swollen with rain, threatening to let go.

"I'll find out soon," Marek said, his words a dangerous promise.

"Over my dead body," Aethan growled just as thunder cracked in the clouds overhead.

And then the clouds opened up, releasing a deluge of rain.

Marek lunged first, his massive fist arcing toward Aethan's head. Aethan ducked, feeling the rush of air as the punch missed him by a hair, followed by a spray of rainwater. He countered with a quick jab to Marek's ribs. Marek grunted, his expression darkening with rage, and swung again. Aethan sidestepped, driving his elbow into Marek's side and then quickly backing away.

The platform's narrowness restricted their movements, forcing them to fight in close quarters. But even worse was the slickness of the platform beneath their feet, already drenched in rain. Aethan's fighting leathers and underclothes clung to his skin. Every step they both fought for control to keep from slipping. Losing footing in this fight would be a certain victory for the other man. And Aethan refused to lose.

The other competitors kept to the edges, watching the brutal exchange but not intervening. They knew this was Aethan's fight.

Exhaustion burned in his muscles and his wounds ached, but he pushed through the pain. He had to win. For Aslyn. At least the rain kept him sharp and cooled his burning hot skin. He pushed rain and hair back from his eyes, never taking his gaze from Marek.

Aethan darted forward, foot slipping on the slick platform, and landed a solid punch to Marek's jaw. The larger man stagger with a spray of rain and blood, his own feet slipping as he struggled for balance. Sensing victory, Aethan moved in, his fists a blur of motion as he attacked.

Just as Aethan was about to deliver a decisive blow, a voice boomed from the Imperial balcony. "Marek, finish him dammit!"

The shout shattered Aethan's concentration. But not nearly as thoroughly as Aslyn's cry of pain. Aethan's head snapped up, landing on Aslyn. She stood pinned against the balustrade railing, the full force of a large older man pressed at her back. He had wrapped his hand around her throat, holding her head steady, forcing her to watch. Aslyn's face was pale, her eyes wide with fear.

The distraction was all Marek needed. Seizing the opportunity, he swung a powerful fist into Aethan's gut, knocking the wind out of him. Aethan doubled over, gasping for air, and Marek followed up with a crushing blow to his back, driving him to his knees. Aethan slipped as he fell, landing on his hands as well. Rainwater made his hair hang around his face, rapidly dripping on the platform beneath him.

Pain exploded through Aethan's body, but the worst was the sense of failure. He had let his guard down for one crucial second, and now he would pay the price. He fought to recapture his air.

Marek gripped his hair in a massive fist, pulling his head back painfully. Aethan's vision blurred, but he could still see Aslyn's anguished face, her lips forming his name in a silent scream.

Marek leaned down, his breath hot and rancid against Aethan's ear. "You're done, Aethan. This is where it ends."

The crowd's roar was deafening, a cacophony of cheers and shouts. The platform seemed to tilt beneath him, his strength ebbing away. A sharp blade pressed against his jugular. Marek would kill him.

"Aslyn will never forgive you for this," Aethan said hoarsely, fighting for every word.

"She doesn't need to. With you dead, she will be my wife either way, and I'll finally find out if she tastes as sweet as she smells."

Aethan couldn't tear his gaze from Aslyn as tears streamed down her cheeks. He would die here, killed by the very man she would be forced to wed. Marek would make her watch.

The roar of the crowd vanished in a heartbeat, and for a moment, Aethan thought he had lost his hearing... or perhaps he was dead already.

"Marek, enough!" Prince Valen's voice was the only thing Aethan heard. Not Marek's breathing in his ear. Not the shuffle of competitor footsteps.

Only the Imperial Heir.

Marek eased the knife back, but didn't remove it. Nor did he release Aethan.

Sybil stood beside Prince Valen, his arm around her possessively as he said, "I cannot allow you to kill my future wife's brother."

Sybil. No...

Aethan could just see Trystain from the corner of his eye. His best friend didn't seem too shocked by the news. He hardly even looked upset. Anger boiled in Aethan's veins. He and Trystain would be discussing this later, for certain.

The news wasn't a shock. Not after his conversation with his father this morning. But if he failed to marry Aslyn, then Sybil's sacrifice would be worthless.

"Release him," Prince Valen commanded. "He will live, as a mercy and a wedding gift to my bride." He kissed Sybil's cheek, and she smiled timidly. Did she actually want this union?

Marek let go, pushing Aethan hard enough for his face to smack into the platform. The metallic tang of blood slid across his tongue.

When he looked up again, Aslyn was no longer on the balcony.

And the rain had stopped.

CHAPTER 41

King Without A Crown

Bast stormed through the halls, hunting for Aslyn after the chaos of the gauntlet. The way the Imperial Heir and his cronies had handled her filled him with a vengeful fury he needed to release. But first, he had to get to Aslyn before she could get to Aethan. He needed that jewel, and he was done playing games.

But as he tried descending toward the competitor hallway to watch for her, everyone seemed to get in his way, as if the world conspired against him to keep him away from Aslyn. Squires darted across his path repeatedly, forcing him to stop. A few made him wait as they hauled heavy equipment across the hall. Servants bustled about, constantly getting underfoot. Even a few healers barred his passage along certain halls.

By the time he reached the right hallway, he saw the swish of skirt vanishing through the door.

He was too late.

Aslyn stormed through the corridors of the arena toward the competitor's quarters as pure fury burned through her. She had a strong dislike for many people she had encountered in her life so far, but never hate. That changed today. Aslyn Kiernan, Crown Princess of Novavito, *hated* Prince Valen and his cronies with the fierceness of a blazing sun and vowed to get her revenge for the way she had been treated. For the way Prince Valen had toyed with Aethan and allowed that despicable fight to happen. For the way Lord Bloodstone had dared to touch her as if she weren't the heir to a powerful kingdom.

And to deny aid for a *king's* rescue! What good was the Imperial Seat if it did nothing when the most valuable servants were in great need?

Fray hadn't even realized the danger Aslyn had been in. When she at last emerged from the Imperial Suite, her face a thundercloud, he simply frowned and asked if she had been harmed. Aslyn had no physical signs, only a raging storm of malice in her heart.

And Fray had been clueless. Whatever had muted sound had clearly kept him ignorant in the hallway.

A few squires milled around the competitor hallway on whatever duties they were given. Aslyn waited for most of them to vanish, until only a few remained in the corridor, before marching straight to Aethan's door. She didn't want any of the Umbr men to know she was here, so she had to be sure none of them nor their squires were within sight.

Aslyn didn't bother knocking when she reached the door. That would leave her in the hall even longer. Instead, she opened the door and motioned for Fray to follow her before closing the door.

The main room was silent. Lamps glowed, but no one sat in the room.

Soft voices from the bedroom caught her ears. Aslyn swallowed. "Stay near the door, Fray," she ordered. "Allow no one who isn't a Starkling through."

He nodded, planting himself directly in front of the door, hand on his sword.

Aslyn took a breath, then headed toward the bedroom. The voices on the other side were instantly recognizable. Aethan and Roric. And Lord Lux Starkling, who kept his voice lowered as if afraid someone would be listening in.

Like I am, Aslyn thought. She couldn't be caught sneaking up on them. That might shatter whatever trust they had with one another.

"I will send Roric with messages for both of you," Aethan said, hissing through his teeth. "Morumbris spare me, Roric!"

"Sorry, sire," Roric said. "It's deep."

Aslyn made her steps resonate against the stone floor so they would hear her coming. Within seconds, all three fell silent.

As she reached the bedroom door, Lux Starkling appeared, blocking the path, his face hard and his eyes murderous. The expression made Aslyn flinch back a step, and she heard Fray shift in her direction. She simply held out a hand to him.

Lord Starkling's expression softened, and he relaxed once he realized it was only her.

"How is he?" Aslyn asked.

"Alive."

The word made her heart ache. Aethan had been a breath from death. His father's chosen word had been well-placed. Did he blame her for what nearly happened to his son? He would be right to blame her. Had she never given Marek such due consideration, he wouldn't have had it out for Aethan.

"Yes, for that I believe we are both relieved," Aslyn admitted. "And most likely he has secured his place as the Champion. You must be very proud of your son."

"I've always been proud of him."

Was Lord Starkling barring her passage? Did Aethan not want to see her? Perhaps she had misread that kiss. Maybe Aethan wanted to remain in Vorovesti. Or maybe he had no choice. A lump slowly grew in her throat.

"Can I see him?" she asked, her words forced out around the swelling in her throat.

Hushed voices emanated from the bedroom as Aethan and Roric spoke, but she couldn't hear the exchange.

"It's okay," Aethan called out. "She can enter now."

Lord Starkling slipped back into the bedroom and Aslyn followed on his heels.

Aethan sat on the edge of an armchair near the cold hearth. He winced as he pulled a loose-fitting white shirt over his torso. Pain etched in the lines of his strong face, a sure sign of the many injuries he had acquired during the gauntlet. His beautiful blue eyes examined every inch of her, clearly searching for signs of injury on her.

Aethan stood, and the pain in his body was obvious to her despite his attempts to hide it. He had changed out of the leather pants he wore during the gauntlet into something loose for sleeping. Was he about to go to bed? Aslyn flushed at the thought.

"Did they hurt you?" he asked as he approached where she stood just inside the bedroom.

His bedroom.

"Only my pride," she reassured him.

But Aethan stopped in front of her, tracing a calloused thumb along her neck with a featherlight touch that made her skin heat. "You're bruised."

"I hardly think I have room to complain about a bruise after what you just went through."

"I fear I brought that beating on myself," Aethan admitted.

Lord Starkling snorted, drawing Aethan's gaze over Aslyn's shoulder. "I will await your message, son." He bowed politely to Aslyn. "Your Majesty."

Then he left the bedroom, striding for the exit. Aslyn's heart stopped as she realized Roric had disappeared during their exchange as well. She was completely and utterly alone with Aethan. In his bedroom.

"I'm so sorry, Aethan," Aslyn gushed the moment she heard the outer door close behind his father.

His fingers traced along her neck, making gooseflesh rise on her skin. "Whatever do you have to be sorry for?"

"You warned me about Marek and I was too stubborn to listen," she said. "If I had…"

Aethan put his fingers to her lips. "Don't do that. You're the victim of his games. Don't blame yourself."

Aslyn wanted to argue, to tell him that if she had just listened to him in the first place, Marek wouldn't have tried to kill him today. But his fingers traced her lips as his body edged closer, heating her.

"Aslyn..." Aethan's blue eyes glittered like jewels, bearing down on her with heated desire.

"Aethan?" His name was a breath from her lungs, a glorious sound even in her own ears.

He swallowed, his fingers trailing along her neck, shoulder, down to her hand. "For years, I believed I knew exactly what I wanted from life, and I thought I understood what love was. It was simple, predictable, and safe. But then you walked into my life, and everything changed."

Aslyn's heartbeat thundered in her chest as the confession spilled from his lips.

"Your spirit ignites a flame in me I never knew existed, one that burns brighter with every moment we share." Aethan's sky blue eyes shone brightly with both hope and fear in each word. "What I thought was love pales compared to what I feel for you."

He loves me! Aslyn's eyes glistened with tears of pure joy.

"For all the stars in the sky, Aslyn, none shine as brightly as you. They are but specks of light in the darkness. But you... you are pure and radiant as the sun, and I can no longer imagine my life without you in it. I want to protect you, to stand by your side through every storm and sunny day. If you choose me, I promise to be your unwavering support, your defender, and your partner in all things."

Aslyn's head spun with heady excitement more with each word.

Then Aethan dropped to a knee, holding her hands in his, gazing adoringly up at her. He brought her hands to his lips and kissed them. She wanted to say something, but all thoughts fluttered from her mind. Instead, she just blinked at him in utter shock.

Aethan licked nervous lips and said, "So here I am, offering you my heart, my loyalty, and my love, should you find me worthy of it."

"Worthy of it...?" Those words stunned Aslyn out of her stupor. She grabbed his hands and pulled him to his feet. "Aethan Starkling, you are already a king without a crown. I've always seen the strength and honor in you, the noble heart and soul that drives you to be the man you are. You are a true Champion, not just in battle, but in every aspect of life."

The intensity of his gaze as she confessed all of this to him made every part of her body hum with life.

And then reality crashed down on her. Prince Valen and Lord Bloodstone had made it clear what she had to do to save her father. "But my circumstances have changed, and despite what my heart might want..." Agony ripped at her as that hope in his eyes flickered, then winked out. "Aethan, my father has been kidnapped, and the only way I can get the ships I need to help him is..."

"Don't say it." Aethan drew back half a step, his face twisting.

Aslyn didn't want to say it. Tears rolled down her cheeks. "I wish I could change this. If there was *anywhere* else to get the aid I need to rescue him..."

Aethan's eyes darkened thoughtfully for a moment, then the corner of his mouth twitched up. "There is. My father said you and I would have the full support of King Orrin. Vorovesti has a wealth of naval ships. If you truly find me so worthy, let me prove myself once more. Choose me, and I will rally ships and bring your father home."

Aslyn had never felt so foolish. Why had she not even considered this option? Of course Aethan would have such sway. He was the nephew of the Vorovesti king! Excitement exploded out of her as she threw her arms around his neck and hugged him tight enough that he sucked in a breath through his teeth from the pain. But he hugged her back.

"Yes, I choose you, Aethan," Aslyn said with conviction. She pulled back, but they still held one another close. "Of course I do." She ran her fingertips along his dank hair. "If I am the sun, then you are my blue sky, the endless expanse that gives my light a place to shine."

Aethan rested his forehead against hers, and a thrill raced through her as she realized this was the first of a lifetime of such tender moments. How had she ever considered anyone other than him?

"My Sunfire," he breathed.

His gaze dipped to her lips, and a moment later, he kissed her. It was not the desperately hungry kiss from last night. This one was slow and tender, teasing and tasting. His tongue flicked against her lips once, twice... The third time, she opened for him and met his tongue with her own.

It began slowly. Gentle, exploratory kisses, but the heat beneath her skin built and built as an aching need pooled in her core. They were no longer in an open courtyard. And she had chosen him.

Aethan Starkling.

Her future husband.

Aslyn moaned his name as his lips trailed along her jaw, then down her neck, pulling her curly black hair aside. Aethan's every touch was heartbreakingly tender. Aslyn pressed her cheek against his damp blond hair, breathing in the all-too-familiar scent of wisteria and blackberry currant that was absolutely him. She had noticed it the first time they met, when his face had been close to her neck. But unlike that time, when he had kept a breath of space between them, now his lips and teeth scraped along her neck.

His hands moved along her back and she cursed herself for wearing a corset today. But it gave him no trouble at all. Aslyn hadn't even realized his hands had been busy with the corset until it fell away. Then he pulled back and the look in his eyes as he stared down at her...

Seven Gods...

His blue eyes were stormy with desire. Aethan brought his hand up to cradle Aslyn's face and she thought that the look in his eyes alone would finish her. Aethan didn't speak, didn't move. His hot breath pressed against her own heated face.

Permission. He wants permission. Aslyn realized this as he continued staring at her. She touched his face and brushed a gentle kiss against his gloriously swollen lips.

"I'm ready for all of you," she said between kisses, harkening her words back to last night.

Aethan hesitated a moment longer as if waiting to see if she truly meant it.

"*I* **'m ready for all of you."** Aethan wanted permission to take things further, as far as she was willing to go. But all of him? Not that he didn't desire her with every piece of his soul.

Aslyn smiled shyly, unfastening the overskirt of her dress and letting it fall to the floor. Aethan swallowed, then peered past her just long enough to see the door open and the guard beyond. He stepped around her and thrust the door shut. When he turned again, Aslyn waited, facing him with her hands folded in front of her completely naked body.

Aethan's heart hammered hard against his chest, unable to keep his gaze from exploring every perfect inch of her.

"Seven Gods," he breathed. "You are stunning." He glided toward her, stopping so close he should have been pressed against her. "Have you done this before?"

Aslyn giggled, and the sound made him ache deep in his core. "I'm no child, Aethan, and suspect you aren't either."

"No," he breathed as his hands touched her smooth collarbone. Once more he kissed her, pouring all his love and desire and aching need from his lips to hers. Aethan took his time, tracing every curve, memorizing everything about her glorious body. His betrothed. Soon to be his wife. The realization released any of the hesitation still lingering within him.

Aslyn pressed her body into his touches, arching against him. As his lips moved down her neck, his hands cupped at her soft, round breasts. Aslyn gasped in such a delightful way as his thumbs grazed her nipples that he did it again, eliciting another gasp that turned into a panting moan as he pushed one up into his mouth and flicked his tongue around the nipple, then over it, massaging with his lips.

"Aethan..."

His mouth moved to the other side, repeating the process, increasing her panting.

"This isn't fair," Aslyn pitifully protested. Her fingers gripped his shirt and tugged up.

Aethan pulled away, and the sight of the wild desire in her eyes drove him mad. And those gloriously swollen lips.

Aethan couldn't resist her lips. He kissed her again, bit her lower lip, then sucked on it for a second before releasing. "Get on the bed, Aslyn."

"Why do you get to keep your clothes on?" she asked, pouting.

Aethan advanced a step, forcing her back toward the bed. "Get. On. The. Bed."

Her amber eyes burned into him with need that went straight to his head. As she strode toward the bed, he followed a breath behind. Aslyn climbed on, closing her long legs as she raised a brow at him.

Aethan yanked off the shirt and discarded it on the floor. Aslyn's gaze immediately slid along his muscled chest, lingering for a moment on each bruise and cut on his skin. None of it seemed to deter her, though. The way she licked her lips made him hard as hell. He dropped his pants and stepped out of them, climbing over her.

Aslyn's eyes widened as she took in the full length of him. A greedy hand slid down his chest as he leaned over her, carefully avoiding his injuries as she reached for him. Aethan took her hand and pinned it against the mattress. She pouted and reached with the other hand. Aethan sat back, seizing that hand and pinning it as well.

"You come first," Aethan said. He flicked his tongue against one nipple. "You always come first." Then the other.

Aslyn whimpered as his lips trailed along her body, delighting in every inch of her skin. As his hands caressed her thighs, Aslyn moaned softly, parting her legs for him. If there was anything in the realm more perfect than Aslyn, Aethan prayed he never found out. He had never desired anything as wholly as Aslyn. It wasn't just a need, it consumed him, just as he consumed her, teasing at her with his tongue.

The way Aslyn's body responded to him made the ache within himself so intense he almost couldn't handle waiting. But he wanted all of her. The sounds and twitches and release. Her fingers clutched at the sheets as she arched into his mouth, panting and moaning.

"Let go for me, Sunfire," Aethan purred.

Aslyn bucked against his mouth, her breathing little more than short gasps that drove him absolutely wild. Then her glorious release poured into him as her back arched off the bed. He drank it all in, intoxicated by her.

Aethan's head spun as he kissed his way back up her body, bracing his body over her. Her glazed eyes peered up at him through hooded lashes. That he brought such ecstasy from her made him want her even more.

"You have quite the mouth on you," Aslyn murmured, sliding her hands up Aethan's arms. He shivered with delight at her touch, aching for more, for his own release. "I could barely breathe."

"A weapon I plan to use on you at my will," Aethan teased back.

Aslyn smirked drunkenly, tracing her fingers along his biceps. For a moment, she closed her beautiful amber eyes as he pressed against her entrance but not inside. "Don't keep me in suspense, Starkling."

"Is that a queen's command?" Aethan purred, pulling back just enough to make her squirm.

But Aslyn didn't squirm without purpose. By the time Aethan realized her ploy, it was too late to stop her. Aslyn pushed down against him while pulling Aethan's body toward her. Glorious slick warmth wrapped around the tip and before Aethan could pull back, Aslyn grabbed him and pulled him in deeper.

"Greedy woman," he teased.

"More," she moaned. "Please..."

Aethan swallowed down his humor at that hungry plea, unable to resist. Aethan's hands roamed over her body, feeling the softness of her skin, the curves and angles that made her so uniquely her. Aslyn's touch was equally fervent, exploring, caressing, setting his skin aflame.

In those moments, there was no past or future, no worries or fears. There was only the present, the here and now, the overwhelming sensation of being with the one person who completed him. They moved together in perfect harmony, each touch, each kiss, each thrust drawing them closer, binding them together in a way that was both primal and profound. A slow, deliberate dance. The world outside ceased to exist; there was only Aslyn, her presence filling every corner of his mind.

Aslyn's moans and whispered affirmations fueled his desire, driving him deeper, strengthened his love for her with a depth and intensity that consumed him as surely as the sun. Aethan lost himself in Aslyn, in the way she responded to him with such uninhibited passion and trust. It was a feeling of completeness, as if they had found in each other the missing pieces of their souls.

Aethan wasn't sure how much more he could take. Aslyn's fingers pressed hard into his backside as she held him in deep. Taking all of him had been painful for her and he knew it, but she refused to be denied an inch. Now, her head pressed back into the pillow, face smoothed in pure ecstasy that Aethan couldn't handle staring at for much longer.

"I need you to come for me, Sunfire," Aethan moaned, his voice gritty with unspent desire.

Aslyn opened her mouth to respond, but instead cried out as he thrust again.

Both of them were slick with sweat, and her damp curls clung to the side of her face. Her brows drew together and she panted for more. He gave it, unsure how much more he had in him.

Aslyn cried out one last time, clinging tightly to Aethan as she pulsed with release around him. A groan climbed out of him as he pushed harder, eager for his own release, feeling it there on the brink. Aslyn still gripped him tight inside of her.

"Sunfire, let go," Aethan growled.

If she didn't, he wouldn't have time to pull out.

Aslyn held fast. "I said I wanted all of you."

It was too late for Aethan to argue further as the release crashed over him as sure as a tidal wave.

Aethan lay utterly spent beside Aslyn, struggling for breath. It took several minutes to steady his breathing.

As their bodies lay entwined, sated and content, Aethan looked into Aslyn's eyes, his heart full.

Aethan brushed a sweaty curl from her forehead. "I love you, Aslyn."

"No Sunfire any longer?" she asked, quirking her eyebrow.

He propped himself up on his elbow so he could see her entire beautiful, perfect face. She was everything he had never known he needed, and he was hers, completely and irrevocably. "Always my Sunfire and no one else's."

A gentle smile grazed her glowing face. "I love you, too, Aethan." Her fingers traced over the tattoo on his chest. "I'm very curious about this dragon. Your sister has the same one, I think."

"Every Starkling has had it for as long as we have records," Aethan admitted.

"Are you born with it?" Her fingers made his skin twitch.

"No. We receive it the day we're born."

Her face contorted. "How horrible! To tattoo an infant!"

Aethan half shrugged, running his hand lazily over her chest. "At least we don't remember it. And it isn't that big when we get it the first time. It... grows with us. I don't really understand how or why, but it does."

"There are ancient runes in it," Aslyn murmured. Something about the way she studied that tattoo felt more intimate than anything else they had just done together. "Does it do anything?"

"No." Aethan peered down as her fingers danced over it. "If you keep doing that, I'll quickly be ready for another round."

Her eyes sparkled with amusement. And Seven Gods help him, he loved it so much. "I'm not sure that's such a bad thing."

"Temptress," he teased, scooping her into his arms and pulling Aslyn against his chest. She settled into place easily. Naturally. As if their bodies were made for one another.

Aethan felt a fierce protectiveness surge within him, a desire to shelter Aslyn from any harm and to cherish her with all his being.

Something dark was headed toward their future. He would be certain to protect her from it.

CHAPTER 42

Broken Bliss

Bast spent far too long chasing down the princess, only to find her tangled up with Starkling all night. She never returned to her room.

There was no good reason for Bast to not kill both of them. A job was a job, and if the only thing standing between him finishing that job or failing was their lives, any other time he wouldn't have hesitated. They would both be dead and the job would be complete. Yet that woman had somehow bewitched him. She burrowed her way into his lonely soul and took up residence so thoroughly that watching her give herself to Aethan again and again had broken something inside of Bast. *This is why attachments are a mistake.*

Staying his hand was foolish for a number of reasons. Not the least of which was that his entire future depended on success.

The city of Stormvalor buzzed with excitement over Aethan Starkling's triumph in the gauntlet. They already called him Champion—their own Stormvalor heir. Nevermind that Marek had nearly killed him, staying his hand only because of the

Imperial Heir's command, a fact that Umbr visitors argued until fights broke out. The divide between Vorovesti and Umbr expanded, thickening with tension that would one day snap.

Bast didn't want to be here when it happened.

A darkness loomed over Stormvalor despite the approaching noon hour. Bast could sense it in the air... the impending danger.

Soon, the Stormvalor Champion would be officially announced.

Bast had no intention of attending the ball. The jewel was his target, and he wouldn't be able to do anything in a room crowded wall-to-wall with people. No, he would have to wait for Aslyn to leave.

Hopefully, alone.

Fray said nothing when Aslyn at last emerged from Aethan's bedroom the next morning, for which she was overwhelmingly grateful. Not that Aslyn was ashamed of anything that had happened between the two of them. They had spent hours worshipping one another, memorizing the other, until exhaustion pulled them both under. Aslyn never knew sex could be so beautifully intimate.

The only potential negative of that glorious night would be facing her mother's anger. There would be no hiding the fact that she returned in the same dress she had been wearing yesterday. A princess should never be seen in the same dress twice. The fact that Aslyn was wandering in hours after she already should have been awake in her own room wouldn't help. Hopefully the news that Aslyn accepted Aethan's proposal would soften the blow.

They would, of course, stay in Stormvalor a few extra days so that her mother and Lord Starkling could hash out the details of the arrangement, but considering how each parent had pushed them together, Aslyn knew that was more a technicality than anything else. Still, the engagement wouldn't be official until it was done.

"You are pure and radiant as the sun." Just the memory of those words melted Aslyn's heart all over again.

Today was the beginning of the rest of their lives together. The thought brought a smile to her face as Aslyn rounded the corner.

"Your Majesty!" Voices called out to Aslyn from along the hallway.

Aslyn froze as several royal guards marched hastily toward her. There were at least a dozen of them milling around the hallway.

"What is it? What's happened?" Aslyn asked, hurrying her steps.

Before any of them could answer, Queen Giata stepped into the hall and her stern gaze swept over Aslyn. It took everything in Aslyn not to wince as her mother's eyes widened as the truth dawned on her.

"Where have you been?" her mother snapped, but there was a layer of sincere, deep worry in her voice. "The guards have been searching for you for hours! After what happened during the event..."

"I assure you I was perfectly safe, mother," Aslyn said with as much courage as she could muster. Aslyn was in her twentieth year. She was not a child! "I've been with Aethan."

As soon as she was close enough, her mother grabbed her shoulder and pushed her into the suite, glaring at Fray over her shoulder. "I will deal with you later. Cornelius, let the guards know she has been found."

Aslyn's heart sank. She hadn't meant to get Fray into trouble. Aslyn was an adult, fully capable of making her own choices. "You'll be happy to know I've procured a husband, as you commanded."

The moment the door to the suite closed, Queen Giata rounded on Aslyn, completely ignoring the admission of her engagement. "Do you have any idea the terror I've been through these past hours?"

"I'm sorry, mother, but I was—"

"I thought..." The queen smoothed her hands over her stomach. "I thought the heir hurt you, or that the rebels came for you, too."

Seeing her mother in such distress when Aslyn had been in such bliss made her heart crack in two. She crossed the gap between them and pulled her mother into her arms.

"I'm so sorry."

The queen hugged her back, clinging to her like a lifeline.

When they finally pulled apart, Aslyn saw the tears her mother tried to hide. Her husband was kidnapped and her daughter vanished. It was no wonder the queen was in such distress.

"I've secured a naval fleet," Aslyn told her mother, hoping it would help relieve some of the stress. "I tried speaking with Prince Valen, but he... he seemed keen on father being replaced."

Her mother nodded, her jaw tensing. "I'm not surprised. Your father has always opposed the emperor in every lawful way he could. It was a matter of time before they made their move. In fact, I wouldn't be surprised to learn these rebels worked under the emperor's orders."

Prince Valen's words sank in as Aslyn considered what her mother said. *"Perhaps it's time for someone new to wear the crown."* If they were behind her father's capture, holding him captive and alive wouldn't put a crown on Aslyn's head.

Unless they had no intention of allowing her to be more than an ornamental queen on the new king's arm. But she had already accepted Aethan's proposal. Aslyn would never marry another. She would sooner die.

The queen sighed. "Go get ready for the Champion's Ball. We are out of time."

She turned her daughter and ushered her toward the stairs to her bedroom to get cleaned up.

"But!"

"No buts. Go, Aslyn." Her mother gave her a final nudge and Aslyn stumbled up the first steps, frowning back at her mother.

There was no point arguing. She would tell her mother the news later.

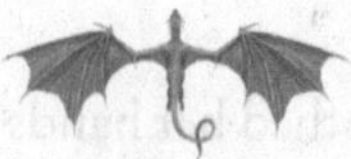

Aethan groaned as he woke, stretching his body and sliding a hand across the bed to where Aslyn lay. Except Aslyn was gone. He blinked and rubbed his eyes, frowning at the empty space behind him. Aethan thumped onto his back again, slinging an arm over his eyes to block out the sunlight streaming in from the high windows.

To call last night perfect would be an understatement. Aethan wasn't even certain a word existed to describe it. And today, he would be named Stormvalor Champion, their engagement would be made official, and his future would begin at her side.

Aethan smiled.

"Sire, you need to get up," Roric called over to him.

Aethan pulled his arm down lazily, wishing he could just stay here in these sheets where the scent of her still lingered.

Roric vanished into the bathroom, and a moment later, Aethan heard the whoosh of water as Roric readied the bath. Aethan gave an experimental sniff and grimaced. Aslyn wouldn't thank him for that smell, that was for sure.

Aethan threw off the sheet and shuffled into the bathroom as Roric finished getting the bath ready. He sank into the warm water with a hiss and a groan. He had worked his muscles too hard yesterday between the gauntlet and his marathon with Aslyn. Now those muscles were screaming at him.

"I'm sorry, sire," Roric said as he set the tray of soaps on the edge of the tub. "I tried waking you earlier, but you didn't even move."

"How long has she been gone?"

"A little over an hour." Roric grinned at him. "I take it things went well."

Well... Such an understatement. "Indeed they did. Send the message to my father."

Lux Starkling wanted news right away so that he could meet with the queen and make the agreement formal. Aethan should have sent word last night, but he had been otherwise deeply occupied.

"Of course, just as soon as I make sure you're ready," Roric said. "There's less than an hour until the Champion's Ball."

Aethan blinked at Roric. Had he truly slept so late? "It's the eleventh hour?"

"Well past." Roric moved toward the bedroom. "I did try to wake you already. I'll get your suit ready for you."

"Thank you," Aethan said, then dunked his head down in the water. There was no time to revel in the soothing bath. He had to get cleaned up and dressed as quickly as possible.

CHAPTER 43

The Stormvalor Champion

If Aethan thought the ballroom had been full at the other events, it paled compared to this ball. So many bodies crowded the room that it was hard to move from one side to another. And finding anyone in this mass was impossible. He hesitated outside the doors—even the hallway was packed!—nervously smoothing out his suit jacket.

The suit his father sent for the Champion's Ball was so ostentatious it made Aethan cringe when he put it on. Lightweight, breathable—thank the Seven Gods—and the purest sapphire blue. Across the back of the jacket, the golden dragon of House Starkling spread its wings in a massive display for all to see. Swirls of golden clouds floated along the sleeves and the pants. Golden stitched bolts of lightning dominated the lapels and epaulets and cut down the outer seam of each leg. The vest shone with golden buttons, and his undershirt was spun golden silk. Aethan was certain that, when the light hit him, it reflected like the sun for all the gold on his body.

The suit clearly made a statement. Here was the heir of Stormvalor, and its Champion.

A low, impressed whistle drew Aethan's gaze to his right. Cormic and Cavis strolled through the crowd toward him.

"That's some suit," Cavis said, shaking his head as he studied it.

Aethan rolled his shoulders. "My father seems eager to remind everyone who I am."

"It certainly will be hard to ignore," Cormic grunted.

Aethan was thankful he had befriended them. Trystain grew distant of late, and having these two had helped him feel less alone. And when he went to Novavito to marry Aslyn, they would be there. His friends.

Iskra emerged from the ballroom, headed straight for Cavis. The joy on her face as she looked at Cavis was plainly obvious. She loved him in ways she had not loved Aethan. Not so long ago, that would have destroyed him. But watching the way Cavis wrapped his arms around her and held her close, it was not jealousy that quickened his pulse. Knowing Iskra would be adored and cared for by someone like Cavis filled Aethan with unexpected delight.

Cavis kissed her cheek, then took her hand.

She turned to Aethan, and for a moment, she looked worried.

Aethan smiled warmly at them. "I'm happy for you both." He stepped closer, taking Iskra's other hand and bringing it to his lips. "Truly." He patted Cavis on the shoulder. "I wish you all the happiness in the world."

Iskra sagged against Cavis with obvious relief.

"And will we be wishing the same for you any time soon?" Cavis asked pointedly.

"You are already a king in my eyes, a king without a crown." Warmth spread through Aethan's chest. He never sought a crown, yet Aslyn's confession had stirred something deep within him. It wasn't about the crown to her either. It was his moral compass that made him a king in her eyes.

"Maybe." Aethan wouldn't give them anything more. Not without Aslyn at his side.

So he plunged into the crowd, immediately corralled by people eager for a word with the next Champion.

A slyn was beyond grateful that Kaiti insisted on sweeping her hair up off her neck. The ballroom had so many bodies Aslyn needed that extra bit of exposed skin on her neck the keep her from overheating.

She moved through the crowd, making small talk with any who spoke to her, congratulating competitors on their performance in the tournament. "It's a high honor just to be selected. Champion or not, you are among an elite class." That statement often soothed their disappointment to some degree.

At one point, she spotted Marek through the crowd. Part of her had a mind to walk up and stick her hidden knife in his neck. But practicality won out. Instead, she turned and moved away from him through the crowd, thankful this many people served at least that purpose.

Not long after, she approached Weylen, noticing him glaring at Marek through the mass of bodies. She stepped up beside him.

"I understand," Aslyn said softly, so he alone would hear her. Weylen and Ryker were friends, from the same kingdom. From what Aethan told her, the two were as close as brothers, spending much of their time together.

"I'm not sure you do," Weylen growled. His anger was not directed at her.

Marek threw his head back and roared with laughter at something someone nearby said to him. How had she ever found him attractive? Even his laugh was vicious.

Weylen's fists clenched at his sides.

Aslyn laid a gentle hand on his arm. "Weylen, you cannot do anything rash. Not with so many witnesses."

He shrugged her off, turning his furious gaze on her. "Let's throw a knife through Aethan's eye and see how you react."

Aslyn flinched, then her lips formed an *Oh!* as she realized the truth. *So not as close as brothers*, she thought. And their king had suggested she marry Ryker? Did he not know?

"Fair point. But my vengeance would not be public." She held her breath, daring to step closer despite the rage pouring from him. "Punish him if you must. Destroy him tooth and nail. Just don't leave a trail. He is favored by the emperor and his heir. It will end in your death."

"I don't care." The rage shifted into grief. Weylen would welcome death. He probably thought it would reunite him with Ryker. And such a waste that would be.

"But is that what he would have wanted?"

Weylen blinked furiously, shoulders tensing. "I told him to stay out of it. But he was too damn noble for his own good."

Henric joined the two of them and Weylen quickly blinked back his tears, masking his grief. Aslyn turned to Henric and smiled. She wouldn't breathe a word of Weylen's secret.

"Weylen is grieving his fallen brother," Aslyn told Henric. "Please keep an eye on him. I worry where that might lead him."

Henric nodded, then leaned toward Weylen and whispered something in his ear. Weylen's jaw twitched, but he turned away from Marek with Henric.

Aslyn watched them go, guilt gnawing at her stomach. His lover died fighting for hers.

A hand fell on Aslyn's waist, and for a moment, a surge of excitement rushed through her. But she had memorized Aethan's touch, his hands, last night. This was not him. Aslyn stepped forward to pull away, but the arm slid around her waist, tugging her back against a hard chest.

"Aren't you lovely as always," Marek purred in her ear. "Almost glowing, even." He leaned so close his lips grazed her ear. "I hope you haven't done anything that cannot be undone, princess."

"Let go of me, Marek," Aslyn said with all the queenly gusto she spent years manicuring.

He simply chuckled softly in her ear, holding her so tight against him she couldn't escape. "Just remember I tried to give you a choice." He nuzzled into her exposed neck and drew in a deep breath. "I really tried."

Why was no one defending her? A few people in the crowd eyed them, then dismissed the behavior.

Because no one knows how much I now hate him. That realization made her heart sink. She spent so much time with him these past weeks that none of these people would think twice about such behavior.

His lips grazed her neck. She wanted to punch him in the mouth. "Enjoy the rest of the ball, princess. I'll see you again later."

"Unlikely. Unless you mean the back of me as I walk away from you for good."

"Oh, it will be the back of you," Marek purred. "But you won't be able to walk for a while."

The words made furious heat rise in Aslyn's face. The audacity to say such a thing to her. And in public! She certainly would punch him in the face now.

Marek withdrew and vanished into the crowd. Aslyn spun around, spotting his dark hair as he marched toward the stage.

They were about to announce the champion and she had yet to find Aethan.

Every minute that passed, Aethan grew increasingly irritated with his inability to evade these people and find Aslyn. He would escape one conversation only to turn around and step into another one. His only hope was her finding him.

A servant of the Gamemaster tapped him on the shoulder. "All competitors are to report to the stage."

Aethan cast one more glance into the crowd. At least on the stage he would see better over the heads of everyone to find Aslyn. He made his way to the stage, politely ducking out of conversations along the way, stating that he had to report for the announcement, which was always followed with sincere wishes of luck. He didn't need luck. The statistics didn't lie. Aethan already knew he won. Everyone did.

"Aethan!" Lord Starkling nudged through the crowd.

Aethan waited for his father to meet him.

Lux scanned the stage and grimaced. Aethan followed his gaze, wondering what he saw.

"Let's go!" Trystain said to Aethan as he passed.

"I'll be right there." Aethan lowered his voice and edged closer to his father. "What's wrong?"

"Your sister is gone." Lux's face was grim, his eyes full of worry. Aethan's heart sank at those words. "Prince Valen took her. He didn't even let me say goodbye. He took her and... they're gone already. They left the arena with all the Black Guards and his entire entourage."

So that was it. His father said the prince was after Sybil, and Aethan couldn't do anything about it any more than his father. Sybil. Sweet, tender, playful Sybil. Aethan closed his eyes and took a breath. He didn't have much time before they forced him onto the stage.

"That's not all," Lux said, lowering his voice. "The Umbrians are gone."

Aethan frowned at the stage. Marek and Bryse were already up there, talking and grinning devilishly. But the other three weren't there. It wasn't required for all competitors to stand for this if they weren't considered a top ten position. Marek and Bryse were the only two from Umbr ranked that highly.

But when they peered out at the crowd and smirked, Aethan knew why they were still there.

"Something is going on," Lux said.

Aethan nodded. "Find Aslyn while they are on that stage. Get her out of here as soon as this is done and take her to your suite. Not mine. They will watch for her there."

His father nodded, then pulled Aethan in for a rare hug. "Take care of yourself, son."

They pulled apart and Aethan turned and climbed the stage steps, passing the Novavito men.

"Stay alert for your princess," Aethan hissed at them as he passed.

They nodded, and he prayed they understood what he meant.

Aethan stood beside Trystain and Calvin, chin high and chest out, hoping everyone saw the proud Starkling heir and not the ball of tension beneath the suit. He scanned the crowd and found Aslyn staring straight at him smiling. Her lips moved and it took him a moment to recognize what she said. *You look dumb.* Despite his worry, Aethan chuckled. He certainly agreed.

Lux made his way through the crowd toward where Aethan indicated he had found her.

"What in the name of the Seven Gods are you wearing?" Trystain asked as they waited. He also wore his house colors, with embroidered patterns, but nothing as flashy as Aethan's suit.

"A gift from my father," Aethan gave Trystain a pointed glance.

His friend chuckled and shook his head. "Old men don't know how to dress." He smirked slightly. "I saw *someone* making the walk of shame barely two hours before the ball."

Aethan watched Aslyn once more. "Believe me, there was nothing shameful about it."

Trystain's expression flickered. "So you aren't returning to Mordelic?"

"There are still a few details to work out but..." Aethan couldn't help his smile. "No. Probably not."

"I'm thrilled for you!" Trystain slapped him on the back and he winced, then glared at his friend.

"What about you? How are you handling what's happened?" Aethan was worried about his friend's broken heart. Sadly, Trystain didn't seem much changed.

He shrugged. "With you off the market, I'll figure something out. And yes, I'll miss her, but nothing I said or did would have changed it. And I was made a few promises in exchange for my compliance."

Promises? "Like what?"

"Ladies and gentlefellows!" The Gamemaster's voice boomed over the noise of the crowd, cutting off all conversation.

But Aethan was dying to know what Prince Valen could have offered Trystain in exchange for Sybil, as if he were entitled to anything. He was not Sybil's family yet.

"For a millennium, the greatest warriors in all the lands have gathered to compete in the name of Justis, the God of War, for a chance to be his chosen Stormvalor Champion!" The Gamemaster stood just ahead of them on the small stage. "And once per generation, this title is bestowed by grace of Justis himself upon just one man."

Aethan felt all eyes fall on him, but his gaze slipped sideways. Marek stood tall and proud, hands folded behind his back just as Aethan stood. But beside him, Bryse eyed Aethan like a starved dog ready to tear apart his next meal. Aethan quickly looked away, finding Aslyn beside his father. He sighed in relief.

"This year, I am most proud to name our Champion, hailing from an honorable and powerful house."

Aethan braced himself for his name and the crowd's jubilation that would likely follow. And the fight with Marek and Bryse.

"Step forward Lord Marek Bloodstone, Stormvalor Champion!"

CHAPTER 44

Chaos

Utter silence filled the ballroom, everyone stunned by the results. The only sound was that of Marek's boots thumping against the wooden stage as he stepped forward to accept his honor. Aslyn was too stunned to think. Aethan had won. He ranked highly enough in all events—even winning a few—and conducted himself with honor both on and off the field of battle.

Her gaze flicked to Aethan and his flashy suit. His expression was stone, utterly unreadable. But those blue eyes tracked Marek's every movement as if expecting an attack.

Her heart hammered. Someone in the crowd coughed.

At Aslyn's side, Lux Starkling had gone completely still. She couldn't even tell if he still breathed, as if the announcement sucked the life from his lungs.

"No," Aslyn murmured, shaking from her stupor. "This is an outrage!"

As the words erupted from her, others in the crowd began voicing their discontent as well. In a matter of seconds, the entire ballroom erupted into a cacophony of angry attendees. Because they all knew the same thing Aslyn did. Aethan Starkling had won fairly and justly. No one would ever accept Marek as the Champion.

Lux wrapped his arm around Aslyn and pulled her back toward the exit. "Time to go, Your Majesty."

"No. Aethan..." But the angry crowd was shifting into an angry mob.

"He will meet with us at the suite."

And Marek stood on the stage wearing his Champion medallion, arms crossed over his massive chest, staring straight at her. *"Oh, it will be the back of you," Marek purred. "But you won't be able to walk for a while."* A chill shuddered down Aslyn's spine. Marek thought if he won, he was entitled to her.

Aslyn stopped resisting Lord Starkling's grasp and turned, pushing through the crowd with him.

"Where is your guard?" he asked as they made for the door.

"Fray should be posted near the doors," Aslyn replied. "It was too crowded for him to trail me in here."

The crowd pressed forward, forcing them to push against the tide of bodies.

"My mother!"

"She left a little while ago," Lord Starkling reassured her. "Said she was feeling dizzy and wanted to get rest and fresh air."

Good. Her mother would be safely ensconced in their suite surrounded by guards. She would see her mother back in her suite.

Aethan's adrenaline spiked as the stage rocked under the pressure from the crowd. He spied Aslyn near the door as his father and her new guard protected her and escorted her out of the ballroom. At least she would be safe. He could meet up with them in the Starkling suite. He shouted for people to stop, trying to calm the enraged crowd, but it had no effect. These people were furious. Likely many of them had lost a fortune, assuming they knew who the winner would be and placing substantial bets.

Bryse jumped off the stage, forcing people back, creating a hole in the crowd. They pushed toward him, but he batted three people back at the same time as if they were little more than flies. Marek followed him, and Aethan saw the glint of steel hidden under his own jacket. If Marek was armed, it was safe to assume Bryse would be as well. Together, the Umbr men pushed and shoved their way through the crowd.

Straight toward Aslyn.

There was no doubt what they were after, and Aethan knew he had to stop them. Bryse bowled a path through the mob so mercilessly that people began parting for them rather than risk his wrath.

A scream from behind him had Aethan spinning. Cormic pinned the Gamemaster against the wall, his thick arm against the man's throat as he demanded answers.

"I'm a priest of Justis! I only speak his will!" The Gamemaster protested.

"Bullshit!" Cormic growled. "The gods are gone and everyone knows it. How much did the Imperial Prince pay you to stack the deck?"

In the chaos, Aethan hadn't even considered the Gamemaster might have been bought off. The Gamemaster's face turned red as he struggled for air.

"Cormic, stop," Aethan commanded, stepping toward him and pulling on the arm. "Stop. What's done cannot be undone and we have bigger problems."

Cormic's furious eyes turned to Aethan. "He's no priest, Aethan. He's a thief who stole what was yours by all rights and gave it away to that Umbr scum."

"Listen to me, Cormic!" Aethan had to shout over the noise of the crowd that the other competitors struggled to hold back. They all wanted the Gamemaster's head. "Now isn't the time. Marek and Bryse have gone after Aslyn. We need to follow them."

Cormic growled but released his hold on the Gamemaster. The man fell to his knees, sucking down precious air.

Aethan turned to see the Umbr men slip out the door. He cursed.

"What do we do, Aethan?" Henric asked.

Aethan glanced at the other competitors. All nine of them waited for his orders, holding back the angry mob.

"Trystain, Kern, and Gorim, take the Gamemaster to the dungeons," Aethan ordered.

The Gamemaster's eyes widened in terror and he stood, shaking his head vehemently.

"Trystain knows the way," Aethan finished. "My father can deal with him later." The stage shook and people started climbing up. Weylen pushed some of them back, but it was no use. These people were furious with the Gamemaster.

Trystain and Gorim seized the Gamemaster, jerking him toward the garden doors instead of fighting through the bloodthirsty crowd. Kern covered their backs to keep the masses away.

"The rest of you are with me." Aethan marched through the crowd on the stage, then hopped down. They parted for him like water around a stone. The other competitors followed on his heels.

The mob slowed Aethan and his companions so much that frustration swelled inside of him, and he was on the verge of resorting to violence just to clear a path. Most of the people fought toward the garden doors where the others had vanished with the Gamemaster. A few called out to Aethan, demanding a meeting with his family—no doubt seeking some form of restitution for a lost fortune. Aethan felt for them, but he wasn't sure what he could truly do. Just like them, he had been certain of the outcome.

Finally, his group emerged into the chaos of the hallway. Aethan turned and sprinted toward the stairs leading to the suites on the upper levels of the arena.

With everyone distracted by the Champion's Ball, Bast returned to the Novavito royal suite for one last search. The princess likely wore the Jewel of Arithia, and Bast had to accept that he would have to either kill her for it or kill his patron. Either way, someone would pay him.

Bast dropped onto Aslyn's balcony from above and popped the lock, opening the doors. Then he set to work.

Bast tore Aslyn's room apart in his search, leaving nothing unturned. He pocketed a few bonus prizes, just in case this went sideways and he needed funds for a while to lie low.

"Who are you?" A shaky female voice asked from the doorway.

Bast reacted instinctively, ripping shadows from the corners of the room to gag and bind whoever caught him before they could raise the alarm. He masked his face in shadows beneath the hood before turning and stalking toward her, yanking his black dagger from his belt.

The girl was young, in servant attire. Probably the servant of the princess herself. She had slid into the armchair beside the door when he bound her with shadows. When she saw his black blade, her eyes widened in terror and tears streamed down her cheeks. Good. She understood her situation.

"Do you know who I am?" he asked, masking his voice in case she heard Zayne Khrahar speak before.

The girl nodded slightly.

Bast stood over her, touching the blade to her neck. Her terror-filled eyes squeezed shut and she would have whimpered were she not gagged.

"Good. Then you know I'm serious," Bast said. "I will remove the gag, but if you make a noise to alert anyone else, you'll be dead before you finish. Understood?"

She nodded, peering into his hood through her teary eyes.

Bast slowly pulled back the shadow gag, and she gasped for breath as if he had suffocated her. "The Jewel of Arithia. Is the princess wearing it?"

"N-no. She s-said it's been w-weighing on her of late."

Some stroke of luck! "Where is it?"

She swallowed, staring up at him. Not that she would see his face as more than a shadowy form, a trace of nose and cheekbone and nothing more. When she didn't answer, he tensed the dagger tighter against her neck.

"In the safe! In the safe…" She whimpered as she repeated the words. "I placed it there myself yesterday."

Yesterday! Bast cursed himself for not checking while Aslyn was rolling around in Aethan's sheets.

"Where is the safe?"

"In Queen Giata's suite," the girl said quickly. "B-behind the stag tapestry."

"And to open it?"

"There's a code, but only the queen and princess have it," she said quickly. "The queen opened it for me when I placed the necklace in it yesterday."

Bast flicked his fingers upward, pulling on her shadow-bound wrists. Her eyes widened. "Where are we going?"

"To the queen's suite, obviously."

She dug in her heels, shaking her head and pushing back against him despite her bindings. "No. Please. I don't wanna go out there!"

Bast narrowed his eyes, not that she would see his suspicious look. "Why?"

Then she began sobbing. Bast growled and stuffed the gag back in her mouth, pushing her out of his way.

Some people had no spine.

She reached her bound hands for his cloak as if she could pull him back, but Bast easily sidestepped her.

When he opened the door leading out into the main living room below, the scent of blood slammed against him. How had he not noticed this before? It was cloying. He tucked away his dagger in favor of Darkheart gripping the sword in one hand as he eased out in a crouch and peered over the balcony rails overlooking the main living room.

The suite was in ruins. Bodies of royal guards laid everywhere, either mangled, twisted, or decapitated. Blood coated the pristine tiles and soaked into rugs. It splattered up the walls everywhere he looked. No wonder that girl had been too terrified to leave the room. Where had she been hiding to avoid that massacre yet not catch him tearing Aslyn's room apart sooner?

There were no signs of anyone alive.

Bast looked across the wide space to the bedroom across the way. The queen's suite. The door was open. Bast moved on silent feet down the steps toward the other side of the suite, careful of the many puddles of blood on the floor. As he moved, he pulled every shadow he could find toward him, setting them around him like another cloak.

The only guard on the stairs lay face up, staring at the ceiling with wide, glassy eyes. A blade had punched through his chin and out the top of his helmet, then been jerked out, leaving his mouth wide open as if in an endless scream. Bast carefully stepped around him, sword at the ready in case of attack.

When he stepped into the room, Bast kept the shadows at his back. They were as useful as weapons in his hands.

Nothing. He eyed the walls but didn't see the stag.

Gritting his teeth, Bast edged toward the bedroom beyond the outer chamber. As he passed the desk, the familiar royal seal caught his eye. Bast picked up the letter and skimmed the contents. The King of Novavito was taken captive by rebels. And when he saw the signature at the bottom, Bast was certain his instincts were correct. It was all lies. He tucked the letter in a pocket to compare the notes later. Right now, he had to get that necklace and get the hell out before anyone caught him.

His gaze fell on the stag tapestry before he crossed the threshold.

Two steps into the room, Bast froze.

Queen Giata slumped against the far wall, a sword falling from her limp hand. Blood coated her chest. The queen had put up a fight and ultimately lost. But what had they been fighting over? Who did this?

Bast's gaze darted to the stag tapestry. In a few long strides, he crossed the room and yanked it aside. The safe door remained firmly closed. He placed his hand against it and closed his eyes, focusing all his shadow magic on the inside of the safe.

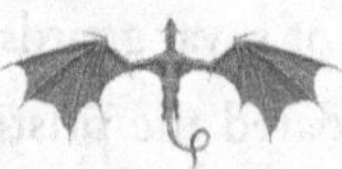

Aslyn hated running in these blasted boots and their ridiculous heels. More than once, Lord Starkling had to grab her arm to steady her steps when her boots rocked the wrong way and she stumbled. Neither of them spoke, reserving their energy for the escape from their pursuers.

They passed several Starkling guards along the way who accepted quick commands to blockade the staircase from Marek and Bryse. One of the guards passed off a sword to Lord Starkling.

"Aethan is on his way," Lord Starkling said as he wrapped the sword belt around his waist. "See that he has whatever he needs."

"M'lord," the guard said with a bow.

And they were moving again.

Aethan would meet with her. He and his father had already expected this, and planned for it. Were she not running for her life, Aslyn would have smiled. Aethan always looked out for her, and he always would. She trusted him like she trusted no one else.

Winded and hoping for a break, Aslyn peered over her shoulder as they rounded the staircase landing. Lord Starkling was in remarkably good shape for a man in his late forties. If Aethan took after him, he would still be in peak physical condition in another twenty years. Not that he wasn't gloriously perfect now.

Now isn't the time for intrusive thoughts, Aslyn, she admonished herself.

Lord Starkling paused to look back. The sounds of a sword fight below rang out, but Aslyn couldn't see anything from where she stood on the wide and winding stairs. Fray gripped his sword, ready for a fight.

And then she heard Aethan, far below, bellowing out Marek's name. If he was going to fight Marek again, she couldn't allow herself to be a distraction like last time. She needed to vanish so Marek couldn't use her against Aethan.

Aethan ran as fast as he could toward the stairs only to find Marek and Bryse fighting their way through nearly two dozen Starkling guards. And they had their swords out.

"Marek Bloodstone!" Aethan shouted, hoping to draw him back down the stairs.

Marek only glanced back at him and grinned.

When they reached the rear guards, one of them handed over his sword to Aethan.

"Your father's orders," the guard said. "We're to give you anything you need."

Aethan wanted to refuse the weapon, but he would need it against those two. A sword was deadly in his hands. Aethan had no intention of playing nice this time. Not if it meant harm would come to Aslyn. He strapped the sword belt on and ordered them to give swords to his companions.

Bryce heaved his sword like a mace, cutting down men far too quickly, and any he missed, Marek finished with deadly precision.

"They cannot be allowed to get past the defenses," Aethan called to the others as swords were distributed. "If you have a chance to slip past, head to the Starkling suite and defend Aslyn."

No one said a word, but he knew they understood their orders.

Aethan surveyed the fight, his heart pounding as he gripped the hilt of his sword. The wide staircase loomed ahead, where Marek and Bryse were making their stand. His friends—Cavis, Cormic, Calvin, Henric, Weylen, and Von—stood ready beside him, their faces set with determination. Behind them, a dozen Starkling guards held the line, providing the space needed for their leaders to advance.

"We have to stop them here," Aethan commanded, his voice steady despite the chaos around them. "Guards, hold the line. Friends, with me!"

The guards nodded, forming a solid barrier against any who might try to flank them. Aethan's group broke into two, with Aethan, Weylen, and Von moving to engage Marek while the others took on Bryse. The clanging of steel and the shouts of battle filled the air as they charged up the stairs.

Marek stood halfway up the steps, a sneer curling his lips. His dark eyes glittered with malice, and he raised his sword to meet Aethan's attack. Their blades clashed, and Aethan felt the shock of impact reverberate through his arm. Weylen flanked Marek, his swift strikes forcing their enemy to divide his attention. But the swings were wild, like a man out for blood without aim.

"Stay focused!" Aethan urged, swinging his sword in a deadly arc. He landed a glancing blow on Marek's shoulder, but it barely seemed to slow Marek down. Von covered Marek's backswings, leaving Aethan and Weylen to do the bulk of the attacking. Despite being outmatched, Marek parried with unnerving skill. A few of the Starkling guards joined their attempts.

Nearby on the stairs, Bryse fought with a savage intensity, his wild eyes darting between his opponents. He already cut down several of the guards around him, but Cavis and Cormic pressed him hard. Bryse held his ground, a sinister smile playing on his lips. Even with his brute strength, he was too slow to take on two vipers and a few guards. Cavis sliced Bryse's side, and the beast roared in pain.

"Use it now, Marek!" Bryse shouted.

Aethan's heart sank as he saw Marek's eyes turn black, an unnatural darkness swallowing the whites of his eyes. Marek lifted his hand, revealing a small, glowing object clenched in his fist. The air around him seemed to warp and shudder as he chanted in a guttural language. Aethan glimpsed the black stone in Marek's hand. The same one Marek's father had given him during the ball.

"No!" Weylen cried, lunging forward to stop him. But it was too late.

Tendrils of black smoke erupted from Marek's hand, swirling and coalescing into the forms of ghastly spirits. They howled as they took shape, their empty eyes fixing on Aethan and his friends. The temperature plummeted, and Aethan felt a chill seep into his bones.

The creatures from the dungeon! Somehow Marek had summoned them with that stone.

"Fall back!" Cavis shouted.

"No!" Aethan hollered. He couldn't fall back. If they fell back, nothing stood between Marek and Aslyn except his father.

Aethan desperately slashed at the nearest spirit. His sword passed through it with little resistance. The creature hissed but did not disperse. Weylen swung his weapon with equal futility, his face pale with fear.

The spirits surged forward, their ghostly forms slipping past the guards' defenses. Aethan's men fought bravely, but their weapons were useless against this new threat. They fell swiftly.

Cormic and Henric grabbed Aethan and pulled him into retreat despite his protests. Marek and Bryse advanced, their confidence bolstered by the dark magic at their command.

"We have to stop those things," Weylen panted through gritted teeth.

Aethan's mind raced. They needed a plan, and they needed it fast. The fate of everyone depended on their ability to counter Marek's dark power. He cast a quick glance at his friends, their faces reflecting the same grim determination he felt.

He cast his gaze upward as the two rounded a curve, their paths unimpeded. Sunlight glinted off the Champion medallion around Marek's neck. Aethan's gaze darted upward at the wide windows. Then he studied these advancing spirits clinging to the shadows, remembering how they had shied away from the torchlight.

"Light. Sunlight! Reflect it back at them!"

Aethan darted for a decorative mirror atop a table, meant to enhance the light of the lamp resting on it. He tilted it, adjusting the angle until he caught the sun and tipped it toward one creature.

It screamed, clawed at its face, and flopped back. Then it vanished in a puff of black vapor.

The rest of the men instantly bolted into action to follow his lead.

"Lord Starkling?" Aslyn's voice trembled when she heard the inhuman shrieks below.

He unsheathed his sword, his back to her, facing the steps below. "They're coming. Run, Aslyn."

"But—"

"Now!" Lord Starkling roared.

Aslyn startled at the tone, but more so at what it meant. So she ran, and Bryse's taunting call up the steps made her blood curdle.

"Where you going, princess?"

But the humor cut off with a clash of steel.

Aslyn paused at the top of the steps only long enough to look back as Lord Starkling wielded his sword with brutal efficiency against two men twice his size and half his age.

"Help him, Fray," Aslyn commanded.

"My duty is bound to you, Your Majesty. And you need to get to the safety of your suite." Fray took her arm gently and encouraged her onward.

Aslyn silently thanked Lord Starkling as she took off down the hallway, sticking close to the wall in case she stumbled in these boots. Fray charged on her heels to cover her back.

If I had a sword of my own, I could fight.

But Aslyn knew the thought was foolish. Marek and Bryse were bigger and stronger, and Marek, at the very least, likely exceeded her own skills. It would be a pointless fight. Aethan would meet her back at her suite and everything would be fine.

It would be fine.

It took far longer than Aethan liked to dispel the shadowy creatures. Cavis bent over beside him, gulping down breaths.

"Reminded me of those things we saw below," Cavis grunted.

Aethan twitched his jaw. He had noticed the same thing. Which meant all of this was premeditated.

"A problem for another time," Aethan said. "Keep your light shields. We might need them again."

The other men hefted their chosen light shields as if they were real shields, and once more they climbed.

At the sound of more steel clashing above, Aethan wondered if his father had ordered more guards. His steps hastened around the bend.

Only two men battled near the top of the steps. Bryse and Lux Starkling. Marek was nowhere to be seen.

"I couldn't hold him long," Lux grunted each word as he pushed back against Bryse's attempt to shove him down. "He slipped past."

Aethan bolted toward his father.

Bryse stepped back and circled, aware of new enemies at his back. When he struck again, Lux parried, but the blade still sliced into his side. Aethan screamed for him, angry at how slowly he moved.

Bryse grinned as Lord Starkling lost his footing and fell back on the steps. He raised his sword to deliver a killing blow. Aethan raised his sword, only a few shorts steps below. He wouldn't get there in time.

But the moment Bryse took to peer at Aethan and gloat had been a costly one. Lux knew Bryse kept his sword in his peripheral vision. Instead, he yanked out his dagger and plunged it deep into Bryse's chest.

The Umbrian Beast stumbled back, dropping his sword with a clang. It skittered down the steps, away from reach. His massive hand wrapped around the dagger. Aethan paused with the rest of his friends close behind.

Bryse stumbled, pulled the dagger, then dropped to the stairs like stone.

"Father!" Aethan fell to his knees beside his father, inspecting the wound.

"I'll be fine," his father insisted. "But nothing stands between Aslyn and Marek except her single guard."

With those words, Weylen took off like lightning.

"Wait!" Aethan called after him.

"Idiot," Cormic grumbled. "I got him."

"Go, Aethan. Now." Lux pushed his son back.

Aethan stumbled, caught by the friends at his back. "Von, go find help. Calvin, stay with him."

They nodded.

"Let's go rescue a princess," Cavis said, grinning as he climbed the remaining stairs two at a time.

CHAPTER 45

Blackblade

Aslyn's heart thundered in her chest by the time she reached the royal suite. Tears rolled down her face.

"Inside, Your Majesty," Fray said urgently. "I'll guard the door and hold Marek off long enough for Lord Aethan to catch up. Lock it behind you."

Aslyn nodded and slipped through the door with an eye on the corridor, then locked it as instructed. She would send more guards out to help him.

The stench hit her first. Aslyn backed away from the door, turning slowly. And what she saw made all hope shatter into a million pieces. Aslyn didn't scream when she saw the massacre of their royal guards. No, it was hard to scream when she couldn't even breathe.

There would be no other help.

A grunt from her mother's suite caught Aslyn's hyper-focused senses. It had been quiet, but she heard it for sure. Remembering what Elisio taught her, Aslyn backed into a shadow and removed her noisy boots, easing them to the floor with an eye on the queen's bedroom door. This was supposed to be her safe space. Aslyn had nowhere else to run. She had to face whoever had butchered her guards.

Once more, she thanked Kaiti for making her wear something so lightweight today. Aslyn hoisted her skirt quietly, gathering the fabric in front of her. She tucked it back between her legs, then parted the material to either side to tie into a knot at her waist in front again. Her legs were utterly exposed, but at least her skirt wouldn't drag through blood or tangle her limbs in a fight.

On silent feet, she tiptoed around puddles of blood. As she passed a guard, she picked up a fallen sword, wincing at the slight ring of steel as it moved. Why was this suite so unnaturally quiet?

The guard on the stairs—her mother's personal guard, Cornelius—looked shocked by his own demise. Aslyn tried not to look too long or she might lose her nerve. What was she thinking engaging someone capable of doing *this*?

The outer room was empty. No dead guards. No sign of her mother.

Her mother. Aslyn's already shattered heart had even more heartbreak to give. The odds of her mother surviving this were almost nothing. *Those are likely my odds, too*, she thought as she moved slow and silent toward the open bedroom door.

Aslyn peeked around the doorframe, holding the sword out of the way.

A man in a black cloak stood at the hidden safe, a strange mist of darkness around him, undulating unnaturally.

Against the far wall, her mother's lifeless eyes stared at nothing. Aslyn nearly cried out at the sight of her mother, just catching herself. She bit her lip hard enough to draw blood, then took a moment to center herself.

"Maybe I will have grandchildren before I die," her mother had said back in the Arithia palace garden. The words haunted Aslyn now. Her mother would never meet Aslyn's children. She wouldn't even see her daughter married. Aslyn hid back around the doorframe, pressing her back against the wall and squeezing her eyes closed to fight off her tears.

What are you doing, Aslyn? Wait for Aethan!

How far behind would Aethan be? Could she even wait that long?

A loud bang from the bedroom made her jump, and she slapped her hand over her mouth and nose to block out any sound. The man grunted again.

He's after the Jewel of Arithia!

All of this death for a bauble? Aslyn blinked her tears back and peeked into the bedroom once more. His gloved hand pressed hard against the safe door. Aslyn took one step. He didn't notice. Another step.

A tendril of that undulating darkness crept across the floor toward her. He tensed.

Shit!

He could use that darkness as a warning.

Aslyn had two choices, and a half a second to make the decision. She could charge him and fight, or bolt and pray he wasn't fast enough to follow.

Lifting the sword, Aslyn broke into a sprint toward him, heaving the sword just as she had practiced a hundred times.

He spun, raising a pure black sword in defense and using her own force against her to shove her off balance.

Blackblade!

Aslyn swallowed as she danced around him.

The sword in her hand felt both foreign and familiar, its weight a reminder of the countless hours spent in training with the palace weapons master. She had never expected to use those skills, let alone in her mother's bedroom against the most feared assassin in the realm.

Blackblade seemed to melt into the shadows. His hooded face was cloaked in darkness so deep Aslyn couldn't see even a trace of a man beneath. He moved with a predatory grace, and as he lifted a hand, tendrils of shadow coiled around his fingers, ready to strike.

Aslyn tightened her grip on the sword and took a deep breath. She had no time for fear.

Blackblade made the first move. His shadowy tendrils snaked toward her. Aslyn sidestepped as Aethan taught her, bringing her sword down to slice through the darkness. To her surprise, the shadows recoiled as if alive, retreating before reforming.

Aslyn didn't hesitate, thrusting forward with a series of quick strikes, each aimed at Blackblade's vital points. He parried with an ease that spoke of both experience and confidence, his shadow magic weaving a nearly impenetrable defense.

For a moment, they danced around each other, Aslyn's agility and determination matching Blackblade's precision. She leaped to avoid a sweep of shadow, landing lightly on her feet and swinging her sword in a wide arc. Blackblade blocked her attack, their blades clashing with a sound that echoed through the room. Was that blade absorbing light?

"Impressive, Princess," Blackblade said, his voice deep and gravely. "Looks like Starkling taught you more than a few new moves."

"Are you disappointed I'm not a helpless woman?" Aslyn spit back.

"Definitely not. I like this side of you."

Aslyn pushed herself back away from him, shoving his sword toward his chest. "Don't speak to me as if you know the first thing about me."

He responded with a wave of his hand. "I know more than you realize."

The shadows surged forward, forming spikes aimed directly at her. Aslyn dove to the side, rolling to her feet and swinging her sword to disperse the dark energy. She closed the distance between them in a heartbeat, her blade flashing in the dim light as she struck again and again.

Each clash of their swords sent strange red and black sparks flying, the room filled with the metallic symphony of their battle.

Yet, despite her efforts, she couldn't land a decisive blow. Blackblade was as elusive as smoke, his shadow magic providing him with an almost supernatural agility. They were equally matched, a fierce storm of light and darkness battling for dominance.

"You might want to hear what I have to tell you about your own family," Blackblade said.

"I would rather send you into the underworld than listen to your lies," Aslyn hissed. She stepped back, circling him, searching for weakness.

He sighed. "I tried."

Aslyn growled, remembering the way Marek had purred something similar into her ear not so long ago. She surged forward.

With a sudden twist of his fingers, Blackblade caught her off guard, a tendril of shadow wrapping around her ankle and yanking her off her feet. Aslyn hit the ground hard, the breath knocked out of her. Her vision dimmed momentarily, and by the time she recovered, Blackblade crouched over her, forcing the sword from her hands.

This is how I die, she thought bitterly.

"If I wanted you dead, you wouldn't have made it those two steps into the bedroom, Aslyn," he growled.

Those words cracked her determined exterior. Those were the only two steps she thought he hadn't noticed. She never had a chance to take him by surprise, and she was a fool to think she was even close to evenly matched with him.

Blackblade leaned in close, his eyes glittering beneath the hood. "I'll give you one last chance to listen to reason."

"Why do you care?" Then she noticed the color in his eyes. Stone cold gray. Aslyn's own eyes widened as she saw through the shadows of his hood. "Zayne?"

Suddenly Aslyn couldn't breathe. She couldn't even think straight. Her heartbeat skyrocketed.

He's a fraud, the prince and his assistant had asserted. And here was the evidence. All this time, Aslyn had been laughing and dancing and sharing secrets with Blackblade himself. No wonder he was so certain he knew her well. Seven gods. She had nearly kissed him, nearly *fallen* for him! This betrayal stung her deeply.

And he was so... young. He had to be close to her age.

When he eased his grip on her, Aslyn didn't fight back. The fight had gone out of her completely.

Zayne stood, then drew in a deep breath and let it out slowly and lowered his hood, removing any doubt that he was, indeed, the famous shadow assassin.

Zayne was Blackblade.

That shattered look in Aslyn's amber eyes crushed a part of Bast's soul. He had allowed himself to get too close to her these past weeks. He spent too much time with her, acting like he cared, like he was interested in her. At some point, she had wormed her way into his lonely heart.

Bast Blackblade was a killer, and he saw that reflected clearly in her gaze. A killer and a monster.

Bast straightened and clenched his jaw. He didn't have time for this. Even now, he could hear the riots beginning in the city with his keen sense of hearing. He felt the coming storm through the strange shadows that crept in every corner of Stormvalor. This ancient city would fall if someone didn't step in and restore order soon.

Which meant he had to get out of here.

But he couldn't leave without the Jewel of Arithia, or without knowing Aslyn was safe—as safe as she would ever be anywhere in this forsaken realm.

"You need to open the safe and get the Jewel of Arithia out of this city, Aslyn," he said, dropping the disguise he used on his voice moments ago.

But she didn't respond. Aslyn studied every inch of him as if inspecting for truth—or lies. She would finds layers of both if she dug deep enough. Seven Gods, he would tell her all of it if he thought she would believe him.

"We don't have time. You know it." He took a cautious step toward her.

Aslyn shuffled backward across the floor until her back hit the footboard of the bed. Then her gaze shifted to the queen's dead body. Tears shimmered in her eyes, but he saw the rage growing inside of her as well.

"You killed them all," she whispered. "You killed my mother!"

When she looked at him, those amber eyes glowed with a dangerous light. Her hand inched toward the discarded sword.

Bast used his shadows to slide the sword out of her reach. "Stop. I didn't. They were all dead when I got here."

"Right." Aslyn wouldn't believe him, and he couldn't say he blamed her.

"I can prove it." Bast prayed he was right, anyway. "Your maid found me searching your room, but she wasn't nearly as scared of me as she was of whatever she saw happen here."

"Kaiti's alive?" Aslyn eyed him suspiciously.

"Yes." He took another step toward her. Aslyn didn't recoil. "I know I don't deserve your trust, but right now, I need you to trust me because you are in danger the second you leave this place."

A fist pounded on the main door to the suite, hard, merciless, and loud. Aslyn jumped, her eyes widening.

"Open the door, Aslyn!" Bast recognized Marek's voice, and the menace in it. And if he was banging on the door, Bast had to assume Aslyn's guard was either unconscious or dead. Aslyn was utterly alone.

Except for him.

Bast reached a hand out to her. "I can help you."

"Who killed them?"

"I've only seen this level of butchery a handful of times," Bast said, waiting patiently as Marek continued pounding on the door downstairs. "By Emperor Oxon's Black Guards."

Aslyn swallowed, staring at him. He could see her trying to put all the pieces together. "Why haven't you killed me yet?"

Bast growled. "Really? I don't want you dead, but your brother does."

Aslyn balked at that. "Dorin? No. He's harmless."

"He wants your crown."

"He wants nothing but his lover."

The door downstairs rattled as Marek rammed into it.

"That man is a rabid dog right now," Bast said. "You can take your chances and continue debating this with me, or you can trust me for the next five minutes to keep you alive. But you must choose now."

"And after those five minutes?"

Bast thrust his hand closer to her. Aslyn glared at him, but her hand slid into his, sending a shock of warmth up his arm. He didn't hesitate a second longer. Bast yanked Aslyn to her feet. She stumbled into his arms.

Downstairs, Bast heard the door crack. Marek would be inside soon. Bast picked up Darkheart and moved toward the door.

"Open the safe and get the necklace," Bast hissed over his shoulder. "I'll cover us."

"And then you'll kill me." She crossed her arms stubbornly over her chest. "No."

Aslyn's stubborn streak was getting on his nerves. Bast strode toward her so forcefully Aslyn stumbled backward until her back was pressed to the wall beside the safe. He towered over her, pressing urgency into her. But this close, his urges fought toward the surface as they always did around her. The Jewel of Arithia called to him even through the walls of the safe. Bast closed his eyes and swallowed, steadying his nerves.

"Please," he whispered. His eyes snapped open again, fixed on her. Impulse drove him. It happened quickly, before Bast knew what he was doing.

Bast dropped a knife into his palm and sliced it open, then cut her own. Aslyn jerked in protest, but the second he clasped his hand over hers, she stilled. The two remained a breath apart, bleeding hands locked together. And the words spilled from his lips of their own accord. An oath that would damn him forever.

"I swear it on my own life, Aslyn Kiernan. I won't allow harm to come to you as long as I draw breath." Bast felt the magic settling over him with that vow.

Fool. What have I just done?

CHAPTER 46

The Standoff

Aethan's heart pounded in his chest as he and Cavis sprinted down the wide corridor toward the Starkling suite. He had lost sight of Marek and Weylen on the staircase and could only hope that Weylen was close enough on Marek's heels to help Aslyn. Every muscle in Aethan's body screamed for rest, and the suit certainly wasn't made for this sort of movement, but the urgency of their mission drove him forward. Aslyn was in danger. He made her a promise. Aethan intended to keep it.

"How much farther?" Cavis panted, glancing at Aethan with a mixture of determination and fatigue.

"Not far," Aethan replied, his voice tight. "Just around this corner and down the hall."

As they rounded the corner, a flash of steel came out of nowhere. Aethan's reflexes saved him. His sword was up in an instant, barely deflecting the lethal strike aimed at his neck. The force of the blow sent him stumbling back as his adrenaline surged once more.

Elisio emerged from the shadows of an alcove, his eyes blazing with hate, his face a mask of rage. Elisio adjusted his grip on his sword, grasping it so tight his knuckles turned white. Why was this man not with the queen and her guards? Unless he was also stalking after Aslyn...

"You!" Elisio spat, his voice dripping with venom. Aethan had always felt some kind of animosity from the guard, but he wasn't sure what warranted this anger. "You think you can take her from me?"

Aethan cursed under his breath, adjusting his own grip as he circled wide, watching how the guard moved.

Elisio was in love with Aslyn. Of course he was. That explained a lot of his behavior. And their arguments in the hallways. *Were they...? No.* And yet, Aslyn had known exactly what she was doing with him last night. She as much as admitted it wasn't her first time.

Cavis skidded to a halt, turning back with his sword raised.

Aethan's mind raced as he prepared for the inevitable fight. Elisio was a skilled swordsman—not as skilled as Aethan, but certainly skilled enough to earn his position guarding the heir of a kingdom—but that hatred in his eyes made him even more dangerous.

"Cavis," Aethan commanded, his voice steady despite the tension. "Go. Find Aslyn."

"But—"

"You can hold your own against Marek." Aethan didn't take his eyes off Elisio for a moment. "Go. Now."

Cavis hesitated for a moment, his loyalty to Aethan clear in his eyes. But his loyalty to his princess won out and he spun, sprinting down the hall toward the Starkling suite.

Elisio's eyes flickered briefly to Cavis before returning to Aethan. "You won't live to see her again," he growled, raising his sword.

"I don't want to fight you."

"You stole her from me!" Elisio roared. Then he charged.

Aethan met Elisio's charge head-on, their swords clashing with a deafening ring. The force of the impact sent a shiver down Aethan's arm, but he held his ground. Their swords scrapped off one another as they both stepped back for another attack.

"I stole nothing," Aethan said through gritted teeth, parrying another of Elisio's strikes. "Aslyn makes her own choices."

Elisio struck again, his frenzied strength forcing Aethan back. The sword screamed off the edge of Aethan's blade, then came back and sliced into Aethan's side. The cut burned, but it was shallow.

"Yes, she chose me for her bed at one point, too," Elisio growled.

Anger burned in Aethan's chest. This man was out of his mind with jealousy. A twisted mix of love and hatred fueled each swing of Elisio's blade, a dangerous combination that pushed Aethan into defensive maneuvers for several steps.

"How long before she discards you for someone else like she did me, do you think?" Elisio growled.

The words etched into Aethan's heart. Aslyn wouldn't do that to him. She loved him. They made promises to one another last night.

Aethan countered another attack, his movements a dance of survival. He couldn't afford to let his guard down for even a moment. Elisio had no intention of allowing them both to walk away from this fight.

The corridor seemed to close in around them. The clang of metal echoed off the stone walls. Sweat trickled down Aethan's spine beneath the layers he wore. He wished he could shed some of them, but Elisio would use that to strike. Aethan blocked a vicious overhead strike and twisted his blade, forcing Elisio back a step.

"She's mine," Elisio grunted. His strikes slowed. "I won't give her up to the likes of you."

"She may have shared her bed with you, but she was never yours to keep," Aethan said, his voice calm despite the chaos. "She chose to marry me."

Elisio's eyes burned with a dangerous glint. "Fucking arrogant, entitled Starkling," he sneered, lunging forward with a renewed ferocity.

Aethan deflected the attack and spun to the side, using the momentum to deliver a swift kick to the back of Elisio's knees. The guard staggered forward but caught himself against the far wall.

"I don't have time for you," Aethan said, raising his sword. "If she hasn't removed you from service yet, I guarantee she will now."

With a roar, Elisio charged again, his strikes wild and forceful. Aethan met each blow with calculated precision, his focus unyielding.

Finally, Aethan saw an opening. Elisio overextended in his fury, leaving his side exposed. With a swift, decisive movement, Aethan struck, his blade slicing through the air and finding its mark. He finished by forcing Elisio to his knees and placing his own sword at Elisio's neck.

Aethan stood over him, his chest heaving from exertion. "This ends now. Stay down."

Elisio glared up at him, his expression a mix of pain and defiance. But he made no move to rise. For a moment, the two of them simply glared at one another.

"Without her, there is nothing," Elisio said. Something about his tone sent a bolt of terror through Aethan.

The sword moved. Aethan prepared to block a final strike.

But Elisio buried the blade in his own gut, then pushed it all the way through until only the hilt remained.

"No..." Aethan wanted to stop him, but by the time he realized it wasn't an attack, it was too late.

Blood bubbled from Elisio's lips, then he slumped forward and tipped over onto the floor.

Aethan cursed violently, but he had no time to spare. Not with Aslyn waiting. The fight with Elisio had cost him precious moments, but he couldn't afford to dwell on it.

Hopefully his friends were able to protect her from Marek.

Aethan murmured a quick prayer to Justis—as if prayers to lost gods mattered any longer—then ran with the little energy remaining in him toward his family suite.

Aslyn tried to retreat, but there was no escaping Blackblade. She barely had time to think before he clasped their hands together and swore himself to her with a blood oath. A *blood* oath! No one offered those any longer. And now Blackblade, the deadly and feared shadow assassin, vowed his life to her. *Why?*

Downstairs, the door cracked. "Aslyn," Marek crooned from the suite entryway.

Moments. They had moments before Marek found them.

But she couldn't look away from Blackblade's stoney eyes. Aslyn flexed her hand as the power of his oath pulsed through her veins. A magic blood oath. They were binding for life.

"Open the safe," he whispered, his breath caressing her skin this close.

Why did he need the Jewel of Arithia so badly? It hadn't held true power since the fall of the Martnarvings during the War of Two Crowns and the rise of Emperor Narcisse. *Yet it warmed around him. Every time.*

Aslyn remembered how the Jewel had warmed in the palace courtyard back in Arithia. Her heart stuttered. *It was him. He was there!* How long had he been following her?

Blackblade flicked his gaze toward the safe, then pulled away from her. With a twitch of his fingers, shadows banded her bleeding hand, staunching the flow. He didn't bother with his own as he moved toward the outer chamber, readying his sword. It was a wicked blade of black so pure light didn't reflect off it. In fact, it seemed to soak into the blade. As Blackblade moved, shadows gathered around him like a second cloak. His heavy boots didn't leave a whisper in his wake.

Magic was forbidden. The few who possessed it were caught and killed by the emperor. How had he escaped their grasp for so long?

Aslyn turned and set to work unlocking the safe as quickly as she could, her hand trembling as she worked.

The power of the blood oath settled fully over Bast by the time he reached the queen's sitting room. He shouldn't have done it. There would be no escaping Aslyn now. Bast would always be drawn back to her because of that oath, no matter how far he tried to roam. His jaw ached and his teeth ground as he clenched them tight.

By the time he reached the door leading to the main living space below, Marek just slipped into Aslyn's bedroom across the way. He peered back over his shoulder to check her progress with the safe. Her hands moved the dials madly, but he saw the tremble in them. He knew what she saw when she looked at him now. A monster. A demon. It was better that way.

Bast slid his sword into the sheath on his back, pushing some shadows into the blade to create a shield against his back around the blade. Knives would be easier in this fight. He flipped his hood up and masked his face in shadows.

Across the way, a woman screamed. Bast mentally cursed himself for so quickly forgetting Kaiti. The shadow gag and binding must have failed during his fight with Aslyn.

Marek dragged Kaiti out of the princess suite by the hair, forcing the girl to half bow and half stumble to keep on her feet. He stopped on the balcony across the main living space. Bast melted into the shadows, dropping a knife into each hand from the sheath around his forearms.

Marek pulled Kaiti in front of him like a shield, holding his sword against the poor girl's throat. If Bast threw a knife, that Umbrian asshole would cut her jugular even as he fell.

Aslyn's bare feet whispered over the floor at his back in a hurry. He melted toward her even as she slipped the Jewel of Arithia into the folds of her skirt. Bast grabbed her wrist and twisted her arm behind her back, holding his knife to her throat.

Aslyn yelped, tugging at his grip as he stepped through the open doorway. Her fingers wrapped around his forearm, trying to pull the knife away.

"Play along," Bast whispered in her ear.

Aslyn's heart beat so wildly she was sure Blackblade could feel it in her entire body. She shouldn't trust him. He could kill her in a second. Yet he had sworn his life to her. None of this made sense. The night they met at the ball, Zayne told her that necessity sometimes dictated things for him. Was that why he gave her the blood oath? But what necessity could it have been?

She stilled in his arms, giving up the fight and playing along as he asked. He hadn't been at the training grounds that day to figure out who might win the next event. He was there to study each of those men, how they moved and fought, just as she had been. How much more deadly *was* Blackblade with that knowledge?

Marek's gaze fixed firmly on Aslyn, and he bared his teeth. Poor Kaiti was a mess. Aslyn couldn't blame her.

"Kaiti, it's okay," Aslyn said, trying to sound reassuring despite the tremor in her voice. "Stay calm and we will get through this. Please."

"Hush," Blackblade snapped, pressing that knife dangerously tight against her throat.

It's a show. It's a show. It's a show. The words repeated in Aslyn's head, but she wasn't sure if they were true.

"It looks like I have something you want, Bloodstone," Bast called across the open space.

Marek growled. "Let her go or I kill this one."

"Go for it. I only want out of here. And I want to make it clear that no one follows me when I leave."

Marek sized Blackblade up. "Liar."

Blackblade's voice took on a dark, dangerous edge. "Do you have any idea who I am?"

The menace in his tone gave Aslyn terrible chills. She whimpered, certain his knife was about to draw blood. Surely that had to be against his oath.

But once more Marek sized him up and squinted, trying to see into the raised hood. His face paled. Even from across the massive room, Aslyn swore she saw him swallow. Hard.

"I just want what I was promised," Marek said, flicking his gaze over Aslyn. "She's mine."

"I'm not!" Aslyn snarled.

Blackblade yanked her back, silencing her. "She doesn't seem to agree."

Aslyn watched helplessly as tears streamed down Kaiti's face.

"The Imperial Heir promised me."

Who did Prince Valen think he was? He had no right.

But his father was after something. And if Blackblade was to be believed, so was her brother. Aslyn wanted answers, and she knew the best place to get them.

"Let me go with him," Aslyn murmured, trying not to move her lips.

"Do you know what he will do to you?" Blackblade asked just as quietly. His breath rolled across her neck.

"I can handle myself. I know what I'm doing."

"Let her go and I'll let you go," Marek said. "I won't tell a soul you were here."

Blackblade snorted softly. He didn't believe a word Marek said.

If she could get to the Imperial Seat, she could save her father, her kingdom, and perhaps find out exactly what the emperor was up to. Besides, Aethan's sister would be there. Aslyn could protect her. It would drive Aethan mad, but it wouldn't be forever.

She felt a slight tug at her waist, but didn't dare pull her gaze away.

"That knife has a strong sedative on the edge," Blackblade whispered. "If he tries anything, use it on him. Just a cut unless you mean to kill him. I'll be watching."

Somehow, Aslyn didn't doubt that.

The two of them made their way toward the stairs. Marek mirrored their movements.

Suddenly, Aslyn had a horrible feeling she shouldn't keep the Jewel of Arithia around Marek. Not when everyone wanted it.

"Take it," she hissed as they reached the bottom of the steps.

"What?"

"The necklace. Take it."

They sidestepped the dead guard, then a pool of blood at the base of the steps. Blackblade released his hold.

When Aslyn spun around, he had already vanished into the shadows of the entryway.

And the necklace was no longer in her skirt.

Aslyn swallowed, making her way toward Marek. "Let her go unharmed, and I will go with you. No more fighting. But there will be rules, Marek."

Marek's lip twitched. "Who says you have any control?"

"I still have a crown to my name. If you want it, you will listen to me." She swayed her hips a little as she took another bold step. "I would be foolish to assume this was all about me, after all."

They stared one another down in a silent standoff.

At last, Marek released Kaiti, shoving her away from him.

Aslyn caught the girl as she stumbled. "She is my maid, and she comes with me. No threats against her. No abuse. She is my charge and I won't have her harmed."

Marek stalked closer. "Is that all, princess?"

"No." Aslyn placed her hands on her hips, feeling the thin bulk of the knife Blackblade had given her. It offered her some reassurances. "People promised me things, too. Aid for my father, first. I won't marry anyone until that is resolved. And if you think you can force me into your bed before we are married, you are in for a rude surprise."

A low chuckle rumbled up his throat as he stopped so close his chest bumped into hers. Aslyn had to tip her head back to meet his gaze. But she didn't back down. He picked up a stray curl, running it through his thick fingers.

"I'm not sure I can keep that promise," he said. "I've been waiting so long already."

"How about this, then?" Aslyn offered. "One month with your family in Lemheller Gap. Wait until that month is up, and we can revisit the point."

Marek's greedy gaze slid down her body. "Fine. One more month."

Where was Aethan? Aslyn's heart sank as she realized he wasn't coming. Some part of her had counted on him storming in and challenging Marek.

Was he dead?

"Let me gather a few things for the trip and we can leave," she said, feeling the shadows around her shift.

Was Blackblade still there watching?

"Make it quick," Marek said.

He followed her up the stairs to her room, following her every move as she grabbed only what she needed—a few changes of clothes, her fighting leathers, jewelry, sturdy riding boots. Some of her jewels were missing. In Blackblade's pockets, most likely. As she finished, Aslyn untied her skirt, catching the knife and tucking it safely in her belt. Something else fell out.

Aslyn bent down to pick it up, finding the letter her mother received bearing the seal of the royal house, as well as a second one she hadn't seen, with the same seal. Aslyn quickly stuffed them into her dress before grabbing her pack and turning to Marek.

"Lead the way, my love," she said, mocking him with each word.

Marek's jaw twitched. "Joke all you want, but you will remember how you felt about me before Starkling pushed his way between us."

Aslyn nearly snorted at that.

He seized her arm, forcing her to lock arms with him, keeping her tight against his side. "Try to run and your girl will pay."

Aslyn smiled sweetly at him. "Why would I want to run from you?"

He glared a warning at her but said nothing else as they marched out the door, a sniffling Kaiti trailing behind them.

B ast followed them along the hall, keeping the shadows close around him so no one saw him.

Whatever Aslyn had up her sleeve, Bast intended to be her shield from danger. And he knew she was riding into the worst den of vipers in all the realm.

CHAPTER 47

Space to Shine

Before Aethan reached the Starkling suite, the rest of his friends ran past him.

"She wasn't there," Cavis huffed. "Nor was Marek."

Aethan froze momentarily. His gaze darted through the group. "Where is Weylen?"

Aethan's heart stopped. No. But she was supposed to come here! Did Marek reach her before she got this far? *I promised to keep her safe.*

Then a moment of clarity struck and Aethan pivoted, sliding the sword into the loop on his belt and running as fast as his legs could carry him toward the royal suite. Perhaps there was confusion about which suite she was supposed to go to.

He passed all his companions, eliciting a few curses and grunts as they tried to catch up.

A slew of horrible scenarios raced through his mind as he ran with every ounce of speed he could muster. None of his companions could keep up, and Aethan ended up leaving them all behind. They could catch him in their own time, but Aslyn had no more time to spare.

Aethan sped past Weylen on the corridor floor, slumped against a wall. A quick glance showed him still breathing. Marek had only knocked him out. A small relief.

When Aethan reached the open door to the royal suite, he skidded to a halt beside the body of Aslyn's new guard. Hope faded when he lifted his gaze and received a glimpse of the massacre inside. Just as he was about to take a step into the suite to search for Aslyn, terrified she no longer lived, he heard her voice distantly down the hall.

"Aslyn," he muttered.

In a flash, he was running again. "Aslyn!"

When he rounded the bend in the corridor, he once more skidded to a stop when he saw Aslyn holding Marek's hand, her body pressed tight against his side. Both faced him. Behind them, Aslyn's maid whimpered and quietly cried. Shadows undulated around the corridor.

Aethan's jaw twitched. "Let her go, Marek. It's over." He rested his hand on his hilt, ready for a fight.

"Is it? Maybe you should ask Aslyn what she wants." Marek smirked.

Aethan didn't like this. The way Aslyn tightened her hold on Marek's hand and stared Aethan down felt so wrong. Could Marek control her with that twisted stone?

Cautiously, Aethan took one step closer, holding his hand out to her. "Aslyn, take my hand."

Tears welled in her eyes and she raised her chin. "I'm sorry, Aethan."

His heart cleaved in two. No. She chose him. She gave him her heart and body and soul. He couldn't accept this.

"Whatever he has over you, we can sort it out," Aethan said, keeping his tone gentle.

Around the bend, he heard his friends calling into the suite doors for him and Aslyn.

"Please," he said, his voice cracking over the word. He hated allowing this weakness to show in front of Marek.

"Don't blame yourself," Aslyn said, yet as she spoke, her words felt hollow. "You are a true Champion, but my circumstances have changed. It's time to bring my father home."

Something about the words she used struck a chord deep within him with a familiarity he couldn't quite place while agony tore at his chest.

"With him?" he asked miserably, his hand falling to his side.

Marek chuckled, raising their joined hands so he could kiss hers.

Aslyn flinched, and Aethan noticed. But Marek didn't.

"To do what needs done, I need the space to let my light shine," Aslyn said. "I wish you luck, Aethan." Then Aslyn turned away from him and Marek smirked devilishly at him over his shoulder as he joined Aslyn, allowing her to lead them away.

Aethan couldn't move.

"You are a true Champion."

His head spun, repeating her words in his mind over and over.

"My circumstances have changed."

"Aethan?" Cavis called gently.

"I need the space to let my light shine."

Cormic placed a hand on his shoulder. "Should we—?"

"No." Aethan was shocked by the word that rushed past his lips.

"It's time to bring my father home."

"You aren't going after her?" Cavis asked, dumbfounded as he stepped past Aethan.

"No."

Aslyn knew exactly what she was saying to him, choosing her words carefully so Marek wouldn't understand.

But Aethan did.

Aslyn hadn't turned her back on him. But her circumstances changed, and she needed him to give her space to do what needed done.

"We have a king to rescue," Aethan said, turning away from the empty corridor Aslyn had vanished along.

Shadows curled around his ankles, then swept away after Aslyn. Aethan didn't know what that meant, but he knew he had to respect her choices.

And he had promised to get her father back.

CHAPTER 48

Shrine of Justis

From now on, Aethan would need to be more careful with his promises. Only a few days had passed since Aslyn left, and his promise to help her father already chaffed at his nerves. All he wanted was to go after her.

Aethan could smell the coming rain and rose to close the window before the Starkling librarian caught him sitting with the window open, letting moisture in with the precious books. A cool, damp breeze blew through the open window, flipping pages on the books laid out over the desk and rustling loose sheets of notes and maps.

Lamplight sputtered among the stacks along the walls and from the chandelier in the center of the massive room. House colors coated everything. Sapphire blue curtains and furniture. Gold gilded table legs and trim. The chandelier overhead dripped gold chains embracing sapphire jewels that sparkled in the light. Bookshelves lined each wall from floor to ceiling. A wide staircase in the center of the room wound up and out along the walls, creating a second-story sitting area—where Aethan currently took up residence.

Aethan felt as if he missed something critical these past few weeks, and that drive for answers was a welcome distraction as he waited for the ships to be ready. He had taken to this library, in the heart of the Starkling Keep in Stormvalor, seeking as many of those answers as he could find. Surrounded by precious, ancient texts, he was sure to find *something*.

His primary questions revolved around the Hall of Champions below the arena, and what might lie beyond the sealed doors. His efforts to learn more had proven mostly fruitless.

But what he stumbled across only raised more questions.

In a book titled "Tales of the Saints", Aethan learned of artifacts created by the Seven Gods. Only those possessing potent magic could wield these artifacts, and they obeyed solely the Saints' commands. Yet the wording around those artifacts remained unclear. Aethan didn't know what they were, or even if they were truly real, physical objects. The verse about Morumbris's artifact made it sound more like a physical space than an object, but still, the wording hinted at something that made Aethan think of a sword. Why couldn't historians and scribes just write in clear language?

Aethan also found an ancient text hidden behind a history book about the War of Two Crowns. He had been particularly careful with that one, but the language was just as ancient as the text and he could only make out a few words. Something about a magical curse and rebirth. It made little sense to him, so he had tucked it back where he found it.

All this research was a means to distract him from his true worries. Lux had sent word to King Orrin the day after the tournament ended, requesting ships and aid in the rescue mission for King Novin of Novavito. In a few days, Aethan would leave Stormvalor and return to Mordelic with his new friends. Then he would take a fleet of ships south to Arithia to return Queen Giata's body to her family and begin his quest. With any luck, Aslyn's brother could offer further aid in the rescue mission. But Aslyn wouldn't be there.

His heart ached every time he remembered that look on Aslyn's face as she turned away from him. What would Marek do to her? What had he already done? Aethan hated how Aslyn bound him to this mission to rescue her father with just a few words when what he truly wanted was to go after her.

But he had promised to trust her. He had to trust that she knew what she was doing. A terrible King Consort he would be if he ignored her first request to do what *he* thought was best. Respecting her wishes was the hardest thing he had done. Every fiber of his soul called to her, yearned to rush into Umbr and demand her release.

Yes, he had promised to petition his uncle for a fleet to rescue her father, but he had also promised to protect her and failed to keep that promise the very next day.

He tried not to let that failure bother him but found it hard to sleep at night knowing she was in Marek's clutches. Aslyn was a capable woman, but Marek was big and powerful. He could out-muscle her easily. Aethan trusted Aslyn more than most—more than anyone—but he couldn't fathom how she thought she could just leave Umbr once her mission was complete.

Cavis and Cormic hadn't been pleased with Aethan's request to help her father instead of chasing after her, but Aethan had pleaded to their loyalty to the crown first and foremost. Until they knew more, that remained King Novin. The brothers had been surly ever since.

Thunder rumbled beyond the windows as the sky threatened to open and drown Aethan's sorrow and guilt.

"Sire," Roric said softly as he slid a tray of toast and tea onto the table. "You skipped breakfast and lunch again."

The steaming mug of tea tantalized Aethan with hints of blackleaf and peppermint. Aethan wrapped his fingers around the mug, murmuring his thanks to Roric as he inhaled the relaxing scent. Roric watched him with apparent worry on his youthful face, waiting for Aethan to take a drink. He obliged, which seemed to put the boy at ease.

Most of the other squires had returned to their ordinary lives once the tournament concluded. A few remained in the employment of their former competitors. Aethan found himself unable to get by without Roric watching over him. Strange to think of a boy eight years his younger as a nursemaid, but Roric had been there these past few days. Whenever Aethan needed anything, Roric was already there waiting—often with food or a cup of tea.

Soon enough I will have to get by without him, Aethan thought as he took another long drink.

Roric wouldn't be coming with him on his mission to Arithia, nor to save King Novin. It was no place for a boy. The dangers of the sea were plentiful.

"What do we know today, Roric?" Aethan asked.

This had become routine as well.

"Master Weylen has questioned the Gamemaster with your father's permission," Roric reported. "The man broke easily enough under Weylen's hands. It's as suspected. Prince Valen and Lord Bloodstone made ridiculously generous donations to the cleric of Justis in exchange for a few skewed results in Marek's favor. He was close enough to make it almost believable."

Aethan snorted, reading the same line in the book before him for the hundredth time. No one believed Marek truly won. It had caused some riots in the city that the guards had to subdue.

Aethan was too distracted to study right now. He rubbed his eyes and turned his attention back to the squire.

Roric remained in perfect stillness, his hands clasped behind his back. Aethan wasn't sure where he learned this stillness, but it gave Roric an air of authority. Perhaps the boy had always had that, and he had just been too busy to notice before.

Roric bit his lip, a tell that the boy was holding something back.

"What is it?" Aethan asked, sighing.

"I don't see why I can't come with you, sire," Roric said, and the sorrow in the boy's voice struck a chord in Aethan's heart. "I can stay small and out of the way. I can pull my weight on the ships with kitchen duty. Let me come along. Please."

Aethan shook his head. "I don't doubt your ability to help, but what we are about to do is dangerous, and I..." The rest of his sentence escaped him as that lump of failure clogged his throat. He cleared it and took another drink. When Aethan spoke again, his voice was softer, defeated. "I can't lose you, too. I'll send for you once I'm in Arithia with Aslyn."

Roric grimaced, staring at his boots, but he nodded. "I understand," he murmured.

The disappointment was painful to bear, but Aethan would take disappointment over death any day.

Death... Flashes of the massacre in the royal suite distracted Aethan's thoughts. That bloodbath on the last day of the tournament had been hard to take in. So much had gone wrong that day. To top it all off, Khrahar vanished that day without a trace. Aethan couldn't help but wonder if he had been an accomplice to the empire after all. The only clues about his disappearance were the words of his servant, who reported that Khrahar had received a letter that morning with a royal seal. Then he was just...gone.

Lux climbed the stairs, settling into a plush armchair across from Aethan. He fixed his son with a worried gaze.

"That's all for now, Roric," Aethan said, dismissing the squire.

Roric didn't seem happy about it, but he left, closing the library door.

"How are you doing today, Aethan?" his father asked, tenderness in his voice. Or was that pity? Aethan didn't want his pity.

Aethan had questions for his father. Questions he had been too distracted to ask about recently. He needed some answers before leaving on his rescue mission.

"Did you know those shadow creatures were being held below the arena?" Aethan asked, closing his book and leveling his blue eyes on Lux.

The confusion on his father's face answered the question before he voiced his denial. "No. But I heard that when the Imperial Heir arrived, his men closed off some corridors for a few hours."

"You think they brought those creatures in at that time?" Aethan asked.

Lux considered it, then shrugged and nodded.

"Some kind of ancient rune I hadn't seen before held them in those cells," Aethan admitted. "If we can learn more about those runes, it might help us control them if we encounter them again."

"I'll have some men look into it."

Aethan ran his thumb along the edge of the pages of his most recent read. Then he drew in a deep breath to summon the courage to ask his next question.

"And you honestly did not know the Hall of Champions was buried beneath the arena?" Aethan asked, eyeing his father.

Again, Lux shook his head. "I've gone back down there since you showed it to me yesterday, but I can't get past that stone wall." Lux leaned forward, resting an arm on the table. "Which only convinces me that your sister is right."

Sybil. Another woman he failed to protect. His failures were stacking up.

"Your fates are linked."

Aethan gritted his teeth. *What did you know that I don't, sister?*

Aethan and his father had tried opening the massive doors on the far end of the Hall of Champions. But, as with Cavis and Cormic, they hadn't budged. Which brought him to another question that nagged at him. *What is on the other side of those doors?*

That night, Aethan couldn't sleep. He tossed and turned in bed, haunted by nightmares of Marek and Aslyn, of those shadow creatures consuming Sybil, of his utter helplessness as everything he loved crumbled to ash.

The restlessness brought him to the belly of the Stormvalor arena in the depths of the night. He passed the magical iron door for the third time, holding a torch aloft to light his way as he descended deep into the earth.

This time, when he entered the Hall of Champions, the lightning trough along the wall sparked with life on its own, flickering to existence. He passed rows upon rows of honored fallen champions, past the ancient king of Vorovesti, as if drawn onward.

Aethan set his torch in a stand near the massive, sealed doors, then stepped back, tipping his head to gaze up at the double doors once more. For a moment, he studied the matching blue dragons sculpted into the doors and knew in the depths of his soul that it had to be Storm.

The last two times he stood before these doors, Aethan had companions at his side. With all their combined strength, they couldn't open the doors. There was no way it would budge for him alone.

Regardless, Aethan wrapped a hand around each handle, a sneaking suspicion crawling through him. Blue light rippled outward from the handles, just as it did on the iron door in the dungeons above. A click thundered from beyond the doors. Aethan's heart hammered as he pushed with all his might.

The massive doors groaned open.

Light from the outer chamber spilled into the inner sanctum, illuminating its grandeur.

Aethan gaped at the sight beyond the doors. At what he had discovered...

The Shrine of Justis, the revered god of war, lay in its own temple-like chamber. Every surface shone with fancy, elaborate reliefs of bronze, iron, and stone, creating an otherworldly glow. On the floor, a magnificent mosaic told the story of Justis in ancient runes, each tile a testament to his legendary deeds and divine power.

At the far end of the chamber, a massive statue of the God of War himself rose atop a grand dais. Even seated, he was nearly as tall as the doors to the shrine. His imposing figure, wrought in iron and bronze, gazed out the doors at his champions with fierce pride. The very air hummed with the power. It buzzed like lightning across Aethan's skin, making the hairs all over his body stand on end.

He moved toward the statue.

Aethan couldn't explain the sensation that washed over him as he crossed deeper into the shrine. It was akin to the sense of otherness, much like he had felt from the statue of Justis outside the arena when he arrived for the tournament. Voices breathed like a whisper on a breeze. Aethan sensed...something.

Something that drew his gaze downward.

At Justis' feet, a sword sheathed in blue leather and wrapped in vines of steel and bronze lay upon an altar. The hilt of the sword held several dark sapphire stones on the crossguard, and rich dark blue leather wrapped around the handle. At the apex of the pommel, another sapphire stone rested in a steel housing. The sight of the sword took Aethan's breath away. He had never seen a weapon so beautiful.

It called to him, pulled at him, and forced him to step closer until he stood before the glorious weapon.

Aethan drew in a breath as he wrapped his hand around the hilt and scabbard. Then he released the breath as he drew the blade from the sheath. It sang as it smoothly slid free.

The hilt fit perfectly in his hand as if made for him. Aethan stepped back and tested the balance and weight of the weapon, slashing at the air. The blade hummed, catching flashes of light from the lightning trough that seemed to ripple with life along the steel blade.

Aethan sensed this sword was meant for him. It whispered a name into his bones.

Stormshard.

Acknowledgments

Those who have known me for years know that Divica has been a long-time-coming labor of love. The world initially came into being when my godsons were born over twenty years ago. Back then, Bast went by a different name and the world itself looked much different. It has taken me a long time to muster the courage to get this story written. Preliminary attempts were feeble, at best. But I couldn't be happier with how Stormvalor not only kicks off this series, but how it slowly introduces readers to a world I have held close to my heart for so, so long.

Getting to this point wouldn't be possible without the help of numerous people. Obviously, for Dawson and Tyler. It's for you I dreamed this world up in the first place. To my husband, for helping me imagine my very first fantasy world.

To all of my friends from NaNoWriMo years ago. You know who you are, and you know these characters better than anyone else. Thank you for helping me flesh them out, even if they have changed a bit in this final version of themselves. To Teagan, you were the first to believe in Bast (then known as Dayen), the first to fall in love with him despite all his faults, and the first to give him hope. To Char, who loved both Aethan and Bast with all of her heart and soul, so much that she could never choose between them. Teagan and Char are the first two women to love Bast, and he will never forget that. A piece of them will carry on in him, even in this series.

A heartfelt thank you to my family for encouraging me when I was down, and being patient with me when I neglected reality to write this book. I hope my kids and my husband understand how much it means to me that I get the space to write. It gives me purpose.

Of course, my beta readers deserve a lot of acknowledgment as well. Jennifer, you have stuck with me through my best and worst drafts, given me frank advice, and have always been comfortable sharing your honest thoughts. I appreciate it so much. Kevin, you always catch on to plot threads I think I've buried far faster than you should. It worries me that I'm not being coy enough. Brenda, Koree, Ashley, and Chloe, I can't thank you enough for taking the time to help me make this better. The four of you didn't really know me as a writer, and it was a big deal that you took a chance and gave me your time.

Therena, your artwork of the characters that only exist in my head is *beyond* amazing. If I didn't love them before, I certainly do now!

They say it takes a village to create something like this. I prefer to think of you all as my generals and commanders

To everyone who supported my Kickstarter campaign, it's because of each and every one of you that this book is so beautifully, utterly perfect. You are my advance footsoldiers, boldly taking that first step for others to follow.

Which brings me to you, dear reader. My soldiers, fighting this battle with my characters. My army, helping this book reach global domination. I will never become an Author Empress like Sarah J Mass or Rebecca Yarros, but each and every one of you brings me just a little bit closer.

About Starr Z. Davies

STARR Z. DAVIES is an award-winning author of over 20 tales that span dystopian realms, epic fantasies, and echoes of forgotten histories. Dubbed the "Character Assassin," she weaves stories where heroes are tested by fire—both emotional and physical.

From her woodland home in northern Wisconsin, she crafts worlds while surrounded by her greatest allies: a supportive husband, two imaginative children, and a curious menagerie of robotic pets. When not conjuring new adventures, she dabbles in home enchantments, swims like a siren, battles through video game quests, and devours books like ancient tomes of power.

If you want to become friends with Starr, dark chocolate, Doctor Who, Parks & Rec, The Office, and the MCU are all fantastic ways into her heart. That or a love for fantasy books by indie authors.

Learn more about Starr and her books.

Keep up with Starr by signing up for her newsletter.

Want to be part of her community? Follow Starr on social media.
facebook.com/szdavies
instagram.com/s.z.davies
threads.com/s.z.davies
tiktok.com/starrzdavies